Everyone has heard ɛ
but what of the Diamonᴜ ᴋᴜ... ᴏ. ᴛ..ᴇ.ᴏ/ᴏ.. ᴏᴘᴜ..ᴇᴜ ᴏ.. ᴜy ᴛ..ᴇ
fabulous finds in the Kimberley Mines in South Africa, many ambitious young men, amongst them prominent San Francisco banker
William Ralston, and in Europe, the great Baron Rothschild, see
the chance to make the United States the diamond capital of the
world. But first they have to find the precious stones....

Philip Arnold and John Slack offer them more riches than they
have ever dreamt of when they deposit rough uncut stones in
Ralston's bank. Ralston will do anything to get his hands on the
men's stake, but first he has to find the secret mine....

About the author

Sam North is currently Senior Lecturer and Programme Leader of the Professional Writing Programme at the Falmouth College of Arts and Managing
Editor of Hackwriters.com, a Cretive Writing website which has won
numberous awards, including the prestigious Guardian award for best student
site.

He is a member of the Writers' Guild of Great Britain, the New Producers
Alliance and The Historical Novel Society (UK). He has just won the Metaplus
Creative   Writing   Award   2001

Also by the author

as Sam North
209 Thriller Road NEL UK - St.Martin's Press, New York -
Ramapo - Nuclear Nightmare Arlington Books and Sphere Books UK
Going Indigo Citron Press

as Marcel D'Agneau
Eeny, Meeny, Miny, Mole, Arlington Books and Arrow Books UK
The Curse of the Nibelung, the Last Sherlock Holmes adventure, Arlington
Books, UK

Diamonds

Sam North

Domhan Books

Copyright USA, UK and Worldwide the author 2001

All rights reserved. No part of this book may be reproduced or transmitted in any form by any means, electronic or mechanical, including photocopying, recording, or by any information and storage retrieval system, without permission in writing from the copyright owner.

This is a work of fiction. Names, characters, places and incidents are the product of the author's imagination, and any resemblance to any actual persons, living or dead, events, or locales, is entirely coincidental.

ISBN: 1-58345-605-8 hardcover
1-58345-610-4 paperback
1-58345-611-2 ION

Published by Domhan Books
9511 Shore Road, Suite 514
Brooklyn New York 11209
www.domhanbooks.com
Please visit us for our latest great reads from writers all over the world. New titles every month.

Cover art by Stacey King, Crystal Moon Design

Printed by Lightning Source
Distributed by Ingram Book Group

PROLOGUE

'Thou shalt not tell any false tales about "good diggings in the mountains" to thy neighbour that thou mayest benefit a friend who hath mules and provisions, tools and blankets he cannot sell; lest in deceiving thy neighbour when he shall return with naught save his rifle he present thee with the contents thereof and, like a dog, thou shall fall down and die.'
No 9 . The Miner's Ten Commandments J. M. Hutchings. 1853

John Slack and Philip Arnold left home to get rich, never once entertaining the idea that they might end up poor. No one who left home young to seek their fortune in California set out with the intention of starving to death from a lack of funds or an absence of luck. It is true that most of the dreamers who crossed the mountains in search of gold didn't find any, and if they did, the publican or the bandit grew fat off them long before they ever got to live the good life. The idea that California was paved with gold was much more compelling than the reality that California was the state where a man could lose everything he had, as well as his health and sanity. The editor of the San Francisco Alta knew well what drew men to his city.

"Bright visions of big lumps of gold and large quantities of them, to be gathered without any severe labor, haunt them night and day before they reach here. Here they hope to find a land where the inevitable law of God that 'man shall live by the sweat of his brow' has been repealed."

It was hope that had brought them out west in the beginning. It was hope that had sustained them in all the years they had not found anything worthwhile. Once folks quit Elizabethtown it was rare they would ever return. Certainly no one ever expected Philip Arnold to return. The fact that he came back a rich man was an astonishment to all. People never tired of talking about it, or speculating on how he had done it, or why he had returned without John Slack. We all knew someone who had gone over the divide in search of a fortune, but almost no one could recall anyone ever coming back.

It was in the summer of 1872 that they first made the newspapers, probably every one in the United States, and certainly every journal in Kentucky. Their news was viewed with amazement in Elizabethtown, for most of us had pretty well decided they were dead. I had to smile, for although they'd certainly grown older, they looked just the same as I remembered them from our days on the prairies.

"Here I am," Arnold would say, " a rich man and here's you, a respected physician, with medals and everything. Who'd believe this of two farm boys? Who'd believe it would turn out like this?"

From the moment John Slack had read to him details of the great diamond discoveries in Kimberley, South Africa, Arnold had become obsessed. He had had to have diamonds, and what Africa had, surely America, rich in every mineral imaginable, would have as well. It was just awaiting discovery.

Slack wasn't so sure. But between them both they'd dug over every last inch of Nevada and California and found no sign of anything, not gold or silver, nothing. There had been plenty of nothing.

Yet, despite their hope and determination, by the winter of 1871, Arnold and Slack had become destitute. They didn't even possess a mule. The leather on their backs was cracked and soiled, their boots had long ago given up any semblance of shape or waterproofing. They had had the fever all right and it was a terrible, cussed ol' bug that had bitten them good and wasn't about to let go.

It is at this dark point in their lives that my tale begins. Other scribes and historians will, no doubt, paint another side of the picture and make excuses for the less than glorious behaviour of the players in this adventure, but none know the facts as complete as told to me by Philip Arnold. I hereby set down the truth as a warning to all who may be tempted to speculate, and as a monument to human greed.

Philip Arnold used to say to me in that boastful manner he had, "One day, Doc, they'll name a big city street after me. They won't forget Philip Arnold in a hurry, I can tell you."

Well, wouldn't you know it, all history recalls is the bankers.

Philip Arnold and John Slack's story is true in every detail. Although sworn to secrecy by Arnold, I hope it will not bring about his final displeasure when it ultimately comes my time to meet with my Maker.

Dr Daniel P Jackson
Dashaway House
Elizabethtown,
Kentucky. 1886

DIAMONDS

CHAPTER ONE
A Matter Of Great Secrecy.

Twelve long years after Philip Arnold and John Slack had departed Kentucky brimful of optimism, life found them stepping off the Oakland ferry into a sea of genuine San Francisco mud. The rain had done its worst, and no matter who you complained to in the city, the roads were a disgrace and seemed set to get worse. These had been lonesome years for our two prospectors, some damned hungry ones too. Folks shunned them as they walked along Market Street. It was obvious to any observer that they'd probably just come down off the hills and had had no success. These two were pitiable, dirty specimens, mere relics of men, closer to beasts than human. Mud caked their hair and lacquered their thin worn leather coats. It was a lucky thing the fog had come in after the worst of the rain, for the very sight of these two men might have frightened horses or brought terror to young children and delicate noses.

Theirs had been a brutal trip, and Slack hardly needed to go through the charade of wearing boots at all, for his toes poked out from both feet. No one would guess that under this mud lay proud manhood. Arnold, the shorter of the two, was brawny, somewhat stocky but deadly handsome; only the thinning of his hair revealed his age, but he was not a man to let that worry him. Slack had seen this man out-stare a rattlesnake and with those same bright brown eyes he could test the nerves of the most confident poker player in a saloon or press the lady of his fancy to succumb to his natural charms.

Slack had none of these attributes. At six feet he stood out among men, but even with the mud washed off, no one would ever think him distinguished or charming or even half-way handsome. Not even his sharp blue eyes assisted his demeanor. Nevertheless, you'd be wrong to dismiss this man because of his appearance, for a sharp brain hid behind the dirt and his plain manner of speaking. The truth of it was, here was a man who was honest and modest, content to leave the show to his partner. This particular day, however, he was a touch vexed.

As they made slow progress through the mire, Slack would pause every so often to stare behind them, as if he were expecting trouble. He'd been especially nervous on the nickel ferry, convinced that every soul knew their business that day. Arnold had done his best to calm him, pointing out that with the fog down on the bay, people were more than likely staring out to warn the Captain of the other boats, mindful of all the times in the past that the ferries had gone down with all hands.

At Market and California streets, the mud and chaos seemed to be at its very worst. Some Chinese laborers stood around a brazier, warming their hands as a crude block and tackle lowered iron rails onto a stack behind them. They looked cold and miserable and probably wished they'd never answered the call of the Central Pacific railroad. Crocker's coolies, they were called, had been imported from China to build his railroad, but now some mean spirited folk were calling for them to be sent back to China. Yet who else would work so hard or so cheaply? The Chinese had been at Promatory when the golden spike had been driven in, yet from the photographs that recorded the event you'd have been hard-pressed to spot them.

Now here they were digging Crocker and Hopkins Cable Car lines - testimony to their continued usefulness. Slack was the type of man to keep his opinion about the Chinese to himself , but Arnold, like many new Californians, was in favor of sending them back. This wasn't so unusual, since he'd said the same thing about the Irish and the Germans. Arnold was of the opinion that America was full enough, it was time to close the doors on all newcomers.

Arnold and Slack kept a wary eye about them as they passed the diggings. Arnold cursed as he nearly slipped and fell. Slack held him steady. Arnold had one or two things to say about the cable car, too. It was one thing for the rich to choose to live up on Nob Hill, but for them to dig up San Francisco so as to provide themselves with transportation to get up there, well, even in Boston you couldn't have got away with *that*. Still, there was a tinge of jealousy there. Arnold kind of admired Charles Crocker. At least the man was a worker; well, not a worker exactly, not with his bulk, but he'd been there, every inch of the way, snow or bake, he'd been at the railhead, and there weren't many rich folks you could say had actually earned their money *and* taken the government for a ride.

It had been with respect that Arnold and Slack had gone along to Crocker's offices way back in the summer of 1870 and had told the big man about their idea of diamond prospecting. Crocker, like Arnold, had read with much fascination about the Kimberley diamonds and the fortunes being made in South Africa, so he had listened to Arnold, considered it, then turned them down flat. He'd built a railroad clear across the Sierra Mountains and up to the foothills of the Rockies. He'd seen gold, he'd seen silver, he'd even seen nickle, copper and quartz, but never once had he seen a diamond, and he for one didn't be-

DIAMONDS

lieve the American continent had a single one.

There was no arguing with that. Arnold knew, right then, that if he was ever to get investors to help him join the ranks of those living on Nob Hill, he'd damn well have to find those diamonds himself. In this quest there had never been two more determined prospectors than Arnold or Slack, nor two more mocked for their obsession. Some scoffed, but it had not stopped the odd prospector, likewise dazzled by the riches being made in Kimberley's diamond hole, taking a closer look at quartz bearing rock and other semi-precious stones that would come their way from time to time.

Yet, it was a fact that between British Columbia and the San Joaquin valley, not a single diamond had yet turned up. Undaunted, Arnold and Slack had combed the mountains and stalked the Indians. Somewhere, Arnold was convinced, the Indians had a secret place and he aimed to find it.

Slack wiped the drizzle from his eyes and again cursed the fog which clung to his body like a wet blanket. He could hear people and horses around him, but only if one actually bumped into them could one actually see them. Fog or rain he could stand on their own, but together they made a man unnaturally damp and cold, likely as not to catch some fever that was always present in these foul-smelling cities. Slack was always loathe to leave the wilderness for the confines of a modern noisy city with its mountains of horse manure. City folks just didn't understand what it was to breathe fresh air, they'd be better off born without a nose at all. Slack turned to Arnold and helped him up onto the boards of California street. All around them mud flowed like a constant stream of lava. There was an awful stench coming from the diggings in the middle of the road. The cable car trenches were filled with city sewage, which having found its way in, could find no way out. Altogether, what with the fog, drizzle, mud and the stench, one had to be a pretty determined kind of San Franciscan to walk abroad in this weather. Not a few citizens had already remarked in the pages of the *Alta* and the saloons, that before they filled in those long trenches, the bodies of a few city fathers and railroad men could well find themselves lying at the bottom of them.

Philip Arnold walked on, one sticky foot in front of the other, slipping and sliding on the irregular boards. Slack began to cough, the years of dirt and dust in his lungs protesting at the damp. He began to wonder if all this was a mistake. A man only had his health; without that he was done for. The cruel contrast with the harsh heat across the bay in Oakland couldn't have been more emphatic. Their destination, however, was but one block away now. It was widely known that the newly-constructed building had cost no less than a quarter of a million dollars to build, and was the most magnificent example of its type. It was hard to make a judgement in this fog. Nevertheless Slack was of the opinion that you should judge a bank by the men behind the facade, not the other way around. He was a hard man to impress with piles of stone.

DIAMONDS

Arnold came to a halt opposite the bank on California Street. An old battered Concord went by, its horse team protesting at the weight of the mud on the wheels. Arnold wondered if coaches would be running at all once the cable car was completed. Perhaps it was time to buy Cable stock. Certainly he'd have to be considering some investments soon. It was a funny thing to be poor so long and then be on the very verge of a fortune, and have to consider ways to protect your wealth. Naturally all this was still in the future, there was much to be done yet, but the seeds had been sown. Suddenly anxious, he patted the coat pocket closest to his heart and was reassured to find a large hard lump still situated there. They'd not been robbed...yet.

Slack was still watching out for trouble. Every miner knew that the most dangerous time was crossing the street to the bank. There was always some scallywag lurking about ready for trouble. But on this miserable day, he'd have had trouble telling these two men apart from the mud, even if he could see through the fog.

Arnold rested his hand on Slack's sleeve momentarily. "Bank's open now. Any doubts, John Slack? 'Cause if you have, best say your piece now, there's no going back after this."

Slack shook his head. He would not change his mind. Enough was enough. Everything they had had been invested in what rested in Arnold's pocket. Years of sweat, and not a little blood. Every last cent they could get out of the ground had amounted to just one small pile and to look at it, it was hard to say it had all been worth it. Twelve years was a long time to live in the bowels of Mother Earth, dining on nothing but promises and keeping a rifle handy in case of anyone trying to make his fortune the easy way.

The fog thinned out for a moment, revealing the Bank of California in all its glory. Good blue stone lugged over from Angel Island had been used to clad the building, lending the imposing two storeys the solidity expected from the state's principal banking institution. Well it had better be secure, Slack was thinking. Not that he seriously thought this bank could fold. He knew enough men up at the Comstock and Ophir mines who'd once been rich shareholders, richer than this bank itself, but each one in turn had gotten into debt somehow, and afore-long it was the bank itself who had become the largest mine owner. Bankers who didn't know one end of a pick from the other owned it all. The thought of it made Slack's blood boil. He reckoned that his time in Virginia City alone had earned him at least six windows and maybe a door at this bank.

Naturally they couldn't stare at the bank forever. Still, it was a moment worth preserving. It had been a long time coming. To get as far as going into the Bank of California was an achievement, considering how they had been living these past months.

Arnold had been contemplating on things more serious. Did they go into the bullion entrance - the logical place for prospectors - or the front entrance?

DIAMONDS

The Bullion entrance was just across the way on Sansome, but it didn't seem right somehow. After all, they weren't carrying gold. He made the decision. The man they would have to see was the chief cashier himself, at the very least.

A thought passed through his head that perhaps they should have paused at the bath house first, but then he quickly dismissed the notion, knowing how ridiculous they'd look with white faces peering out of these muddy clothes.

"Come on," he muttered, nudging Slack off the sidewalk.

Slack followed, ever vigilant, holding his rifle before him as if sure they'd be robbed in the bank , never mind five steps away from it.

Inside the bank things weren't as cool, calm and dusty as one might expect. This is because just a moment before Arnold and Slack set off across wide California street toward the main entrance, a Mrs. Jennifer Bond, wife of William Bond, ship chandler and as a consequence a weathly man, had entered the bank in wild confusion. She'd swept in with the fog still clinging to her pretty skirts and had been unable to speak, she was so much atwitter. It was all she could do to wobble her eyes and issue a plaintive squeak as she pointed behind her back into the fog, perhaps regretting she'd not taken flight the moment she'd glimpsed the robbers.

The bank employees weren't entirely stupid; no sir, when any woman came in there squeaking hysterical. The assistant cashier, Mr.. Thomas Brown, immediately stepped over to the stack of gold and silver coins beside the tellers nearest the door. In those days there were no grilles and tellers weren't kept in cages. The double eagles were stacked twenty high, worth four hundred dollars a stack, conveniently placed so that tellers could scoop them up off the wide, highly-polished mahogany counters. Banking back then had the air of a gentlemen's club, but Thomas Brown was a worrying soul. The fact that they had never been held up didn't mean they wouldn't be, and with that woman throwing terror into every tellers heart, it strained no imagination to surmise the very worst. Mr.. Thomas Brown, normally impassive and resolute in his stiff collar, paled. All eyes focused on the doors.

Mere seconds later, the squelching footsteps of Philip Arnold and John Slack were heard slapping the boards. Thomas Brown hurriedly began scooping up double eagles and thrusting them out of sight. Several other tellers took his cue, and there was a great flurry as silver and gold disappeared off the counters. Their foresight was rewarded when in through the doors came Arnold and Slack in their muddy garb. Threat became reality when customers and bank tellers alike saw Slack's rifle held at the ready and the furtive look in Arnolds eyes. The atmosphere was so charged that if Slack had said as much as boo, the tellers would have pelted him with the same gold coins to save their own skins. Instead, Slack swung his rifle over to his other hand and the tension rose perceptably around the banking hall.

11

DIAMONDS

Not a word was said, but there wasn't a soul in that hall who didn't believe this was an armed robbery. Certainly the security man , expressly hired for the purpose of keeping the peace, was regretting the day he'd ever needed a job.

Imagine, if you will, the look of astonishment on the faces of Arnold and Slack as they stood in the banking hall with the brass-plate doors swinging behind them, whilst in front women customers fainted, tellers flung themselves behind the solid mahogany mass of their counters, with the occasional disembodied hand coming up for the last of the double eagles. Such dedication in the face of danger.

Slack turned to Arnold and wondered himself if they had walked into a robbery. Arnold watched with bewilderment as people shrank from them in horror and regretted they hadn't stopped off at the bath-house after all. Clearly the people of San Francisco had developed some very fine and sensitive noses since their last visit.

"Anyone going to attend to us?" he called out, not hiding his irritation.

The ashen face of Thomas Brown, the assistant cashier appeared from behind the counter. He stuttered nervously. "Wha...what do you want?"

Arnold stepped forward towards him and Slack likewise, his rifle cocked and ready. Something was going on in this bank, he didn't know what, but he was ready for trouble if it came.

"We want to make a deposit, of course," Arnold told Brown.

They could see the color rise in the man's face.

"A deposit?" he asked in an embarrassed whisper.

Slack could hear people exhale all over the room. And if they'd had a mind to, they'd have seen a dozen or more red faces as timid cashiers bobbed up from behind their counters. There was much coughing and shuffling too.

"I'd like to speak to the cashier," Arnold explained. "Got some business that has to go *into* your vault."

Thomas Brown was recovering now, especially as Slack was busy lowering his rifle and resting it against the counter. Brown caught the eye of Mrs. Bond, who turned away blushing. It was her panic that had caused this upset. She knew the town would gossip about it, and it hurt her to think she'd be the focus of that gossip.

"It's a confidential matter sir," Arnold was saying. "Whom am I addressing?"

"Thomas Brown, sir, assistant cashier. My apologies sir for any misapprehensions we may have had, but we are unaccustomed to gentlemen entering this bank bearing arms."

Arnold stared back at the man as if he were mad. "Mr.. Brown, sir, it's obvious to me that you never tried to make a deposit at your branch in Virginia City. There's days a man needs the entire Union Army to get across C Street just to pass the time of day."

DIAMONDS

Thomas Brown had indeed heard tales of wild times at their Comstock site. He did not expect an apology from these men. This was the way they made sure they kept possession of what they had, and it was their right to protect themselves. Still, there was no shame in being cautious. His heart still beat wildly beneath his vest.

"If you'd come along to the end counter, sir, I'll attended to your business personally." His voice was as controlled as a pastor at a Sunday service.

Arnold, well pleased with the answer, signalled to Slack to accompany him. Elsewhere in the banking hall, business returned to normal, and once again the coins were stacked on the counters, ready for business. People gave Arnold and Slack a wide berth, to be sure, but only on account of their embarrassment They lived in interesting times. Two wild men from the hills had come in wanting to make a deposit. A wide berth was given, but not too wide...these two men had found something, and they were behaving mighty cautious about it. Perhaps a new discovery. Some new lode of gold or silver. Something they wanted to keep secret for a while until they laid claim. San Francisco had not yet sated its curiosity for new wonders and investment opportunities.

Arnold had all of Mr.. Brown's attention by now, and with one final check around the huge, highly-ornamental room for prying eyes, he brought out the large buckskin pouch that had warranted all Slack's security arrangements.

Arnold lay the warm overstuffed pouch on the counter and kept his hand over it. He was not a man who would trust anyone easily, not even a cashier of Brown's publicly-known honesty.

"I'd like a receipt, Mr.. Brown, and for this pouch to be placed in your vault this morning. I'd like to purchase one of them tin boxes I know folks like to keep their valuables in and have this pouch placed in it, before me and John Slack's eyes, so we know it's our pouch and not some substitution."

If Mr.. Brown was offended, he bit his lip rather than showed it. He wanted no more raised rifles in his bank. "It will be no problem to supply you with a lock-up box, sir, but we have regulations at the Bank of California, sir. We have to have sight of what has been placed in our vaults. I regret this has to be, sir, but ever since the Parker gang saw fit to place ten sticks of dynamite in the Western Bank, we have instituted a simple sight procedure."

Arnold appeared alarmed. "I don't think you want our business, sir. We came to this bank because we reckoned on it being one we could trust. Now I see you want to poke your nose into our private business. Even Bill Sharon wouldn't have stooped to that kind of business. He'll vouch for us. He got enough of our money from us when we was in Virginia City."

Mr.. Brown lifted a hand to halt the flow. He was used to this. "It is unusual, sir, I know, and I for one regret it is so. But since I suppose you'd not like to see our new London manufactured vault blown to pieces any more than would I, you'll realize that I have to have sight, sir. It is only I who will look, and you can rest assured that you can rely on my complete discretion in this matter. I, and only I, will know the contents."

Arnold looked at Slack and Slack looked at Arnold. It seemed a long way to come to not put the pouch in the bank. It was a dilemma, to be sure.

Mr.. Brown waited patiently. There was not much money to be made out of placing valuables in their vault, and the greater the value the greater the risk. The Bank of California could survive without these two miners' business.

"If it is a matter of bullion gentlemen, we do have an assayer in the bullion room. Our vault is safe, and we would be prepared to offer you the very best price in the city."

Arnold smiled, not that the smile was so easy to see under all that mud.

"Bullion it isn't Mr.. Brown. If you don't know us, you soon will, for we are Philip Arnold and John Slack; this here is Slack. I've a mind to go elsewhere: Mr.. Brown: but we have come a long ways and we are tired. You have given your word on privacy in this matter, so you may take a look."

Mr.. Brown quickly untied the knot securing the buckskin pouch. Miners could be so secretive, it was tiresome. Gold did not spill out, nor silver, nor anything Mr. Brown had ever seen before, or in such quantity. He was clearly astonished. Diamonds poured from the pouch, small, irregular translucent , along with other colored-stones. A less experienced man might have dismissed these stones as quartz or marble, but their shapes were irregular, and just in some, there was a hint of a sparkle.

"Diamonds, Mr.. Brown. In the raw, as found. They lack the glitter of the jewelry store at the moment, Mr.. Brown, but I can assure you, sir, that what you are looking at is pure, elegant *American* diamonds."

Mr.. Brown quickly shovelled the stones back into the pouch. His heart beat just a little faster. "You said *American* diamonds, Mr.. Arnold?"

Arnold smiled. "Mr.. Brown, I said nothing and your word on this matter has been accepted in good faith by us. This is a private matter until we have them verified by experts and a legal stake to our claim."

"My lips are sealed, Mr..Arnold. Sir, any assistance the Bank of California may be able to offer you, please feel free to discuss with our chief cashier William Ralston. I know he is most keen to see all Californian resources developed to the full. I want you to rest easy that these precious items will be as secure in our vaults as if they were the valuables of President Grant himself."

"Now that's what we came to hear," Slack commented. He had no liking for Grant, or his politics, but he had a lot of respect for his money.

Arnold watched as a tin box was brought. The pouch was placed in it and then all of it was locked and a receipt issued. The diamonds were now in the safe keeping of the Bank of California, and their secret was sworn to by the assistant cashier. All was right with the world.

DIAMONDS

Arnold bid Mr.. Brown good day. He and Slack were already on their way out of the bank when in came another man out of the filthy fog, who stared at Arnold for longer than was exactly polite. "Is that you, Philip Arnold?"

Arnold was taken by surprise. He would have been surprised if his own mother had recognised him let alone George D. Roberts, mine owner and proprietor of the hardware store down by Bush Street.

Roberts shook his head, adopting an amused expression. "'Well I can see you've returned from the wilds again, Arnold. Them Indians told you where they are hiding the diamonds yet?" He chuckled much amused by his remark. Slack noted the man's wig had slipped to one side under his silk hat.

Now, here was a tricky problem. It was one thing telling everyone you were *looking* for diamonds; it was half of what prospecting was about, but when a prospector had finally found some and just secretly deposited those same diamonds in the bank, the very last thing he needed was some blabbermouth telling the whole world about it .Arnold just shrugged. After all, Roberts would know in good time that he was laughing at them in vain.

"Good day Mr.. Roberts," was all he said, as he and Slack walked by.

Mr.. Roberts was still chuckling to himself as he walked over to greet Mr.. Brown. "Not seen those two dreamers for quite some time, Mr.. Brown. Never met two men more determined to discover diamonds in my life. If there are any, the Indians aren't trading 'em, and I've yet to see an Indian who wouldn't trade anything to get at the firewater or a straight shootin' rifle. My guess is Arnold and Slack will end their days out in the wilds and never find a one."

Now, for the first time, he detected something was amiss in the bank. "You look a little flustered, Mr. Brown. Arnold give you trouble? Want him run out of town?"

Mr.. Brown simply raised an eyebrow. But Mr.. Roberts was no fool. He had noted which part of the banking room Mr.. Brown was situated in, and the locked tin box clutched in his hands. There was something else too; a man like Philip Arnold didn't come into a bank without a purpose, and for him to want to see the assistant cashier, well, it indicated business of a serious kind.

"You don't mean to tell me that Arnold has found his diamonds, do you, Mr.. Brown?" He tried on his most disarming smile.

"Now, Mr.. Roberts, you know this is a private matter between myself and Mr.. Arnold. All business is confidential at the Bank of California."

"But Mr.. Arnold did make a deposit, Mr.. Brown, and it was something of value or else you wouldn't be toting that tin box in your arms like it was your youngest child."

Mr.. Brown looked down at the tin box momentarily and was surprised to discover that he was indeed holding it just like a new-found babe.

Mr.. Roberts had made his point. He knew he wouldn't get past Mr.. Brown, and it was no use trying. He let Mr.. Brown go about his business, and he

15

DIAMONDS

strolled over to the nearest teller unoccupied with any customer. He explained that he'd like a private word with the chief cashier, William Chapman Ralston.

It wasn't so unusual for a customer to ask for William Ralston, and Mr.. Ralston was a very accommodating man, visible to all in his inner glass office. He was there at this moment talking with the financier William Lent, a man famous for his knack of knowing not only how to get in on the ground floor of a thing, but knowing when to quit too. 'Getting out timely is as important as knowing when to jump in', he was known to quote whenever asked financial advice and his opinion was much respected.

The teller walked around the glass and signaled to Ralston. He briefly smiled when he saw Mr.. Roberts nudge his silver-topped cane in his direction. He indicated for him to give him a minute and Mr.. Roberts took himself to a quiet corner to wait. What he had to say had best not be over heard. He took a deep breath in an effort to curb his natural enthusiasm. By god, diamonds! If Arnold had really found them then fortunes would be made. There had been countless expeditions to find these precious stones ever since Kimberly had inspired the big rush to Africa, but nothing had been found, no evidence of even a small stone. That was the main argument against Arnold succeeding. How had he found them when no one else had? Was it true the Indians thought they had magic properties and wouldn't like for the white man to get hold of them? Arnold had suggested as much more than a year ago when he'd tried to track the Hopis to a secret burial ground. He'd gone and gotten an arrow in his back for his trouble. Mr..Roberts was determined that he would discover Arnold's secret. The two prospectors could be bought off easily enough. He knew miners who'd spent ten years or more looking for gold, and then six months after finding it were absolutely flat broke again, if not dead from too much good food and loose women.

Mr..Roberts' thoughts were interrupted by a jog on his elbow from the banker, who smiled and shook his hand firmly as was his custom.

William C. Ralston was no ordinary chief cashier, but the *de facto* Director of the bank. It was a fact that there would have been no Bank of California at all without him and that San Francisco would be a smaller, less prosperous place without his faith and enterprise. He was the life saver of many an ambitious scheme. The Cornwell Watch Company and the West Coast Furniture Company owed all to him, as did Kimballs manufacturing, the famous California Theater, and the fabulous Palace Hotel. This was under-construction at this time, with its two and a half miles of corridors and eight hundred and fifty rooms. Even now it can be considered the most ambitious building constructed in the United States and the envy of New York. Mr.. Ralston was a legend in the city. His baronial estate at Belmont quite astonished everyone. It held accommodation for 120 guests, all lit by gas from his own gas-works on the estate. Ambassadors and kings vied with each other to be guests there.

DIAMONDS

Ralston, like most Californians of that time, had not been born there, but it did nothing to dim his devotion to the new state. An Ohioan native of Plymouth, Richland Country and son of a riverboat family, young Ralston had learned his rivercraft from an early age and just how fickle fortune could be. When gold had been found in California, Ralston and the two Captains had intended to follow the hordes out there, but there was too much profit to be had transporting the thousands who went by way of Panama. Ralston's business skills were learned on the Isthmus but by 1856 San Francisco had boasted a growing bank organisation known as Garrison, Morgan, Fretz and Ralston, dealing primarily in gold bullion, gold dust, and exchange dealing.

The Bank of California had grown out of the amalgamation of several other banks and the Darius Ogden Mills bank in Sacramento. Ralston, with his ' ring' of friends soon contrived to put a stranglehold on the source of California's wealth, Nevada's gold. Soon they controlled most of the producing mines, the mills, even the very railroad to the mines and held the all important voting rights on just about every enterprise in Virginia City.

It was no accident that by the time Arnold and Slack walked into this very building, the Bank of California was the third largest bank in the entire Union, and had the most solid financial base. The East Coast might have been shaky, but out west business was at a peak and looked set to continue that way for all time.

Mr.. Ralston was known to be the best kind of American, keen to further the wealth of his state, as well as the bank and his own pockets. His judgment was reputed to be sound. In short, he knew a good thing when he saw it and wouldn't shy away from the cost. He was a handsome man too, despite a receding hairline. The ladies liked his sharp bewhiskered face, unsullied by a moustache. He was by all accounts a strong, healthy ox of a man. He made it his business to become everyone's good friend. Although his wife 'Lizzie' was more often than not to be found in Paris, she was the linchpin of San Francisco society and their summer residence at Belmont the social epicenter of society.

Ralston searched Roberts' face with interest. "You look feverish Mr.. Roberts, what's put the color into your cheeks? Not this weather, I'll be bound. This damn fog has been sitting like this for three days now. Each hour I expect a breeze to get up but every time I look out I'm a disappointed man."

He checked his watch, there were things to do, he didn't want to spend too long passing the time of day with Mr.. Roberts, even if he was a good customer.

"It's a quarter after ten, sir, but what I have to suggest will stop your pocket watch for good," Roberts declared, inclining his head toward Ralston so he could speak in the lowest most confidential tones. "I have reason to believe that diamonds, American diamonds, have been deposited with this bank not more than fifteen minutes ago."

DIAMONDS

Ralston blinked. It was not often someone was able to tell him something about his bank that he didn't already know. "Diamonds y'say, in my bank?"

Roberts could tell he disbelieved him.

"I'm telling you, I saw Mr..Thomas Brown scurrying away to your vault just this minute and the prospector Philip Arnold walking out of here with John Slack."

Ralston frowned. "There are no such thing as American diamonds. You were with me yourself when we heard that German geologist say it was unlikely they'd ever be found."

"Yes, yes, but what if they have been found? You don't mean to tell me that all the diamonds in the world are only to found in Araby and Africa? Why, until Kimberley, geologists would have probably sworn that not a one would be found in Africa. Now they have, and some as big as a cat, I hear. Don't you think that if Arnold has found diamonds, we should be there to help him get them out? He'll need capital, expertise, all kinds of things, and it would be a shame if he went to someone else for it."

Ralston allowed himself a thin smile. He knew Roberts' game. "If they've placed these so called diamonds in the vault, why then, it's a matter of trust between the bank and Mr.. Arnold."

Mr.. Roberts smiled, rubbing the top of his cane on his forehead. "Now, there's the rub, sir. We may never know if there are diamonds or not, unless we get a look into that tin box. It would be a black day for you if it came out one day that you were ignorant of one of the most important happenings in San Francisco's history."

"I haven't been amiss as yet, Mr.. Roberts. Comstock and Ophir didn't entirely escape my notice. I'm sure that if Arnold has made an important find he will be making his claim."

"Yes, sir and then there will be a million souls climbing all over our backs again in the scramble for it. I'll sell a lot of picks and, no doubt find some new customers, but how much better, sir, for us to get a share of it now, dig that mine over before the hordes arrive and make the profit for ourselves?"

"I'm a fit man Mr..Roberts, but as yet I've felt no desire to go digging. There's good pickings enough in a bank."

"I'm aware of that sir, but perhaps Arnold and Slack might be persuaded to share in their new success and be satisfied at being rich whilst others dig."

"It would hardly be ethical, to go making offers on something I am not supposed to know anything about. A reputation is not made or kept that way."

"But fortunes are," Mr.. Roberts answered him. "Or are you rich enough?"

Ralston laughed. It was a ridiculous notion. Who ever had enough? He considered the situation a moment, then inclined his head toward Mr.. Roberts, dropping his voice to a mere whisper. "Perhaps you'd like to find Mr.. Kavak and have him at the bullion entrance by half-past noon."

DIAMONDS

Mr.. Roberts smiled. He'd achieved more than he'd hoped. "He will be here, sir, you can depend on it." But Ralston was not finished. " Mind you tell him nothing. Be there on time, Mr.. Brown usually takes his luncheon at Mrs. Fields' dining rooms. We can be sure of thirty minutes privacy, no more."

Mr.. Roberts understood. "If they be diamonds, Kavak will know. Meanwhile I will put out word that I want the address of Philip Arnold. He'll not be far from his precious hoard." Ralston straightened up and turned away to glance out of the window.

"I recall something about this Philip Arnold. Something to do with Charles Crocker. You ever hear about that?"

Mr.. Roberts did seem to recall something about that, but he hadn't known it had been Arnold who'd asked the big man to put up the fees for a diamond expedition in the Rockies. "Crocker ever give a reason?"

Ralston shrugged. "Charlie's made enough out of the railroad; he never was one for a gamble." He smiled suddenly, recalling something, "Unless of course it has four legs and a tail."

Mr.. Roberts laughed with him, but he was aware that William Ralston and Charles Crocker had probably wagered and lost more on the horses than most men could hope to earn in a lifetime. Quickly though Roberts thoughts returned to the diamonds. He was truly excited by the prospect of a new fortune to be made. It really was too good an opportunity to miss.

"Well, it looks like Arnold's gone and found them without Crocker's help. Those two boys sure looked as though they'd been out of civilization for quite some time. Slack looked as though he's ready to grow roots. I wonder if they found the Indians' hoard.

"That was Arnold's theory y'know. The redskins had been hiding them from the prospectors."

"Well, maybe so, but I'll guess it'll take more than beads to trade with those two savages, Mr.. Roberts." He stuck out a hand and pumped that of his visitor. "I want to thank you for drawing my attention to this matter, Mr.. Roberts and er, naturally I can rely on your discretion."

"Wild horses, Mr.. Ralston sir, it would take wild horses to get it from my lips."

Mr.. Roberts tipped his cane in the banker's direction again and made his way to the door. More customers came in wiping the mist from their eyes. Ralston watched Mr.. Roberts go and felt the presence of someone at his side. Mr.. William Lent, the financier, stood there, having grown tired of waiting in Ralston's office. Here was another fit man, yet grey with years.

"Our Mr.. Roberts seemed a little excited, Bill. Anything I should know?"

Ralston turned to face him and smiled. "What would you say to making another million, Will? How would your wife like to wear diamonds to go with her pearls?"

DIAMONDS

"Diamonds, Mr.. Ralston? Not a field we are familiar with surely." Mr.. Lent was a cautious man.

"Perhaps not, but neither can we let others reach that field before us, Will. You're in my confidence now. Sound out a few of your friends, see who wants to come aboard a little mining venture."

Mr. Lent frowned. "You're not saying much."

"When I have something to say, you'll be the first to know. You know yourself Will, it's a long way from hearing a rumor to confirming another Ophir."

Mr.. Ralston then shook Mr. Lent's hand and walked back towards his own inner sanctum. He stopped at a messenger,s desk on the way. "Have Mr.. Brown come to my office, Harold. As soon as he's free."

Diamonds, he was thinking, were just what San Francisco needed. Why, the city could become the very center of the financial world, and the Bank of California the greatest jewel in the whole collection. By God, if only it could be true.

DIAMONDS

CHAPTER TWO
'Your company is requested...'

The ferry left the dock, and Arnold and Slack were glad to be on it. Half way across the bay the fog thinned and the sun broke through, immediately warming their backs. As the city shrank behind them, they looked forward to getting back to Oakland and its quiet streets. They were warmed by the thought of their destination and the idea of a change of clothes and a hot meal, both long missed. Arnold tapped Slack's arm and pointed out some fish passing alongside the ferry. "Sturgeon, Slack. By God I'd like to taste that again. No finer fish than boiled sturgeon."

"I'd like to see you catch a fish," Slack remarked, scornful of Arnold's way with nature.

Arnold smiled. Let Slack think what he liked. He knew he could catch a fish as well as the next man if he wanted to. All it needed was... well, whatever it needed, a rod and a hook, and a hungry fish.

The ferry finally approached its destination and there looked to be quite a few people gathered ready for the return journey. Arnold inspected his pocket watch and checked the time. "The Central Pacific must be on time. Now there's a miracle, Slack. Things must be right in heaven today. Got themselves quite a haul of passengers too."

"Immigrants. Look at 'em, look worse than we do." Slack declared.

Arnold laughed. "Then you haven't seen yourself, John Slack. By God, them folks look as though they're dressed for the California Theater, compared with you."

Slack smiled He knew how bad he looked, but he'd grown attached to these rags, even if they were rapidly reverting back to nature. "You remember you promised to take Alyce to the theater when we returned. She'll remember."

"Hell, I'll even take her to the Grand Opera and book the best room in the Grand Hotel to wine and dine her. What do you think of that?"

"How many diamonds are you figuring to sell to pay for that?"

Arnold grinned, turning a little to get the full warmth of the sun on his sore neck. "Well, maybe not just yet, Slack, my friend, but we'll be rich soon

21

DIAMONDS

enough, you'll see. Then you'll see a difference, mark my words."

Slack made no comment. Right at this moment his stomach was sending out distress signals. He would have traded a diamond for a steak if pressed. It seemed to him that they'd spent an unnecessarily long time without eating. He wondered too, whether the leather boots he'd left at Moses Chase's house would still be there. Someone had won them off him at cards and he sorely missed them. There was another thing he'd trade a diamond for.

The Southern Pacific ferry finally docked at the bottom of Harrison Street where the sounds and smoke of the Southern and Central Pacific locomotives filled the air. Arnold and Slack disembarked and they had to walk up to 8th Street before cutting east toward 4th Avenue on the shore of the swamp some folks liked to call Lake Merrit. It was just here a new settlement was going up, and on the banks of the mud flats lived Alyce Wentworth, spinster. It was just a modest home. Four rooms and a veranda, but she was proud of it and kept it clean. Two other families had built close by and another was under construction. Alyce had planted trees in her yard, and there was good fishing in the tidal basin at high tide. But Alyce was no old maid; cast that notion aside. A more comely woman it would be hard to find in all of Oakland, let alone across the bay. She stood proud, dressed with care and a dash of flourish, although she was often without the means to buy anything new . Because she grew much of her own food, she had an unfashionable sun burnished face with freckles from all her time spent tilling the soil and chasing chickens. Yet, she never looked the part of a country woman. She herself thought she was demur and lady-like, which no dancer ever was. Her prominent brow, delicate nose and handsome profile should have featured on romances in the city galleries, not lie wasted in the barbaries of Oakland. She might have looked unapproachable to the locals, but her nature was loving and kind. She was a beauty in the wilderness.

She'd arrived in the city by railroad as the fiancee of one Thomas Kravis, prospector and quarter owner of a mine in the Ophir region. It might have been that Thomas Kravis would have become as rich as James Flood, or any other on Nob hill. When Kravis had to journey to New Orleans to pitch shares in his new mine to investors there, he had met and fallen for Alyce. He had seen nothing wrong with her being a showgirl. He'd returned to San Francisco engaged to her, promising to send for her when he made his fortune. He had kept his word and had immediately done the honorable thing and sent for her.

Alyce had come as soon as she could, happy to put aside dancing for wifely duties, but as luck would have it, she arrived on the very day her fiancee had been crushed to death in a rockfall. He had died so cruelly they had nothing but his bloodstained woolen cap to give Alyce as a keepsake.

Naturally she had moved into Kravis's modest home. She had pretty soon got to know that Kravis had done nothing much else than talk about her for almost six months since he'd returned from New Orleans. Men Kravis had worked with came agawking, but none offered to marry her; she was too fancy for them, and they judged they couldn't afford her. Pretty soon she was reduced to taking in lodgers to pay bills as lawyers chewed over her dead fiancee's estate. She'd been surprised to find herself an heiress, but she didn't expect much, and it was just as well. Alyce had always considered Mr.. Kravis an orphan, for he'd never talked about his family before dying. So she was surprised, more than anyone, when about a hundred Kravises arrived to make their claims on his estate. There was only so far a quarter share in a small mine can go, of course, and Alyce, as advised by one Philip Arnold, settled for the modest home in sunny Oakland in lieu of any further claims she might have made. (And even this the relatives bitterly contested, although greed won out as she let them squabble amongst themselves).

So Alyce's boarders provided her living, and her two most regular customers were Philip Arnold and John Slack, when they returned from prospecting. She never knew when they'd be coming back, but there was always space for Arnold, especially, for Alyce fancied that one day Arnold would ask her for her hand in marriage. She'd told him that he didn't have to wait until he was rich, for she knew that that could be a long wait indeed. In short, Miss Wentworth loved Philip Arnold, and to be frank, assumed they were married, for Arnold shared her bed. She had a soft spot for an ambitious man and Arnold could be tender if he was in the mood. Besides it was the best a woman of twenty-five could hope for. She thought that he returned her affections, but sometimes, on lonely evenings she did wonder that she might be a 'convenient' woman and no matter what he promised, one day he might forget. She knew that Arnold had a wife called Evaleena somewhere back in Kentucky, but she also knew that that marriage was over and could never be fixed. John Slack always referred to her as the "second Mrs Arnold " and she kind of liked the jest.

So it was to this address that Arnold and Slack were heading and dreaming of steaming hot food, clean sheets and all the comforts of home. The wilderness was all very well, but home sweet home was better.

Fog there might have been, but Alyce must have been born with witching powers for she was standing on her stoop well before Arnold and Slack came into view, and when she saw Arnold, never mind the way he was dressed and the months of grime, her heart soared and she dashed along the short path into his open arms. "Arnie, Arnie, I just knew it was you, I did. I felt it all day."

Arnold clasped his woman tight and almost squeezed the life out of her as they kissed right there in the open. Slack just sailed on by. He'd seen enough of these long lost lovers' reunions and he just wanted to get inside.

"Arnie, it's been four months, longer. How could you go so long?"

Arnold laughed and kissed her again. "My God woman, it's a fact I'd have been back a long time before this if I d remembered the taste of your kisses "

DIAMONDS

Alyce blushed. It was the nearest she'd gotten to hearing that Arnold loved her Arnold turned her around and took her arm as he walked her back to the house.

"Oh, Arnie, I so missed you."

Arnold didn't mind being called Arnie. He returned the favor by calling Alyce, Al. Al and Arnie sounded so cozy somehow.

"Al, you can start making plans for that next grand trip. Time to get yourself some fancy clothes too."

Alyce laughed. He always came back telling her these things. She knew it meant nothing, but she liked to hear it nevertheless, 'cause it meant he wasn't beaten yet.

"I mean it. Slack and me have made it this time. The Injuns were sure they'd shaken us off, but Slack has a nose like a fox. He tracked them all the way to the creek that I guarantee no white man has ever gotten sight of, and that's where we found them."

"Indians?" Alyce asked, confused.

"No, diamonds, my angel pie. There's diamonds out there as big as your pretty little fist."

Alyce laughed, shaking her head. "Then where are they, Arnie?"

Arnold frowned, pausing a moment on the wooden stoop. "I can see you don't believe me, but haven't Slack and me just come direct from the Bank of California? " He brandished the receipt that Mr.. Brown had issued him. "Now, would Philip Arnold and John Slack go to the bank if we didn't have proper business there? I'm telling you, Al, diamonds rest in that vault, you never saw the like of 'em. Slack and me have proved every doubting Thomas a liar. We found diamonds, and you know why the Injuns never traded 'em?"

Alyce's eyes were as big as saucers now. He'd always said he'd find diamonds, but he never before categorically declared that he positively had done it. "Why, Arnie? Why?"

"The Injuns sit on them, lie next to 'em, their little braves probably play marbles with' em, but I'm tellin' you those Injuns don't even *know* those are diamonds. They can't tell one from a pebble. They knew gold, but diamonds passed them by, Al. We walked in there and took all we could find in one day before they came back. It was as easy as picking daisies. All these years, angel pie, I've been thinking those Injuns were trying to hide them and keep them secret, and all the while they just didn't even know they were there. Makes you want to laugh or cry, don't it?"

Alyce shook her head. "You telling the truth, now, Arnie?"

"As God is my witness, Alyce, we is going to be rich, and you are going to live in a palace as big as William Ralston's Belmont. Bigger!"

She laughed again and pulled her man into the house that smelled of fresh baked bread. Arnold inhaled deeply; there was nothing quite like that smell, and it fair made a man giddy just to think about it after so long out in the wilds.

"John Slack, you come out of that kitchen, the bread isn't cooled yet. Before either one of you touch a thing in this house you are going to soak in a hot tub. You both smell badder than two old bears."

"Hot bread and a good soak," Arnold mused. "There's times when even diamonds seem worthless, Al. I've dreamed about this for more than a month. Times I would have paid with diamonds for the pleasure of your pies and hot tub up in those mountains."

"Well, you can pay with diamonds here, " Alyce told him, looking as though she meant it.

Arnold held up his hands. "Patience, Al, a few days yet and we will have more than enough for us all. What say you, Slack? How many diamonds would you say a hot tub is worth?"

Slack frowned. He looked into Arnold's face and at Alyce's smiling eyes and he knew they were mocking him. It was well known that bathing and Slack were not best of friends. Slack was a hard man to civilize. There are bears who would not care to consort with him on a hot day.

"Don't you worry about me," Slack told them. "I'll bathe tomorrow."

Alyce feigned horror. "John Slack, you will be first into that hot tub, and then I'm a going to burn those moldy old clothes of yours. Both of you look like tramps.I wouldn't have let you into my bank dressed like that. I'm crazy to let you into my house at all."

Arnold laughed to see the discomfort on Slack's face. "Better bolt the door, Al, afore this critter makes a run for it. We caught a wild one here."

Slack shook his head. Let them joke at his expense if it amused them. What he really wanted was some of that hot bread. That was what could make a man happy, not water.

William Ralston of the Bank of California was anxious for another reason entirely. It was twenty minutes since he'd brought Mr.. Roberts and Mr..Kavak into the bullion office behind closed doors. It would be ten more minutes before Mr.. Brown returned, but he didn't want his assistant cashier to know that he'd betrayed a trust, leastways not so openly. Perhaps it might have been wiser to wait until after the close of banking hours when all the staff were gone, but it was too late for that now. Mr.. Roberts smoked a cigar and stared with a monumental lack of patience as Mr.. Kavak examined the contents of Arnold and Slack's buckskin pouch.

Mr.. Kavak was not a man to be hurried. His manner was polite, respectful and his clothes were plain. But Mr..Kavak's beard, black and fierce, hid most of his face; only his overly crimson lips added color to his wide countenance. A watchmaker by trade, his acquaintance with diamonds wasn't extensive, but

DIAMONDS

his small store traded fine jewels, watches, and silverware for the wealthy of San Francisco, so if anyone in the city was to assess the value and determine the genuineness of what was in the pouch, it was he. To be truthful, Mr.. Kavak made most of his living as a pawnbroker, but that was no shame in a growing city where a man might be rich one day and poor the next. This was an optimistic city. Many a man had pawned his last precious piece for a chance to buy shares in the mines. Mr.. Kavak gave a fair price and was only too happy to redeem a good piece to the rightful owner, for he knew the value of repeated custom. For this reason he was a good judge of whether something was genuine or not and this had taught him a great deal about people's characters, too.

It is not recorded what Mr..Kavak thought about the ethics of the chief cashier and a customer examining the contents of another customers's valuables. It was a salutary lesson in how private a man's business was at this bank, and Mr.. Kavak was glad now that he kept his gold buried in a sack under the old well at his home.

"Well?" Mr..Roberts inquired, not for the first time.

"What have we got here, Mr..Kavak? " Ralston wanted to know, picking up a red stone and holding it up to the daylight. It cast a red glow about his hand.

"What you have there, Mr..Ralston, is a ruby, if I am not mistaken, this one here," he held up a small, brilliant green irregular stone, "this is an emerald, and a fine specimen too."

"So it's not diamonds," Mr.. Roberts exclaimed, almost disappointed. An emerald or ruby mine would have been just as pleasing.

"Oh the majority are diamonds, Mr.. Roberts, there's no disputing that. As genuine as they come. But diamonds need to be cut and polished, sir, and there's no one to do that outside of New York. There's a sprinkling of rubies, garnets, and just a few emeralds, and my judge is that although they are small, these could be considered good specimens. Look here, this is a sapphire, I believe. A very pretty sparkle to it, even unpolished. If this was colored glass we'd know it gentlemen, for natural abrasion would dull it.

"You're saying these are *genuine*, then? All of 'em?" Mr.. Roberts asked.

" I cannot pretend to have seen such quantities taken out of the earth before, but I know what is real and what is not. This stone here, is this a diamond?"

He handed it to Mr. Roberts who studied it in the window light a moment before handing it to Ralston. The light caught it and there was a momentary sparkle. "I'd say yes." Ralston answered for the both of them.

"Then you'd be poor men if you'd paid for it," Mr. Ravak replied. "It's fluorspar, and I know they already found much like it in Illinois. I have heard nothing of emeralds or diamonds being found anywhere in the Union. Garnets yes, they can be found in many places I believe, but rubies? Nowhere I know of."

DIAMONDS

Ralston picked up a diamond from the table and looked more carefully at it. "This is a momentous occasion gentlemen. American diamonds."

"How long will this stay secret?" Mr. Roberts asked no one in particular.

Ralston turned on him . "We are all sworn to secrecy. All three of us never saw these stones. Mr. Roberts, Mr. Kavak, your word on this is vital."

"I saw no diamonds this day," Mr. Kavak declared, beginning the task of restoring the stones to their pouch.

"Nor I." Mr. Roberts agreed, less convincingly. "But Mr. Kavak, do you not place a value on all this?"

"These are rough, uncut, primitive stones, Mr. Roberts. They only gain value when they have been cut and polished. I could make an estimate, but I won't be held to it." He waved his hands to absolve himself.

"No one is holding you to anything," Ralston reassured him.

"Then," he said, putting the last stone in, taking it from Ralston's hand and tying up the pouch in the exact way he'd found it, "I'd guess the diamonds alone are worth one hundred and twenty five thousand dollars."

Both Ralston and Mr. Roberts looked at each other in astonishment. They hadn't been prepared for that. It made this hoard more valuable than gold. How many more of these were there? Only Arnold and Slack would know. It made them dizzy to think about it.

Ralston consulted his watch and saw that it was one o' clock precisely. "Perhaps I could stand both you gentlemen to a lunch?"

Mr. Roberts accepted, but Mr. Kavak had other matters to attend to. He accepted the fifty dollar fee from Ralston without comment. Both men could rely on this being secret between them: less sure were they of Mr. Roberts, but that was the risk they had taken.

Outside the bank Mr. Kavak bid them good-day, and Mr. Roberts watched him disappear into the haze. The sun was making progress through the fog at last.

"Can we trust him?" Mr. Roberts wanted to know. .

Ralston struck out across the boards toward the hotel dining rooms.

"Mr. Kavak is an unusual man, Mr. Roberts. Not your ordinary emigrant. Besides, he speaks better English than you or I. He's a cultivated man. His uncle is a close friend to the Czar, and Mr. Kavak is quite an asset to this town just for that. Besides, who else could translate the occasional business we have with Russian traders?"

"And much good that does us. They never have money, and I always have to resort to barter."

"Trade is trade, Mr. Roberts. Come on, let us talk of carboniferous compounds and Mr. Philip Arnold."

Mr. Roberts smiled. "It's good to be in business with an educated man, Mr. Ralston."

DIAMONDS

"Ay, but you'd better hope Mr. Arnold is lacking in that direction. It's better if he doesn't know his worth. I hate a prolonged haggling."

John Slack was not a happy man. He sat sulking in a full hot tin bath while Alyce washed his wild hair. He'd been shaved, insulted, and even now was being embarrassed by Arnold's jokes about his dusky complexion. Well, it was a fact that Slack liked to work with his shirt off. He saw no point in sweating it out like Arnold did, and if it made him deep brown down to his waist, well, so what, he was healthier for it, and anyway hadn't they both as boys spent days, if not months each year swimming in the creek stark naked? They'd been browner than good old Kentucky earth most of the time. Arnold had grown stuffy in his growing up, was all.

"Didn't you ever wash out there?" she complained.

"We swam in the rivers when there was one, " Slack pointed out, "but some of that water is as cold as ice and a man could lose a few fingers and toes in there if he wasn't careful. The wilderness isn't exactly full of steambaths and piped water. You through yet?"

"No, I'm not through, we've got to rinse yet."

"Slack, quit griping. You got a free haircut, free hot bath, and the prettiest barber in the West. Be grateful, it's not a mountain lion who's pawing your hair."

"Now, that was something," Slack recalled, suddenly much animated. "Alyce you should have been there. I was trying to get to sleep, just staring up at the stars as I generally do, when suddenly I sorta felt something warm at the top of my head. I didn't move a muscle. It's best to be cautious in mountains, 'cause you don't know what's acoming. So I turned my head sideways a little, and I could hear real close to my ear a heart beating that wasn't mine and it certainly wasn't Arnold's, 'cause I've known him as long as I've lived and I'd seen no sign of a heart yet."

Alyce smiled at Arnold. She knew better. Arnold pulled a face at her and laughed, enjoying Slack's retelling of the familiar tale.

"Anyways, this critter beside my head is making funny sounds in its throat, like it was real keen to eat and the only thing to eat was Arnold and me, I knew from the smell and the noises that it was a member of the cat family. Normally they wouldn't come near unless they were starving or crazy, but this was summer and a warm night. I just couldn't figure out what a mountain lion was doing sitting practically on top of my head. I turned some and saw he had a paw on Arnold's head and he seemed pretty damn interested in his hair.

"I thought he'd been using the bear grease again. It was an astonishing thing to see this animal practically combing his hair. I thought he was going to tear Arnold's head off. I was reaching for my knife when I became aware of

28

two more of the critters very close by, impatiently bouncing from one foot to another, like they just couldn't wait to eat us for supper. I swear, I thought we was gonners for sure."

"I was still asleep," Arnold remembered, "which was a lucky thing, for who knows what might have happened if I'd moved. A mountain lion has got some pretty mean claws and they are real strong. You'd lose if you tried to arm wrestle one."

Alyce laughed, throwing up her hands ."Liars. Arm-wrestling mountain lions. You two are terrible to me. I was really believing you."

She got her revenge quickly enough, heaving up a pail of cold water and splashing it down over Slack's head. Slack roared, but Alyce was quicker than he and she had the second pail over his head before he could do anything about it. It was quite a shock to see Slack so clean. Now you could see his scars, some still vivid and raw. Prospector's medals.

"Get him a towel Alyce, I reckon you've seen enough of him for one day."

Alyce handed him a towel and Slack hauled himself out of the bath affecting great injustice. He rubbed himself down as Alyce, eyes averted, went back into the kitchen to put another log under the range.

Arnold stood up and looked down into the bath. "Best get this water on the roses Al. Enough rich soil in there now to make 'em grow six feet tall."

Slack looked back down at the contents of the bath and pulled a face. It was carrying more silt than the Mississipi. Hard to believe it had started out clean. Slack was decent by the time Alyce returned to the room.

"What happened to the mountain lion, Slack ?" she wanted to know, teasing him, but half of her fascinated by his tall story.

Slack grinned at her and rubbed his chin as he tried to recall.

"Arnold woke up, " Slack answered. "He had a lion's paw on his hair, and he lay there blinking at me, wondering what was happening."

"Thought I was about to be scalped," Arnold told Alyce. "I couldn't move my head. I saw Slack had a knife in his hand and I was just about to reach for my own when..."

Slack jumped in to continue the tale "When suddenly the mountain lion made its move and it knocked Arnold on the head with such a force he rolled away yelping with pain. I was just about to make a rush with my knife, but before I could move, the lion had sunk its teeth into Arnold's canvas sack and made off with it, quickly followed by two cubs skirting around us to make sure there was no trouble. They moved liked greased lightning. It was all over in a second."

"But what was in the canvas sack?" Alyce wanted to know, now transfixed by the story.

"Venison Deer I shot the week before. I'd been saving that piece until it was good and ready." Arnold told her.

DIAMONDS

Alyce frowned. It sounded disgusting. "You were using the meat for a pillow?"

"Best place for it if you don't want it to get took in the night. That lion had a smart nose all right. He knew what it was, and he was trying to get it without waking us up. He didn't want trouble, and he knew he'd get trouble if he woke Arnold. They say animals are dumb. Not this one."

"It was a she," Alyce remarked, confidently. "A lioness with her cubs. A male wouldn't have been so smart."

"Hark at her," Slack said, laughing. "A lioness. You never once been in the wilderness and you know whether it was a lion or lioness that was combing Arnold's hair." He turned to Arnold and shook his head. "You got yourself a clever woman, Arnold. She's got the sight."

Arnold smiled and took Alyce's hand. "I think she's right. Neither one of us stopped to look, but I'd say it was a lioness, now I thinks about it."

Slack scowled. Now Arnold was on her side.

"Well anyway, I'm sure it was very frightening. Why, you both could have been eaten." Alyce declared, mostly to mollify Slack, who looked a tad hurt.

Arnold laughed. "Even if they'd bitten us, we would have given them a good fight."

Slack pulled on a pair of old boots and wistfully thought again of his lost pair. "It's the lion I feel sorry for." He was ignoring any advice about the lions sex. "Eating that canvas sack . Damn hard thing to digest."

"Oh,the poor thing," Alyce wailed, genuinely concerned.

"The cubs didn't get much either; it's a tough school in the mountains." Arnold told her. He saw her puzzled expression and wondered, "What's wrong now Alyce? We didn't touch a hair of that lioness, if that's what's worrying you."

"What I can't understand is how she could smell the venison out with you two lying on top of it."

Slack and Arnold roared with laughter at that, their eyes falling on the clothes they had discarded. There was a strong scent coming from that quarter and it was a wonder they'd lasted so long.

"I'm burning those," Alyce told them, putting her fingers to her nose.

"There's still life in 'em yet," Slack complained. He'd grown attached.

"That's what I'm afraid of, John Slack. I don't want no bugs setting up home here."

Arnold laughed again and stooped to pick up the tin bath. He looked at Slack tying on his boots and let out a yell of joy. "By God it's good to be back in civilization again, hey Slack?"

"Speak for yourself, Philip Arnold. I'm civilized enough for one day. There was no call to cut *and* wash my hair. I'm telling you, there's many a folk in Oakland city who look clean but whose business couldn't wash as clean as mine."

Arnold picked up the tin bath and steadied it in his arms. "Now that's a fact, Slack. There's truth in your words." He cocked an eye at Alyce as she opened the kitchen door for him. "What do y'think, Alyce? What about this Mr. William Ralston, chief cashier of the Bank of California. Can we trust him?"

Alyce smiled sweetly. "All I know is that Mr.. Ralston is reckoned to be the most honest banker this side of the Divide."

Arnold's eyebrows raised a little as he struggled with the bath. "Is that so? Well, you go ask Mr. Adolpho Sutro the same question. He's been villified by Ralston and his pal Bill Sharon for ten years or more on account of his Virginia City tunnel. You ask him if he thinks Ralston is an honest man."

Slack was walking up and down in the room they'd just left, trying to get comfortable in his boots. He saw them looking at him and raised his arm as if he were about to make a sermon. "I'll tell thee Alyce, a man's a fool for robbing a bank when for the price of a good suit he can open one."

Alyce acknowledged this pearl with a respectful smile. Arnold just stepped outside and threw the water over Alyce's dog roses, satisfied to see the ground soak it up thirstily.

"Now that'll do 'em good Al. I once had some wild roses growing back in Kentucky. I'll tell you that there's many a night I'd come in from the fields in summer and the porch would be full of the scent of 'em. He sighed. "It was like stepping into the arms of the most beautiful woman in the world."

Alyce laughed, shaking her head and letting her hair fall loose a moment before she quickly pinned it back. Arnold set the bath down and smiled awkwardly. "You look real fine, Al. Come here."

For some unaccountable reason Alyce suddenly felt shy, and she retreated into her kitchen asking, " Now who's for pancakes?"

"With maple syrup?" Slack called out.

"Anyway you like it."

"Pancakes, " Slack was heard muttering to himself as he continued to walk in his shoes. Then he suddenly popped his head around the corner. "Don't cook 'em without me, Alyce. I want to watch."

"You want to eat them, y'mean. Last time I cooked, you ate everything before I had time to serve it up. You attend to your boots, John Slack."

"Yes, you attend to your boots, Slack. Time we opened up a bottle to celebrate our homecoming. What you say, Al?"

"Celebrate all you want, but don't mess up my parlor."

Now, would we do that?" Arnold teased her.

"And you tell John Slack to keep his room tidy this time. I think he was raised by hogs."

"There's a few hogs who'd take exception to that," Arnold remarked

DIAMONDS

Alyce smiled as she fiddled with pots and pans, readying herself for cooking. She looked out of the window and pointed out the new house going up at the end of her yard. Something narrow, but quite grand in its own way. "You see the new house. Revellini."

"The Italian? Old Garibaldi's pal?"

"The same. Only now he's a stonemason and he's brought twenty stone cutters over from Torino to work for him. His wife is pregnant again. Sixth child in eight years. Poor woman."

"Six? " Arnold protested. "Imagine clothing and feeding them. You'd need to find diamonds every week just to stand still."

Alyce fell silent and busied herself with the batter. She wanted a child more than anything else, but unless Arnold married her it wouldn't be. She couldn't have a bastard. Well , she could, and she was almost willing, but she couldn't continue to live in San Francisco and stay respectable.

Arnold sensed he'd said something to upset her . He came up behind her and slipped her arms around her, kissing the back of her neck. "We'll be rich soon Alyce. We'll be wanting to be respectable."

Alyce said nothing, but she loved his hot lips on her neck and the feel of his warm body held tightly against hers. She thrilled to his touch. What exactly did he mean by respectable? There had never been any promises, nothing he could be held to.

"I know, I know. I never did get a divorce from that wife of mine, but I would, I truly would if I knew where she was. Alyce, you know I'd marry you tomorrow if you'd only forget about her. No one would know. Most people already think we are married already. If Slack and me make money this time; and I'm convinced of it, as convinced of it as I am that there is God up there watching over us, then we can make a new home back East and raise ourselves a family. I mean it. You just say it and I will make you mine."

Alyce still said nothing. She was astonished. Arnold had never said this much to her before. He had never talked of homes and family. It was a shock, but at the same time it was a thrill.

Arnold kissed her neck again. "You know, when I go away from you I forget what a beautiful woman you really are."

"You do?" Alyce asked, sounding concerned.

"Yes I do. I don't mean disrespect by that, Alyce, the Lord knows I don't. But I look at the trees in the forests and the lakes and mountains and they are beautiful. I can see rivers disappearing into far-off valleys and clouds scouring the tops of hills and sometimes it all takes your breath away, it's so beautiful. I mean it. I come from Kentucky, where they think an anthill is halfway to a mountain. I never tire of how beautiful the West is, or how hostile. When I see the deer and wild blossoms I try to picture you to compare, always I forget a detail here, or the way your eyes look when you smile, and I just can't see it.

DIAMONDS

So when I come home and I see you again, it's a shock, woman, a real shock to see you so real, so radiant. I just know that if you were up in the mountains with Slack and me, the entire world would look so dull in comparison, and we'd be amazed at just how much we missed being out there all the time.

"Alyce, forgive me for being away from you for so long, but I just want to say thank you for being so beautiful and being here for me when return."

Alyce could hardly move. She couldn't whisk, she couldn't speak. It was the prettiest speech that any man had ever said to her; or anyone she ever knew, for that matter. And to think it had been said by Philip Arnold, who she'd never thought had a romantic bone in his body. She knew they had to be true words. Arnold didn't need to waste any on her when he had her body and soul already. She leaned back into him some more and he spun her around to give her a kiss. They pressed together with surprising force, their passion aroused, sharpened by the months apart. Alyce held her man, never mind the whisk on one hand and the sticky flour on the other. She held him as if she never intended to let him go, and if she could have produced a child for him right there and then, she would have and called him Arnold Junior to boot.

"What happened to the pancakes?" Slack called from the other room. He looked into the kitchen and saw the blissful scene. "Put him down, Alyce, before you squeeze him to death."

Alyce blushed and turned back to her range. Arnold smiled, his heart beating with passion and longing. "John Slack, I reckon it's time you found yourself lodging some place else. Perhaps Mexico City would be near enough."

Slack laughed, retreating back into the parlor "And leave you alone with that woman? Before you know it, Philip Arnold, you'd be a father of twins and working in some office, wearing a brown suit."

It wasn't so very much later that Alyce was serving up steaming hot pancakes to go with the fresh coffee and brandy that Arnold had placed on the stoop table. She returned to sit with them as they ate and she couldn't help but laugh to herself at how clean and respectable these two men looked, compared with the two wild men who'd wandered in only a few hours before.

Slack sat in his chair with his back to the sun, his eyes on the wild fowl settled on the lake off in the distance. She admired the way he was so attached to wild creatures.

Arnold ate with relish. He was comfortable in Alyce's home, and now and then he glanced over at Alyce and gave her a smile. She'd never seen him so happy and secure. She reflected on how it would have been if she'd met him ten years earlier. How handsome he would have looked in uniform. All she could remember of her youth was the best men getting into uniform, riding out East and never coming home. The best of them had always died and families were forever mourning

But Arnold was hers now, and she'd hang onto him. She turned her atten-

33

tion to Slack for a moment to catch him cramming more pancake into his mouth than was strictly necesssary. It would be a tough woman who could tame Slack, she was thinking to herself; he was far gone in the matters of manners, but he had a good heart and a sharp brain when he wanted it, and that wasn't to be sneezed at. It was comical to see him in boots and dressed like a gentleman, like a bear wearing a suit. It looked nice, but it was plain wrong.

Arnold was suddenly looking down the road at an approaching figure. "You expecting a visitor?"

Alyce shook her head. "Might be for the neighbours."

Arnold pushed his plate away and expressed his opinion with a satisfying belch. "That was mightly good, Alyce. Mighty Good."

The visitor turned out to be a boy, a uniformed bank messenger, all puffed out from his quick trot from the ferry landing. He had his face buried in a scrap of paper, and everyone could see he deeply uncertain that he was in the right place.

Slack stood up as the boy stopped outside the gate. "You got no dog have you?" the boy asked nervously.

"No dog," Alyce replied. "Who are you looking for?"

The boy seemed to grow in confidence. "I'm looking for two gentlemen. A Mr.. Philip Arnold and a Mr.. John Slack."

Slack turned to Arnold, but he shrugged; he didn't understand it either. Why would the bank want them? They'd deposited the diamonds legally. There was no dispute about ownership.

"It depends." Slack told the boy, "Who wants to know?"

"Bank of California, sir. Mr.. William Ralston."

Slack looked aggrieved momentarily. "It ain't burned to the ground is it?"

"No, sir," the boy answered, puzzled.

"It ain't fallen down?" Slack asked.

"No sir, it'd take more than two hurricanes to do that."

"Then it must have been robbed. That's why you're here."

"No sir, it hasn't been robbed either." Now the boy was really puzzled.

Arnold smiled at Slack's questioning. The man could be quite exasperating sometimes. "Spit it out boy. Tell us why your here."

The boy was relieved to get some sense out of the men at last. He'd already given up hope of a tip. "I have an invitation, sir. Mr. Ralston would like to know if it is convenient for Mr. Slack and Mr. Arnold to join him for supper at Culpepper's this evening at seven o'clock."

Arnold could not act anything other than surprised. They had never met this man Ralston, and here he was inviting them to dine. "Funny thing, wouldn't you say, John Slack. We make a deposit at the bank, and suddenly Mr.. Ralston is offering us food. Would you call me a suspicious man, Slack?"

"Cautious, Arnold, cautious. Who knows the heart of a banker?"

DIAMONDS

Arnold smiled, nodding at Alyce as if to say, *This is your most honest banker this side of the Divide.*

"He might just want to meet you, Arnie," Alyce told him. "You've just come into town. You could tell him how things are in the wilderness. A banker needs to know these things."

"Not now there's a railroad, he doesn't. No, Slack and me know why he's asking. We ain't fools."

Slack shrugged. "I ain't ever dined with a banker afore."

"You will tonight, Slack. Boy? You tell Mr. William Ralston that John Slack and Philip Arnold will be honored to join him at seven o' clock."

"Ay sir. Thank you, sir."

Slack dug deep into his new pants and found a coin, which he tossed to the boy. The boy caught it, inspected the quarter, and was impressed.

"You're a gentleman, sir. Thank you."

Arnold laughed as the boy ran off along the road. "Called you a gentleman, Slack. Best stop off and get you a topper and cane before we dine tonight."

Alyce laughed and Slack blushed. He didn't know why they always made fun of him. Never knew why at all.

Arnold took Alyce by her hands and pulled her close to him. "Alyce, what did I tell you? Bankers come a courting us today, tomorrow it'll be kings and queens. Me and Slack have got what they want. Diamonds, my fairie queene, sparkling diamonds. Soon we will be rich, richer than anyone."

"But how does he know?" Slack asked, returning to his chair. "It was supposed to be a secret."

Arnold suddenly turned pale and struck his head with the palm of his left hand. "Slack, we're a couple of prize fools."

"Why so?" Slack couldn't think of anything they'd done wrong.

"'Cause we didn't count our diamonds before we deposited them, that's why. Old Ralston's got himself in an excited state, and there's us trusting this bank with our hard-won diamonds."

"Don't take on so, Arnie," Alyce remonstrated. "Mr. Ralston doesn't know you haven't counted them. Besides, he's an honorable man. He wouldn't cheat you. After all, he's invited you to supper, hasn't he?"

Arnold frowned, still discouraged. "Ralston has probably got his pockets filled with our diamonds right now while he hunts the city for bits of glass to put in their place."

Alyce wouldn't hear of it. "I tell you, you can trust him. He's a good man. Judge others as ye would judge yourself, Philip Arnold."

Slack snorted. "That's what's worrying him. Still , it's no use frettin'. If he knows, he knows. We knew we'd never keep it secret for long."

Arnold shrugged. He wasn't unhappy about this; he'd expected something like it. News of a gold strike traveled like a prairie fire. There was no reason to

35

DIAMONDS

suspect that diamonds would be any different. The essential thing was secrecy. He and Slack were the only two people in the world who knew where the diamonds had been found. That information they had to retain for as long as possible. No money on earth could prise that away from them. Well possibly, but certainly no small amount. Arnold knew one thing about diamonds. They were no earthly use to a man unless he could sell them. He and Slack had damn near starved to death carrying them around, and more than once they'd felt tempted to sell just one for food. But all that was past now.

Slack was hunting around for something.

"What you lost, Slack?" Alyce asked.

"You get the *Alta* today? You keep any for me like I asked? There's a whole lot of news me and Arnold have missed."

"There's news of the war," Alyce told him." The French and the Prussians are having a terrible time. There's a Prince Otto Bismark who says the Prussians will win and crush the French. The war must end soon, I think."

Arnold remembered. "There's a few fellows up in Oregon who don't like the Iron Chancellor. You read all about it, Slack, and then you can chew my ear off when we next get stuck in some godforsaken hole."

Alyce laughed; she knew Slack just loved to read and discuss what he read. Must be his fate that he had a partner who didn't care a fig for news of any kind, still less a debate about it.

Arnold grinned. "A man doesn't need no books when John Slack is about. I seen him read a newspaper and tell you what was in it word for word. It's a gift, only I don't know what use a gift like that is to a man."

"Well, John Slack, if you look in the trunk by the parlor door, I believe there's a month or more of newspapers for you. Today's is lying on top with a lively speech made by Mr.. Horace Greeley of the *New York Tribune*."

"Now there's a man who'd make a good president," Slack declared.

Arnold shook his head. "It's Grant. You ain't going to shift that rock, John Slack, especially not with a newspaper man."

"Well I'm looking forward to the day when Mr. John Slack and Mr. Philip Arnold make the *Alta* California. It'll read "The Discoverers of the Diamond Fields.""

Arnold laughed. "No, no, the American Diamond fields. I tell you, Al, you'll be wearing diamonds bigger than those pretty little fists of yours sooner than a cat can catch a fly."

Alyce smiled, and the pleasure in her eyes lifted the spirits of both men. Arnold took hold again and squeezed her, looking down into her eyes with a look she knew only too well. She looked sideways a moment, still pretending to be shy.

Slack made his way back to the stoop then. In his arms were twenty yellowing newspapers or more, and he looked happy. Arnold winked at Alyce.

DIAMONDS

There would be plenty of time to make hay. He moved her backwards into the parlor.

Alyce pretended to be shocked. "In the afternoon, Philip Arnold?"

"It's bedtime in the East, Al. If the president of the United States can go to bed now, well it would be downright ungracious of us not to emulate him, wouldn't you say?"

Alyce giggled. The argument was riduclous. "Well, if the president says it's all right."

"He does, Al, he surely does, " Arnold answered her as he steered her into her bedroom and bolted the door behind him. Arnold had his shoes off with a loud thud before Alyce had time to even think.

"Besides, I have four months to catch up on. Could be there'll be little time for us, what, between the banks and the deals."

Alyce lay back on the bed and discarded the last of her clothes. Arnold shed his newly-ironed shirt and lay beside her propped up on his elbow. "Al, I swear you're more lovely than ever." He stared at her white skin and cupped one small breast in his broad hands, grinning as he watched her nipples firm up under his fingers.

"Aren't you going to kiss me?" she asked, teasingly.

He smiled and did as he was summoned. Alyce had only one question. "You sure there was no Indian squaw who won your heart out there?"

Arnold laughed. "There was many, Alyce. I told 'em it was no use. They begged me to stay and court them, but I explained, you haven't tasted Alyce's apple pie. It was pitiful to see the disappointment in their big brown eyes. They knew they was licked. Not a one of them can bake a pie."

Alyce smiled and kissed her man's broad chest. Arnie was sure a one for tall tales. But, and this did cause her some concern, she couldn't ever recall baking him an apple pie.

CHAPTER THREE
The Price Of A Man's Pride.

The hour was fast approaching seven o'clock. The streets were still damp, but the sky was clear, a moon was on the rise, and there was no sign of fog rolling back in off the bay. It was a touch cold but not excessively so, and neither Slack nor Arnold remarked on it, the cold being one of the many things they had long put up with.

The boardwalks were full of people going hither and thither and the streets full of carriages and individuals on horseback hacking through the interminable mud. Many a foot was turned toward the same destination, namely J.C. Culpepper's Fine Eating Establishment, with public dining rooms to seat three hundred at a time, private booths on request, orchestra six nights a week and the finest chefs this side of the Divide. Culpepper's was no ordinary restaurant. Even the waiters had something of a reputation for being the richest of their kind, for it was not unknown for miners and the like to pay in gold dust ; indeed a scale was provided in the cashiers box for just such an occasion.

At Culpepper's a man could enter rich and exit poor. It was not the food or the wine that stung a man's wallet but the gaming table, which only a few gentlemen had access to, and besides all that, the many private transactions that took place in the private booths between businessmen and lawyers, or prospectors and bankers. There's many a time when the arguments were solved with bullets, ignored by waiters rushing on by with hot food in their hands. Culpepper's was a place to meet, swap gossip,and spread vile rumors.

So it was with a certain anxiety and curiosity that they approached this glittering eatery. Considering its reputation, it was all the more confusing that Mr. William Chapman Ralston, chief cashier of the Bank of California had chosen it as their rendezvous.

"Why here?" Slack complained as he peered in through the windows.

Arnold had been thinking the same. "Lot of noise. A man could get shot and no one would notice." He'd fretted since leaving the Oakland Pier.

Slack slowly nodded. He believed it. The restaurant was packed to the gills with men and not a few women in fine fancy clothes and all of them were eating, shouting, grabbing, bustling and haggling, every damn one of them talking louder and louder as the orchestra tried level best to beat back the din. It was a proper circus in there, and hot too. The blast of human warmth mixed with the pungent aromas of cooked hams, sides of beef, and fresh fish was so great, it was like a solid wall you had to pass through with the knowledge of a secret password.

"Afraid of what he's going to ask?" Arnold asked Slack as they paused in front of the doors, letting others go before them.

"Yeah, I am. Have you ever seen such a crowd?"

Arnold smiled and put his arm around Slack's shoulders. "Slack, old buddy, you're going to have to get used to this. We're going to be rich men, and we'll be eating like this every day, cutting deals, swapping small talk, big talk. "I think we should be opening a restaurant when we get rich, Slack. Right across the street. What d'y'think?"

Slack crossed his fingers. He hated it when Arnold talked big. He wanted to know that there was money in the bank before he went off imagining what it would be like to spend it.

"Ready?" Arnold asked him.

Slack shook his head, but Arnold stepped forward and dragged him over the threshold anyway.

Arnold was impressed. The *maitre d'* approached them with a hostile expression on his sweating face. Slack could see that he was about to try and turn them away.

"We're here to dine with Mr. William Ralston, banker, " Slack informed him.

The *maitre d'* adopted a new more generous expression. He pretended to check a list he had on a high desk by the door

"Table 82, gentlemen. Please follow me."

Arnold dug Slack in the ribs and made a funny mime of the *maitre d's* walk. Slack laughed, and it helped ease him into the place. The floor was sticky underfoot; no one had much of an aim for the cuspidors in this place.

William Ralston sat alone at his table, a bottle of wine chilling beside him in an impressive silver ice bucket, nibbling on some bread as he waited. He seemed to be enjoying himself as he kept an eye on some ladies gathered beside the orchestra's podium.

"Mr. Slack and Mr. Arnold sir," the *maitre d'* announced, just as the orchestra struck up a waltz. Arnold wasn't sure what was said, but he shook hands and sat down alongside Slack anyway. Ralston looked impressive to Arnold, every inch the successful banker, and judging from the number of people who passed by just to nod and smile, he was a well-known figure. If this was to be private conversation, more than a hundred folks would be in on it.

"Glad you could make it, gentlemen. Some wine? Pay no attention to the music; if you want to be heard talk as loud as you can, everyone always does.

Slack was amused. He'd expected many things, but such a casual and friendly meeting had not been it. Alyce was right, Ralston did look like the kind of man you'd trust on instinct, and there weren't too many of those born on God's earth.

"Some wine would be good," Slack told him.

"Yes, sir, some wine would be good," Arnold echoed, his eyes on stalks as he watched a woman slip her hands down a man's pants and cackle with laughter at his public surprise and private delight.

"Welcome to the club, gentlemen." Ralston lifted the bottle and poured three glasses full to the brims, waving away a waiter who was concerned for his job. "French Chablis, Mr. Slack. War raging in France, and still they can send their wine all over the world. Kind of admire their determination, don't you? The French will have to look to their business in the future, though. There's a lot of determined men aiming to make California wine best. I've got a few acres planted with vines myself."

"California wine?" Arnold asked, sure he hadn't heard right.

"Yes, sir, there's vineyards planted right now. The Buena Vista vini-cultural society has six thousand acres planted for wine grapes in Sonoma County. Mr.. Leland Stanford is talking of planting millions of vines. Europe has the rot, and he believes our native soil is better than French soil. Now, what do you think of that? My friend, Captain Olmstead of the North-West trade, is interested in settling in Napa Valley. He says that one day he's going to invest up there and better the French at their own game,"

Arnold scratched his head. He'd never expected to come here and discuss wine. He knew something about whiskey, but wine was a mystery to him.

"Tell me when they start a whiskey farm, Mr. Ralston, I'll go for that."

Ralston laughed, glad to have reached an understanding with Arnold. He was studying their clothes. They were respectable, but hardly from the best tailors. Mr. Roberts had said that Arnold and Slack were the worst kind of ruffians, uncouth and uncivilized, yet here before him were two gentlemen as clean as any he'd seen of late and as respectable as any man could hope to be. Mr. Roberts seemed poorly informed. Offers would have to be adjusted accordingly upward.

"Risky business, establishing a vineyard," Slack announced. "You have to wait seven years before you get a crop worth drinking, then it has to mature, and on top of that the phylloxera louse is killing off the French vines. Perhaps Mr.. Stanford has the right idea, Mr.. Ralston. Arnold and me know something about farming. If you can keep a pest out when others have it bad, then you'll make a killing."

Ralston studied Slack, amazed. The man had a plain appearance, but to discover he was well read-up on the latest developments in France and skilled as a farmer. . . well, further revision of his offer would be in order. Clearly he was dealing with two well educated men who happened to be diamond prospectors. One thing was for sure: this would not be a wasted evening.

"I shall pass your remarks on to Mr..Stanford. But I still say it's one thing proving you can grow wine in California, but quite another thing making a man drink it. I'm proposing we adopt some standards of quality."

"If it's cheaper than Madeira they'll drink anything," Arnold remarked. "I've seen men drink poison up in the mines and go back for a second bottle."

Ralston smiled, raising his glass. "To poison, then. May it make us rich."

Arnold and Slack grinned, liking the joke. They raised their glasses and drank to each other in turn.

"Being a banker is about taking risks, gentlemen. You have my admiration. How many years have you been out there in the mountains looking for er..." Clearly Ralston was about to say diamonds, but he remembered just in time to say gold to save his honor.

"We came out here over ten years ago We've broken our backs with the best of 'em," Arnold told him. "Sooner go back to farming than waste my time searching for that particular poison. Slack's the same, eh, Slack?

"We found some, but nothing that was worth freezing to death in winter for, or being eaten alive by flies bigger than buzzards in summer. Man's a fool digging for gold at four dollars a day, when he can get other folk to do it for him."

"He means owning shares," Arnold explained. "Like the bank."

Ralston conceded the point. "Bank of California has always been bullish on Virginia City, Mr. Arnold. Gold has built California, and silver will do the same. Can't say I'd like to dig it out with my own hands,"

"Thank the Lord there's folks who do." Slack told him.

Ralston nodded, taking another sip of his wine. "Glad we have an understanding, gentlemen. Now perhaps you'd like to order up some food? The beef is prime and the fish is fresh, nothing but the best here. "

Slack squinted up at the wall and swore. "Can't see any board. You know what the special is?"

Ralston looked most amused and shook his head. "Menu is printed on a card here, different every day. Take my word for it, the beef is best."

Arnold agreed. "We'll take the beef."

Ralston did the ordering and had more wine poured. Arnold sensed he was trying to keep them both sweet.

The food arrived along with more wine before Ralston could bring himself to speak on the subject of why they were invited, and even then, Arnold could see the man was having trouble getting it out.

"My cashier tells me you made an interesting deposit in my bank this morning gentlemen."

DIAMONDS

"Did he say how interesting?" Arnold asked, laying down his fork.

Ralston held up his hands. "Now, Mr. Arnold, I am an ethical man. A man's business is his business, but I'll come straight out with it. Another gentlemen with whom you are acquainted drew my attention to your deposit and he made a speculation as to what might be in our vault. You'd think me a strange man Mr. Arnold if talk of," he lowered his voice a moment, "stones- didn't excite me some. I am as aware of the fact as yourself that no such... er stones have been found on the continent as yet, so I immediately said to myself that if two resourceful fellows such as yourselves could find them, then I wanted to be the first to congratulate you both."

Slack looked at Arnold. Arnold looked at Slack. Ralston could tell at once that they were angry.

"We expected secrecy, Mr.. Ralston. That Mr. Brown swore he'd say nothing."

"So he did Mr. Slack. He said nothing. But I share the keys to the vault."

"It seems to me," Arnold began, backing away from the table, "that our possessions aren't secure at the bank, Mr.. Ralston. Perhaps the caretaker and the messenger boy are playing marbles with them right now."

Ralston sensed disaster. "No, no, Mr. Arnold. Mr. Slack I implore you both to calm yourselves. It is all my decision. My responsibility. I took the decision to have them valued."

Arnold was stunned. Slack slapped his wineglass down on the table, speechless.

"You did *what*, sir?" Arnold asked. " I am flabbergasted. You had the temerity to have our valuable possessions looked over by another gentleman? Whatever happened to trust and honor? How is a person expected to keep a secret? We are insulted men, Mr. Ralston."

"Gentlemen, gentlemen."

"You said we could rely on the Bank of California, Arnold. We're marked men now. How we ever going to keep our claim?" Slack declared, slumping in his chair.

"Now Mr. Slack, I have not compromised you. Your possessions are intact. They are safe."

"That's not the point, Mr. Ralston and you know it," Arnold protested, aware that he was causing a commotion. People had their heads turned their way and the orchestra was between tunes.

"God damn it, sir, that was our business. What we place in your bank is *our* business, and no one gave you the right to make it *your* business."

Ralston shrugged, trying to pass this off as though it were a friendly quarrel . He smiled at the gawkers and tried to make Arnold sit down again. "It's my bank, Mr.. Arnold, did you ever think of that?"

Arnold blinked at the audacity of it. Of course the shareholders might take a different view, but then Arnold knew California bankers. They'd be more likely to fire Ralston for not looking in the vault than for investigating it. It was a Mexican stand-off.

Outside, tramps pressed their noses against the windows with covetous eyes and empty stomachs. Such opulence. They couldn't understand why a man would argue over such a feast and risk walking out without eating a scrap. But Arnold was close to it. He was damn near shaking with anger, and Ralston knew that he'd miscalculated.

Slack was less passionate, however, and what's more, hungry. The beef arrived, and it immediately set up camp in his nostrils, fixing him to his seat. "How much, exactly, did your friend value our 'friends,' Mr.. Ralston?"

Ralston took a breath. Yes, stick to money. These men would be poor after months out in the wilderness. What they needed most was money. Of course there was no reason to tell them the full estimate. Best to play cautious and allow a margin for error. The rubies were second rate, after all.

"I believe the figure was marginally in excess of ninety thousand dollars, Mr. Slack "

The orchestra suddenly set up again, adding something brassy to its range, and Arnold was out on a limb. He was caught between moral outrage and urgent materialism. Ninety thousand dollars. It was a small fortune. He dared not look at Slack's face for fear of bursting out into laughter. Instead he steadied himself and looked Mr. Ralston in the eye. "That, sir, is an insult. Everyone knows our 'friends' would fetch a better price than that in the East. I'd venture to say that they are worth closer to a hundred and twenty thousand."

Ralston smiled. He began to relax a little. Arnold was coming around.

"That might be so, sir, but I'm a banker. Best to err on the side of caution. I'd only value them at ninety. Now please sit down, Mr. Arnold. Let's keep this matter between ourselves. As I said, I merely wanted to celebrate with you. Please reconsider. Drink your wine, eat your beef. I wish to be your friend, nothing more. This I can promise you, sir: You are going to need friends in the coming months. If there's more of these, then you'll need all the friends you can get. Or had you in mind throwing open the mine to all comers and letting the rabble take the glory and the stones?"

Arnold said nothing. But he did sit down again and inspect his beef. It looked good. The wine certainly was drinkable and the place just as he'd always imagined a fancy restaurant to be. This wasn't such a bad evening. Ninety thousand dollars, well that was certainly something.

Slack ate and eyed Ralston and Arnold alternately. He'd said his piece. Let Arnold juggle with the ball now.

Arnold suddenly put his knife to the meat and looked across the table at Ralston. "This supper doesn't buy us, y'know."

"No one is buying anyone, Mr. Arnold. I am merely trying to get acquainted

I want you in my confidence and I am merely trying to gain yours."

"Like your Mr. Thomas Brown gave us his confidence."

"Mr.. Brown, sir, would be mortified if he knew I had abused his word to you gentlemen. Believe me, gentlemen. I took the risk only because I know what is best for the development of the West. If you have made a genuine discovery, then I want you to come to me first. You have worked as miners, you know the risks. You know the costs. You'll need a bank behind you, you'll need partners you can trust. I want you to know that at all times you have my word, my confidence and my friendship."

"Fine words, sir. Fine words. What you say, Slack?"

"Fine beef. You were right, Mr.. Ralston. Best beef I've tasted in a long time."

Arnold scowled at Slack, but he'd made enough fuss. He ate the beef and drank some wine whilst Ralston discussed the future.

"The city is growing, Mr.. Arnold. Getting bigger every year. It's being fed by the mines, the banks, and shipping; the railroad plays its part too. Every week hundreds arrive in San Francisco and all of them need work, a place to live, money, food, there's no end to it and they can't go anywhere, except back, and almost no one goes back across the Divide. I have a vision that this city should be the finest city in all the States, one that will rival any in Europe. We are the new Europe, and San Francisco will be the new Rome."

"What's your point, Mr. Ralston?" Arnold wanted to know.

"My point sir, is that this fair city of ours needs new rabbits to pull out of the hat, to keep the wheels turning, as it were, and I'm betting on you and Mr.. Slack here, having a lot of little rabbits for us to get fat on."

Slack grinned. He liked rabbit, stewed especially. He sat back in his chair and thought about it a moment, then leaned forward so he could speak a little more confidentially. "I got one piece of information for you, Mr.. Ralston: these so called rabbits don't live in California."

Arnold shot Slack a look that begged him to keep his mouth shut. Ralston had caught it and it encouraged him. He speculated on whether everything was rock solid in the partnership. Could one be split from the other?

Slack wiped his mouth and pushed his plate away. He'd fairly wolfed his beef down and was looking forward to something sweet to follow. He looked at Ralston and said, "Our rabbits could make a lot of people rich, Mr.. Ralston, but like I said, they ain't close by."

"And we're not about to say how close either," Arnold interjected. "Our rabbits stay in the hat."

Ralston smiled, conceding that they had all the aces in this game. He also felt that all these rabbits were getting a little out of hand. "What I mean to say, gentlemen, is that San Francisco can provide the finance to get this new venture off to a good start. We can provide the labor, transportation , the market, and bring in the expertise to make it succeed from the beginning. I want to be your partner, gentlemen, and if you care to ask around you will discover that I've been a good partner in a number of schemes. No one ever lost money yet, and a lot made a fortune. Tell me, Mr. Slack, what is your estimation of the difficulties of getting our rabbits to market?"

Slack indicated to Arnold to answer that one, but he wasn't in any big hurry . He searched his pockets for some tobacco, but Ralston beat him to it and shoved over his own box of cigars. Arnold took one but Slack declined; he was busy with a toothpick. Beef always got stuck in his long-neglected teeth.

Arnold struck up a light and sucked on his cigar as he pondered and gave his answer. "Aside from the inhospitable terrain, and the Indians, there's no difficulties at all, Mr.. Ralston. You agree with that, Slack?"

Slack paused with his pick and searched the ceiling for inspiration before giving his answer. "Well, I guess I'd have to confess, Mr.. Ralston, finding rabbits ain't as hard as you might think. Once you'd found where they live, that is. Seemed to me that it was as easy as picking mushrooms. If they aren't lying on the ground, they're in the creek and if they ain't in the creek, they're in the ant-heaps. Arnold and me couldn't believe it at first. Thought it was a trick of the devil himself, but they was there, ripe for the picking."

Ralston stared at Slack, incredulous. "You mean they just lie on the ground?"

Slack nodded, shrugging his shoulders. "Been there since God fashioned the earth, I reckon. It was just like being the first men to arrive in Kimberley. As I hear tell it, they found the first stones on the De Beer farm and just kept on digging, on their way to the biggest damn hole outside of the Grand Canyon."

"You're saying you've found another Kimberley on the continental United States?" Ralston could hardly contain his excitement.

Arnold finally got a good head of steam going on his cigar. "We make no such claim, sir. We found a few rabbits, we might find a few more rabbits, but we ain't saying there's rabbits a mile deep in that hole like Kimberley. You'd think us liars and boasters out for a quick buck. I want to remind you, Mr. Ralston, we didn't come to you, you came to us. We make no claims whatsoever. If it's another Kimberley, well God be praised, Slack and me are going to be rich. If not, well we already got ourselves ninety thousand dollars' worth for our trouble and we'd be fools to sneeze at that."

But Ralston had heard the word Kimberley and he did not heed any warning signs nor hear any disclaimers. Kimberley in a few months had made men fabulously wealthy and generated millions upon millions of dollars for prospectors and diamond dealers in Africa and London, and it looked set to continue doing so for many years to come. But an *American* Kimberley. Why it fair staggered the imagination and to think he was dining with the only two men in the world who knew where it was. He had to know. Why, in one leap he and the Bank of California would become the richest body in the Union, even the world.

Ralston shook his head in a happy state of confusion. He'd not felt like this since the Ophir mine had fallen into his hands when others had thought it finished. All that silver still in the ground, and men had walked away from it for lack of gold. What would be their price to reveal the source?

"Look. I'm interested in helping you obtain verification of the claim, gentlemen. I want to help you set up an efficient company that can exploit it to our mutual benefit. You know it can't be done alone.

Slack emptied his glass and wondered if there was any coffee. He wasn't used to so much wine after their months out in the wilds and he felt heavy with it. "I'm not sure it should be... what was that word...*exploited*? Arnold and me can go back there anytime we like and get more, more than enough to see us through our time."

Ralston adopted an irritated look. "Now, Mr. Slack, that is a thoroughly selfish attitude, worse than a man owning an orchard and letting all the fruit rot rather than share it."

Slack smirked. "If we lived a thousand years, Mr. Ralston, I doubt we'd see our particular apples rot."

Ralston smiled and conceded the point. Now the rabbits were apples. How confusing life could be sometimes. Perhaps things could have gone easier if he'd entertained them in a private booth.

"Mr.. Ralston," Arnold interposed, "you're concerned and I know how keen you must be to help us make a fortune, but Slack and me, well, we will be approaching a few prominent citizens in this city. We'll be looking for the best offer we can get to help us get started. Mr. Flood and Mr. Mackay might be interested."

At last Arnold was talking language Ralston could understand. "Mr.. Arnold, I am the last person who would advise you to consider only one offer; why that would be imprudent. But, the more people that know, the more who might be tempted to go looking for themselves. Can you afford to risk others finding your orchard?"

Slack laughed. "If they can find it without us, then they deserve it, Mr. Ralston. We searched for years. It's not something you can just walk up to and stake your claim on."

Ralston held up his hands in approbation. " I understand you want to preserve the fruits of your labor and protect yourselves. But I'm telling you now, gentlemen. I will make you the best offer. I'd be cautious of any offer that Flood or Mackay might make you. I trusted them once and that would be a mistake I'd not make twice."

"What exactly would this offer be Mr. Ralston?" Arnold asked, attempting to blow a smoke ring with his cigar but not quite achieving it.

"The exact nature of my offer would depend upon two things."

"Two things?" Slack asked. "What two things?"

Ralston leaned forward, beckoning them in closer so he could talk more privately. Slack and Arnold quickly exchanged glances wondering what the banker would say.

"The first is, I would have to send with you my own appointed agent to verify the claim and give me an independent assessment of the commercial problems associated with extricating the um, rabbits and getting them back to this city in sufficient numbers to make it all worthwhile."

Arnold narrowed his eyes a little. "And the second thing?"

"If it is a viable proposition, I'd want an equal partnership with you gentlemen."

Slack's mouth fell open. Ralston's terms had knocked the wind out of him. "A one-third share for nothing?" Arnold exploded. "I heard bankers were greedy, but that's worse than highway robbery. You got more nerve than a Boston politician. And as for verification; well, sir, if you think we are going to lead you to our claim, you can wait for a blue moon, Mr. Ralston. We may look like country bumpkins, but we ain't about to let city bankers run rings around us."

"You don't understand," Ralston protested. "In the matter of verification, any investor would want that. You know that. If my appointee has to go the entire way blindfold, well, so be it, and as for my getting a third, well, gentlemen, I'm not asking you to put up a penny. The Bank of California would pay for every cent from the day that claim is verified. You'd never have to do another days labor in all your lives. Every, er, rabbit we get out of the ground would be counted and independently accounted for, so neither one of us would feel cheated. We'd form the company, operate the mine and market the rabbits, and you'd get two-thirds of the profits. If that isn't a fair deal, then my name is not William C. Ralston."

Slack mulled it over. It wasn't quite the way Arnold had said it would be. He studied Arnold's face and saw his familiar scowl when he thought things over.

"I'll concede that you have made a reasonable offer, Mr. Ralston. I don't say we can't best it, however, and you're right, the mine would have to be verified. Slack and me are prepared to take one of your representatives to the site, but I warn you, it's practically two days by railroad and another three or four on horseback after. From the railroad on he'd have to travel blindfold. No question of it."

"So best make sure it's a man who can ride in the dark," Slack remarked, with a sly smile. "Best he has a soft head to fall on."

Ralston was smiling, however. They could joke now. He'd gotten through the first blockade. Arnold and Slack wanted to do business.

"When can your representative be ready?" Slack wanted to know.

"Within the week; earlier if I can find him sooner. I'm keen to get on with this venture, gentlemen."

Slack groaned. He'd hoped for a bit of soft living before he went out to the wilderness again.

"Who's paying?" he asked, looking Ralston directly in the eyes.

"My representative will pay his own way, and I'm prepared to advance you the cost of the railroad journey, gentlemen, but it's your task to prove to me that this claim is genuine. As I said, from that time on, you'll never have to spend another cent."

Slack frowned. He had hoped for more than the price of a railroad ticket. He looked at Arnold, expecting him to argue, but Arnold was agreeing and setting a time to meet before the Friday train back east.

"Who would your representative likely be?" Slack asked, cutting Arnold off mid-sentence.

Ralston gave the matter some thought. "Well, I'd hope to get General Colton. You know him of course, quite a hero here with the Union Army, and since."

Both Arnold and Slack knew of the General, as he was generally well known. The Sutter mine had been a bone of contention from the time it opened up and had fallen into the hands of the banks. The mine bosses had brought in General Colton as strikebreaker to force the men to take a cut in wages to two dollars and fifty cents a day. His men had mounted a cavalry charge and cut the rebels down, literally.

"Just the man. I would never have chosen him in a hundred years. We was working miners once, and we wouldn't work for no two-fifty a day.

"That man is a swine. I don't like this at all," Slack remarked, angrily, staring at Arnold as if he'd like to add more, but was too angry to get it out.

"Like I say, Mr.. Ralston." Arnold continued. "We wouldn't chose him, but I know the General to be a man of his word. If he verifies our claim, then you can be sure it is everything we say it is."

Ralston nodded, admiring Arnold's tactics. General Colton was the most objectional man he could think of, especially to former miners like these two. But Arnold was right, the General was a man who took his honor most seriously. If there was the slightest suspicion about this find, then he'd say so and take pleasure in running Arnold and Slack out of town.

Arnold put a hand out to Slack's arm. "We'll take the old buzzard, Slack. We have nothing to fear. We make the trip and the General won't be on any wasted journey."

Slack conceded that; then he adopted a sly smile. "But the same conditions apply, Mr.. Ralston. The General will be blindfolded. Agreed?"

Ralston laughed, his large frame straining against his chair. He saw the humor in sending off the General blindfolded. "As long as you don't lead him off a cliff, gentlemen. If he comes back with so much as a hair missing, then we have no deal."

Arnold smiled. The telling of the trip would be pleasure enough. A lot of men would take pleasure in knowing they'd led the General by the nose.

"I think this has been a satisfactory supper, Mr. Ralston."

Ralston poured the last of the wine into their glasses and raised his own, waiting for them to join him. "May this be the first of many," he said, drawing breath, granting them his most brilliant smile, "partners."

There was something of an argument brewing at Alyce's home that night. Alyce made coffee and kept well out of it as Slack paced up and down, an angry man.

"You said they'd pay us to make this trip, Arnold. You said we'd never have to pay for anything ever again. You said once we had deposited the diamonds they'd be falling over themselves to put money in our hands."

Arnold took his head out of his hands and shrugged. He had said all those things, it was true, but what could he say, it hadn't gone the way he'd figured it, that's all. Slack had been there right with him all the time. If he didn't like it, he could have said something.

Slack took up his coffee and then put it down again without tasting it. "I mean you know I can't afford any more expenses. Neither one of us can."

"That's their game, Slack, don't you see? They want to squeeze us so we give in easy. It's no more than a tight game of poker. Ralston is going to make us wait for money so we will come cheap. I know that's his game. Don't crack now. We got the railroad fare, didn't we?"

Slack appealed to Alyce. "Your Arnie has gotten me into more scrapes and financial pits than any other man I know of. Diamonds are a sure thing, he said. So we find diamonds and still we're broke. Better yet, we got all our stones locked in the bank and we ain't making any attempt to sell 'em like any sensible person would."

"That's because they're our collateral."

"You said that when we went into supplying water pumps to the mines without the steam engines to make 'em work. You said something like it when you had me packing mules to the mines ."

"They paid good for the mules, Slack, you can't hold that agin me."

"Yeah I can, you invested that money in the pumps."

Alyce smiled, remembering the pumps. They'd sat stacked in her yard for a year before they'd finally been sold for probably less than they'd cost. She felt sorry for Slack. He'd looked forward to getting rich and living comfortable, now to be sent back into the wilderness with nothing, ... well, he sure looked miserable.

"Slack, we will get our money and more. I know it. Hell, we could sell the diamonds we got and go back to Kentucky, but what fools we'd be to let Ralston get the whole damn thing so cheap."

"Why didn't we sell the diamonds to him? Like you said we would."

"Because this is a game of poker, Slack. He knows we need money. He knows we want to sell the diamonds. They are genuine, he knows that, but he wants the diamond field. If we sold to him now, well, he might think he got it all too easy. Besides which, you know damn well that half of ninety thousand dollars is no compensation for what we've been through."

Slack knew that. He'd started off with a horse once and a change of shirt when he left Kentucky. Later on they'd sold their share of the Kentucky farms to invest in a gold mine and now all he owned was the suit on his back or in the bank locked away. Better if he'd stayed a farmer.

"And if General Colton doesn't verify our claim? What if we can't find no more diamonds? What about that? You think Ralston will still want to buy what we have found? Or will he sew up his pockets?"

Arnold wouldn't take any doubts. "He'll verify. Damnit, Slack, don't be so sore. We know what we got. He'll verify. Alyce, soothe this nasty old bear down won't you. Remind him that plain old-fashioned faith is what is needed here."

"Faith?" Slack protested. "Faith in what?"

"In another man's greed, Slack, another man's greed."

"Better worry more about General Colton." Alyce told them both. "No friend to miners and prospectors."

"We don't need friends," Arnold declared confidently. "Only believers."

CHAPTER FOUR
The Bear Sets a Trap.

William Chapman Ralston stepped out of his stylish lightweight buggy and tethered two muscular grays to the iron hitching post outside an imposing Nob Hill residence. He saw that the offside gray was sweating badly, but it was no surprise. He looked back down the steep muddy slope of California Street and surveyed the almost completed cable diggings at the junction with Taylor Street. Life would be a great deal easier with the cable car functioning at last, not to mention the tidy profit he'd made on land speculation along the route. There would be more of that in the future; right now he had an important meeting with General David Douty Colton.

The General's title was honorific; he'd never actually gone into combat. He was renowned in the city for his ability to involve himself in almost all the major doings. He liked to make himself useful, and indeed his not inconsiderable fortune had been founded on a particular service he'd rendered to Senator David C. Broderick back in '59. He'd been the senator's second, in a duel against the prominent Judge Terry, on the sand hills south of the city. The senator had come off second-best, and many had thought that the senator's political organization would dissolve with his death. However, young Colton, who had been just twenty-five at the time, held the dead man's organization together. No one knew quite how, but certain valuable parcels of San Francisco real estate belonging to the late politician ended up in Colton's hands. These waterfront parcels formed the basis of his fortune.

The General was at the very epicenter of power, not quite possessing it, but able to touch it, and those who wished to gain favor with the powerful knew they could get word via this man as long as there was something in it for him. Those he counted among his friends were Mark Hopkins, Charles Crocker, (a future neighbour) and Leland Stanford, (somewhat reluctantly on Stanford's part). Indeed, the General already represented Mark Hopkin's railway business and had proved reliable in that respect as manager of the Southern Pacific company since 1870.

Naturally he counted himself a friend of Ralston's and inevitably turned up

51

on invitation lists at all the Belmont banquets. For Ralston's part, whether he liked the General or not was by the by; he needed him, and he knew as well as any man that the true way to success lay in greasing wheels. It wasn't an easy task to get those diamonds out of the ground and to market. Arnold and Slack could not comprehend just how hard a man like Ralston would have to work for his third share. Anyone could stumble across a diamond, but not everyone would know how to juggle it into a fortune to rival all fortunes.

Ralston surveyed the house a moment and considered that this was not the home of a modest man. Of course, Ralston was the least modest of men, but he considered himself to be the arbiter of taste, and this wooden monstrosity with its towers and turrets was just a little too ambitious. Nevertheless the carvings on the front door were amusing and certainly captivated one's attention.

He had no need to announce himself. The pig-tailed Chinese servant admitted him and showed him to the long-room. The servant was dressed in yellow silks and certainly no expense had been spared on the staff. To Ralston it reminded him of nothing more than an exotic log cabin, the highly polished redwood interior walls being its only distinction. It was unexpectedly dark too, the only window in the room being north facing and curiously small. A fire burned brightly in the grate and Ralston made his way over to the warmth, his eyes alighting on a pool of resin on the Delft tiles surrounding the grate.

The Chinese servant brought in some tea and placed it on a lace-covered table where, Ralston noted, also rested a crystal decanter of whiskey, the stopper left on crookedly, as if someone had sneaked a drink and had had no time to replace it.

Ralston glanced at his pocket watch. The meeting was set for five o'clock. The General was late. Usually the man could be relied on to be punctual. He began to feel a tad annoyed.

He arrived eventually wearing a curious afternoon suit made of white cotton, the sleeves turned inside out, the tailor's stitches exposed.

"Bill.. Bill, you'll think me rude, I'm sure, but this damn fool tailor has kept me this past hour with his nonsense, and I can't move for all the pins stuck into me."

Ralston smiled, for it was a comical sight to see the General so pinned up and stiff in his half-completed suit.

"Think nothing about it General. A white suit, eh? There'll be talk you're taking up a theatrical career, I'll be bound."

The General frowned. "Yes, exactly what I told my wife. She swears it's the latest thing in Paris, and since we are planning a trip to New York this summer on the cars, she has me all tricked out like a show pony in 'cotton creams,' she calls them. I try to tell her I've always worn black, but she won't be deterred. It's cream, or I'll hear the worst of it."

Ralston knew Mrs Colton, and could well believe the General had little say in the matter. The worst of it was, if the style caught on, Ralston would have to wear one too, eventually, curse the meddling woman.

There were tiny drops of sweat on Colton's forehead and nose, and his red hair was decidedly long on the collar. Time had thickened his neck, and good food had filled out his frame. He was not the blade of old. Indulgence had a price.

"*The Bulletin* is full of its usual lies I see. Pickering and Fitch are determined twisters. I should like to see *The Call* and *The Bulletin* run short of paper, or burn. They seem to be willing folks to lose faith in business with the banks here. The East might be shaky, but at least here, General, every dollar is backed by gold or silver, and in my opinion the price of either has a long way to go yet before it finds a top. What do you say, General, or are you one of the doomsayers too?"

The General said nothing. He was desperately trying to understand why the banker had come to tea. Had he overlooked some debt? There were debts, but he thought them secured by a speculation he'd made... Ralston was still talking as Colton poured them both a cup of tea, adding lemon to both cups.

"Fitch is a scoundrel of the highest order. Horsewhipping would be too good for him. I was hearing in the club that Charlie Crocker is less than happy with his grand tour. Think there's a possibility of him coming back to the city soon? "

Perhaps this was a friendly visit after all, Colton persuaded himself. He tried to relax as he passed Ralston his cup.

"It would take a mighty jolt to get him back so soon after selling out his share in the railroad, Bill. I fancy his share of nearly two million dollars will keep him amused for some while yet. The rail-business is still bad here. Hasn't brought the profits we predicted. Freight is down, passengers too. It pulled into Sacramento with just thirty passengers yesterday. Why, at this rate it would have been better not to have bothered at all."

"As long as your locomotives crash, General, people will prefer to take ships. I've taken the cars to the Sierras myself and truly a man needs courage to look down while taking some of those bends around the cliffs."

"The railroad is our future, Bill. People must realize that. The horses won't get any faster. Our locomotives will get faster and safer. You'll see."

Ralston smiled and drank some of his tea. "Well, I suppose we have progress, General. I can get to go three hundred miles between sun-up and sundown by the railroad. It took the children of Israel forty years."

The General looked astonished. He did not pickup Ralston's attempt at humor, and took it utterly serious. "Forty years, you say, is that so? Three hundred miles . Can that really be true?"

"Well they didn't possess a compass, unlike the Mormons; and there was much hither and thither, I reckon. I rather think if those congressmen and senators in Washington had to do the same, General, it might take even a few years longer yet."

At this the General did manage a smile. He could tell a jape, and this one he knew was not at his expense. Everyone knew that Washington took a devil of a long time coming to a decision about anything, anything at all.

"So," Ralston sighed, relaxed now, positive he had Colton's attention. "The business at hand," he began.

The General halted him, however, choosing that moment to bring out a box of cigars. Fine specimens they looked, too, but Ralston declined. The General didn't take offense and lit up anyway, filling up the room around him with a thick cloud as he tried to ignite the tobacco. Ralston watched and waited until the whole business was completed, and even then he couldn't launch into his proposal, since his host also took it upon himself to recall his Chinaman and have two glasses of whiskey poured and set down beside them both should they want real home comforts.

"General, I'd like you to make a journey for me, and the rub of it is, I can't tell you where you're going or how long you will be away."

The General laughed, thinking this a good joke, but it soon died on the wind when he saw Ralston's earnest face.

"No, sir, no idea at all. What is more, what I am about to say is in strictest confidence, General, and you'll soon see the reason for that. Should just one word leak out about this business, we would lose a considerable advantage and live to rue the day. Of this I can assure you."

"What exactly is it that you propose, Bill? What do you want me to do?"

Ralston then told him, omitting nothing; for he knew that for the verification of the claim the General would have to be offered something substantial, and one could hardly let the man be led clear across the Sierras to the Rockies to see diamonds without admitting him to the business of owning shares in them.

"So you see, General. If everything is as dandy as they say it is, then I'm going to be needing a trustworthy general manager for the diamond company. You'd have a chance to be in on the profits and take up shares at a discount. What do you say to that?"

"Diamonds, you say. And only these two know where it is?"

Ralston affirmed that this was true. "They'll part with the information by and by, but that's not so important as you verifying that it is true. I want you to dig deep mind, take a good walk around the mesa, give me an accurate report. We want to be sure what we are getting into. You know mining. You can tell me how much it will cost to get in there with the railroad and whether the water supply is regular all year. Watch out for Indians, too. They might give us an argument."

"I never heard a thing about diamonds before. In all the years they were building the railroad, we never came close to finding one. You sure this man Arnold is honest?"

Ralston smiled preening back hair that was no longer growing on his head. "He's a prospector. Been out here since the rush of '59, and George Roberts tells me that he's had business with the man on occasion with Nevada gold. He made a profit, so we can conclude that Arnold and his partner Slack are genuine enough. As for the diamonds, General... well, the ones they fetched in are genuine enough. So, it's down to you; if you'll take the job on. I want your candid opinion as to whether their claim is genuine or not."

"And how far will you expect me to dig? My back isn't what it was, and my hands are softer now. Surely you want a man used to the hard life."

Ralston held up his hands to protest. "It's a matter of trust. I can ask a thousand men to go, General, but how many could I trust not to go to some other banker, or to shoot off his mouth and start a rush, so that no one gets to make a fortune without first having to buy out ten thousand small claims? No, sir. We have first crack at this one, and I want you to go. I'd like to have your answer now, if you will."

"When would you be wanting me to leave, Bill? I have accounts to prepare and new freight charges to assess in the south."

"Get the accounts prepared and set your new rates at five percent above the last price. You did it last time. Everyone will squeak, but they'll raise their prices to match it. That's the joy of a monopoly."

The General shook his head in wonder. The way Ralston cut through things to the very heart. But to go on this wild scheme, blindfold. It was audacious, it was preposterous, yet such an opportunity.

"I could leave in five days."

Ralston rose at once and shook the General's hand. "I knew you'd accept, General. Believe me, no other man would I rather have on this venture. I will await your return with great anticipation."

The General also stood and for just a moment felt quite proud he had accepted. Yes, if this thing came off, Colton could be quite a famous name. Perhaps even a city named after him like Kimberley. .

"We can leave on the Monday train then," Colton remarked at the door.

"Take warm clothes," Ralston warned. "The snows haven't disappeared yet."

"They almost never disappear from the Rockies," the General asserted. "If it's too high you'll never work the mine in the winter."

"It'll work all year General. Believe me, even if I have to melt the snow myself,

it'll work all winter."

DIAMONDS

Ralston took his buggy back down California Street, reflecting that the business with Colton had been resolved to his satisfaction. He did not go immediately home. He had guests due for dinner, some London investors; but there was another detail to attend to before he could leave the city. He pointed the buggy towards the Grand Hotel, hurrying his horses as he noticed the time on the Hibernian Bank building.

The Grand Hotel was yet another of Ralston's interests. A handsome combination of two buildings on Montgomery and Market Streets. It was topped off with an elegant mansard roof and it boasted four hundred rooms, most with a private bath and all with telegraphic communications between each room and the main office. He had no part in its running, but was a quarter share owner, the rest being owned by his friend and financier, Asbury Harpending, his former partner also in the Montgomery Land Company, which was the basis of his latest venture, the Palace Hotel. But that does not concern us now. For the moment the Grand was the best hotel in San Francisco, and there was profit enough in that.

Ralston entered the busy lobby of the Grand and was immediately greeted by several folk who regaled him with hearty hellos and how-d'you-do's, as if they were his bosom pals. But it would have been a rash fellow indeed who didn't acknowledge the banker in his own hotel. Ralston did not tarry long in the lobby, but went upstairs to his office, a room he usually shared with Harpending. It showed neglect, but no matter, the building would be sold soon enough when the right buyer came along, or when land prices improved in general.

He inspected his pocket watch once again : twenty-five minutes short of seven. His appointee was late by five minutes.

A minute later the door knob began to turn and a man entered silently, closing the door behind him quickly, exchanging no word of greeting.

The man, Henri Jean Decker, was dressed in a brown suit one size too small for him that seemed to cramp him dreadfully under his arms and chest. It really looked most uncomfortable. Decker had shaved, and Ralston could tell the man had taken trouble to make himself as respectable as he could manage.

"Got a small job for you, Decker, a confidential task."

Decker might have been interested, but his face showed no trace of it.

"It's simple enough," Ralston continued, quite used to Decker's impassivity.

Mr..Decker had proved useful and reliable before; he was trustworthy. "I want you to follow a party of three men leaving this city on the Monday Central Pacific and stick with them. I don't want them to know you're there, y'understand. They must never suspect you are there. They are going to get off somewhere after Salt Lake City and head off into the Rockies. You will follow,

56

at a distance, and observe. I want to know the route they follow, and when they finally get where they are going and set up camp, I want you to watch."

Decker showed a little confusion. "Watch, Mr. Ralston?"

"Yes, Decker, watch. Now, these men will be looking for gold or silver, you can generally tell when a man has found what he's looking for."

"But I must watch and wait for how long, Mr. Ralston? Prospecting can be . ."

Ralston cut him off at the pass. "Two of the men already know what's to be found. The third is there to verify whether the claim is good or not."

"Yes sir." Decker resumed his dead fish of a face.

"Then when the third party is satisfied, Mr. Decker, that is when I want you to quit your perch and get back to the telegraph as fast as you can. I want the exact location Mr.. Decker. You have a compass?"

"Yes, sir. I can give an exact location sir. I was a scout for the army for three years."

Ralston knew that well enough. He also knew that Decker had been damned good, too, and done the Confederates proud, but they'd ditched him when he'd been wounded, left for dead, like so many others they couldn't care for. Decker had lived, but he had lost three fingers and half of one ear. Making a living had been a problem until Harpending had taken him on as detective in the hotel. The odd thing was, Decker could still shoot straighter than most, and no one liked to argue with him because he'd never understand another's view. Decker had an unusual dedication for keeping the peace in the Grand Hotel and a great respect for the two men who paid his wages.

"I know you can do this little job for me, Decker. Now, I'm placing you in a position of great trust here. I know I can rely on you to keep this little business to yourself. You will speak to no one about this. It will remain a confidential matter between the two of us."

"The men have the claim posted, don't they?" Decker asked.

"Perhaps they do, Mr. Decker. I'm not concerned with that. It's the land that surrounds the claim I'm interested in and the source of the water. A claim is all very well, Mr. Decker, but what value has it when a man has to cross another's to get to it." Ralston smiled, and suddenly Decker began to comprehend the importance of his mission.

"And my arrangements, sir?"

Ralston was not a man to cheat those who served him. "Two thousand dollars in gold coin, Mr. Decker, all costs paid and a ticket to Charleston. Charleston is the object of your desire, is it not?"

A light that had long died flickered in Decker's face. There was a woman back home, a woman who still loved him, despite his wounds and disfigurement, but how to go back without money or knowing who'd employ half a man such as he?

"How the devil d'y know about about that, sir?"

Ralston waved his hand in dismissal. "It's a banker's privilege to know, Mr. Decker. I hope she is as pretty and deserving as they say. Two thousand's good enough to get you on your way in Charleston, I believe."

Ralston left behind him that night an astonished and happy man. He did not question the honesty of the business. Here was an opportunity for one Henri Decker to make good, put his miserable life in order.

If gratitude was the measure of one man's appreciation of the other, then Slack would rate very low on the scale indeed. John Slack was in a foul mood. For one thing, they were expected to go into the city and meet this General Colton and then come back on the same ferry, to the same place, and catch the Oakland eastbound train. Why General Colton couldn't simply cross the bay by himself and meet them he didn't know, but he suspected it was Arnold's fault for agreeing to such an absurdity. To cap it all, the fish were really biting this morning, and what was the point of catching the slippery things if there was no time to eat 'em? Though to be sure, he, John Slack, was going to eat his for breakfast.

Arnold eventually tumbled out of bed at seven o'clock and was a little surprised to find Slack all dressed and sitting out on the back porch fishing already. There was a healthy stack of fish smacking the boards with their tails, too.

"Been up long?"

"Since an hour before sun-up. Couldn't sleep, and I could hear the fish a-calling to me."

Arnold shook his head. Slack had an unnatural obsession for sea trout. Nevertheless, they would make an uncommonly fine breakfast.

"Good day for travel, I'd say, " Arnold remarked.

"Just as well," Slack muttered to himself. "We're set to travel a thousand miles or more." You could tell from the way he said it that he had no stomach for the journey. Fishing had a better pull this day.

Alyce was up then, pinning back her hair and fussing over giving her men a good send-off. It was no easy journey to the diamonds. Arnold took out his map and spread it about the table. Alyce did her best to ignore it, she knew better than to try to sneak a look and build any distrust between them. But Arnold wasn't so bothered this morning. The map would require detailed studying before anyone could make out any kind of sense of it, and even then making a decision as to which state it was in well, a man would have to be mightly familiar with the West to even take a guess at it and then you'd be wrong by five hundred miles.

The fish was dished up and many compliments tossed out to Slack for his morning's work. Alyce grew sad, for she'd gotten used to having her menfolk back with her, even if they hadn't exactly paid her a cent in rent for some time now. She was always willing to extend credit to Arnold, and besides, with Slack around there never was any shortage of fish to eat.

She would have walked them to the ferry, but the house had to be tidied and sheets washed for new guests arriving that morning for a week.

"Take care now," Alyce whispered to her man. She pressed into Arnold's hands a cheese wrapped in muslin for the journey. Arnold hugged her once again and drew in her body scent. "Alyce, when were done on this trip, we are taking the city by storm. Never will there have been such a celebration as we shall have. We will drink the town dry and dance the night away until we can't stand no more, and then we'll eat the biggest breakfast in the Grand and begin all over again."

Alyce laughed and hugged him back and said how much she'd look forward to that, but in her heart of hearts she wondered if she should ask him to promise to pay the money he owed first, before he had this blow out on the town. She loved the man sorely, but there were times when money would be better proof of his affection for her. She cried then.

Slack put out a fishy paw and comforted her too, but Arnold got Slack out of the house to clean his boots so he could give Alyce one last kiss. Knowing how to leave a woman was just one of the skills Arnold had acquired over the years, not that there had been many women at all up in the hills. But he imagined that this was the way to leave 'em, and this was his way accordingly.

Slack stood outside in the dust cleaning his boots on the back of his trousers, unable to see much wrong with them anyway. He sensed Arnold was being too particular and fussy about meeting General Colton. Slack knew that it didn't matter if they pitched up naked as the day they were born for the meeting, as long as they took the General to the diamonds. He amused himself a moment with the thought of actually taking a ride on the ferry stark naked.

Arnold and Slack had long been delivered by the Oakland ferry to the Central Pacific landing at the Embarcadero. They lolled about impatiently in the morning sun which had already done much to dry the streets and harden the mud. Ralston, who had insisted they be on time, was already five minutes late, and the ferry would be leaving again in fifteen minutes.

Arnold attempted to get his pipe lit, but an annoying gust of wind kept on at him and he gave up in disgust soon after, preferring to just suck on his pipe as usual. Slack had purchased himself the *San Francisco Alta* and was keeping it creased and safe in his pocket lest he be tempted to read it before they got onto the train. He liked to study every word, and there was no place better to do that than on the Central Pacific as it took its time a-twisting and curling around the Sierras. He'd probably purchase a paper in Sacramento, too.

At exactly thirty minutes past the hour Arnold spotted Ralston in his buggy jostling its way through the ferry traffic. Beside him, straight as a giant redwood, sat General Colton. And wasn't he dressed for show, morning coat and top hat. Slack had seen it too, and he gave out a little groan that said a lot without saying much at all.

"I'd like to see that get-up sat on a mule," Arnold remarked, amused.

"You're going to," Slack told him, easing himself off the barrel he was sat on. "If the mule don't take fright first."

Ralston was waving to them and pointing them out to the General, who only just seemed to have taken an interest in them, as much as if to say, 'Well if I have to, but not for long.'

Arnold knew the look well, but didn't care. Everyone was equal up in the mountains. They had a way of leveling everyone. Kings and generals.

Ralston dismounted, shook hands, and made a big thing of his hellos and introductions, treating Arnold and Slack as if they'd been lifelong buddies. The General was less enthusiastic and his handshake unusually clammy.

"Now, I want you to take good care of the General, Mr.. Arnold, you, too, Mr..Slack. He'll treat you fair if you treat him fair."

"Fair do's," Arnold replied

Slack was studying the boxes and trunks being unloaded from the buggy by the General's Chinaman. "These all yours, Mr. Ralston?"

The banker showed a little surprise and turned to look at what Slack was referring to. "Mine, sir? Why, yes. Is there something wrong?"

Slack looked at Arnold and Arnold looked at Slack. Slack knew no fear.

"Well General, if these be yours, as long you'll pay for the mule train over the mountains and don't expect us to carry anything, you can bring the entire contents of Coleman's store."

The General surveyed his three boxes, the two trunks, and his leather portmanteau, not to mention the leather coat he'd brought along to keep him warm in the train. It was likely that it was only at this exact moment, right there on the jetty, that the General first put his mind to considering his journey and the difficulties ahead. That and the problems of leaving one's Chinaman to pack for you. He noticed that Arnold and Slack were carrying but one set of mining tools and a battered leather sailor's bag between them. Embarrassment didn't come into it.

"I suppose it is a trifle too much," the General mused. But that was all. He pointed to one of the boxes and the Chinaman went over to struggle with it, not expecting any help, nor getting any. All four men watched him seize the box with his two short arms and go very red in the face. The box appeared to be filled with rocks. The servant made no progress at all, then all of a sudden, the box left the ground and the Chinaman staggered right, staggered left, then

DIAMONDS

lurched backward five, six, seven steps, straightened momentarily, and then with no warning at all fell over backward, the box crashing down on top of him, pinning him to the jetty. A terrible, singular groan was emitted, yet not such a groan you knew it had to be mortal.

"Well, I reckon the Chinaman thinks you've got one too many collars for your shirts, General," Ralston remarked climbing back up onto his buggy. He tossed a look over at the ferry and saw it was near full. "You three better get on; the ferry won't wait, not even for its own."

The General just didn't like to admit he'd gotten his trail arrangements wrong. Certainly he didn't go to the aid of the Chinaman, and the Chinaman wasn't about to make a move from under the box in any hurry.

The General made a fast survey of his possessions and then swallowing his vast pride, untied the first trunk and took out a canvas sack. He then stuffed no more than two shirts into it, along with some jerk beef. He totally abandoned the rest, put on his leather coat, tossed aside his topper for something close approaching a gaucho's leather hat, and stood before Arnold and Slack a different man, a man who looked as if he were headed up into the hills. A last thought made him pick up his compass, his digging equipment and a flask of brandy.

"Time to go gentlemen."

The General said no more, instead walking manfully toward the ferry with not a glance back or a farewell to Ralston. Arnold watched Ralston's face, expecting him to be showing signs of irritation at the lack of respect, but no, Ralston was as astonished as Arnold and Slack and just as amused.

The two adventurers nodded at Ralston and followed after the General. Slack noting the Chinaman was still pinned down with not a soul to help him.

Ralston had one last word, however. "Mr. Arnold, the General has your railroad warrants. You travel free as long as you're with him."

"Then we will stick close," Arnold called out behind him. "Good day to you, sir."

Within four minutes the ferry had sailed and not a soul looked back. It was as if the last sermon they'd heard had concerned the fate of Lot and his wife, and none could take the risk that their city would suffer the same fate. So no one saw the banker come to the aid of the Chinaman, nor saw the Chinaman's shame.

Arnold and Slack stood by the rails, the rush of cool air pleasant to their faces and keeping from their nostrils the worst of the common crowd, a mixture of horses, cattle, and ordinary working folk rubbing shoulders with the finest cloth and their fine sensibilities. Somewhere in the middle of this, on a raised platform reserved for Central Pacific personnel, the General stood in his customary rigid manner surveying the distance with a visible longing to be on dry land. He was, no doubt, wondering if he had done the right thing in the

61

heat of his irritation with the Chinaman. He was perhaps feeling he'd committed a terrible and rash deed, that perhaps he should go back for at least some of
his clothes, or his shaving brush and blade. By God, he'd just abandoned all
the standards of civilization in one strike. He felt like a pioneer of old, like
Lewis or Clark, or, if he cared to think of less pleasant memories, Donner.

Standing at the prow of this less-than-magnificent vessel, another pair of
eyes studied all three of our would be adventurers. Henri Decker was wearing
the most non-descript outfit it was ever the misfortune for a traveler to wear. A
person would as soon turn his eyes away rather than stare, for fear the man
might suddenly get it in his mind to start begging for his supper. Or possibly,
he was a seasoned frontiersman down on his luck; either way, no man could
chance a look, or risk conversation. To look at him would be to miss him; ones
very eyes would slide off him onto something more interesting; a fly biting the
backside of a cow or a man scratching his nose, both scenes considerably
more riveting than two seconds of staring at Henri Decker.

Decker had fixed in his mind already the features of Philip Arnold and John
Slack. The General he recognized from his nocturnal visits with various painted
women to the Grand Hotel. Little escaped Decker's eyes. And now he would
be there, practically alongside them for the rest of the journey. He'd not forget
a detail about them, not a one. Even if he were shaken, boiled, and thrown fifty
feet in the air, he'd not forget one jot or let them escape from his sight. He'd
follow them to hell and back, and they'd never know he'd been there. As close
as their elbows, their neighbor at lunch, their very shadows in the afternoon.
They'd never know.

The locomotive was all fired up and building up a good head of steam
when they finally arrived at the Central Pacific station. The matter of stepping
aboard the cars and making sure they got a corner to themselves was over in
minutes. The locomotive pulled out in five . They were finally on their way,
riding Silver Palace class as well, all velvet and mahogany, not forgetting the
comfort of a wood stove.

CHAPTER FIVE
Arnold's Great Trek

To say the cars lurched a little would be to disappoint the most feeble of imaginations. The cars fairly rocked and shook, nay, trembled at every turn around the mountains. Switchback tracks caused the cars to buck and jig. One moment a passenger was scraping his or her head off the tobacco-stained ceiling, or else apologizing to all and sundry for crashing them to the floor. Experienced passengers had long learned to brace their legs against the opposite seats and grimly hold fast with both hands, expecting that any moment the whole carriage might depart the rails and plunge down the cliffs. It was a known fact that the wrecks of previous Central Pacific trains lay at the bottom of the canyons as testimony to this ever-present danger.

The promised magnificent views were but glimpsed nervously between the great belches of black smoke billowing from the locomotive. The very track seemed perilously close to the mountainside, and leaned so far over the cliffside around corners that the lengthy journey became just too arduous for words. It was a miracle the train survived any distance at all.

Sacramento had long been left behind, as had Emigrant Gap and Donner Pass, where the going had been reduced to a crawl due to a sudden and unwelcome snowfall. Not a passenger could see Donner Pass and the snow without thinking of the fatal Donner party in which old man Keseberg had eaten men, women and babies to stay alive in 1846. The fact that he had gone on to establish a restaurant and hotel in Sacramento hadn't seemed to worry folks much, though no doubt winter diners grew nervous at the first sign of snow.

Truckee was gained and dismissed. Slack always claimed he knew a man who'd been in the immigrant party the old Indian guide Truckee had gotten through to Sacramento. If the eye cared to look, the riverbed was still strewn with abandoned wagons, settlers' tools, rotting books and a plentiful supply of graves. Arnold and Slack knew this territory well. They'd walked it up and down for years, prospecting and pocket mining. Pocket mining consisted of going over abandoned claims for little pockets of gold that had been missed. Looking for diamonds for as long as Arnold and Slack had, it was no surprise they'd come across more than their fair share of generous pockets, but nevertheless it had always been a disappointment that it was gold, and not diamonds that they had found.

As the train rumbled through the Humbolt Sink during the night, many passengers were of a mind to call it quits and take the stagecoach. It was only the promise of breakfast at the next eating stop at Elko that held them there, and the lack of a stagecoach.

A bright moon shone as they went through another pass in the northern Sierras. Even so, the Shoshone range was visible behind them, glistening in a frozen tableau. Before the railroad, this journey would never have been attempted in winter. The western territories were isolated by months of snow and then even more months of avalanches. Even by rail, treacherous conditions prevailed in this country: washouts, snowdrifts, mountain slides. A railroad journey was perilous enough without any of these threats. All through the night, folks tried to sleep, other folks' elbows and feet permitting. The General was a most democratic fellow. It was quite possible for him to have taken his own car and have it hitched to the train for his own privacy and comfort. But no, he felt that as he was on a secret mission of great importance, modesty was essential. Naturally, the conductor recognized him and despite the General requesting he be treated as any other passenger, word soon spread that he was on the train. It thus ensured that the rules were observed, the train traveled on time (as best it could), and news spread up the line by telegraph that the General was aboard, so that the necessary adjustments were made to the eating-stops. Fresh bread instead of stale, a smile instead of a scowl. No doubt they all considered his curious plain attire, his occupation of a seat with common travelers, and his lack of trunks and boxes as some test of railroad employees. It was cunning, but they were more than a match for him; not for a moment did they believe he was aboard because he wished to see the Rockies in all their winter splendor. No man went on a grand tour without baggage, and no man went on a grand tour to the Rockies. If a man wanted to travel he went to Europe, that was where men of the General's caliber went. Any other move was far too suspicious. There was therefore much speculation as to his true purpose.

With their careers firmly in mind, complaints were dealt with expeditiously, instead of ignored and shrugged off as if God himself could do little to improve on the perfection of the Central Pacific.

Slack sat in the corner, not three feet from the General, experiencing a different kind of journey. He had read not one, but three newspapers, and listened to two passengers arguing fiercely as to whether Mrs O'Leary's cow had been black or white, and as to whether it was right to rebuild Chicago at al, since God had seen fit to burn it to a crisp less than a year before. As near as damn it three hundred thousand citizens had been made homeless, yet William

DIAMONDS

B Ogden, the great rival of the Central Pacific, was predicting they'd build themselves a new city twice the size within five years.

Slack's only remark was to say that he'd sooner prefer the three hundred thousand Chicagoans stayed exactly where they were, rather than having them go and cause trouble and more fires any place else. This simple statement endeared Slack to both parties for the rest of the journey. There were many who shared Slack's low opinion of a city so careless it could let itself be devastated by a single cow, whatever its color.

Slack and the General had fallen asleep at about ten, despite the stopping and starting, lurching and bucking as the train descended one mountain and climbed the next. Arnold had been unable to sleep and found himself a card game. Poker. Played with a rough looking crowd with little money among them but a mighty ambition to make some. The conductor had looked in but seen he wasn't welcome so he'd gone to safer quarters. Now, it so happened that Arnold had won himself seven games in a row, and he was thinking how pleasant it was to play with such simple sheep as these, when some among them began to grow edgy. Not only edgy, suspicious. It never occurred to him that their card playing was piss-poor. He wasn't to know Arnold had learned his craft from a Mississippi steamboat gambler, one who'd been so successful, not a boat would carry him, nor a port would let him land. In desperation he'd gone west to play for a fortune in the mining camps of Ophir and Comstock, only to get his left leg shot off by a man none too pleased to lose a months' labor in gold at a game of cards. Now this gambler's curse was about to visit one, Philip Arnold.

When he slammed down his eighth royal flush there was a sudden, rather awkward silence. The roughest and loudest man whose name Arnold had never caught, couldn't take anymore and so took the law of averages into his own very broad hands.

No matter the train was traveling at that time at a good lick of at least twenty-five miles per hour; the stranger seized Arnold by the throat with one hand, his fingers encirling his neck, and with the other grabbed the two hundred dollars in coin that Arnold had won. Then without a word, dragged Arnold to the door conveniently opened by another and flung him out.

Arnold would have cried out had he been able. The last sound he heard was the door slamming shut and a hoot of malicious laughter. Then, with a whoosh and a wild, uncontrolled slide, Arnold was deposited in three or four feet of snow, landing hard at the foot of a cedar tree that deposited half a ton of snow over his head.

Arnold was a man of action at the best of times, of which this was hardly one. He was in pain, his neck hurt, he was cold, he was buried up to his neck in thick snow and he was stunned, shocked and benumbed. Events had transpired so quickly he thought perhaps this was a dream, but a glance to his right

65

where he saw the train fast disappearing out of sight soon brought home his terrible circumstances.

To add troubles to misery, it was four o'clock in the morning or thereabouts. Dawn was still an hour away, and the train wasn't scheduled to stop until Elko, miles away. There was no way he'd be able to catch up, and not another train would be going westward for possibly an entire day. Arnold was aware that he was in the wilderness without a weapon, without his thick leather coat, without food, and at the mercy of the coyotes. If he hadn't had to dig himself out of the snowpile he'd have been deeply concerned for his fate. He reflected that things couldn't have been worse if Jonah himself had organized his luck.

It took a few minutes to get his bearings and dig himself free. His hands were but blocks of ice on the end of his arms. He'd spent enough time in these parts to know that it would be fatal to sit still. Even to stand and think one ran the risk of dying of cold. And it was bitterly cold. His very breath seemed to form clouds that would cause yet more snow to fall. He began to walk, stumble, run , rejoining the railroad track and lumbering after the train. There was no time to inspect his body for damage; nothing felt broken, so he took it that nothing was. As he ran he began to curse. As he began to thaw out the curses grew more inventive. He brought every curse he could remember, since childlood and beyond, down on that brute who'd flung him from the train.

By God he swore, cursing himself, too, for being such a lucky fellow. If they hadn't been such terrible poker players he'd not be in this predicament. If a man was to ignore his innate skills with the cards just to save the ignorant from loss, what a shame the world had come to this! Fling a man from a train, shoot him, fill his widow with lead, too, if he cheats, but to do the same to a man who won fair and square, well, the devil himself wouldn't contemplate such bad sportsmanship. The brute on the train must be of the most villainous stock. Perhaps one of those Ukrainians who inhabited Chicago; no, even they were God-fearing. This brute must be at one with the devil or else after his job.

He walked, he ran, he slipped and fell, stumbled on, getting colder yet working up a sweat. He reasoned that this nightmare need not have happened at all. He would have been prepared to argue the point, even return half the money on account of their lack of experience, but to sling him out just like slops, there was no question of it, if he ever saw that brute again the man would get a slug for every lousy mile he'd made him walk, and two more for luck.

Snow melted down his collar and slid down his back. Arnold even cursed John Slack for sleeping on, unaware of what had befallen his partner. Oh, how they'd wail and lament if he, Philip Arnold, froze to death out here. Slack would never find the diamonds on his own, not in years, and the General would soon lose patience. Oh, how sad they'd be they hadn't stopped the train and made it come back for him.

Arnold lumbered on in this manner for one mile, two miles, yet more miles, never daring to stop, yet quickly tired at that height, in that cold. He kept himself going with the thought that Slack would soon awake and go looking for him. What a surprise awaited Slack. Would he have the sense to take himself and the General off the train and wait for him? Or would they assume the worst and think him dead, given up to the coyotes?

And then he was cursing all over again as it began to snow.

Slack was already awake. First light had taken him by surprise. That and the fact that the train seemed to have stopped. People were walking up and down outside the train, and two children were making sport with snowballs, much to everyone's disgust. The air was frigid; some fool had let the car door open, replacing a warm fug with vigorous fresh mountain air. A light snow was falling as Slack stepped outside. He discreetly took a long piss behind a rock, along with several other similarly inclined passengers, and then woke himself up with a quick snow-wash nearby. The General followed suit a few moments later. "Where are we, Mr.. Slack? I can't get my bearings with this snow falling."

Slack knew what time it was, because his stomach was demanding something that couldn't be had. As to where they were, he couldn't hazard a guess. Some distance from Elko, he guessed, or else Elko had had a terrible time of it with the snow.

"Still the Humboldt, is my guess, General."

The General showed some recognition. " The old bullion trail is about here some place. Spent a summer out here supervising the digging of a shaft, a while back, mind in '59 or '60." He smiled. "Six of us thought we'd all be millionaires, Mr. Slack, but the best we could find was silver, and precious little of that. About a year after we quit and went east for the war, they discovered gold by the ton here. A personal blow for me. And what a terrible road it was. Switchback with sinkers. There's not a wagon in the Union that would survive the old bullion road without shedding a wheel or an axle."

The General strained to see up the line. "Any idea of what's holding up the train, Mr.. Slack?"

Slack didn't know, but he was prepared to take a look. His legs were stiff from all that sitting. By God, it was too damn cold to stand outside for long without moving. The General joined him and together they made their way through the thick snow, creating deep holes in the railside deposits.

"You seen your Philip Arnold lately? " The General asked, by and by.

Slack had been wondering at that very second where Arnold could be. The card game must have ceased, of that he was certain. He conjectured that Arnold might have decided to sleep elsewhere, but that was not too likely. They had made a pact to stay together for safety. One couldn't make a deal without the other, and for that reason alone they had to keep company. It was unlike Arnold to be gone so long.

The conductor intercepted their stroll. "Ah, General, only a momentary delay, sir, we've got volunteers digging now. Just a snowfall, common enough this time of year. Couldn't be more than fifty feet."

Slack queried, "Fifty feet high or, fifty feet long?"

The conductor ignored him. "Franklin says we won't be more than half an hour delayed. It's too thick to take a run through it, and besides, it should clear as we descend."

"Descend, Sir?" the General queried. "We are not yet at Elko, and the elevation at Ruby Dame is more than eleven thousand feet, sir. The snow will be with us a while yet, I think."

The conductor didn't contradict him. Somehow he hadn't expected the General to know the very height of the mountains in these parts. Of course snow was irregular in the Nevada territory. Mostly it was dry, but there was always the risk of snow and delay. He retreated, leaving the General to walk on toward the diggings.

When they passed the locomotive, hissing and creaking at rest, Slack observed that nearly ten men were digging to clear the line. The conductor hadn't exaggerated any. Fully fifty feet of snow covered the track both up and down. The diggers were making some headway, they didn't have to clear the lot, just make it possible for the train to get in there and force its way through.

"Now, if we had a pipe under pressure," Slack mused aloud,"we could steam the snow and melt it away like a knife in butter."

The General looked at Slack with surprise. "Well, sir, you might have come up with the most sensible solution that it has ever been my fortune to hear. Why, beside us stands one of the very largest locomotives in the West, and there's an excellent head of steam in her, why, if one could but attach a fireman's hose to the boiler, surely your idea would be an excellent one indeed."

"We lack a hose, General and don't know a one that could survive the boiling water."

"Nevertheless, Mr.. Slack, it smacks of good American inventiveness, and I shall put it to my engineers when we return. These delays play havoc with our time-tables, and I'd like to think we have a way of dealing with events like this."

"Of course you might then have a problem with ice," Slack told him as he surveyed the sky looking for further clues about the weather. There was definitely more snow on the way.

The General turned back to the snow on the line again and thought that one out. "Ah, yes; ice. Yes, I see what you mean. Ice."

DIAMONDS

They didn't discuss the snow much after that. The volunteers declared that they'd done enough, and the train driver, Franklin, reluctantly agreed. He thought that perhaps if they backed up a ways and then made a run for it, they'd most likely get through the snow.

Folks climbed back aboard, likely as not having had enough of the cold.

Slack did spy out one curious incident as he climbed aboard:a knot of men at the rear of the train laughing and calling out a name that sounded very like Arnold's. But the distance being far and the locomotive sounding its whistle while letting off steam, well, he could have been mistaken. Still, as the train began to back up for its run up to the snow, Slack was strongly aware that Arnold was not aboard.

He was suddenly, extremely apprehensive. What if those men had done some mischief to Arnold? His rifle was here with Slack. Little a man could do to defend himself unarmed. There was no question about it; Arnold had to be sought and proven to be aboard the train. Without a word to the General Slack stood up and walked through the cars.

Arnold was desperately cold, undeniably sweating, out of breath, completely out of curses, snow-blind, ravenously hungry and mad as hell. He'd run on now for miles, and even he thought he was being a fool. It was better to lie down and die. Just curl up in the snow and surrender to the inevitable. That was his uppermost thought before the sound of a train whistle sounded extraordinarily close. For a wild and terrible moment Arnold thought a train was bearing down on him. The westbound train wasn't due for days, but how could this be? Was he dreaming? Was this the final stage of exhaustion, was this the way death came?

He ran on, stumbling in the snow, his feet frozen stumps, yet still moving, one in front of the other, willed on by a sudden surge of hope.

It snowed thickly, but it was near daybreak now and it was already brighter. There was definitely something up ahead. It was too big to be a cow, and besides,what would a cow be doing out here in this cold? He was not thinking clearly at all. Again he heard the familiar sound of the Central Pacific locomotive, and it seemed to him that it was closer than ever.

He stopped in his tracks momentarily, willing his heart and lungs to be silent a minute so he could listen. All he could see was snow. Flakes dissolved upon his eyelids and tongue, but the surroundings refused to take on shape. Not a tree, a rock, nor even the rails stood out a different color from the all-covering snow. Arnold was about to admit that he had finally gone raving mad, that God may as well do for him now, when... almost without warning something large, rumbling, beautifully brown lurched out of the white opaque and fast bore down on Arnold.

69

DIAMONDS

A train, the train, his train was coming back for him' Oh, joy of joys, how wonderful the world was, God really did answer prayers! But wait, the train wasn't slowing none.

Suddenly Arnold had to fling himself off the rails and immediately he was plunged down a slope, buried under a mound of snow, and completely disappeared from view.

The train meanwhile came to a shuddering, aching halt, sliding the last few feet on the snow covered rails. Then, with a desperate jarring, it started forward again with one toot of the whistle and a clashing of coupling as the wheels spun on the locomotive.

It was at this moment that a less than happy Philip Arnold realized that it was possible the train, his train, was there for some reason other than picking him up. The fact that it was beginning to leave as fast as it had arrived, practically stopped his heart. And him still at the bottom of this snowy bank.

He jumped up. He fell, farther than before. He shouted, leapt up, he fell again, even farther than previously. He almost burst into tears as he tried to scrabble up that slope, the train quickly gathering speed above him.

"Stop, stop " he yelled, but only one startled, snow-white jack-rabbit heard.

Arnold hauled himself up on his belly, pushing with his boots. He snaked his way up that slope until at last he found crabgrass under it to hold onto to pull himself up faster. In a trice he was up on the tracks where he'd been only moments before, but alas the train was already a hundred feet away.

Arnold wasted no more breath on shouting. He ran, he positively flew after the train, slipping, losing ground, gaining ground, falling back and running faster again, the snow on his clothes shedding all the while, making him lighter. But, agonies of agonies, the train went faster and faster, and it was not easy to run between the sleepers. At last he felt he was gaining. The train must have been up to practically full speed, but Arnold was a fit man; no man who'd walked the mountains wasn't. He made one final surge, hands outstretched to grab something when he misfooted and went crashing down, head first into the snow. The impact crushed the wind out of him and with one terrible groan he realized all was lost.

The train sped on, rounded the bend, and with one tortuous roaring catastrophic screech of metal, steam and snow, it hit the bank of snow covering the tracks. Of course, seasoned travelers were ready for this and braced for it, but there are always those who care little for common sense or their personal safety. Many therefore sprawled about the cars only to find themselves pinned up against the walls and floors as the train met impenetrable snow.

Yet the diggers had achieved something. True, the cowcatcher was now nothing more than twisted metal, but the train was still moving and making headway. Cheers went up as once again the train began to move forward.

Behind, Arnold was up again,winded, to be sure, with a hand bleeding from where he had grazed it on a sharp rail. Might it still be possible to catch that train?

He began to build up steam, with something of a fanatical relentless energy radiating from within him now, and Arnold made no mistake of looking ahead to where the train may be. He watched each step as he gathered speed, sure now that here was another chance, most likely the very last chance. He felt he *deserved* to die if he didn't get it.

Slack reached the end of the train and by now was sure that Arnold was not on it. Furthermore, he thought he knew who was responsible. There had been much joshing and laughter when he'd come through the second-to-last car, and he recognized one of the men as a miner from Virginia City, Nevada. Arnold might not have known him for he was grown fat now, but there was no mistaking him or the fact that he was known to have killed at least two men to Slack's knowledge. If Arnold had been playing cards with them, well nothing but a shoot-out would get a straight answer from them.

Slack turned around and decided to pay a call on the conductor. He'd know something, and if Slack even suspected he knew that Arnold had been ditched, that conductor would find himself walking that track too. Never mind what business they had with the General.

The train was suddenly through the wall of snow, and it celebrated the fact with a blast from its whistle. A cheer went up everywhere as the train immediately gathered speed. All in all, they'd lost but two hours.

There was a man on the back of that train, standing out on the cold platform. You'd never notice him unless you had to, but he was there and watching. He was there when Arnold had nearly made it the first time, and he was still there when once again Arnold loomed close, head down, almost in danger of overtaking the train, never mind catching it.

"Up here, friend," the man called, setting down the chain and extending a gloved hand.

Hardly able to believe his luck, Arnold found himself hauled up onto the rear-car platform and there he stood, covered in snow, his hair a mess, his eyes wild.

"Stand easy, stranger," the man said, "gather your breath, shake off the snow. The stove's burning hot inside."

Arnold followed these instructions, almost without thinking and with a sense of relief equal to redemption itself. Arnold shook the snow off him, stamped his feet until life resumed in his toes, wiped his face clear of snow and ice, and shook out his jacket . All the while he drew deep breaths to fill up his lungs as he spat out more phlegm than he thought was possible. It was only when he'd finished with all this that he turned to thank the man who had undoubtedly saved his life. But that man was gone, and try as Arnold might he knew that as long as he lived he'd never be able to recall the man's face. A pair of black gloves was all, and a thousand souls wore those in winter. It was a puzzle, but no matter. Arnold lived. He'd caught the train. Now there was just the matter of vengance.

Decker made his way from the rear platform to the car beyond the next. He wiped the snow off his gloves and settled down in a corner seat with a newspaper over his face. Something was about to happen here, and he wanted to watch. He didn't know whether Arnold was armed, but he'd be an angry man all right, and the gamblers still laughing about their nefarious deed were in for a great shock indeed.

Arnold took his time. He had the element of surprise. He knew as well as the next man that to go into a confrontation without his trusted rifle, well, there were simpler ways of committing suicide. But he was canny. He had no intention of going through the cars unarmed. What he needed was his rifle, and his rifle he meant to get.

The snow had tailed off considerably by now, and the train was making up for lost time at a good tilt, considering the terrain. Arnold had spent the best part of two hours outside and not died of cold, what could a few more minutes do? He seized the ladder and did what any self-respecting man would do, seeking to regain his honor. He climbed up to the roof of the cars and, gritting his teeth, made his way on foot along the top of first one car, then another and another, until he was at the self same one that he'd started the journey in with Slack and the General. He descended, made a brief attempt to wipe the soot from his eyes and then entered the car as if nothing had happened at all, hiding his bloody hand behind.

Well, hardly nothing. His jacket was torn, damp and his hair was a sight, but there was nothing to suggest he hadn't just been sleeping rough and gotten covered in snow.

"Morning, General, worked up an appetite for that breakfast at Elko?"

"I surely have, Mr. Arnold. I trust you slept well."

"Seems to me I missed some action."

"Just a little snow on the line. We might make up time after Montello."

"A ways to go yet, General." Arnold told him. He turned to Slack and smiled. "Got a fellow I'd like you to meet, Slack. He's hoping to catch us a jack-rabbit and I says he'll never beat you with a rifle."

Now Slack knew that Arnold had not been on the train. Arnold looked a mess, as if they'd been up in the mountains for months. At some point he'd rejoined the train. Everyone knew, except possibly the General, that trying to shoot a jack rabbit with its white winter jacket from a moving train was something close to spitting at the moon and landing it, so something had to be up and it was their rifles he needed. So Slack took them both down, made sure they were loaded, and with not another word to the General they headed back down the train.

Arnold didn't need to explain much. Arnold knew he could rely on Slack to shoot if he had to, but he was hoping it wouldn't actually come to that.

The brute and the gambling party were utterly surprised. They were practically winded with shock when Arnold came through the connecting doors of the cars and pointed his rifle. When Slack followed suit and covered the rest you could have heard their cowardly knees knocking as far back as Sacramento.

"Now, I'm going to count to ten, gentlemen; and I'm doing an injustice to the word gentlemen, if that two hundred dollars ain't on the table by the time I've finished counting, you are all dead men. When the two hundred dollars are on the table, gentlemen, you may leave...." He indicated the door that he'd been forced out of earlier. "You may leave by that door alive or dead."

The men could see that Arnold had had a terrible time of it. His face was beginning to swell now, his hand was still bleeding from where he had cut it on the rails and there was a terrible cool look in his eye that better belonged to a stone-hearted killer. They believed Arnold. They didn't have to discuss it among themselves. Arnold had come back from the dead. They had little choice and even though the offending brute was in fact armed, he had the sense to know he'd be dead before he could reach for his pistol.

The two hundred dollars found its way onto the table by the count of three. By six, one man began to yelp a little, but Arnold continued counting. When Slack snapped shut the breach of his rifle and took aim. Their nerves snapped.

At ten the door was open and one by one they jumped out, the brute last of all. Not a smile, not a laugh now.

Slack was the one to slam the door shut as Arnold picked up the money. So it was him who observed that the train was crossing a bridge at this time and it was a mighty long way to fall to the ice below. He didn't think Arnold would want to be bothered by such petty details.

Decker, Arnold's saviour that morning, was impressed by these two men. They didn't notice him lying feigning sleep in the corner, why should they? They had other things to do. Certainly he resolved there and then not to cross these two. He couldn't fault their right to take revenge, even if it had been a bit extreme.

By the time Arnold and Slack had rejoined the General and apologized for missing the jack-rabbits, there was a definite atmosphere of expectation in the cars. Twenty minutes later it resolved itself.

"Elko. Eating stop," the Conductor called out. "Fifteen minutes. Breakfast time, folks. One dollar. Breakfast."

Now, breakfast is an important meal for folks who've had nothing to do but stare out of a window for more hours than seems possible. The rarified air and excitement of the snow blockage on the line had cut a fine edge into their appetite. It was the same food for everyone for the price of a dollar, and there wasn't a soul who didn't make a bee-line for the ramshackle Refreshment Saloon. This was a crude log cabin kind of structure that could squeeze in a hundred people sitting down as long as they didn't move their elbows or turn their heads. There being a chronic shortage of knives, just a spoon and fork was provided for all, to last the entire meal, which consisted of nearly stale corn cake, hard-boiled eggs, and hams. There was coffee, too, but no sugar, which set many agrumbling.

The rush to eat was so great that the entire trainload was watered and fed within twelve indigestible minutes and was reckoned good value. But had you been particularly hungry and had even ten dollars to spend, there was no more food to be had.

There was, of course, nothing in the way of washing facilities, so Arnold had to content himself with washing the blood away with snow melted on the side of the locomotive. Franklin, the driver, raised an eyebrow. Men did not survive long in the West asking awkward questions.

For Arnold's part, he'd already put aside the incident with the gamblers. He'd taken his revenge, and that was a man's right. No need to dwell on it, or crow. He may have put it aside, but the gossips on the train hadn't and word was going around that the train was a few passengers short on account of some of them having been put off at gunpoint and dashed to their deaths in an icy gorge. Eyes flashed to Arnold and Slack, but no accusations were made. The conductor did nothing. There were apparently no witnesses. Besides, the gentlemen were traveling with the General. It was not worth his while to surrender his career on the railroad by making false or embarrassing accusations over a game of cards.

The General was not happy, however. For one thing, he had an attack of dyspepsia from the hurried breakfast. Here was a man used to a leisurely intake of food. "We're running late and breakfast was far from good value for a dollar. I shall have to speak to the contractors. At the very least the bread should be no less than a week old, or else none should be provided at all."

Slack was standing with him outside the saloon attempting to pick ham from his teeth. "General, you're getting too picky. That was quite a feast for these parts. Not so many years since all a traveler had for breakfast was his companion."

The General looked at Slack with surprise, then saw the smile and understood it was a jest. "Yes, well things have improved a little since those days, Mr. Slack."

"That's right, General, at least now you get coffee to swill it down with."

The General didn't particularly care for this kind of humor.

"I'd like to see the Pullman cars hauling all the way west instead of quitting at Ogden. Think of how much time the railroad could save if we didn't have to stop to eat."

"Still stop for water," Slack pointed out.

"But not always do we stop for water at the same place we stop to eat," the General pointed out, although at this very moment the train was taking on water ahead of them.

"There's times I've wondered about the efficiency of the railroad myself, General. Now if you was to carry the water with you behind the locomotive, or routing a train along a shallow riverbed so it could suck the water up as it went along well, now, you'd really be saving time."

The General again regarded Slack with surprise. "Mr. Slack, you are a veritable mine of original ideas. You're wasted, sir, absolutely wasted in this prospecting. If ever you desire an occupation on the railroad, you come and see me."

Slack smiled. It was the first time anyone had ever offered him a job. A strange sensation indeed.

The bell sounded then, giving notice to all to re-board.

Slack was disappointed by the Central Pacific's attempt at a morning newspaper, on sale for a few cents. He declined the offer. He knew that once they changed to the Union Pacific he'd be able to obtain the *Great Pacific Line Gazette*, altogether more informative than the Western rag. He still didn't see why, if they went to all the trouble of making up a newspaper on a train they didn't just telegraph the pages of the *New York Tribune* and have done with it.

The General was still grumbling as they mounted the steps.

"Something has to be done to get the Pullmans running west, Mr. Slack."

"Well, first you'll have to straighten out all the bumps, General. Your fancy passengers won't take kindly to spilling their Krug champagne everytime we round a bend or straighten up. Unless you intend to supply them with straws."

Arnold greeted them between cars, holding some brightly colored Indian blankets. "Need these up in the mountain, General. I told the Indian you'd pay him a dollar apiece."

"A dollar?" the General protested.

Slack felt them and thought them good. "The Indians know what it takes to keep warm, General, and believe me, it's still mighty cold out where we're going."

The General saw the Indian standing outside waiting, nervous in case the train pulled out without him getting money for his blankets. The General paid, sickened by the thought of a trunkful of blankets left behind in San Francisco.

"You won't regret this," Arnold declared, settling down in his seat. "Wake me when we get to the next stop, boys. I've a desperate need for some shut-eye."

DIAMONDS

The rest of the journey was less eventful, although Slack did get to witness an altercation between one English traveler and the conductor. As the train descended it picked up speed, and the general estimation was that a good thirty miles an hour had been attained. Certainly, judging from the shaking of the cars the train had reached its limit of endurance, and the traveler was now wishing he'd taken out an accident insurance. The conductor didn't think it was warranted at all. "Sir, we have not had as much as a minor derailment in almost six months."

The traveler was not convinced. "But don't you see, by the law of averages the next train smash on this line is overdue by four weeks at the very least."

The conductor then pointed to the General as his trump card.

"Sir, if the management of the railroad can travel with us with confidence, I believe you can be sure that we will arrive at Ogden in complete safety."

The Englishman was not convinced. In his experience, he said, the very presence of management on the railroad was proof positive that an accident was long overdue and he was there just to make a face of it. He made a resolution there and then to get off the train at the very next stop. Since he'd chosen to disembark at the most inhospitable spot in all of Utah, a place thick with alkali dust, if ever a man was overdue for an accident it was that Englishman, and Slack wondered about him for many miles thereafter, wishing he could send a raven or two to sit on his shoulder to help him await his doom.

The General busied himself with reading a manual. '*The Recognition of Diamonds, Corundum and other precious stones as found in the Kimberley region of South Africa*' by Col. H.J. Lyall-Ollins, DSO. But the ride was now so rough at these high speeds, one page had to be read a number of times to get any sense of it at all.

Slack took to day dreaming about what he'd do with his money once he'd made his pile. This required much thought on his part because, being practical and down to earth, he found it hard to picture a life of ease. He rather considered a wealthy man was one who owned a draft-proof cabin up by Lake Tahoe with a plentiful supply of logs in winter and fish in summer. It was a problem knowing what to do with money when it had been such a long time since he'd had any. Perhaps he should travel the world, go to Hawaii or someplace. But he wasn't sure what he'd do there if he went. The idea of seeing women in grass skirts tickled him some though.

Slack did meet a man who'd just returned from Virginia City. He'd been delivering vital new parts to Adolph Sutro, the great tunnel dreamer himself. The man, whose name was Garnett, was formally the number two man to Sutro and was now on urgent tunnel business for him. Talk fell to drills and Slack was astonished to learn that the drills came from Germany and they were boring with a diamond drill whose rod weighed several hundred pounds.

DIAMONDS

Naturally Slack was interested to know where the diamonds came from. Garnett didn't know, but he was convinced the whole enterprise would be a lot cheaper if the diamonds could be found on the continental USA, but he'd never seen a one.

"I can tell you, we've bored 9000 feet into Mt Davidson with only 3000 feet to go to reach the Comstock and never seen one single precious stone. Nevada won't yield anything but gold or silver. Plenty of quartz mind. But no diamonds."

Slack shrugged. He was glad that the General hadn't met this man. He didn't want the General prejudiced in any way.

"The tunnel should have been dug years ago. It's those bankers, Ralston and Sharon's doing. They set themselves again it and Sutro's been battling ever since. Someone should take on the Bank of California and bring it down a peg or two.

Slack pretended to be offended on the bank's behalf. "Nevertheless, Ralston's the man whose built San Francisco."

"Maybe he is, but with whose money? Whose labor? Do the people own San Francisco, or Bill Ralston?"

"And will Sutro ever finish his tunnel?" Slack asked.

"You'll see, in five years time, every Sutro stockholder will be so rich, they'll be living on Nob Hill."

Slack made a mental note to buy stock. The man looked convinced.

"Now what business are you in sir?" Mr. Garnett wanted to know.

"Land, sir, real estate."

"That's the business these days. So you'll be hoping we will run short of it, by the bye."

Slack smiled, recognising the man's ironic tone. " By the bye," he returned and they both laughed heartily as another million acres drifted slowly by their window.

So it was in this fashion that the adventurers finally reached Ogden, Utah. Only when they gained the luxury of the Union Pacific and the spectacle of Echo Canyon did they really get warmed up to the idea of finally nearing their destination. Echo Canyon is the express part of the mountain journey, twenty miles at the bottom of a long, narrow natural street with a gradual, descending grade. The sides were four hundred feet high in some places, and one sensed it would be much like this to ride the ramparts of some medieval giant's castle. Green River was next, and the General thought for sure this was where Arnold and Slack would disembark, but, after a more satisfying meal of antelope steak and fresh coffee, they reboarded the train and didn't seem in any rush to strike out for the diamonds at all. Even as they passed through the very heart of the Rockies, his companions showed no sign of wanting to leave the train. He thought that perhaps when the train finally reached New York they'd laugh and let him know it had all been a huge joke and they'd only wanted a ride east. At Rawlins Springs, a two bit town and the very last place the General had considered as his destination, Arnold awoke, took one look, and quickly had them all off the train moments before it took off again. The ostler was there to greet them by name, and he had mules ready. Arnold had sent word by telegraph.

Neither of the three noticed a fourth person disembark and vanish into the sparse buildings surrounding the station. They were too busy with the mules and getting re-acquainted with their limbs and muscles after sitting for so long. Rawlins was no coming metropolis, then or now: a telegraph station, the most primitive refreshment saloon at the railroad station and something like a hotel, half empty even when full. There was a church, but it doubled as schoolhouse most days and on wet days as a barn. A handful of log cabins made up the street and if you counted the hogs, cows, and horses, it was quite a sizable place.

The General didn't like the look of the mules they'd hired. A few days on the grasslands were desperately needed to get them to the state where they'd look well enough to carry even a man, let alone transport him a couple of hundred miles over the steepest mountains in the Americas. But they would have to do.

Arnold, making liberal use of the General's purse, organized provisions for the journey, whilst Slack filled their flasks with sweet water. There'd be plenty of fresh water up in the mountains, but before they climbed that far a man could get awful thirsty.

The very last task was to blindfold the General. Arnold had the decency to wait until they'd ridden a few miles out of town. Folks could be mighty suspicious if they wanted to be.

"Now, mind you don't nod off, General. The mule will know where it's going, but since you're behind us, we may not notice if you've gone, and a lot of time might be wasted a going looking for you, assuming we can find the same track."

The General said nothing. The cloth was darker than sin, and he didn't like this part of the deal at all. Nevertheless, he did not feel he was in any danger. Arnold and Slack needed him to give a good account of the diamond field and they'd have to take good care of him, of this he was sure.

"Now, General," Arnold continued, an amused look sliding onto his face, "it's pretty dark in there, but when you finally clap eyes on our diamonds you will be dazzled so much you'll think yourself in paradise itself."

The General was not amused, not at all. "I've held my tongue, Philip Arnold, but I have to tell you that I am not altogether convinced about this magical diamond field of yours up in the mountains. It's my opinion that the diamonds are in your imagination, but Mr.. Ralston is bewitched by the subject."

DIAMONDS

Slack laughed, setting off on his mule, giving the General's mule a casual slap that set it off at quite a lick. "Now, hold on there, General, this ain't no gallop."

Arnold dug in his heels and quickly followed, highly amused by the way the General hung on for dear life. They drew level with the General and both mules settled back into a regular rhythm. Arnold looked across at the General and saw he was uncomfortable. "Y'know, I told Mr.. Ralston myself, 'Give us a man who is a disbelieving cuss, a man who'd need to see God himself before he believed He exists and ten miracles in case one was a fluke.' You know what? he immediately thought of you, General. He said, 'If the General says they are diamonds, I'll take his word for it, and his word alone.'"

The General rather liked the tone of all that and appreciated the fact that Ralston thought him so difficult to please. He turned to where he thought Slack was riding, but missed him by a mile. "And you, Mr.. Slack? Do you believe in your diamonds, or has Mr.. Arnold here got you seeing visions too?"

Slack hadn't been listening. He'd been looking up at the mountains above them and begun to worry that bad weather was closing in. He was concerned about his mule, too. It was one sorry-excuse for a mule, and sore where it had been rubbing itself up against a pole somewhere, so that the nasty abrasion was attracting flies. Might even have been a snake bite to begin with, it looked mighty red.

"What was that you said, General?" Slack called back.

The General turned his head again, happier to know Slack was ahead of him. "I wanted to know your opinion about the diamonds, Mr. Slack."

"My opinion, General, is that God took his time in choosing a place so inconvenient to get to. But I'm thankful all the same, 'cause if he'd put them down here, likely as not the railroad would have had them by now, and it's my opinion that Mr.. Hopkins and Stanford an' all have altogether enough by now without adding to it further."

The General puzzled over this reply. He decided that it was possible Slack had answered in the affirmative, although he couldn't be positively sure.

"How long a journey is it?" the General asked.

"Two days, three nights, maybe a little more. Hard to tell. 'Fore now we always walked. Mules is a luxury Slack and me never could afford."

It was still morning, the sun was burning mist off a small lake nearby, and the first ridge ahead rose before them shrouded in a foggy haze.

They rode on in silence for a while but the sight of wild geese rising and making a curve across the rising sun did lift Slacks heart some. His eye followed the birds until they disappeared into the dark clouds, hanging heavy to their left.

"Don't like the look of that," Slack said, turning to Arnold and pointing.

79

DIAMONDS

"General, there's cold weather coming. Make the most of this sunshine."

"Thought I heard birds, Mr. Slack. Not buzzards , I hope."

Slack laughed. "You should see this land in spring , General. A real picture it is. A regular carpet of silver and blue lupins. God's own Indian blanket, I reckon."

Arnold was leaning forward studying the mountain peak covered in snow, a cloud rising up to cover it. "We want to aim for that peak for about a day. Hope we don't lose sight of it. If that cloud closes in we could be in trouble."

"I have a compass," the General reminded them.

"A compass is a nice idea, General," Slack told him, "but there's some terrible magnetism around these parts, and a man could follow due south for ten days and find himself in Kentucky or Tennessee. No, a man has to trust his instincts around here."

This information did not cheer the General up any.

"There's a kind of trail to the first ridge," Slack remarked. "The deer go through to a valley behind the forest to breed. I reckon they think its safe from the Indians."

"Nothing is safe from the Indians," the General declared emphatically.

"Oh, they won't make a kill when the does are dropping," Slack told him. "They don't go in for indiscriminate killing like some folks do. Not so long ago a man couldn't move around here for buffalo, but where are they now? Makes no sense to shoot every last one of them. Animals should have a right to be left in peace someplace."

"You're quite a radical, Mr. Slack." the General remarked.

"You live as long as we have in the mountains, General,... well, you learn to respect the ways of nature."

"If you were that respectful, Mr.. Slack, you'd be leaving the diamonds where they were."

Slack laughed. Arnold chuckled too. "We're respectful, General, but we ain't stupid."

They rode a while, the mules making steady progress on a considerable incline. They gained the ridge by mid-day and didn't stop to rest until they'd reached the edges of the forest.

The General fiddled with his blindfold, but Arnold wouldn't release him from it, not while there was still a view behind them he could take a bearing on.

"We still in Wyoming?" the General asked.

Arnold smiled. "Could be. Hard to tell. It's all right for folks in Washington to draw their lines on the maps, but unless they draw them on the ground, how's a man to tell whether he's in Wyoming, Utah, or Colorado?"

"Well ..." the General frowned, "I'd like to know, Mr. Arnold. I'm not trying to cheat you, I'd just like to know whether your diamonds are in the Colorado mountains or those belonging to Utah. It's all a matter of legislation, you see."

"You mean if it's in Mormon territory, you're scared that the Avenging Angels might make trouble ?"

"Them too."

"Well, set your mind at rest, General, the diamonds are not in the state of Utah. But even if I confess to them being in Colorado, I couldn't be sure, the way the maps are drawn."

"But they're definitely not in Wyoming?" the General asked.

"Sir, if Wyoming has diamonds, may I be struck dumb twice over. The railroad didn't find any diamonds, the cattlemen didn't find any, and neither have the farmers and settlers. My guess is that God didn't intend the people of Wyoming to get lucky."

The General was happy to know the diamonds were not in Wyoming or Utah. Colorado was not a difficult place to obtain legislation necessary for them to extract diamonds from the ground. There were no special interests to grease as far he knew.

"Ho, let's git going," Slack called out. "We've many miles to go yet."

The first night they camped in the shadow of a huge cedar forest. There was no trail, so it was a question of picking their way through the trees and looking out for that mountain peak. Mercifully, the clouds hadn't grown any thicker, so its snowy peak was still visible. No closer, but visible. In Arnold's estimation they'd covered thirty miles, which was good going by any standard and testimony to the stamina of the mules. But they all knew that from here on they'd not be so lucky. The mules feasted on grass growing beside a mountain stream. Judging from the way they went at it, it was their first good meal in weeks.

Slack made up a fire and heated some coffee while Arnold stirred a mess of beans with wild mushrooms they'd found close by. The General removed his blindfold and sat silent, nursing his saddle-sore thighs.

"Tomorrow we'll clear the trees and reach the snow," Arnold declared.

The General groaned. The journey had been arduous enough without encountering more snow.

"We had to surrender the mountains to winter these past years, General, but it was mighty mild this year, so we took our chances and got up higher than we normally do. That's when we found our diamonds."

It was getting markedly cooler now, and even though the General sat near the fire he was shivering. Slack noticed. "If it gets too cold for you, General, get close to a mule, but watch out if it decides to roll."

Arnold had to chuckle at that, but again the General wasn't amused.

DIAMONDS

Soon after they finished eating they went to sleep on a bed of fir-cones. Slack wouldn't keep the fire going. He banked up the ashes with rocks; that way there'd be some heat left for the coffee in the morning.

Arnold had one thought for the General before he slept. "General, you think this country of ours will ever fill up so much folks would have to live up here?"

The General thought about it a while as he shivered under his blanket.

"It would have to be mighty full, Mr. Arnold, but then there is the matter of the Mormons. They spread pretty thick these days."

"Yep, that's what'll take," Slack commented. "One man, a hundred wives, eight hundred kids. Why, there won't be a tree or a blade of grass left without a Mormon standing in place of it."

"Now there's good a nightmare as any you'll have, General," Arnold declared, "and not a one will buy a diamond for fear of incurring God's wrath."

The General thought some more. "Maybe so, Mr.. Arnold, but if you gave one diamond to the youngest wife, the husband would be obliged to purchase ninety-nine more to keep the others happy."

Arnold and Slack were much amused by that and cackled on it for some minutes, concluding that the General was a good fellow after all. The three fell to sleeping with a smile on their faces.

The next day progress was slow. Slack wasn't so sure Arnold was leading the right way, though the mountain peak was stil on their the right , so it had to be.

By the third day the General was beginning to sense Arnold was lost completely. It didn't inspire him much, and his good mood had long gone. The mountain peak was as far or near as ever, and now they were riding in wild, sparsely vegetated land.

They came to stop by a ridge overlooking a broad, sweeping valley of endless trees. On their immediate left, wild, coarse grass grew, breaking through the snow. The mules fastened onto this and were not to be moved on until they'd cropped it short. Slack dismounted and began filling the flasks from a clear mountain stream.

Arnold had gone ahead some hours before to get his bearings. He insisted that he wasn't lost, but reminded Slack and the General that it wasn't easy to find your way back to a place you'd been to only once before. There was no trail or signposts.

The General was sucking on an icicle, wishing he was back home in a hot bath with a full roast waiting for him down in the kitchen. Tonight he'd be eating jerk beef, and even though it was prime, somehow it wasn't quite what he was used to.

DIAMONDS

"I've got to tell you, Mr. Slack, your Philip Arnold is lost. Furthermore, I dispute his calculations. He says we are two hundred miles from the railroad, but I swear it's only a hundred, and if we were flying as high as the buzzard I'd swear it was only forty."

Slack broke off an icicle for himself and narrowed his eyes at the General, sat awkwardly in his saddle. "You're welcome to fly anywhere you like, General, so long as you take your mule."

By midnight the mood was black. The moon was dying away, and with it the light, but even so the snowy peak was clearly visible. It was Slack's private opinion that there'd be a heavy frost once the moon had gone and certainly it was cooler than the first night.

The campfire was hardly adequate either. Fir cones were hard to find up here and the ones Slack had found were wet. Still what warmth they gave was entirely welcome. The General sat close to a sleeping mule, a happier man now that his blindfold was removed. There was a frostiness developing between himself and Slack , and Slack could sense that the General was afraid of the forest, the sounds of the coyotes and other nocturnal animals. The General kept on looking behind him as if expecting some wild creature to sneak up and pounce. Even at this moment the man was staring back into the darkness with a look of alarm on his face.

"You'll not find any trouble behind you, General. The bears are probably still hibernating or leastways afraid to come close and the coyote's a real coward too. It's too cold for snakes, so if you're going to perish, all that's left is the snow...that and your shadow."

The mules snored awful loud too, it didn't make him any happier. Sleep seemed out of the question. The cold didn't seem to make a difference to mules.

The General was envious of their indifference. "Where is Arnold?" he asked impatiently.

"He'll be here," Slack reassured him.

But a good hour passed and there was still no sign of him. Neither man could sleep and Slack was doing his best to keep the fire going. The cold was biting hard and his toes felt dreadfully numb.

"What was that?" the General called out suddenly.

Slack listened. He could hear a distant shriek. It had traveled far.

"That's the train, Mr.. Slack. I can distinctly hear the Union Pacific."

Indeed Slack had thought it sounded much like the locomotive's distinctive note, but it flummoxed him as to exactly how that was possible. He knew for certain they were at least a hundred miles south of the railroad, if not Arnold's generous two hundred.

"Sound travels a long ways at night General."

"A hundred miles, Mr. Slack? Two hundred? I think not sir. Admit it,

You've had me riding in circles since the day we left the train. We are no more than an hour away from the train." The General was getting hot under the collar now and working up a good head of steam. "By God, Slack, we are probably still in Wyoming. Is this your idea of a joke? Where is Arnold? Hiding out in some hotel, sitting by a warm fireside laughing at us, and me in particular?"

Slack smiled. The idea of it appealed to him, only he wished it was himself sitting in the hotel, not Arnold. "General, see for yourself. No blindfold prevents you from looking now. If you find that hotel, you have my permission to burn it down with Arnold in it."

The General stood up, walked ten paces to the top of the ridge, and saw for himself that they were in the middle of the wilderness, and if there was a hotel here, it would be more likely St. Peter's, they were up so high. That damn mountain peak was still up there buried under a thousand years of snow. Now instead of being angry, he worried that Arnold was lost and Slack would never know how to get them back to civilisation again. Yes, Arnold was lost. By God, they'd traveled so far he wouldn't be surprised if the train he'd heard wasn't one serving Texas.

Slack found a few sticks and got them burning on the fire pretty quickly. The General soon gave up his anquished pacing and joined him by the fire.

Slack looked up and caught his eye . "Tell me, General, when you saw the hotel, could you tell if the bar was open?"

Arnold returned thirty minutes later. He was practically frozen to his saddle, he could barely speak for ten minutes as he and the mule stood close to the fire.

"Damn it, Slack, if you hadn't kept that fire going I might have spent twenty nights trying to find my way back here. Hell, I'd thought we'd overshot the diamonds and got ourselves too far south by the Yampa river. Which would make us very lost indeed. But when I looked again, I discovered we couldn't have got here straighter if we'd sailed over in a balloon." Arnold smiled. "You hear about 'em adventurers traveling around the continent in a hot-air balloon, General. It could be the coming thing, what you say to that, eh?"

"I'm sure I don't know, Mr.. Arnold. But you were saying about the Yampa River?"

"Don't get ideas, General. The Yampa is in Colorado. If you think you can find this diamond field on your own, feel free, General. Shouldn't take you more than a hundred years."

The General said nothing. Arnold knew he was trying to narrow down the area. Well, he'd let slip the Yampa, and the Yampa was most definitely in Colorado. At least the General could be sure of what state they were in now.

DIAMONDS

Arnold tethered his mule to a lone bush with the others and got out his blanket. He huddled down beside the fire, just a dim glow by now.

"Tomorrow, General, I mean, later this morning, we will be dining on precious stones."

"We're that close?" The General sounded surprised.

"No more than an hour's ride in daylight. I found that old Indian trail at last, and my trail markers. Old Sitting Bull will be sick soon enough when he discovers we've found his secret hoard."

"There's no proof the Indians hoard diamonds," the General asserted.

"You ever see one try to sell one for firewater or a rifle? You know they'll sell their own women for a rifle."

"No, sir, I haven't witnessed either transaction. I still don't think..."

Arnold cut him off. "Sitting Bull doesn't want us to find diamonds. They don't want the white man to walk in their mountains. They know that once we've got them, they'll never get their mountains back."

"The Indians have the plains," the General explained. "They don't need mountains."

"The Indians think the great white spirit lives hereabouts," Slack declared.

"It's altogether too cold for gods, I should say." the General muttered.

Slack grinned, thinking the remark amusing. He watched the General shiver. The man certainly couldn't abide the cold; left alone he wouldn't survive two days.

At some point during the night, all three men found time to doze off, but come the frosty morning they were all as stiff as the cedars around them. It was with great reluctance and not a little pain from aching muscles that the mules were remounted and the last stage of the outward journey commenced. Arnold began by insisting that the blindfold go back on, but the General was asking so many damn questions and the track was so difficult to navigate that Slack drew alongside and took it off. "There you go, General. Seems a pity to miss such a grand sunrise."

The General appreciated Slack's gesture and was surprised to discover they were riding along a narrow rock canyon, no more than six mules wide. On either side cliffs towered above them, glowing pink in the sunlight. The ground was a tangle of thorny scrub and sage brush and the mules thought they were in heaven, mooching their breakfast on the hoof. The men envied them, all they'd had was cold coffee.

"Interesting geology," the General remarked. "Ice must have cut its way through here in time past. Quartz-bearing rock, if I'm not mistaken. You didn't find any gold hereabouts?"

Arnold shook his head. "Quite a freak of nature this canyon , General. I reckon a lot of that snow up ahead finds its way through here in the summer months. Ten thousand more years of that and you could be looking at another

Grand Canyon."

That was when they came upon the remains of an immigrant's wagon and three unmarked graves. There was a fresh mark on the side of the wagon: *A and S.*

Arnold pointed it out. "I remember when we first came upon this, General. Felt mighty spooked by it. Some pour souls must have thought this was a God-sent route to California. Only it peters out at the foot of the mountain peak and there's no hope in hell of getting a wagon over that, summer or winter. Getting the wagon this far took some doing."

They rode on by. Farther up they came across the rotting remains of wagon wheels and even the would-be settlers' trunks, long ago looted by the Indians. Slack thought the wagon might have been a breakaway from Manly's immigrant train, but the General disagreed. It was a sobering sight and took the edge off their anticipation.

By around ten o'clock the sun was giving off some real heat, and aside from the gnats, it was a pleasant ride. Suddenly Slack was shouting up ahead, and Arnold let out a rebel yell. This was it. They were there.

Arnold was still whooping and Slack laughed. They were quite drunk with good humor and relief that they'd found the place.

"I tell you, General, I could have sworn it was another mile. Just goes to show how cussed a man's memory can be."

As the General looked about him, he was confused. He was aware of a heightened sense of disappointment. If he'd been expecting to find Ali Baba's cave, he couldn't have been more wrong. All he faced was a natural break in the cliff face, a tree making good on a patch of soil left behind by the ancient snows, and one crooked man-made (and crudely made at that) wooden cross with words scrawled on it with what looked like blood: Arnold and Slack's notice that this land was theirs.

NOTICE

'We the undersigned claim two claims of 600 feet each (and one for discovery rights) on this carboniferous-compound bearing rock extending north and south from this notice, with all its undulations, spurs and angles, variations,and water supplies (including the sources thereof), together with fifty feet of ground on either side for working the same.

John Slack. Philip Arnold.

"Got a notice posted in six places, General. By our reckoning we've got the whole plateau legally covered, and the only reason you were blindfolded is because if we were to register this claim in the recorder's office, you and a million others would be here so fast well, a man would only have to blink."

DIAMONDS

The General understood. He smiled at the term carboniferous compounds. That would have any other stray prospector good and foxed.

"We've got a name for the mine, General," Arnold pointed out. "Vermillion Creek. On account of the rock plants. It was Slack's idea."

"Name's fine gentlemen, but all I see is a notice written in blood."

Slack smiled. "Got to confess, General, it's rabbit blood; and mighty tasty it was, too. Slack walked on around a tree out of view. The General followed, stumbling a moment, but when he looked again, he was astonished.

He would never have imagined such a place could ever exist. Not up here, not in the mountains. It was a meadow. Oh, the grass was short to be sure, and coarse, crushed by the winter snows , but it was a meadow nevertheless, and wild flowers were already showing, tiny, bright vermillion creatures. It looked as though the Indians had forgotten their most precious rugs in wild flight from some danger. At the edge of the plateau a stream cut its way through, and the sound of small rapids could be heard. The mules could smell grass and were already making their way through the gap in anticipation.

Slack strolled alongside the narrow creek that emerged from the rocks behind them to cut its way through the plateau and eventually fall, two, or three hundred feet to the rock pool below. The creek flowed on for miles, snaking its way through the rocks to disappear in a sinkhole. This was an area of outstanding natural beauty, replete with many rare plants he couldn't put a name to. Slack looked back over the plateau proper and scratched his head. It looked different without the snow. Thirty, perhaps forty acres in extent, it was a curious spot. Plumb in the center stood a flat rock of black quartzite rock surrounded by the meadow of flowers and coarse grass. Normally this was a haven for all kinds of birds and animals, but their arrival had scared them off. Arnold led the mules over to the water and partook of the same himself.

The General was well pleased with the general aspects of the claim. Fresh water, flat, quartzite in evidence. He looked over the edge and squinted in the sun as he sized up the great redwood forests all around them. Plenty of timber handy for mine shafts.

Slack joined Arnold in the water and began to soak himself, shaking off the dust and grime of the journey. He looked back at the General and observed him poking at the dirt with a knife.

"What do you think, General? Ain't it as pretty as a picture? Reminds me of old fairy tales. Arnold here calls this the giant's footstool. What d'you think?"

The General nodded, slapping his neck as gnats began to gather 'round him. He walked over to the creek and waded in, drinking and washing himself.

"It astonishes me that you found the place at all. This water run all year round?"

"This is run off from the snow, General: the snow is permanent. There's a spring over by the fringes of the forest over there and the creek below us is

87

deep, fed from springs and run off from all over. No shortage of water up here. Flows thataways a while, then disappears down a sinkhole."

"Disappears?" the General queried.

"Slack here reckons there's an underground lake half way down, but it's rough country down there. The mosquitoes here are the fattest, meanest-looking buzzards that you ever met. There's places down there that the Indians won't go near it's so hostile. Critters down there, General that have not yet got into the natural history compendiums. Wouldn't be at all surprised if they didn't find dinosaurs, or something like, from those pre-historic times."

"The dinosaurs all died long ago, " the General declared dismissively.

"Tell that to the dinosaurs, not me."

The General could believe it; the forest was thick and spread out below them for miles.

"Tell him, Slack. The drop here's damn near three hundred feet."

"You ever see Flaming Gorge, General?"

"No, Mr. Slack, I have not, but I hear it is a spectacular sight."

"It's more than that, General. It's steep and this is spring. That creek can turn into a torrent fiercer than that fateful day when the Red Sea closed in on the Egyptians and drowned the lot of 'em. Besides, you ever try getting miles up a creek? I've been down it, sir, thought we'd find diamonds, but all we found was gold."

"*All?*" The General was taken aback.

Slack took out the last of his chewbaccy and popped some into his mouth. "When a man's looking for diamonds, General, gold is a poor substitute. Heck, it's natural that somethin's gonna turn up in that creek. We got ourselves five ounces of gold in seven months of panning for precious stones. So my guess is that it's no Comstock."

He was looking about him now with greater interest. A red-tailed hawk flew by, curious and unafraid. He saw strange sandy colored formations dotted around the plateau that aroused his interest. Around four to six feet high, they didn't look as though they belonged on the plateau at all. "What are these rock formations?" he inquired of Arnold, still sitting by the stream.

"Anthills, General. You must have seen them before."

Well, of course he had, but he'd never conceived of them outside of a desert. "No need to be afraid. The ants made a mistake I reckon. It's too cold up here. The snow must have got'em. Take a look," Arnold encouraged him. "Slack, find the man a stick."

"No need, General, give it a kick."

The General did just that. The shower of dust and bits of sandstone that covered him set Arnold and Slack off real good. They laughed so hard they nearly fell down. The General stood there, pale as a ghost and just as angry.

His anger quickly turned to joy, however, when he suddenly spied some-

DIAMONDS

thing in the dried mud and scooped it off the ground. "What's this? What's this?"

Arnold looked at Slack and smiled.

"Gentlemen, I think I've found something." The General's voice began to rise with excitement. "It's a ruby, Mr. Arnold. It's a ruby, Mr.. Slack or I'm a Dutchman."

Arnold walked over slowly, taking care not show any emotion.

"Of course an anthill is made up of the ground below it, so it's possible you got lucky , General, but hell, we was here a week before we cottoned on."

"It's a ruby, I tell you," the General insisted, exhibiting the stone as big as a thumb before Arnold's eyes.

Arnold wouldn't say yes or no until he'd washed it. He didn't want the General thinking he was tricked. He wanted everything to be sure and certain. He took it along to the water, with the General in close quarters behind. He gave it to the General to wash, and even though the water was near frozen, he held it under and rubbed at it until all the mud was gone completely.

When he took it out and held it to the sunlight it was just as he'd predicted. A stunning wine-red ruby, like glass, but as yet in need of a polish to bring up its natural beauty.

"You're a lucky man, General," Arnold declared, somewhat wistfully. "Wish we'd had you with us when we first started looking in these mountains. We'd be rich and sitting by warm fires many months ago."

The General was just too excited now. Slack was getting up a campfire and Arnold was talking of setting up a camp and getting them some shelter, but he couldn't abide it. "I must search every inch of that anthill. There might be more. Have you tried others?"

"General, I have personally demolished about twenty, but never found a stone as good as you found straight off, " Arnold confessed.

"Then where, where did you find those stones you brought in? Where are the diamonds, Mr. Arnold. Tell me, sir. I want to know."

Arnold shook his head. "General, I could tell you the vicinity of the diamonds, but you'd accuse me of being a conjurer if I told you the exact place. I told Mr.. Ralston that a keen man could find the stones lying on the ground, and I'd like you to bear me out, General. I've brought you up to prove our find, and it's not becoming for us to do your work for you."

The General pondered this reasoning a moment and knew Arnold was right. Ralston would be asking him all kinds of awkward questions when he returned and he'd have to give a good account of how he came across the precious stones. He'd want to know what part Arnold and Slack played in their discovery."

"If I was you I'd stick close to the water," Slack volunteered when he came back with some branches and twigs from the pinetrees on the ridge. "But you

89

search that anthill good an' proper, General. If there's one ruby, I reckon there's going to be two."

The General ran back to his anthill, certainly no place for ants anymore. He practically fell onto the dirt, and Arnold and Slack watched him with some amusement as he sorted through every particle, making a pile of stones on one side and precious stones on the other. Or at least what he thought was precious.

"If it shines, General, it's probably quartz. Diamonds don't..."

But the General wasn't listening. He'd found something and grabbed it, turning for the stream once more, his passion aflame. "It's a diamond I swear it, I swear it."

He ran into the stream and plunged his hands in to wash away the mud.

There was no stopping him now.

Arnold stepped over and confirmed that it was "probably" a diamond, but more likely a sapphire. He made no other comment. He didn't want to stand falsely accused of working up the General's enthusiasm.

The General hardly noticed how cold he was getting. He finished with the anthill after about an hour, then moved into the stream itself, panning with a sieve that Slack had brought with them especially for this purpose. "Have to use a fine mesh, some stones no bigger than a tear drop and harder to see, too."

After they'd been there for just six or seven hours the General had amassed himself six small diamonds, two rubies, perhaps one or two sapphires, and a stone not one of them could recognize. He was beside himself with excitement and by nightfall, utterly exhausted.

Later, when they sat around Slack's fire and ate a mess of beans and herbs, fresh picked from the surrounding area, the General couldn't contain his pleasure. He was a total convert to the word of Arnold and Slack. He'd found everything just as they'd said. Diamonds in the stream, rubies in the anthills and other precious stones literally lying on the ground around the big rock in the middle of the plateau. It was America's Kimberley.

Sitting around a campfire can be pretty inspiring for the soul of a man, and here were three who had much to be inspired by. The General held his precious stones all crammed tightly into a leather pouch, held them so tight Arnold worried he'd bust its seams and scatter them all over.

For his part, Arnold smoked the last of his plug tobacco, musing over what he was going to do with his new fortune, perhaps wondering about what size palace to build on Nob Hill. Slack had other concerns at this time. He was worried that perhaps he'd rather overdone the wild herbs in the beans. He was beginning to suffer from gas and knew he'd have to move.

DIAMONDS

The stars were out. The moon was expected any moment, but for the present it was hidden by the mountain peak. All was peace and contentment. Arnold tapped out some ashes from his clay pipe, then pointed at the General's leather pouch.

"General, I don't want to diminish your obvious pleasure any, but I notice you've adopted quite a proprietary manner as to those diamonds and rubies in your possession. I have to remind you that this claim is the property of Arnold and Slack and, that all diamonds, rubies and sapphires and what have you are the sole possession of the aforementioned gentlemen. That is to say, ourselves. And as much as I hate to disappoint you, the fact that you found 'em doesn't mean you can keep 'em or profit by 'em. If you understand me."

The General understood, all right. He sat there open mouthed, his jaw flapping in the wind. Not his? There never was a man more disappointed than General David Douty Colton. A day's hard labor worthless. The ruination of his Mexican leather boots. All for naught. Arnold and Slack had watched him dig up their precious stones for them, and they'd done nothing to stop him, said nothing about their proprietary intentions. From acute disappointment he quickly traveled into anger and stood up to deliver what he believed would be a stinging rebuke of their business methods, but just then Arnold smiled and jumped in there to beat him to the punch.

"You see, General,'" he puffed up a hit of smoke before continuing, "the point of this exercise is to prove we have located the site of American diamonds. That's all. Now, we could spend a week here, and each day I'd guess you'd find one or two, maybe six or seven like today, hard to say. But that's not why we're here. Of course I'd like you to explore every inch of this ground, as Slack and I have done, just to verify that this claim is just and true. But that wouldn't be right. To let you go on finding our diamonds. You'd only feel cheated. And I'll tell you something else, too. You can walk a hundred feet east and you'll find not a pebble worth a cent. The lode, if that's the correct term for diamond bearing rock, seems to be west of the line from the gap over there to the southernmost ledge. So my guess is there's a few more gone down to join the creek. I'm telling you this so you don't waste time or make a false report. What I'm really saying is take as long as you like, but as soon as you're satisfied that the claim is genuine, we should think about getting back before the weather closes in again. Think about getting this diamond company launched too."

The General stood there digesting these remarks, and as he did so his anger seemed to evaporate. Now he thought about it, the diamonds were valuable to be sure, just like a railroad was valuable, the locomotive and the cars. Arnold was right. The sooner the diamond company was launched, the more money could be made. Arnold was no simple prospector, to be sure. He had a smart head on his shoulders.

DIAMONDS

The General sat down by the fire again and looked at the leather pouch rather wistfully. "Nevertheless, Mr.. Arnold, I will hold onto these precious stones. Mr.. Ralston will not take my word half so well if it's you who hands over the diamonds."

Arnold grinned and kicked the fire to get a few sparks into the air so he could see the General better. The General was beginning to play his own game. It was more sportsmanlike this way.

"Fine with me, General; but Slack here will have to record 'em first. We like strict accounting. Just as Mr.. Ralston does, I'm sure. Couldn't have faith in a banker who didn't know down to the last cent what was in his bank, now, could you?"

The General laughed, shaking a finger at Arnold. "I don't know, Philip Arnold. You have the darndest way of accusing a man of theft and making it sound as if it were the most reasonable thing in the world."

"Sir, if I thought you a thief I would not have done business with you. Your integrity is beyond question, General, but once that pouch leaves your hands and gets into the bank well, a clerk might have himself a look and who knows, might need a pretty diamond for his sweetheart. Just the smallest one, mind, but one nevertheless, and then there's his sweetheart's sister who just must have one too. Just about anything can happen in a bank, General. You recall in '63 when they blew up the bank in Virginia City, I think it was. Some boys got skinned one night, and just because they didn't like the man who ran the bank they burned it down. Sure, they all pulled to and built him a new one once they'd sobered, but there were some mighty original claims as to what might have been in that safe that mysteriously got blown. I don't reckon they've gotten the matter settled yet."

The General shook his head. "You shall have them for counting, Arnold, every last one. And tomorrow, first light, I propose we leave and take the good news to Bill Ralston."

"That's a real pleasure to hear, General. What you say, Slack?"

But Slack had gone. Nature called and was most pressing. He knew that he'd better get a long way down wind too, because he didn't feel good at all. He hated it when his stomach churned. Herbs didn't seem to affect the Indians the same way. Perhaps their stomachs were different. What he needed was some way to carry potatoes or something like that with him. You take the water out of a potato, then you got something real easy to carry. He remembered reading particulars 'bout the Incas in *Kelly's Universal*. They'd solved the mystery of the potato, all right. Used to boil 'em up, put them out to cool in the frost, and then trample them good until all the moisture had gone. All you had to do then was add boiling water when you wanted to eat 'em and they'd taste good as new, leastways that's what *Kellys* said. Often times Slack thought on these things and wondered if he could make another fortune one day by inventing a food everyone would want to eat everyday, just like bread. A man could live well for a long time on a simple idea like quick mashed potato.

Slack attended to his needs and felt marginally better for it. He made his way slowly, appreciating the moon sliding out from behind the mountain to light his way. Over on his right he caught site of meteorite burning up as it hit the atmosphere. Slack made a wish on it. As a kid he remembered his long departed ma would say, 'It's a shooting star, Johnny; make a wish your father comes home soon.' Pa didn't come home, but it had never stopped him making wishes.

He didn't immediately rejoin Arnold and the General by the campfire for the good reason that the fire needed fuel and he had to walk over to the trees by the ridge to gather sticks and fir cones. He had more than enough after ten minutes of gathering fuel, yet he was reluctant to return. It was good to stretch his legs and inhale that singular scent that always hovered over the pine forests.

He wandered along the ridge for a hundred yards or more, kicking at the odd stone, making a mental note to inspect the loosened soil the next morning; old habits .

Slack was just at the point of turning for home when he heard a cough. Now a cough was all right in itself, coughing was fine, but what Slack had just heard was a horse coughing. Well, even a horse would cough up here in this cold, but one thing was absolutely certain: it was no wild horse. They just never did venture up this far unless they were ridden up, and if it was ridden up, who rode it? Dammit, him and Arnold had been up in these parts for months on end and never seen a living soul.

Slack gently placed his sticks and cones down on the ground. Alert now, he made his way through the trees to a large boulder that masked a bend in the ridge. Careful not to jolt any loose stones, he mounted the boulder, aware as he looked across the sky that it afforded a remarkably clear view of their plateau below.

The horse, a grey, stood its ground in a clearing, plainly illuminated by the moon. It was saddled up, blanket rolled up behind it, it stood pawing the ground and snorting. Slack knew something about horses from his days on the farm and his guess was the ride up the mountain had been too much for it and it was footsore. There was a rifle lying beside a canvas sack on the ground. Slack had the impression that someone was almost ready to go. Slack had no intention of letting the stranger go. With five quick steps, Slack seized the rifle, snatching it up off the ground. He turned and gave the startled horse a slap on its rump and with a startled whinny it turned and swiftly moved off.

"Wo steady " came a whisper from the bushes and a man stepped out hitching up his trousers. He came face to face with Slack. If there had been any color in his face it would have drained away completely.

" I seems to recognize you from somewhere mister, and if it's from a place within two hundred miles of San Francisco you are a dead and gone man."

Arnold was in mid-conversation, when he suddenly stopped short at the sight of a horse galloping onto the plateau and turning circles, seemingly out of its wits.

"What the ...?" Arnold began.

"Where's Slack?" The General asked in alarm, immediately standing up. "That horse is saddled, Mr. Arnold. What's this?"

Arnold stood and began running in the direction of the ridge. "Slack"? He feared the worst. Slack had left without his rifle.

The General went for the horse, softly calling to it. He didn't want it breaking its legs on the rock-strewn open ground.

"Now this looks bad, I know..." Decker stuttered, backing up against the bushes, "but..."

"No buts, you can keep yourself to yourself, mister. If this here rifle is loaded, I've a good mind to plug you now and have done with it."

Behind him in the dark, Slack could hear Arnold calling his name. He was happy they were alerted to the situation. He nodded to the unfortunate Decker. "I'm mean, mister, but my partner is a real bastard when he's crossed." Slack stepped forward and kicked Decker's canvas sack to one side, noting the contents as they spilled out onto the ground. It was dark to be sure, but he could still see the rocks he'd collected and a small sketch-book.

"What have we got here, mister?"

Decker didn't know what to say. He almost wished he were dead already. He knew he would be soon enough. If he confessed to being Ralston's stooge, he was condemned. If he confessed to spying on his own account he was equally condemned. To claim he was innocent would be to stretch credibility to an extreme. He had none of the tools common to a prospector. It was mortifying that he'd been found out, and he was ashamed. He'd claimed to be the best tracker in the West, and here he was caught, literally, with his trousers down.

"You got a name, mister?" Slack asked; his inclination was to kill the man outright, so a confession wasn't strictly necessary. Either the General had ordered him to track 'em, or Ralston. Either way it was bad.

Decker said nothing. Even his name would give the game up. For if they didn't know him, the General surely did. Wasn't it only a month past he'd brought the man a bottle of wine to his hotel room where he had been entertaining a certain dancer from the show at the California Theater?

Arnold arrived on the scene first and instantly took in and understood the situation. Glad to see that Slack had the upper hand, he quickly seized the canvas bag and its contents, holding them up to the light of the moon.

"We got ourselves a spy, Slack. Shit, and I thought we was dealing with gentlemen. Who the devil is he?"

"Didn't say. Do I plug him now, before the General gets here?"

Decker stepped back. Perhaps he was thinking of escaping; certainly he was casting his eyes every which way to see if it would be possible. Slack saw it and quickly checked to see if the rifle was loaded or not. It was, and he snapped shut the breach, taking a closer aim at his charge.

"You move as much as an inch again you're going to lose a lot of weight, mister."

As Arnold examined Decker's possessions, the General rode up on Decker's horse, calmer now that it had someone in control.

"What the devil have we here?" he demanded to know. "Who is this man?"

Arnold whipped around and showed the General the open pages of the sketch-book. "See this, General? What kind of a trick do you think you're playing with us? Who the hell is this man? You and Ralston think you can play us for suckers? You think you can have us followed so you can cheat us out of our rights?"

Arnold was real worked up now and practically shouting at the General, who was far from impressed with the situation. "See this. He's gone and sketched our plateau. Got his compass points on it an' everything. Now this ain't no coincidence. Ralston and you were just out to get us to reveal our claim so you could then cheat us. I knew we couldn't trust you. The deal's off, General. We're heading back, and the deal's off. It's my final word."

The General dismounted, a growing anger rising within. There was one thing he prided himself on, his integrity. Moreover, he was in distinct danger of losing out to the millions that were obviously on offer here. Something had to be done to rescue an very bad situation. He advanced closer to inspect Ralston's man. (He had no doubt it was Ralston's doing; there was no question of the man being innocent.)

"You there, what is your...." It was at this moment he recognized exactly who it was. "Decker. What the? ...Decker, is this possible?"

Arnold took it the wrong way. He appealed to Slack. "See, he admits to knowing him. It proves everything. I say we shoot them both Slack an' have done with it."

The General quickly stepped back out of Slack's firing range. These were angry men; justifiably so, in his opinion. Ralston had played foul. The General felt distinctly cheated. Somehow he had to regain Arnold's trust, or all was lost. He could see that.

"Decker, you have an explanation for me?"

Decker shook his head. "No, sir, I don't. You might as well kill me now. I

95

couldn't expect better."

"At least someone speaks the truth, " Slack remarked. "Care to explain to me how come you know him, General?"

The General welcomed the opportunity from Slack, but what words of reassurance would work? These men stood betrayed. Decker, too, for surely Ralston must have known this might happen. Or was it another? Who else knew of Arnold and Slack's discovery?

"This man is Henri Decker, detective at the Grand Hotel. You both know him, I'm sure."

"Decker?" Arnold stepped forward to get a better look. There was something about the man that was familiar, but he couldn't say what or why. The black gloves...

"Three Fingers Decker," Slack remembered. He was sure he remembered something else about him too, but it escaped him right at this moment. "Ralston's got a share in the Grand Hotel. You work for him, Decker? I hope he paid you good. Pity you can't take it with you. Ralston set you up good and proper. I just knowed you didn't do this on your own account. Got to tell you, you're good. Arnold rode out last night to make sure we wasn't followed and here you are. Well you're going into the next life quicker than any of us, Decker. I hope you've been making your peace well and good."

Decker had been praying, but he knew it wasn't going to save his neck. He addressed the General, perhaps hoping for a better hearing.

" I'm sorry to git you into this mess, General. I know you didn't know I was here. The other party relied on me not being discovered. I was just leaving..."

"Now he's trying to make out the General is a saint. Won't do, Decker," Arnold complained. "The General ain't going to save your neck. His own is vulnerable enough. You're a cheat, and anything you say is a damned lie."

Decker looked severly pained by this remark. "Mr.. Arnold, I've never cheated a man in my life, sir."

"Then you are a saint." Plainly Arnold would not be mollified.

"Sir..." There was an element of pleading in his voice now. " This was a job sir. It was going to be done whether I accepted or not. This is open territory. A man can come and go as he pleases."

"A man can go to hell when he pleases too," Arnold informed him. "Decker, you had it easy in the hotel, you should have stayed there." He turned to the General. "General, do your duty."

The General didn't like the sound of that. It looked as though he was meant to be executioner. Well, what else? How else could he prove his innocence?

"I will have to have this out with Ralston when we return. This is disgraceful. It's almost piracy. I know it was him who put you up to this, Decker. It is better to confess."

DIAMONDS

"The Lord knows my guilt, General Colton. He missed taking me on the battlefield, so maybe he'll take me now. But I couldn't go if I betrayed a man before I died."

"One thing I can't abide is a blessed saint," Arnold declared with disgust. "General, I don't care how you do it, but it's got to be done."

The General was rapidly coming to the same conclusion. He hated to do it though. Decker didn't deserve to die. But what was a man supposed to do with him. One couldn't just take him back to San Francisco and put him on trial. Besides all he'd done was spy. No court would convict him of that, and anyhow, all he'd have to do is blab about where the diamond claim was and the city would be empty within the space of a day. You'd be hard-pressed to find a judge or jury in the whole city. Not a man would be left who could heft a pick and shovel. No, the deed had to be done here. He placed a hand on Slack's shoulders and indicated to Slack he was taking over.

"I'd like to do this on my own, if you please; Mr.. Slack."

Slack relinquished the rifle easily enough, but he didn't readily leave. "Can't leave you, got to be a witness. Ain't that right, Arnold?"

"Darn right. General I'm not persuaded you're not in partnership with this Decker. So if Decker's going, one of us better be there to make sure. It's only right in case you fancy giving him a sporting chance to run for it."

"You know I wouldn't, " the General declared. But he'd been thinking of doing just that.

Perhaps it had only just occurred to Decker that he really was to die. If they were to kill him, well it was only right he should try to make it as difficult as possible. Just as the General put his eye on Arnold to argue, Decker darted backward, through the bushes and began to run. The General tried to get a shot off, but he was way too slow.

Slack spat on the ground with disgust, took the rifle from the General, and set off in pursuit, cutting around the bushes to gain time.

The moon was on Decker's side. It chose that very moment to disappear behind a cloud. Slack came to a stop within inches of a fir tree. He could see neither left nor right. He stood, listened, and heard Decker's feet to one side running, stumbling blind. Heard him collide with a tree and yell with pain. Left, one hundred feet. Decker was traveling fast. Perhaps he thought he really could get away. Well now he had to be killed. He'd tracked them with the cunning of an Apache. Slack knew that if he didn't get him quick, they'd lose everything. Decker would talk; it was in his interest to talk. Once he reached the telegraph station everything would be lost. He didn't even have to call Ralston. He could get practically anyone; the army, anyone; who'd give him protection in exchange for information.

Slack listened some more, then sloped off at a steady pace keenly listening for Decker's footsteps up ahead. His eyes were adjusting to the dark now.

97

DIAMONDS

Decker ran in a panic. He just wanted to put distance between himself and his pursuers. He knew he was better than any of them at blending into the undergrowth. He'd work out later how to survive without food or his horse. Once he'd alerted Ralston to the problem he knew he'd get help. After all, he knew where the diamonds were and he could lead anyone straight to it...and not take four days about it, either. He knew Arnold had been leading the General in circles. There was a better way back, less than eighty miles to the railroad. All right, it was a steep journey and difficult through the snow, but it would be possible. He stopped and listened for his pursuer. He heard nothing. It wasn't possible they weren't coming after him. He listened again but all he could hear was his heart beating wildly and the wind through the tops of the trees. They'd not catch Henri Decker, he'd never make such a stupid mistake again.

He took two, three steps, then felt nothing under him. He tried to stop. He struggled to turn, he clawed at the branches of a tree growing out of the side of the cliff, but they slipped through his desperate fingers. Suddenly he was falling, falling. He began to call, "Help," before he remembered there would be none forthcoming.

The moon leapt out from behind the cloud and shone brilliantly over the scene. Slack arrived at the cliff edge in time to hear a plaintive cry, but Decker was gone. He stood and waited. Sure enough, there was a final yell and a sudden, sickening crunch as Decker hit the rocks three, four hundred feet below. Slack felt kind of sorry for the man. He had a sad face, and missing three fingers was no kind blessing from the gods either. As he turned and began the walk back to the campfire he thought how lucky it was the horse couldn't sketch or talk either. Otherwise it too would have to join Decker in the creek.

"Slack?" Arnold's voice was calling. "Johnny Slack, you all right?"

"You'd better not have let that fire go out, Philip Arnold, or else there'll be hell to pay."

Slack emerged into a clearing and saw Arnold astride Decker's horse. The General stood at his side. It looked as though the men had had strong words. "He's gone. Went down the fast way," Slack told them.

"Dead? You sure he's dead? "Arnold queried.

"You remember when Jacob Hazlett fell off Ward Peak and crushed Spike Garvey's chicken coop?"

"As bad as that?"

"Worse. I reckon Decker wasn't as good a tracker as he thought he was. I always say if you're careless enough to lose three fingers, the bettings evens you'll lose something else."

The General shook his head. "I hate to see a man's life wasted so easy."

"Not wasted, General," Arnold reminded him. " If he'd lived, we'd be poor men and you'd be ... you'd be a lot wiser."

DIAMONDS

The three ambled back to the campfire in silence. Arnold walked beside the horse, reflecting that the grey would be a more comfortable ride down the mountain than the mule.

Flakes of snow suddenly began to fall out of the sky. It was going to be a real cold night. Back on the plateau the campfire was most definitely out. Slack was not impressed.

CHAPTER SIX
The Gentlemen Need A-Courting.

"The answer is no, absolutely no. As far as I'm concerned, you ain't a man who can be trusted."

William Chapman Ralston was angry and disturbed. Things had gone plenty wrong, to be sure. Decker being caught and plunging to his death was tragic, but need it be the ruination of a potential fortune? He thought not. Arnold sat alone in a barber's chair, all lathered up. After a terse discussion the much-aggrieved barber had gone outside at the insistence of Ralston, who stood inside, leaning up against the door. It had taken two days to find Arnold and Slack, and Ralston had to believe Arnold meant what he said about not doing business with him, but he meant to change his mind anyway. The small barber shop was baking in the sunlight, its thin wooden walls revealing gaps through to the sunshine outside. It was a dirt-poor barber shop, really no place to do such important business, but he felt desperate.

"Mr. Arnold. Firstly, I have denied having anything to do with that man Decker. You said yourself he never admitted it was me who sent him, and he had plenty of encouragement from you, no doubt."

"Mistaken loyalty don't mean you're innocent."

"But I *am* innocent. I will tell you plainly, there are a few others who knew you were headed out toward the Rockies. Will Lent, George Roberts; you said yourself that Roberts was most curious about what you'd placed in my bank. I resent your accusation, Philip Arnold. I resent it because it shows you don't trust me."

Arnold was watching Ralston's face in the mirror, enjoying seeing him beg like this. Quite a turn up for a poor prospector to have a banker begging at his knees. "I'd like to talk about trust, Mr.. Ralston. It's us who trusted you. It's Slack and me who put the diamonds in your bank. It's us who trusted you when you took a look at 'em without our say-so and had them valued. It's us that took your word for what they are worth, and it's us who left them in your bank without getting a penny for 'em. On top of that, it's us who brought back

DIAMONDS

more and some rubies and emeralds too. So don't talk to me about *trust*, Mr.. Ralston. I'm all out of trust. I knows it was you who sent Decker, and now I want my diamonds back or a hundred and twenty-five thousand dollars. You takes your choice."

Ralston frowned. He wasn't getting through. "Philip, listen to me."

Arnold noticed he was getting the first name treatment now.

"Decker was a foolish episode. I'll swear on a holy Bible that I had nothing to do with that disgraceful incident. The General has plagued me for two days about his honor being besmirched, but I tell you Decker did not follow you on my orders. I have shaken hands with you. We have a deal. I have no intention of breaking it. If I'd been there, I'd have shot Decker myself."

"Well, I should have liked you to have been there, Mr. Ralston, I wonder if Decker would have been so loyal then, huh? " Arnold smiled. He enjoyed having the upper hand. "I have to tell you, er..Bill...," If Ralston could use first names, well damn it, so could he. "that Slack and me are pretty damn disgusted with 'Western business ethics,' to quote the General. Slack thinks we should take our diamonds to New York and find some investors there. Got to be at least one honest man in the East. Perhaps Jay Cooke? I know there's some pretty rich folks who'd like to get their hands on this claim of ours. What's those bankers called in Europe? Rothschilds? Now, they'd be pretty interested."

"We have a deal ," Ralston reminded Arnold, trying to control his temper. "And besides Jay Cooke is in no shape to assist you. My associates in New York say he's all but bankrupt, won't last another year."

"Maybe so, but the fact remains that our third partner sent Decker to spy on us. Hardly the spirit of a trusting partnership ...Bill." Arnold liked to see Ralston wince every time he called him by his first name.

"We can start afresh. No harm was done. The day is yet saved."

"Now, I don't know, Bill. These diamonds haven't made Slack and me a red cent yet - we did everything you asked and more, yet you or another sent Decker. I would have to be a real cotton-head to trust you again. Fact is, Slack and me don't care for this way of doing business. Either we develop the claim as we originally intended or else we sell out entirely, and if we do that, well, my guess is New York is the place to go to raise the best price."

Ralston wiped some moisture off his upper lip and stepped forward to blot his sticky hands on a towel. "Our ideas are not so very far apart, Mr.. Arnold. I had always had in mind attracting New York finance for this enterprise. On the matter of your own situation: it is intolerable, of course, that you alone bear the burden of providing the diamonds and receiving no recompense. With the diamonds and other stones, not forgetting the new ones the General has deposited, I am sure we can accommodate your demands."

Arnold was still translating that when Ralston simplified it for him.

DIAMONDS

"That is to say, the Bank of California will advance you the sum of $125,000 dollars on security of the precious stones already deposited."

Arnold settled back down in the chair. "I think the barber can come back now ; the soap's drying out."

"Then we still have a deal?" Ralston inquired.

"I'll have to talk it over with Slack, but I'm sure he'll see that you are being reasonable at last."

Ralston inwardly breathed a sigh. The situation had been rescued, at least for the moment.

"But I still reckon New York's the place," Arnold asserted.

"If we're going there, we'll need more diamonds than we've got so far," Ralston told him. "What we have is impressive, but what we need is something to dazzle them. I propose floating ourselves a major mining company, Mr. Arnold. Kimberley started with more than this."

"Kimberley was over-run in weeks and they'll keep digging that hole until they reach the center of the earth. But so far there's been just me and Slack and the General up there. The haul ain't so bad."

"No, no, I didn't mean to disparage what you have found. I meant that to launch a company, Mr.. Arnold, a little showmanship is needed. The rest is imagination. No rising share-price is without a healthy dose of imagination."

Arnold took it the wrong way as a matter of course. "Our diamonds are the genuine article, there's not a man in this world who could say they're not."

"This I acknowledge, but I'm talking about shares, Mr.. Arnold. What is a Comstock share but a piece of paper? A gold dollar is, well...a gold dollar. Back east they use paper, and as people are discovering to their cost, paper money often isn't worth the ink. Here we are proposing selling paper to people instead of diamonds. It's one of the curious phenomenons of our times that a man can get rich by buying and selling paper."

"Then it's a pity Slack and me didn't find you trees," Arnold declared.

Ralston laughed. "Diamonds are a good second best, Mr. Arnold. Believe me, your discovery will be the most sensational talk of this city once word gets out. That's why I want you to go back and get us more. Something like a million dollars' worth."

"Why," Arnold declared, sitting up in his chair, "if Slack and me worked for a month or more we could probably get you two million. They're there for the asking. Why didn't you say when we left with the General? We had no need to hurry back."

Ralston shrugged, taking out his handkerchief and wiping the perspiration from his neck. "It is only now that we have verification that your claim is genuine. Now we can go forward and plan. It would be so much better if you could go back, find us the very best that you can find, larger stones. We need to impress. You understand me?"

Arnold understood. "But you'll pay for what you've got now. Slack and me have debts. We have plans. I can tell you, Bill, we won't go back to the claim until we've got our business affairs in order."

Ralston held out his hand for Arnold to shake. "Mr.. Arnold, you have my word. Facilities will be made available to you and Mr. Slack to come to the bank tomorrow and draw coin or gold certificate, whichever you please."

"Coin." Arnold said. "It's been a while since I had any to hold."

Ralston backed off and turned to open the door to admit the patient but puzzled barber.

"Just one other thing, Mr.. Arnold."

"Yes, Bill?"

The 'Bill' immediately impressed the barber. Arnold saw his eyebrows shoot up to his bald pate. He obviously knew who Bill Ralston was. Who didn't?

"If you can find your friend Mr.. Slack today, I'd very much like yourself, your good lady friend and Mr.. Slack to attend a small dinner I'm giving tonight. It'll be discreet, a few friends, some you'll know of, I'm sure. It'll be my pleasure if you'll attend."

Arnold smiled to himself in the mirror. "You have a time in mind, Bill?"

"Seven. I'll have a carriage meet the five o'clock ferry. The journey is possible in less than two hours, but it might as well be a comfortable ride."

"Five o'clock it is, Bill. We'll be in the city on time."

With that, Ralston was gone, glad to shake Oakland soil off his shoes. He instructed his buggy driver to get to the ferry as quickly as possible. There was much to do and a ferry leaving in five minutes. Now he knew that Arnold was keen for money. Ralston knew a lot about a person who was keen for money. It meant he could be bought for a price. He now saw a way to get the entire diamond claim off them. It would be a pleasure. All that was required was to establish what that price was. He seen it on the faces of other prospectors. They'd found what they'd been seeking, but how many of them wanted to stay and develop it once business and banks got involved? Not Henry Comstock. Not John Sutter; though, truth tell, he was a farmer who'd just been swamped by men with gold fever. He'd lost the day his boss carpenter found gold on his land. Niether Sutter, nor the carpenter got rich, if he recalled right.

One day he'd like to read a book about that, but for now, it was best to thank God for sending him two more prospectors whose hunger for money outweighed their common sense.

He had no doubt that the dinner would be amusing, but it would serve its purpose. Belmont had been built to intimidate and Arnold would soon realize who was master of the situation. Soon there would be no more 'Bill' being bandied about by the likes of Arnold.

"That would be Bill Ralston the banker?" the barber asked.

"It was, Gully. Old Bill and me are in business now. I'm so important to him he has to come all the way to Oakland just to pass the time o' day."

The barber thought on this a moment as he refreshed Arnold's lather.

"Well if you're that important, Philip Arnold, best you pay your bills in cash now, eh?"

Arnold smiled. "How much do Slack an' me owe you now, d'y 'reckon?"

The barber thought on this a while too, making a count in his head.

"Well, there was two cut and shaves last year. Slack's back tooth, that was two dollars alone, and your front tooth you had filled with gold, that was a dollar on account of you providing your own gold."

"It fell out when I got caught in the rapids in the mountains."

"No matter. I put it in, you lose it for free. Then there's this haircut and the one you're probably gonna make me do for Slack to make him presentable tonight, so I reckon that's a clear twelve dollars fifty cents you owe me."

Arnold shook his head. "An' I told Ralston that you was the most reasonable barber in Oakland. If he come back here for a cut, he's going to get a shock when you give him a bill."

"Now, if you was Bill Ralston, I'd cut and shave you for free."

"Now, why would you do a thing like that?"

"On account of him coming here, everyone else will want to come here."

"Who's to say he didn't get a cut today?"

"Well, if he did, you must have done it, Philip Arnold, 'cause I think the entire town saw me locked out of my own place while he was in here with you."

"And I thought it was a private meeting. Twelve bucks, fifty. I suppose you'll be wanting it paid in gold."

"And it better be San Francisco mint. Remember, I got the scales. I can weigh it out here, just like the old days."

Arnold laughed, but not too hard, for the barber was using the blade. "Those days were the best, eh? Remember when people used to pay you in dust? Time, back in '68, I was real sick and needed attention to my gums. They was bleeding bad. Anyway, barber up in Sonora, he was a cussed old bastard. Wouldn't tend anyone if they was sick unless he got paid in gold dust, and he carried scales with him, too. He wanted an ounce before he'd even look at me. An ounce, mind you. I called him a robber and kicked him out. Said I'd rather rinse my mouth out with gold than give him a smell of it. I was a mad as hell, I can tell you, and Slack was no help because he was all for paying it. Rattlesnake Bob, that was his name. Well, just to show how mad I was, I did rinse out my mouth with gold. Though to tell the truth there was zinc and quartz and all manner of things in that mixutre there too. Rinsed it, spat it out and Rattlesnake Bob he swore at me, took off saying I'd be dead of poisoning by the morning anyway.

"Next morning I woke up, no bleeding, no irritation, and Slack had dried it and gotten all the gold back into his pouch anyway. If I had any sort of scientific training, well, I could patent some cure and go selling it like those medicine men out on the trails. What do you think?"

"I think you're crazy, that's what I think. There isn't enough gold in all the world that would fit into all those bottles you'd need.

Arnold grinned. "That's the point, don't you see. I don't reckon it was the gold, it was all the other stuff. Gold couldn't fix a thing by itself, but you mix it with all the other stuff, you got yourself a natural cure."

"And a mighty expensive one."

"You could afford it, charging twelve dollars fifty for a few cuts and shaves. Why, I'm surprised this place isn't a grand palace by now, and you got ten folks working for you and ten more just to keep people in line."

The barber just shook his head and shaved the man. "I suppose this all means you don't have twelve-dollars fifty?"

"Tomorrow. Ask me tomorrow, and you'll be a happy man."

"Tomorrow I might die of shock, Philip Arnold, that is what I might do."

"Then you'll die a wealthy man. Er..take a little of those sideburns off, will ya, they been itching something bad of late.

Getting Slack off his jetty and away from his precious fish was nothing compared with getting him a cut and a shave, and even that was a mere insignificance compared with the terrors of putting Slack into a borrowed gentlemen's suit of clothes and polished boots. He protested something terrible, swore, demanded assistance from passing strangers, threatened life and limb to both Arnold and Alyce, but it was Alyce who finally tamed him. She had to sock him with a good left hook to get him to shut up and put up. Naturally, Slack wouldn't strike a lady, but he nursed some mighty large grievances by the time five o'clock came around.

Arnold was the very stylish man about town. He'd prevailed upon Mr.. Thomas Marshall, a leading light in Oakland business (dry goods) to lend him his suit, fresh out from tailors in New York. It was a tight fit, but the transformation of Arnold from wild prospector to city gentleman was so acute, Mr.. Marshall just had to comment that he'd be wearing that suit every day hence to boost his own public image.

Mr. Marshall wouldn't have let it out of his sight at all but for the fact that Arnold was dining at Belmont. It was a singular privilege for any man from Oakland, who wasn't a landowner, or famous in some way or another, to be invited to Belmont, and there was much speculation about why two hitherto much-ignored individuals would be so picked out. Local opinion was divided between the idea that Arnold and Slack now owed so much to the bank the banker had to make a good face of it and treat them like other rich folks, who could borrow as much as they liked without putting as much as a wooden peg in for collateral. The other idea was that Arnold and Slack had struck a bonanza somewhere and Ralston was trying to wrap it all up before word got out. Not a few fully intended to stake out Arnold and Slack's place and follow them when they left the city.

Arnold knew there'd be talk, but he didn't mind. He was playing his own game. If Ralston did have any plans to cheat him, well, he wanted to make sure plenty of people knew who'd been doing the courting.

Alyce had a woman's perspective on the situation. This was probably the only time in her life that she was going to get to go to a supper with the cream of San Francisco society. The very fact of it would boost her social standing and improve her boarding house business. Folks would want to know her, and only good could come from it. She, at least, didn't have to borrow a dress.

So there it was. Everyone, saving Slack, had a reason to go to dinner with the banker, and when the time finally arrived to go shortly before five, all three were gussied up like Thanksgiving turkeys.

It was back on the ferry again, but Ralston's carriage was waiting for them the other side, just as he'd promised. There was a man waiting inside, Judge Wallace.

"Plenty of room," the old judge remarked as he made way for Alyce to climb inside. "Happens I've got papers for Bill Ralston to sign and I missed him at the bank today, so since this carriage was going to Belmont anyway, I hitched a ride."

"Fine with us, Judge," Arnold declared. "I'm Philip Arnold, this here is Alyce Wentworth, my fiancee, and this here is John Slack."

Alyce squeezed Arnold's hand. This was the first time she'd been introduced as Arnold's fiancee and it pleased her no end. This was an important day in her life. She made a note to remind Arnold later that as yet she had no ring.

"Dining at Belmont?" the judge inquired.

"Yes, sir."

"Bill usually stays in town week days. Got himself a place within a short walk from the bank. Seems he's taken to riding home at nights. I try to tell him that it isn't safe; all manner of folks and brigands are about these days. I fear one day he'll be caught in an ambuscade."

"Not Bill Ralston," Arnold reassured the judge. "From what I hear he can outride even the San Jose locomotive. Be a fast brigand who'd bring him down."

"Don't talk of such things, it might happen." Alyce told them .

Slack boarded the carriage, which took off with such a lurch he went sprawling across Arnold and Alyce. No one made comment; it was a common enough event.

"Heard the news?" the judge asked them in general. "Things really on fire on the big board today. Pine Street was fairly buzzing this afternoon. Lots in a claim adjoining the Consolidated Virginia sold for two hundred dollars this morning, but by three o'clock they'd sold for two thousand and tomorrow they say they'll double again. Quite like old times, eh? They say Ophir is old hat, but I've staked twenty thousand on Consolidated and Ophir this very day, and if I've the nerve, it could go to a million. What do you think of that?"

Slack was looking at the judge with surprise. If this judge was prepared to blab so about his finances, well, either he was a fool or he assumed the party he was traveling with to be fellow investors privy to Ralston's inner circle.

"We're cautious men," Slack told him. "I'd prefer to have an ounce of gold in my pocket than a pound of paper."

The judge beamed at Alyce. "It's caution that separates a rich man from his fellows. Why, if I were cautious, Mr.. Slack, I would be forced to live on a Judge's income, and I'd be a pauper. The market is the thing, sir. My advice is to get into it now before the rest of the world knows. Believe me, my ear is to the ground. The time to buy is now."

"How cool it is this evening," Alyce remarked, hoping to steer the conversation away from high finance.

The carriage finally cleared the city outskirts and headed on down El Camino Real, the tree-lined southern highway to San Jose. Daly City, first call. This was the vegetable garden of San Francisco, hard-won land by farmers who'd had to fight off the plug-uglies sent by land speculators in 1859. It took until 1866 to get it back and it had been Judge Wallace who had helped the Supreme Court make up its mind. In this area the judge was a hero. At San Bruno they stopped at the old stagecoach halt to rest the horses and water them. Before the railroad had come, the former San Francisco-San Jose line, now the Southern Pacific, the stage would change horses here, but there were no such luxuries for a simple carriage and four. Besides, it was half the weight of the old stage and could travel almost half as fast again.

Slack sat under an old twisted sequoia and tried to get comfortable in his stiff suit. Arnold and Alyce went to pick some spring flowers for her hair, relieved to be out of the cramped carriage. The judge read *The Call*, mindful of the time, since he intended to return this same evening.

About ten minutes after they'd stopped, four farmers' wagons trundled by, pulled by enormous cart-horses. In each wagon sat twenty or more Chinese coolies, looking exhausted from their day's work. Arnold watched them making their way north and wondered who could afford such a plentiful supply of labor and such magnificent dray-horses. He asked the carriage driver, who'd not appeared to notice anything go by at all.

"What's their business around here?"

The driver spat some, then reluctantly addressed Arnold as if it were a big

107

favor he ever spoke to anyone at all. "Be out of Mills House. Yep, Mills build-ing himself a dairy-farm. Building levees down by the bay. He reckons to be reclaiming the land down there for his dairy-cattle. Got himself an army of coolies working down there. They say it's the latest thing in dairies. Got a Dutchman supervising."

Judge Wallace knew something about the Mills place too. "I've been there a few times myself. Darius Ogden Mills is quite a man. Made himself richer than anyone else in the West. Getting tied up with Bill Ralston was the best thing he ever did. You should see the lawns of his house, friends. Cast-iron shepherd maids with petite flower baskets, Himalayan cedars, it's a real pic-ture, I can tell you. He brought over some kind of special tree from Australia, too. You've smelled nothing until you've got a whiff of eucalypti on a hot summer's evening."

"Australia?" Slack asked. "Where is that exactly? I always wanted to know."

"It's quite a ways I guess," the driver remarked.

"Well, it's certainly not on the railroad route," the judge agreed, not exactly wanting to admit that he couldn't rightly answer that question. "Mills estate is impressive, but farther along the Howard Estate in San Mateo is better, and old Fred Macondray's. I've got business with John Parrot down there too, but he's in China, they say, buying treasures for his mansion. It's becoming quite the thing to build a mansion in these parts."

"Well, don't mind, Judge, " Arnold remarked, " you'll soon make your fortune, then you can stick up a tower to dwarf them all."

"Oh, no. I've already bought at Burlingame. I've bought myself a five-acre lot, the roads are in already, and a fresh water main. I'm to build a house there in the summer. It's going to be the place to live. If you boys are in sight of money, now's the time to get in there. They aren't selling to just anyone, y'know. Bill Ralston has to approve every purchaser himself."

"I'll bear it mind," Arnold replied. "What you say, Slack?"

"How's the fishing, Judge?" Slack asked.

"Plenty of sturgeon in the bay."

"Reserve me a lot, then," Slack declared, but he was only joshing. To his way of thinking, either you lived in a city or you lived in the wilderness. Buying a lot ten, sixteen miles out of town was neither one thing nor another. You'd always be in the wrong spot whatever the choice. If you were out in the wilderness, at least you'd be right half the time.

"Time to go," the driver announced.

The relief was felt by all. They wanted to get on.

The carriage made a gradual ascent now, but the road was no more than thirty feet above sea level. It afforded good views of some of the growing estates, and when they finally reached San Mateo, Slack was impressed by the sight of wild deer browsing in the Howard Estate. He'd heard about the prize stallions installed in the rosewood and mahogany stalls in the extravagant stables. Diamonds could buy him all this and more.

Finally the road breached the wooded hills overlooking Belmont, Ralston's magnificent home. Everyone craned their heads to get a look. It was evident from first sight that Ralston hadn't stinted himself. They entered by the tree-lined driveway.

"It's like one of them French Chateaus you was showing me," Arnold told Alyce. "My God, how many bedrooms does a man need?"

"At the last count I heard there were one hundred and twenty," the judge informed them, adjusting his coat and smoothing down his moustache and beard so as to appear untroubled by the twenty-three miles from San Francisco. "Originally it was a small villa, built for Count Lussetti Cipriani here in the Canada del Diablo. I doubt you could find much of the original structure at all now. It's all wings and corners. He's even built a little copy of it in the grounds for his Chinese servants."

"It's all the rage, I reckon. We used to see them up on the mines, but the Union drove them out of Virginia City once Bill Sharon got the Virginia and Truckee railroad built. Reckoned they were working too cheap," Arnold remarked, sitting back in his seat and following the judge's example by preening for the big arrival. It was near dark now, so it was easier to hide the journey's dust.

"But why would a man want so many rooms?" Alyce asked. She'd been impressed with the journey so far, the trees lining the Mission road, the beautiful mansions glimpsed and many strange folk she'd never known existed. She reflected on how she'd really shut herself in of late and must get about more. No one answered her question.

They were within a hundred yards of the house when it began to glow with light. Room by room, the gatehouse, the entire ground floor, every room was ablaze with gaslight. The effect was magical. Alyce couldn't but help clap with delight. "Why, every room is lit with gas! Have you ever heard of such a thing? Arnie, have you ever seen such a thing?"

Arnold hadn't. Neither had Slack. They were more than surprised. They knew what expense it would be to fetch gas all the way from San Francisco. Never mind the size of Ralston's place. This man was truly rich to afford such extravagances. It was simply a stunning sight against the black canyon beyond.

The judge had seen it all before. "Well, he built himself his own gas works over there, near the woods. No man for small gestures is our Bill Ralston. If he wants light to come home to, he'll get it. He's built a dam up in the hills to irrigate his gardens."

"Even Napoleon didn't live like this," Slack muttered, happy for once that he was wearing a clean suit of clothes. For the first time he could remember, he felt overawed. Arnold must have noticed or felt the same because he nudged him in the ribs and his face was set like he was trying to figure out an approach here. "We're gonna have to get used to this, Slack. Ralston could teach us a thing or two."

The carriage proceeded up the long twisting drive and never were four people so silent or so awed by a place. Ralston's four-in-hand was briefly glimpsed being led toward the stables. The great white mansion was simply too great to take in all at once. They came to a stop under the great *porte cochere* behind two other carriages that had also made the long journey from town.

"Take a tip from me," the judge said suddenly, making sure he was the first to alight. "Don't mention the fleas. Mrs Ralston is very particular about her home being clean, but if there's one thing she can't abide is a man scratching in her home."

"Nice to know the rich have fleas just like us," Alyce said, amused.

"Not to worry," Arnold told them. "Slack's wearing a new suit. They won't recognize him tonight."

They all had a good laugh at Slack's expense, and so it was that the four entered the great white mansion a lot less tense than they had been a few minutes before.

Immediately they were set upon by Chinese attendants. With ordinary servants you knew they hated you straight off, but these Chinese were so polite and studious, that it was impossible to think badly of them; and since you had to do just what they asked, because you didn't want to offend, they probably thought you pretty good fellows too. Eventually, after washroom facilities were provided in a discreet and lavish bathroom off the entrance to 'get the dust out', they were herded into the library, and given some refreshing fruit punch. The judge went about his business without another word to them.

Arnold felt they were safer where they were. 'Let Ralston find us,' he told the Slack. However Alyce felt she needed to stretch her legs and wandered out into the terraced grounds.

Half an hour later Alyce had climbed the hill overlooking the house and entered the Orangery. There was a heavenly, thick scent in the air and a breathtaking view of the bay in the distance. From her vantage point she thought the house looked much like the sort of vast homes she usedto see in New Orleans and it made her feel unaccountably homesick all of a sudden. She turned to leave and found herself face to face with a strange, none other than the Mayor of the City of San Francisco, Mr..William Alvord.

He tipped his hat and smiled at her. "Good evening Miss, Mayor Bill Alvord. It's a pleasure to meet such a radiant face up here. One of the best views of the bay anywhere, don't you think? Bill Ralston's got himself quite a little nest here."

Alyce curtsied. She didn't know what else to do. "Alyce Wentworth, your honor, I..."

He smiled. "No formalities here. We're all friends of Bills." He pointed out a sea- eagle circling in the heat above them. "This is some paradise isn't it? I could retire here myself, get a little shelter from the Coastal Mountains, listen to the wind passing through the magnificent oaks and the distant rumble of the surf in the bay."

Alyce saw a deer grazing nearby. "Did you see it?"

"There's more in the hills"

"This place is a palace. The princes in Europe couldn't live as well."

The mayor smiled, more to himself than Alyce. "That's our Bill, the best of everything, the best Dresden, the finest Sevres china, Aubusson carpets, peacocks on the terraces. I stand here Miss Wentworth and imagine a Caesar of Rome standing here and calling it home.

"If there's time, make sure Bill takes you riding through the hills of Half Moon Bay. His horses are the finest in California. You do ride out ,Miss Wentworth?"

Alyce smiled, trying to be non-commital, not entirely sure if he was making fun of her.

"Do you like the theater, Miss Wentworth? The great actor John McCollough was here today and he was telling me that he would like to bring Shakespeare out here, perform in this very amphitheater."

Alyce thought about this a moment, another idea had occured to her. "I think on the shore by Fort Mason would be altogether more useful to people."

The Mayor nodded to himself. "Capital idea. Summer theater by the shore. I like it, get us out of that stuffy heat. Thank you Miss Wentworth." He examined his pocket-watch. "Regretfully I have to return to the city, so I shall miss dining with all of you tonight."

"That's a pity."

"My loss, I think, with yourself as a dining companion." He took her arm. "Shall we go down?"

Slack was in some kind of heaven. On the long rosewood table, rested not one newspaper, but a hundred at the very least, and not a one was from San Francisco. *The Times* of London. *The New York Tribune*, the *Herald*, French papers, German, even Russian. Mr.. Ralston obviously placed great store by keeping his finger on the pulse of the world. With gas light a man could read all night.

"What's happened in the great world of ours, Slack? Anything worth getting in a sweat about?"

Slack rattled off some headlines. "Earthquake in Greece, kills thousands.

111

DIAMONDS

Thames freezes, hundreds die in unseasonable weather. Paris Commune brutally crushed, who now will govern France? Greeley declares he'll take on Grant. Chicago lumber shortage -riots quelled by city guard."

Slack paused momentarily, then snorted with a mixture of disgust and pleasure, usually reserved for some outlandish news item. "Some English professor has predicted the world is running out of coal and in ten years people will freeze to death in their homes unless they stop producing gaslight."

"Well, they never saw the State of Virginia. Can't move for coal, and practically nowhere to sell it. Just goes to show, Slack, never can trust the word of an expert. Got anything in the paper about Kimberley? I'd like to know what the going price for a diamond is these days."

"I'll look."

A servant entered the room with a silver tray laden with cordials and offered them around. Arnold took two, for the journey had left him with a thirst.

Alyce amused herself by admiring the pictures on the gallery walls. She particularly liked one by William Holman Hunt, entitled '*Love at first sight*' which seemed to have been painted on an estate much like Ralston's and another by an artist called John Everett Millais showing a young woman in the arms of her medieval lover. It was entitled ' *The Huguenot*'. How luscious, how tragic and wistful she looked.

Arnold peered at them but didn't much care for the pictures, and declared that they were too mushy for him. He was too busy sizing up the room to figure out the price of everything. The library alone was worth all he'd pay for the state of Kentucky. The ballroom was bigger than the Grand Hotel's, and who knew the value of all the marble and bronzes, some come from as afar Egypt and Ancient Greece.

The Chinese houseman entered silently and caught his attention.

"Mr.. Ralston regrets he is delayed sir. He has urgent business matters with the judge. If you'd care to utilise the gymnasium, or take a Turkish bath before dinner is served, I would be happy to organize this for you, sir."

Arnold couldn't get over how well the Chinese houseman spoke English. He must have stared at the man for a good minute or more. Suddenly he snapped to. "I'll be hanged if I'll go to a gymnasium, but a Turkish bath, that sounds like something. Lead on. It's been a hot day, I could sweat out some dust. How 'bout you Slack?"

Slack just waved his hands. He had a month's worth of newspapers to read and meant to devour them all.

"I'll come." Alyce offered.

Arnold pretended to be shocked. "What, men and women together?"

"This is possible, sir. Mrs Ralston believes that the European custom of mixed bathing is permissible."

"As long as God turns his back, we'll be fine," Arnold joked.

112

DIAMONDS

"I'll stay," Alyce declared. "It would not look right. Not here."

Arnold shrugged, but he would be damned if he wasn't going to partake of this house's amenities. "Lead on, boy, Arnold's going Turkish."

The Chinaman led Arnold out and Alyce looked rather wistful about it. She'd have given the world to take a Turkish bath in such a grand house. It all reminded her of Cleopatra or something similar.

William Chapman Ralston stood talking with William Lent and General Colton. His business with the judge was done and the judge was already on his way back to the city. Ralston had made no attemt to urge him to stay for dinner. Judge Wallace was a useful man to have on your side, but hardly an asset when the subject of diamonds was under discussion.

Lent smoked a cigar, and had the air of a man who had just recovered from some ghastly malady. His doctor had warned him off cigars, but he had no will to surrender to logic or good health.

The General partook of some of Colonel Agoston Haraszthy's wine from Sonoma. He was thinking of investing in vineyards now that Leland Stanford had shown the way. The Reisling had a distinct German flavor. "You know, I think this Haraszthy's wine is better than General Vallejo's native stuff. What you say Bill? You're growing the mission vines here, but the German vines they brought over seem altogether more subtle to me."

"Buena Vista's got it right, Harazsthy is going about it scientifically but who is to say that the vines he's imported won't have the same pox as Europe. The Mission vines are disease free."

Ralston for his part, was impatient to get things done, but he had to stay calm for the sake of appearances.

"The situation is this, gentlemen: Arnold and Slack are to be advanced $125,000 exactly, to be paid by the Bank of California. In return we keep the precious stones already deposited. I have had our Mr. Kavak in to look over these stones you found, General. He says the new ones are of a better quality than the ones found before, and the ruby is worthy of display. Things may come to that later. But at valuations we have now, we are advancing $125,000 for stones worth within the region of $200,000 to $300,000, if they are to be sold."

"Then you are adequately covered," Lent remarked. "Tell me, do you think Arnold and Slack know the true value?"

Ralston shook his head and sipped at his wine taken from a long-stemmed crystal glass. "I'd say not. They do not have the services of any expert in this field, but do not make the mistake of underestimating Arnold. He's a smart one. I've done some checking. They've been working the gold fields for some years. George Roberts, who's got a lot of interests up in the mines, as well as his store, brought them to my attention. Arnold and Slack sold him some lots in a gold mine they'd claimed back in 1870. Both came in good and are still producing. It was a bad bargain for them, but Roberts isn't complaining. He paid $50,000 for it and sold it on last year for $200,000."

The General was frowning. "They never mentioned this to me on the trail."

"I gather they're none too pleased to have made such a poor deal, General. But they seem regular types, and George swears by them. You've spent the most time with them, General. Can you say anything agin' them?"

"Can't say I can. They took that fella Decker hard."

"I can't get to the bottom of that," Ralston declared with some conviction.

"It's a disgrace it happened. Obviously, we have to be more guarded about this subject. Who do you think Decker was working for? We don't want Flood or O'Brien pipping us to the post, gentlemen. This is just show tonight, gentlemen. I want them to get to like us and want to stay with us. If anyone is going to come in with other offers, we have to appeal to their sense of loyalty."

"But surely you have secured an interest " Lent protested.

"Yes, sir. But after this Decker incident, the ground is shaky. I told 'em we don't have enough to get the show off to a good start. I want more diamonds, better quality and most of all I want them out of the way whilst we organize. Now we know it's genuine, thanks to the General here, I want the best people on this I can find. For that reason I intend to contact Asbury Harpending."

"You'll not get him back from London. He's settled there, shut up his house," Lent told him. "He wants no more business here."

"Once he knows what's at stake, Will, he'll come. By my reckoning, we've got a fifty-million-dollar investment here. If we play this right we can get control of the world diamond market. Think of that. San Francisco will rival and overtake the rest of the world in finance. Arnold and Slack just don't know how big this is."

"But they own two-thirds," the General pointed out.

"It's my intention to buy them out, General. Money means a great deal to 'em. I know their type. They are short-sighted. Look what happened to them on the gold mine they sold to George. They'll come back with more diamonds and I'll make them an offer. We all will. We will buy them out and sweeten the deal with stock or, whatever. They know they don't have the resources to develop this. We do and we can. Believe me these men are ripe for the picking. You'll see." He smiled. "Meanwhile, let's entertain them, get them feeling happy. What do you say?"

"I'd say they're no match for you, Bill," Lent assured him.

"I'll second that," the General added. "Yes, sir. You've got 'em plucked and stuffed, just ready for the oven.."

Ralston looked pleased. "I'll call the ladies. General, if you like that wine, wait until you taste what we're having with the beef. It was a gift from Mr.. Greely of New York. He wants to impress us with their New York wine, but we're going to give them a run for their money. I'm going to send back some of Dr George Crane's special reserve and some bottles of Haraszthy's finest. We shall see who produces the best. I'm betting on California.

Arnold didn't really consider this a Turkish bath. It was more a blistering hot lake fenced in by acres of Italian marble. He wondered how many miners had sacrificed their dreams of fortunes to pay for this marble palace alone. He floated in the water stark naked, his white flesh now pink as a winsome piglet. Sweat poured off his face as he reflected that life wasn't so bad when you were rich. He'd done this once before in a hot-springs up in the mountains in Utah, but it had hadn't been so fancy. For one thing he'd had to share the spring with seven of the sweatiest mud-encrusted prospectors that were ever collected into nature's crystal-pure waters. The odd thing was, that experience had been one of the highlights of a six-month ordeal. Now he'd come to the conclusion that you had to share a hot bath if it was to be any fun.

He wondered how Slack was getting on with his newspapers. He counted himself a lucky man to have a partner who took the trouble to keep himself informed. Information sometimes proved useful. Otherwise, it was like school learning, easily forgotten and best left that way.

With reluctance he hauled his dead weight out of the steaming water and walked without pause to the cool-off pool, plunging into it with the grace of a polar bear. The shock of it practically killed him. It was worse than being shot at dawn. He roared and skittled out of there as fast as he could . It was cold sea water, heavily saline. Arnold had to look back at the water to make sure there wasn't an iceberg in there ; or a polar-bear. He stood shivering on the tiled floor and wrapped a huge white Belmont towel around him for warmth. His cry of shock must have been loud, for seconds later three Chinamen arrived at the run, ready to dive in and save him. They stopped short when they saw him shivering by the pool. "Cold water. Salt water very cold," he admitted.

One of them bowed, concealing his amusement behind a cupped hand.

Arnold heard their laughter as they walked back to the main house and wasn't impressed. Someone could have damn well warned him.

The library was full now. Alyce had been quite calm hitherto. She accepted that she was not society but she knew her dress would create comment. The other ladies looked positively plain beside her and none could match her looks, not even Mrs Lizzie Ralston, and she had the means. Her silks were fine and elegant, but so dull. But, the great error was in Alyce dressing French at all. In this year society ladies did not look to Paris, which was still in chaos following the war, but New York. It was all the rage to dress American. The lace and frills of Paris were suddenly entirely wrong. Sly whispers remarked on her skin. She may have been a natural beauty, but to allow the sun on her skin was a terrible mistake in their collective opinion, and their white powered faces stared at her with a very critical eye.

If Ralston had known what a terrible job the ladies were doing to the harmony of this occasion he'd have banished them to an attic room.

Slack was discussing the merits of establishing a sales office in Paris, Berlin, and London to sell Californian real estate. Particularly land south of San Jose and on the coast as far as San Diego. He'd been thinking about this for some time, and not just Ralston was surprised to hear it.

"You see, Europe's running out of land," Slack told them, warming to his subject. "I was thinking about what to do with my share all the way back from the creek."

Ralston made a mental note to ask the General about this creek.

"Well, I thought at first I'd like to own me a hotel like the one you're proposing, Mr.. Ralston. The Palace sounds a real swell affair. There's cities that'll not match up to that in a hundred years. I hear you even plan to build a promenade up on the roof and plant trees up there."

Ralston smiled, glad to hear an encouraging voice for his magnificent venture. "The Palace will be the biggest and best hotel in the world Mr.. Slack. Hot and cold water in the bedrooms , four hundred and thirty seven bathrooms complete with tubs, eight-hundred and fifty guest rooms and two and a half miles of corridors. Carriages will be able to ride right into the central courtyard and the guests will dismount under cover. I tell you it's got the Europeans agog and it isn't even built yet. Seven stories high, Mr.. Slack. It'll be some years before anyone caps this. But you tell me, what of your plans?"

"Well, I kind of think I should leave hotels to them that likes folks and wants to be with them everyday. I've got this idea of buying land in the south, coastal, as well as inland. It sells by the mile and no one can see any use for it right now. Well, that's where I think they're fools."

"Water's a problem," Mr. Lent pointed out. "One can't farm with sea water and there's precious little else."

"I admit water is a problem, but it can be provided for, Mr. Lent. You could build a dam or two up by Lake Arrowhead or farther north at Santa Felicia. More importantly, they're going to build the railroad farther south one day all the way to San Diego. So all you have to do is pick the best land you can for farming and selling in lots, put in your water and wait. One day for sure you're going to make a fortune."

Mr.. Lent was less enthusiastic. "Well, it's one thing to divide Burlingame into lots, Mr.. Slack, in the expectation of a profit. Here there is a growing city. What such prospects have you in Los Angeles or San Diego? Why, there are scarely a thousand people spead throughout the territory."

"That's where the advertising comes in. We set a price, show 'em some pretty pictures, tell 'em they can catch a train there, but they can't come over to inspect, they'll have to take it on trust. My guess is you could sell land at a hundred, two hundred dollars an acre and they'd consider it cheap. And as far as profits go, in the south you can buy land at the most for ten dollars an acre, for two dollars or less in swampland, hell they're giving it away at La Habra. I heard there was land for the taking there. Put in sheep they'll soon have five or six thousand acres smoother than a hog's back. When folks arrive they'll soon see the possibilities."

"It's not the wildest idea I've ever heard, " the General admitted. "But tell me, Mr.. Slack, while you're waiting for the railroad to come to you, what will you do?"

"Fishin', General. A man can never get tired of fishin'."

"Well, I predict you'll never find people who'll want to live down south, Mr.. Slack, not in a hundred years; let alone pay two hundred dollars an acre for the privilege," Mr. Lent asserted firmly. "It's a desert."

"I don't mind if they don't come, Mr. Lent. I'll still own the land. I don't care if the railroad takes twenty years to reach San Diego. I'll still be fishin' and land will be even scarcer in Europe. I'll be looking for something to sell to keep me in my old age. I reckon land's going to be worth more than diamonds by then."

"Ridiculous," Mr. Lent snorted, but Ralston put an arm around Slack's shoulders as he walked him away from the group toward the women.

"Mr.. Slack, you're one constant surprise. By golly, you're more bullish than me on California. I can see we're going to have to make room at the high table for you and Arnold."

Slack was amused by that. "Oh, I wouldn't come to the city myself, Mr. Ralston. I like it peaceful."

"Remind me to show you my stables, Mr. Slack. I have the best thoro'breds in the West. Well, why be modest? They are the best anywhere. Didn't I just last week sell three stallions and a mare to Lord Tussock for stud in England's Newmarket? Now what do you think of that? The New World selling new blood to the old."

"I like it fine, sir. I hear you have a fine selection there."

"Indeed I have. In fact, you three shall stay the night. I must insist. It's foolish to go back in the dark. The arrangements have been made. I believe I might have a few spare rooms somewhere."

This remark drew laughter from the ladies.

A gong sounded somewhere deep in the house and seemed to grow louder by the second until it reached a crescendo, and then abruptly stopped. Dinner was served.

Miraculously, a lobster red Philip Arnold reappeared at the very moment, hair all slick and shiny, his face all smiles,

"I have a serious case of hunger, Mr.. Ralston. Them Turks knew how to

117

live, eh? I could use one of them hot dips every day."

"You look to be in rude health, Mr.. Arnold."

"Sir, can't say I ever felt better." He turned to the ladies. "Ladies, the name's Philip Arnold. How do you do?"

Plainly, society ladies were not used to this homely approach and rightly snubbed him, sailing on by without a word. Arnold looked at the men, ready for another snub, but Mr.. Lent was smiling. 'Now, if my ladywife would ignore me so thoroughly, Mr.. Arnold, I'd be the happiest of men. Lord knows I'd welcome the peace. How do you do, sir? I've been making the acquaintance of your partner John Slack here. And if you are as half as forward-thinking as he is, well, all I can say is San Francisco has got to look forward to some exciting times ahead."

Arnold beamed, a trickle of sweat falling off the tip of his nose. "Sir, if Philip Arnold can't liven up a place, well, no one can. Mr.. Ralston," (he couldn't bring himself to address him as Bill in this company) "that marble in your Turkish bath, it come all the way from Italy?"

"It did, sir, it most certainly did. How did you know?"

"Only green marble I ever saw came from there."

"Nothing but the best for Belmont," the General drawled, but Arnold could detect a hint of jealousy in his remark.

There then came the business of seating around the grand table. Ralston bowed to his wife's seating arrangement, but he did insist upon having Slack sit across the table from him so they could talk. Mrs. Ralston wasn't at all impressed by this.

"I don't like talk of business at the supper table, Mr. Slack, but if you ask me, you're going to lose your money into the greatest sink hole you ever saw. I have been as far south as San Juan Capistrano and I can tell you that people would rather live in hell than settle there. There is still a lot of space left in Europe, believe me, think again, Mr.. Slack."

Arnold suddenly realized what Slack must have been talking about.

"Slack been and sold anyone half the Mojave Desert yet? " He laughed. "Slack's got some good ideas, mind. But you just can't sell land, even to ignorant foreigners, if there's no water for irrigation."

"I told you, Philip Arnold, it's quite possible to dig a canal or what the Romans call an aqueduct from the San Joaquin River south as far as you want. Gravity'll take it." Slack felt a little peeved at Arnold's remarks; he had been rather enjoying his new status as a real estate developer.

"Now, that's what I call a man of vision," Ralston declared. "Mr.. Slack; you're my man. An aqueduct, it's perfectly natural. We could get federal money for a thing like that and land grants. There's a thing to finance, General!"

"And I want the construction contract at twice the money the railroad gets a mile, no, three times. Unlike the railroad, a canal can't afford to lose its freight. It'll have to be a tight ship, no leaks."

"Then there's work for lawyers too," Mrs.Ralston pointed out, "trying to stop it, some to start it and others between for those whose path it crosses."

"Now, is this water free?" Arnold asked. "And if it isn't, how much can I get for the San Joaquin River?"

At this everyone laughed and the tension in the room seemed to drift away as the Chinese servants brought in the first courses, lobster bisque, fresh fruit, hot biscuits, sauteed kidneys in red wine, and a cheese souffle. By the time they got onto the second course, grand salmon stuffed with brook trout and baked in rose leaves, Slack was already satiated, but the food kept on coming, as did the wine, both French and domestic. The roast was beef sirloin. The game was canvas-backed duck . This made quite a change from nights spent with a bottle of Old Continental and cold beans.

The finest ice-creams followed, set off with apple pie and slices of cheese. There were nuts and chocolates to follow, but not a one could swallow the tiniest morsel more. Arnold and Slack could not remember a finer meal. Alyce had tasted something of everything, but was conscious of the constrictions of her tight bodice. A woman in the possession a comely figure had to endure much torment, she felt. She watched the other women push their food around their plates, no doubt also thinking of their stitching. There hadn't been much conversation. It seemed eating and drinking were the thing, with the odd comment on the pluses and minuses of the household staff and what plans were being made for the next grand tour. On the whole, it wasn't a great deal to make a fuss about. Not as much fun as sitting around a campfire of an evening and swapping tall tales about the millions you'd missed and the zillions you would make, if only your luck would change.

Only after the ladies had retired to the drawing room and the men were smoking did serious conversation start up again. Ralston somehow got it back to the business at hand.

"When you go back this time, gentlemen, I want you to go at this thing scientifically . You understand? Now, I've obtained a book from the Dutch. The diagrams are very good. It's all about diamonds. I have another about geology. Philip Arnold, I'm going to send you back to the diamond fields with the best tools and the most scientific books I can muster. It's not enough to dig anymore, one must go at the thing with trained eyes, map the terrain. I want to know the geography of a diamond field so that when we come across another we will know it straight away."

Arnold smiled as he twirled his brandy in a crystal balloon. "I'd like to know the geography of a diamond field myself, Mr.. Ralston. I'd like to know the geography of a gold field. There is one thing that's for sure, I've never yet met a man who could describe with any certainty what a gold field looks like before it's proven. I've seen gold in flat land, rivers, mountain peaks, the bottoms of canyons, seen nuggets turn up in a farmers cornfield, and I couldn't say if I learned anything about any specific geography. Once, me and Slack were digging up by Nevada City, working over old placers and looking for pockets, when Slack stood up, swore at me for talking him into ever leaving Kentucky, and then said that if ever a rock formation looked like one that should produce gold this was it."

"And did it?" Ralston asked, keen to hear the result.

"Did it, hell. All we found was four pounds of almost pure silver for a ton of diggings."

The punchline sank in somewhat late. "Four pounds of silver to the ton of ore? Why, that's quite a haul," Mr. Lent said, impressed.

"I tell you, we thought we'd hit the mother lode itself. I was all for scooting down to the registry and starting another rush, but wouldn't you know, it pinched out as fast as it started. We dug out every side, we dug under it, but there never was another ounce. So, in answer to your idea about recognizing the geography, Mr. Ralston, nothing is ever going to replace the instinct of a prospector, and even that ain't infallible. But we'll take your tools. "

Ralston smiled. "Mr. Arnold, this great nation of ours is ever in debt to prospectors like yourselves. If it weren't for your dedication and perseverance, we'd be a lot poorer. Worse, we'd be bankrupt. San Francisco would still be a little fishing village."

"Hear-hear," Arnold rejoined. Slack said nothing, nor did the General; they'd both dropped off to sleep.

"Got to be the brandy, " Ralston said with a smile. "Shall we join the women, Mr. Arnold? The General's wife will tell you about her terrors on the evening train down from the city today. She was covered in soot and weeping uncontrollably. General wasn't affected a bit. We need more efficient boilers, altogether a better class of locomotive. All that damned smoke and yet who can ride with the damn windows closed? If they don't bake you, they freeze you. You think the airship will ever come, Mr. Arnold? I was hearing some great ideas about an airship that could travel all the way from New York to San Francisco and carry a hundred passengers. Would that be possible?"

"Not until the Indians make rubber arrows, Mr. Ralston, not until then."

Laughing, the two men deserted their own and crossed the divide to join the ladies. Their arrival was welcome, female conversation having run dry awful early that night. They were all discussing the actor, John McCollough and the latest play at the California Theater. "Of course our Mr. McCollough *is* excellent, but it is only a San Francisco production. We just have such a way to go to compare to the heights of London dramatics. Don't you agree, Mr.. Arnold?"

Mr.. Arnold had never been to any dramatic performance of anything in all his born days, and had drunk enough to say so this evening, but for once he was thinking before he spoke. "Never cared for dramatics, Mrs. Ralston. Opera is the thing for me. Nothing quite gets one off for a good nap than something really musical."

And that closed the subject of culture for good that night.

It wasn't long before all succumbed to the weight of the food and claimed their bedrooms. Alyce of course had her own room, and she knew from the condition Arnold was in that he'd not be padding along the heavily-carpeted corridors. In this particular corner of paradise, she'd be sleeping alone.

The same carriage that had delivered them took them to the morning train. The Ralstons didn't linger long abed, despite their good fortune. As soon as the sun touched the eastern horizon, bells were clanging, house staff bustled. It would have been impossible to sleep through it.

Breakfast had been almost as lavish as the dinner the night before, but fortunately they'd had the benefit of riding out on the horses beforehand and worked up a tremendous appetite. Alyce still hadn't quite gotten over the stables. It had so many grooms and ostlers, she couldn't count them all. The stables were redwood outside and carved mahogany inlaid with mother of pearl inside. The glass-enclosed harness room sported silver pegs for each horse, upon which monogrammed harnesses and top-coats hung. She'd never seen *people* treated this well, never mind horses. The entire effect of the Belmont trip had quite crushed her. Perhaps before, she'd found some dignity in her own poor life. After all, she did own her own home, and the views couldn't be bettered, But compared with life at Belmont, well, it was like comparing a flea with a buffalo and just as pointless. She rode home quite subdued.

Slack went back much richer than he'd left. Ralston had so taken to him, he'd let him keep the leather boots he'd borrowed to go riding in, in fact he'd insisted upon it. Slack didn't resist. They were the best, most comfortable boots he'd ever had the pleasure of placing on his long-neglected feet.

Arnold was of two minds about his experience. He couldn't decide if he could live like Ralston, or go for something less extravagant, like the General, who had his home in Nob Hill. Of course he still had a weekend place too; a ranch house on the slopes of Mount Diablo. There looked to be a devilish lot of organization in running a place like Belmont, not to mention the outgoings. Why, Ralston would have to be earning in excess of ten million dollars a year or more to live as he did. He wondered how many others in the world could boast such an income. Even Jay Cooke would be troubled to match him.

The rest of the day was spent most profitably. Ralston was as good as his word and he paid over the $125,000 in gold coin and didn't question where it went. They took the money over to the Western Bank for safekeeping and made their arrangements there. It was no disrespect to Ralston, it was just that they were clients of the Western and thought it best to keep the money out of reach of Ralston should for some reason he try to change his mind.

As planned beforehand, they bought new equipment for their prolonged stay on the diamond field. Picks, shovels, graders, broad mesh sieves, tight weave mesh sieves, anything that could be strapped to the side of a mule and gotten up a mountain. Geology books and Ralston's book on gems were packed too. All this they took to Oakland by way of the ferry, and left with officials of the Central Pacific to stow for the journey east the next day. They purchased Silver Palace tickets through to Ogden and took pleasure in knowing that all those who'd follow would have to fork out their precious dollars to do the same. Slack had considered buying them only as far as Cisco then quickly getting back on the train to laugh as others scrambled to re-join. It was the one way of knowing for sure, just how many there were spying. They anticipated at least half a dozen. It was the way of the West. If ever the US Army wanted volunteers, all they had to do was come west, dip a soldier in gold dust and half the state would follow him half way around the world and thank him for it to boot.

By nightfall they were pretty much ready, but there was a surprise to come for Alyce. It was after supper and Slack was out of the house deliberately, leaving Arnold to talk to her undisturbed. He was sat out by the water listening to the night, waiting for sounds of trouble. There weren't many stars and no moon to speak of, so he couldn't see too well, but he was sure there was someone outside, hoping for new tidbits to feed the grapevine. Arnold and Slack couldn't make a move without the whole of Oakland being informed now. Well, so be it. They'd outfox them all, somehow.

Inside, Alyce was near to tears.

"What do you mean? Arnie, don't josh me." She fell into Arnold's arms. She was overwhelmed; he'd known she would be. Whether she accepted or not, he'd finally asked, but it was asking a great deal. He knew that, so he hugged her hard and whispered that if she declined he'd hardly hold it agin her.

"Oh, Arnie," she finally sighed, tears welling up in her misty eyes. She wouldn't let Arnold look at her, not in this state. "I'd be in the way, wouldn't I?"

"Well, it's no picnic, it ain't like visiting Belmont, Alyce. There's no soft pillows, it's hot as hell during the day and freezing at night. The bugs will bite your ass off if you let 'em. We'd expect you to cook and clean and sort the gems, and I'm not offering you a share, 'cause that's between Slack, me, and Ralston. But you'll get a share of our profits through me and a grand home to live in ; that is, if you'll agree."

Alyce stiffened. "Does that mean you're asking me to marry you, Arnie? " She fixed her eyes on his face, searching for clues. "I know you said I was your fiancee..."

Arnold reeled back momentarily. "Now, did I mention the word marriage? Alyce, you got my heart lock, stock, and barrel. I'm offering you a home with me, asking you to share any money I make from the diamonds. I'm kind of shy of marrying after my first, and besides, that ain't over legally. I like things as they are between us. You got your own house; you live more secure than Slack and me have done since we was kids."

Alyce wasn't so sure about all this. Many women did it, but the shame she'd felt at Belmont hurt. She was sure the ladies knew she lived in sin, though nothing was said. She'd been introduced as Arnold's fiancee, but she'd sensed it wasn't believed.

"We'll be moving away from San Francisco, if that's what is worrying you. If you want to tell folks we're married, well, that's your business, but it wouldn't be true. Alyce,there's never going to be another woman, of that I can promise you. "

He leaned forward and kissed the top of her sweet -smelling hennaed hair. "Just don't insist I marry you, cause if that's the way it's got to be, well we will have to part, and that'll be worse than losing my diamonds, Al. Honest, woman, you've got me landed and filleted, just don't make a meal of me."

Alyce didn't know what to make of her situation. She buried her head into Arnold's shoulder and one awful sob escaped, but he held her tight and they stood that way a while as she considered her future with one Philip Arnold.

Meanwhile, Slack had spotted a figure moving no more than twenty, thirty feet away from the house. Some man had gotten himself up on the roof of the neighbor's shack, and it could be for no other reason than to spy on Alyce's place. Slack did nothing for a few minutes, just to make sure the man had no friends with him. Then, secure in the knowledge that he couldn't be seen in the pitch dark, he made his way around the back and silently gained on the man by stealth.

A few minutes later he was standing on the water barrel just a foot or two below the man himself. The man hadn't heard a thing. Slack was surprised to see what an excellent view he had of Arnold and Alyce locked in some kind of embrace. He didn't like to think of the interloper spying on them.

He threw a stone into the water to catch the man's attention. It did. Slack got a quick glimpse of him looking over the edge of the roof, and immediately Slack's hands shot up and grabbed the fellow by the neck, hauling him off the roof. Together they fell hard to the ground.

Slack was up in seconds, ready to fight, but this man he'd brought down didn't move a muscle or make a sound. Slack got down for a closer look. It was a man all right, he recognized him as the eldest son of Hazlewood, the dry goods storekeeper an Oakland's main street. For one moment Slack thought he was dead and there'd be hell to pay, but he felt the boy's neck and a heart was still pumping blood around the body. The neck wasn't broken, the boy was just stunned. Just as well for Slack. There was only one thing to do. Get the hell out of there, leave the boy to puzzle things out on his own. Slack ran for Alyce's house the long way, making sure there were no other prowlers. As far as he could tell he was alone out there in the still night.

He arrived at Alyce's house looking wild and all puffed out. Arnold saw him first and realized there'd been trouble.

"Shall I fetch my revolver?"

"No, kid from Hazlewood's up on the Davey shack next door. I reckon he was spying for his pa."

"Where's he now?"

"Face down in the dirt, hurt some, but he don't know who done it to him. You have to burn that lamp so bright? See you and Alyce all the way clear from San Francisco."

Arnold smiled, but turned the lamp down half. "She's coming, Slack."

Slack frowned. He hadn't been consulted about this.

"It took some persuading, so I'd appreciate it if you'd look a bit happier about it. She's a good woman, Slack, and she knows too much now for us to leave her behind ."

Slack rubbed the back of his head as he thought about it. "Well, I suppose there's some sense in it. We'll be gone a while. She would be another pair of hands."

"And don't fret about our friend Hazlewood, or any of the others. I don't care if Ralston sets ten spies on us and half of Oakland, they'll not know when we're due to get off the train. The General ain't stupid, he'll keep silent. We have to use Rawlins Springs again. Hell, the entire State can follow us, but we'll outwit 'em."

"Think we should leave the kid alone?"

"Folks fall off a roof all the time, don't they?"

"I'm nervous about you bringing Alyce along. I've got to tell you that. She's good company but we'd be taking a risk."

Arnold smiled, sitting by the table and taking out a pack of cards.

"Slack, you worry too much. Look at us now. We're $125,000 in pocket. That ain't something to sniff at is it? Money's in New York now for sure and there's going to be more. We'll be rich men yet."

"These are powerful men we're dealing with, Arnie. They'll strip us bare if we don't come up with the right stones, and they'll probably cheat us if we do."

"Well, I don't think so. Hell, they got a bargain with those diamonds, you said so yourself. We aren't greedy men. We don't need mother-of-pearl on our stable doors. We've got the sense to know a horse couldn't care less. Partner, we're in this to the end. Don't we deserve to get rich? What's a few more months in this diamond game ? We'll sell out when they offer us enough, and believe me, they'll offer enough. Then we can quit this game forever. I don't care if I never see another mountain again. Still less silver or gold or diamonds. My God, Slack, think of the years we've dreamed of getting this far. Well, here we are. Only we mustn't let Ralston know we're sick of the life or he'll beat us down on price. We got to make him believe we'd rather die than give it all up to him."

"You're missing your vocation, Philip Arnold. You should have been a politician."

"Well who knows? Soon I'll be able to buy myself a place in the Senate like Sargeant or Bill Sharon did. What do you think of that? Senator Arnold, it has a kind of ring to it, don't you think?"

Slack was smiling again. "Yeah, yeah. So, you ready?"

"Ready as I'll ever be. Alyce is packing. I'm giving her another twenty minutes and then I'll go in and throw half of it away. She thinks she might need a parasol and Sunday dress up on the mountain."

"You tell her?" Slack asked, raising an inquisitive eyebrow.

"No, sir, I figure I'll leave all the shocks until later."

Slack nodded. It was probably best. Better still would be leaving her behind. Not that he didn't like Alyce. In actual fact, in his own quiet way he adored her Arnold looked back at Alyce's bedroom. "Al, make sure you pack your sun hat. The broad-brimmed white one. The sun gets mighty fierce up there in the mountains." He cast his eyes back to Slack. "I know you don't hold with this, but Alyce will bring us luck, you'll see."

Slack would like to have been consulted, but he held his tongue for the sake of peace. He considered that spending time with Alyce would be better company than just plain Arnold. Nevertheless, he would like to have had his say. To speak up now would only upset Alyce for no reason.

"Any coffee left?" he inquired, heading into the kitchen.

CHAPTER SEVEN
A question of hats

Any serious prospector would have known from the equipment stowed aboard the freight car that Arnold and Slack were now big time prospectors. Slack had taken the precaution of covering the book on diamonds in thick brown paper and tying it securely. He wanted to keep their secret for as long as possible. They'd made it to the train in plenty of time and selected good seats nearest the stove. It would be cold crossing the mountains, and Alyce wouldn't be used to that. The Silver Palace was unusually full, but most of the passengers were traveling only as far as Sacramento or Nevada City. Arnold figured that if anyone was going to take the trouble to follow them, they'd travel either in the next car, or, to save money, in the returning immigrant cars; crude, drafty, poorly sprung; already legend for the amount of discomfort they inflicted on the long transcontinental journey. So much so, that some folks still preferred the old route to California by way of the Gulf and across the Isthmus of Panama. It was slow, but sometimes less hazardous.

Arnold told them that he thought he'd recognized at least five individuals who could be spies. He was more amused than annoyed."

"Which one's Ralston's man?" Slack asked, trying to make out a face in the crowds on the station platform.

"He wouldn't send another, would he?" Alyce protested. "He's such a gentleman."

"Maybe so, but a gentleman likes to cover his bets," Arnold told her. He pointed out a particular man in a shabby leather coat and muddy boots. "That's Dutch Pete. Now I know word's out for sure. He's the wiliest son of a bitch I know. Jumped a claim of Rib O'Conners, and O'Conner challenged him and got his head blown off for his trouble. The claim was worthless, so I guess O'Conner had some kind of revenge."

"Well, we've got shotguns and this old navy revolver you picked up yesterday. Should be some kind of protection," Slack pointed out. "If they follow us, I'll not be shy of peppering them with some lead. Should discourage them a while."

DIAMONDS

"You'd kill a man to keep your diamonds?" Alyce asked, suddenly all hushed at the determination in Arnold's voice..

"Kill two or four," Slack told her and meant it.

"Don't look so shocked, Alyce," Arnold told her. "Hell, they'd kill us given half a chance. Go count the graves up by the mines, half of 'em are filled with peaceable men who just happened to find the gold before another who had a gun. Some camps had law, most didn't."

"And shaking this lot won't be easy, especially Dutch Pete," Slack pointed out. "But we'll do it. Arnie's got a plan, eh?"

Alyce smiled. "A plan. Now you're talking like those great mysteries everyone is reading these days. Do tell."

"Later. Just enjoy the journey, my sweet. Smile at everyone like we didn't know half this train's passenger's are only here on account of us."

Slack was looking strange, as if he'd lost something. "What's up?" Arnold inquired, worried some new development may have occured.

"I was just thinking, I kind of miss the General. At least he was an educated man."

Arnold took immediate offense. "And I suppose I'm not?"

"I've spoken enough with you to know everything you have to say, Philip Arnold."

"And all you're full of is yesterday's papers."

"Now, now, you two, no dog fights, " Alyce intervened. "Let's keep this journey pleasant."

"That weren't no dog fight," Arnold reassured her. "When we have a spat I gets real mad, and Slack, he just sulks." He laughed. "One time he didn't speak to me for more than six weeks, and all it was over was me losing a bag of nails."

"Our *only* bag of nails," Slack corrected him. "We had the wood, we had the floor, but we had no nails and it was the wettest month of May you'd ever known. We had to sleep under a lean-to that leaked more than if we'd slept out in the rain. That's why I didn't speak to him."

"All rust and rotting timber now." Arnold mumbled.

The train pulled out with its usual fanfare of whistles and steam. Dense wood smoke swept past their window as the coupling jerked, contracted,and generally made a regular hash of a smooth exit. Arnold made the sign of the cross. He wasn't normally a religious man.

Slack had his newspapers spread out already, and he'd be lost to them until every last word was drained from its pages. Alyce settled down to reading *Alice in Wonderland* , a book that was all fashion in the city at this time. She had no concerns about her house. Mrs Kelly would tend it as if it were her own and split the profits if any rooms were let meanwhile. Alyce was sure she was honest, but even if she wasn't, the house would be secure and not empty. That was the main thing.

Arnold, affecting a new responsibility now that he had money in the bank, was reading a New York publication on banking practice; or lack thereof.

"That's all you brought to read?" Alcye inquired.

"I wanted to know how a bank works. I want to know if we can get our money back as easy as it went in or, whether we have to string these cashiers up first and count the coins that fall out of their pockets

"Trusting kind of individual, isn't he, Slack?" Alyce commented with a wink.

"Man's got a right to protect his own," Slack returned.

Not another word was exchanged between them until the train gained on Sacramento. Alyce thought she'd like an ice cream and was about to step off the train to fetch one, when Slack suddenly spotted the Hazlewood boy he'd dragged off the roof the night before. He was skulking behind a stack of mail sacks, trying to get a good look at them to make sure. Slack was happy to note a good-sized bandage on his head for his troubles.

"Hats on," he told the others, and they quickly responded. This had been one part of the plan that Arnold had revealed to Alyce. She flourished her white bonnet Arnold had insisted she brought along.

Slack and Arnold fixed on broad-brimmed felt hats that were one size too big so no one could mistake 'em.

"It's the Hazlewood kid. He's keen, ain't he?"

"Take a stroll with Alyce," Arnold told him." We've got five minutes before the train leaves. I want them to get a good look at these hats."

Alyce and Slack needed no encouragement to get out for some fresh air. They could feel eyes fixed on their backs, burrowing into them.

"Hope they're getting a good eyeful," Slack muttered, and Alyce giggled.

As she purchased ice-cream, Slack got himself a copy of the *Sacramento Bee*. The lead story concerned Grant's election campaign and discussed the fact that no matter who was pitched against him, he couldn't lose. Greeley and all his friends millions weren't going to make a dime's difference.

Slack didn't care much either way. There had been talk of California seceding from the Union before the railroad came, but not much had come of it. Still, it was big enough, rich enough, and hell, who needed the east anyway?

Alyce handed him an ice cream and smiled. "Best eat it quick, heat's not doing it any good."

"Best enjoy it, Alyce. Won't be any luxuries like this over the hump."

"Oh , I'm quite willing to forgo civilization for two months. Arnie wants me there, and if it brings us closer, then I'm happy."

Slack just smiled. Alyce would see a different side to Arnold soon enough. He could be a cussed brute sometimes; she'd learn a lot about him she had never known before. For that matter, she'd discover more about Slack too, and that wasn't so bad. Maybe she'd be more patient with him.

The whistle blew, flags waved, loved ones waved good-bye, doors slammed for the last time. They were finally on their way. Now all they had to do was find a million dollars worth of diamonds!

There was nothing eventful about the journey to Ogden, although Arnold and Slack played some good games with their little spies. This involved getting off at remote stations, walking up to the freight car and taking off some of their picks and shovels, standing around in their ridiculous hats as if they really were taking leave of the train. They'd done this six times and each time seen the 'spies' panic and decamp with all their possessions. Only when the final whistle blew and the train began to haul out did the three of them hand back their tools and quickly re-board. Six times they'd witnessed a mad scramble by their camp followers to get back aboard, and by Arnold's reckoning they'd managed to get rid of quite a few of them, who had either grown tired of the game or miscalculated Arnold's intent. Alyce had laughed so hard about this game she feared for her heart and Slack had joined in when they saw a hapless spy left stranded on the platform with all his possessions.

By Arnold's deduction they were left with Dutch Pete and the Hazlewood boy. They'd seen this trick enough times now not to fall for it again, and besides a joke six times was enough; they'd milked that particular cow dry. That and the fact they were traveling through Salt Lake and everyone knew there was nothing worth having in that particular desert.

The wait at Ogden was much longer than anticipated. The Union Pacific train had been delayed by rain and flooding at Grand Island, and it was going to be at least six hours late. Well, these were not unexpected delays. It was an unusual transcontinental journey that had none, and who could begrudge Grand Island its rain. Or Ogden for that matter, for the same clouds had approached the town, and there was much anticipation about it, for it had been a good six months since the last rain.

Alyce had but one demand of Arnold: a hot bath. A few other travelers had the same idea, so there was quite a rush for those hotels with tubs available. Arnold took a room, organized them hot water and the best wine he could find. If they were going to be clean, they well might as well get themselves a comfortable bed and make an afternoon of it.

Alyce didn't demur. This was an adventure to her, and love making in Ogden was as good as love making at home. Certainly it would be better than up in the mountains with Slack ever about to spy on them.

For his part, Slack didn't care for the luxuries of a tub. He'd had enough of sitting around letting his body grow weak. As it began to rain he struck out for a walk in the desert. He stripped off to the waist and got himself one of nature's showers. If that didn't freshen him up enough for Alyce's nose, then he didn't know what would. Either way, it would rid him of the stench of the sweat and wood smoke from the cars

These unexpected expeditions prompted by the Union Pacific delays had caused not a little confusion among the spies following them. Dutch Pete, being the more intelligent of the two, had stayed with Arnold and Alyce, in fact, stationed himself in the bar of the very same hotel Arnold and Alyce were canoodling in. Young Hazlewood chose to follow Slack in the rain. A mile out it really began to pelt it down and the ground quickly became sticky with mud and fast running streams. The soil, having been baked good and hard by the summer and compacted by the winter, wasn't about to absorb water, even if it sorely needed it.

Slack didn't turn back. It was just as he liked it after the confines of the train. It was quite possible he sensed Hazlewood was behind him, too, so after about four miles of this drenching he suddenly ducked behind a huge rock and took shelter under a prominent overhang. As he waited there he noted a fat slate-gray lizard had gotten the same idea. They stood there looking at each other, hard to tell who was the most surprised.

Aforelong Hazlewood walked by, peering into the distance, possibly wondering if he'd let Slack get too far ahead of him. Slack noted the determined look on the boy's face, as if he meant to dog Slack to the ends of the earth if he had to.

Slack made light work of his return journey, running most of the way. He'd lost track of the time some and was afraid the Union Pacific would have been and gone already. His fears were groundless, however. There was still time for him to warm up by the stove of the nearest saloon and get his shirt dried and ironed by a Chinaman.

Finally the train arrived. There was much rejoicing, if only because most folks had feared they'd have to pay overnight in a hotel, and the hotels were fixing to make a killing on account of that.

When the train finally pulled out, it did so without young Hazlewood. Slack had watched and waited, but that boy didn't show. Slack reckoned he was still out there searching for tracks long washed away by the rain.

"Look, a rainbow," Alyce announced excitedly. She was looking cool as winter snow. Slack could hardly believe the transformation from the tired woman who'd left the Central Pacific just six hours previously.

Arnold was looking good too; the love making had relaxed him, given him quite a glow. He was looking at the rainbow and smiling. "I wish we could lose Dutch Pete. Got to admit you did well, John Slack. I reckon that Hazlewood boy will fetch up in Canada aforelong. Have to admire his persistence."

"What will you do with the last one ?" Alyce inquired. "If it is the last one."

"I say it is, " Arnold said. "Unless the other brought their mother along too." He laughed at that idea and Alyce just had to smile.

DIAMONDS

"Now will you tell me why we have to wear the hats?" Alyce asked. She was restless already and the hat Arnold insisted she wear made her too warm.

"You'll see," he said, winking at her. But he didn't explain. "Meanwhile, Slack, did you organise us beds?"

"Two dollars fifty each they wanted, but I beat him down to two. It's still robbery."

Arnold was looking about the car and seemed impressed. "These Golden Palace cars are quite the thing. Got to admit, the Union Pacific knows a thing or two about building a railroad. The rides better, the seats are softer, and the conductor is polite. The woodwork has got a good polish on it too. Pity they didn't get to build the railroad all the way west, then we wouldn't be held ransom by the Stanford's cowboys."

"Now what did Leland Stanford ever do to you Arnie?" Alyce asked. "You're just like everyone else down on the Central Pacific, just because you didn't think of building it first."

"I'd like to see Arnold build a railroad," Slack commented with a sly smile.

"I'd like to see you try to run one," Arnold countered.

"And I'd like to see you both stop picking on each other," Alyce stated, holding up her hands. Then she was sighing.

"Why the sighs? Ain't you happy?"

"I wished we'd seen Salt Lake City. I wanted to see the Mormons."

"Ain't nothing to see except a lot of men who wished they'd stayed single. Besides, I told you Al, this ain't no jaunt, it's business."

As the train was running late, it was already dark when they cut through the mountain pass. Arnold and Slack now made getting rid of Dutch Pete a priority. So for that reason, when the train reached the Green River supper stop and watering for the locomotive, they took the opportunity to retrieve all their possessions from the freight car, not forgetting to wear their precious hats as they did so. Dutch Pete was familiar with this routine by now, and must have guessed they were getting close to a disembarkation point. Slack caught sight of him watching from the corner of the refreshment saloon, his canvas bag at the ready.

"We'll have to ditch him soon, or else do the other thing," Arnold whispered as they walked back to their car.

"Well, I hope it don't come to that," Slack replied. "Remember O'Conner. I hear Dutch is a crack shot."

"Hearing ain't seeing, and he can't shoot two of us at once."

"Well, I don't fancy it being me, " Slack told Arnold.

"Don't worry, we'll flush him out. We'll ditch him."

They put the plan into action when the train got under way again. As it sped east toward Rock Springs most passengers were asleep, tuckered out after a good meal. Slack wandered through the cars to check if Dutch Pete was in place. He was, feigning sleep in the second-to-last car.

Arnold, meanwhile, had found his three stooges, Mr. and Mrs Wendle and their son, Joe, all of sixteen and "big for his age." Mr. Wendle was a teacher hired by the optimistic citizens of Rock Springs to educate their offspring. It was always the sign of a settlement going permanent when they hired a teacher from outside the community in the hopes he'd know more than they did. This one coming all the way from Sacramento must have needed the job pretty bad. His wife and young Joe had no choice but to accompany him.

Arnold had wished them luck. Rock Springs wouldn't be his choice of a place to go, but then it took all sorts to make up a world. The important thing was that the Wendles were good-natured folk. Arnold told them his cousin Aaron had ordered all these prospecting supplies from San Francisco, he, Arnold had agreed to bring them. But now, he'd learned by way of the telegraph at Ogden that his cousin was delayed further down the line. The upshot of it all was, that Aaron had ordered these items and they had to be got to him. A man called Jackson had been asked to fetch 'em from the station, but what with the train being late it was likely as not he'd be gone by now, Jackson not being a patient party. So would the Wendles take the equipment belonging to Aaron and hold it all until claimed.

They would, of course they would. They had a mountain of possessions themselves a few more wouldn't make any difference either way. Arnold had one other request, however. The hats. Aaron had lent them these hats last time they saw him, and it was only just and right that his wife and son get them back. Mr.. Wendle couldn't agree more. A man should get back what was his to begin with. Arnold had a bit of a problem to get the Wendles to wear the hats, but as he put it, if Aaron did get there in reasonable time, how much easier would it be to recognize them as they walked down the road. To sweeten the pill, Slack offered them ten dollars for their trouble nay, forced them to accept ten dollars. The Wendles made quite a stand about this. They'd do everything Arnold asked, but take his ten dollars. It was just not something they'd do or expect.

Of course, the more they protested, the more Arnold and Slack were convinced they needed the money. At one time Arnold thought he'd lost everything and they'd refuse to take a single item, but Alyce saved the situation by explaining that it was custom to pay school teachers in arrears in these parts ; in fact, she'd heard the last one had been hired in return for free lodging and as much bread as he could eat. As it turned out, he ate too much bread and they had to let him go. That clinched it. They took the ten dollars and were still thanking Arnold when the train gained Rock Springs at about midnight.

Arnold gave a boy riding in the rear cars a dollar to help the Wendles unload and get set up on the station platform. Obviously they could not be seen doing this themselves. The Wendles couldn't have departed happier and true to their word they wore the hats, which unaccountably, fitted each one of them perfectly. Slack thought this was something to do with schoolteachers having to carry a lot of unnecessary information around in their heads.

If the Wendles were surprised that Arnold, Alyce, and Slack hadn't stuck around to say goodbye, well, it was just one more oddity. They'd done all right by them.

Naturally the idea of all this was to make Dutch Pete believe they'd finally gotten off the train. The hats would confirm it, and Arnold doubted Dutch wouldn't be getting too close to see he was in error. They figured he'd stay aboard the train until the last moment, just to make sure this wasn't another of their games .

Not everything went according to plan, however. They hadn't reckoned on a welcoming committee for the Wendles, for one thing, and neither had the Wendles. Luckily, they were whisked off the station platform at some speed, their possessions left to some volunteer townsfolk to carry into town.

All this Dutch Pete witnessed and puzzled over. He had to follow now. It was not strictly customary for prospectors to be feted when they arrived in a strange town, but just because it never happened didn't mean it couldn't happen.

When the train pulled out of Rock Springs, Slack caught sight of Dutch Pete slinking off into the stationhouse with his canvas sack slung over his shoulder. They'd bested him at last. Now there was no one left to fool no more.

"What I don't understand," Alyce wanted to know, "is why we ditched our picks and shovels and everything? Why would your cousin want them?"

This had Arnold and Slack bursting into a fit of uncontrollable laughter for longer than was decent. Alyce grew quite peeved about it.

"Well, what is so funny? Please let me know what the joke is."

Arnold recovered enough to slap his knees and plant a quick kiss on Alyce's lips. "You're quite the precious one, my sweet. Yes, ma'am."

"What's the game, Philip Arnold?" Alyce protested. "Arnie, tell me, don't hold out. When are we going into the mountains, and how shall we dig if we don't have tools?"

Slack said nothing. He felt it was up to Arnold to explain.

"We're going to get the diamonds, Alyce. That I promise. Only we don't exactly need the tools." He flashed his best smile at her, but she still looked confused.

"I know you said they were just lying on the ground up there, but surely..." She turned to Slack and slapped his knees. "Slack ,explain to me. What are you and Arnie up to here?"

"Well .... " he gave his slightly bemused look and scratched his head a little. "You remember how you used to tell us how you once missed a chance to go to Europe with a dance show?"

"Yes?" Alyce couldn't believe Slack would bring this up now. "I remember it well. I shall always regret I had chicken pox. I only kissed the child but once."

"Well, you're going to Europe now," Slack explained.

The expression on Alyce's face was a picture? She couldn't comprehend this turn of events at all. "Slack, you're not making sense." She practically shook with frustration. "You two are impossible !"

Arnold grabbed her again and hugged her, despite her protests and wriggling, then just as quickly released her. "Alyce, we're going to London. I've always promised that one day I'd take you, well, now I am. Ain't you pleased? Don't look so sad, you've always wanted to go, I know it."

"London? But..." Really, this was impossible. "But what about fetching Ralston's diamonds? He's paid you. He'll be expecting you to return with more."

"And so we will, Alyce, my darlin'. And so we will."

Alyce blinked as it all filtered through to her confused brain. She stared at Slack a while, then Arnold. "You mean...you are going to..."

"There's no trickery, Alyce well, not really," Arnold tried to explain. "We sold Ralston some diamonds, and we mean to sell him some more. That's all, that's business."

"But the diamond field. The General proved it. He said it was genuine, swore an oath on it."

"And so it is." He leaned forward and lowered his voice to a whisper. "There are genuine diamonds and rubies up there, Alyce, 'cause Slack and me put every last one of them there."

Arnold watched and grinned as Alyce frowned, truly puzzled by this turn of events.

"I just can't believe this," she whispered. "You mean the entire... you deliberately put the diamonds there. It's a salt?"

"Cost us every penny we ever made from selling our gold claims too."

"But that's dishonest," Alyce protested, he heart beating wildly, her breath suddenly constricted. It was dawning on her that her man was nothing more than a criminal and she'd placed so much hope and trust in him too.

Arnold was taken aback. "Why, Alyce, how could you say such a thing about us? Didn't both Ralston and the General declare the diamonds genuine?"

"Well yes..."

"Well, there you are, then. We sold him genuine diamonds, rubies, and sapphires. He got 'em all at a fair price. We made hardly a profit at all."

Alyce was confused now. "You're saying you're not doing anything dishonest?"

Slack smiled. "No more dishonest than the bank's way of refusing to extend a man's credit and taking his claim."

"Put it another way," Arnold explained with some patience. "We're selling Ralston an idea. That idea is that there is this fabulous diamond find up there by Vermillion Creek. The fact is ,the only diamonds there are the ones we bought and put there. The General saw 'em, we ain't selling fakes or nothing, they are the genuine articles. I seen dumb salts before where they put no thought into 'em. Remember that gold salt up by Lucky Boy Pass, Slack? Fool says he's found gold almost ninety percent pure, lying in a hole by a water spring. Well, he'd found gold all right, he'd melted down some gold coins he'd stole from robbing the Wells Fargo stage. Even that would have been all right, but on close inspection of this 'pure" gold, the words US mint were still clearly visible in one part of it. Now, nature's good at making gold, but as yet I never seen her coin it."

Alyce wasn't sure this foolish story justified anything.

"Arnie, what you're doing is against the law. You're saying a thing is one thing when it plainly is the other."

"Alyce, the General confirmed the claim. Who am I to argue with General David Douty Colton?"

Slack suddenly sat back in his seat and waved as a man entered their car, where they'd been alone up until this point.

"Thought I was alone tonight," the stranger stated. "Almost everyone is asleep and the stove's out of wood next car. Mind if I sit a while with you all and get warm?"

Slack made him welcome. "Sit yourself down, stranger."

The stranger didn't sit straight away, though. He smiled at Alyce and glanced around the car as if he was looking for something. "Any of you feel like a song? It's a miserably long journey and I just feels like a turn on the cabinet organ, if you're in a mind to join in."

Alyce pulled a face, Arnold stifled a groan, and Slack tried to look half way enthusiastic. There was no avoiding it however. And so it was, before anyone could do anything to stop it, they were all singing 'Oh Susannah' and 'Clementine' up to all God's hours. All the while Alyce fretted and wrestled with her conscience. She'd had a great shock, and her two companions didn't seem troubled at all.

When a moment came for the stranger to draw breath, Arnold squeezed Alyce's hand and try to reassure her thus; "We'll be in Halifax in five days and London in two weeks after that by steamer. You'll see, Alyce, it'll be the biggest adventure you'll ever have."

Nevertheless, Alyce couldn't help thinking of Arnold and Slack in a totally new light. Somehow they'd gone from being honest prospectors to despera-

135

does in one quick, fatal leap. It was going to take some getting used to. No wonder they'd gone to such trouble to ditch Dutch Pete.

An hour later the stranger moved onto hymns and dirges. Slack called it a night and Arnold soon after. Alyce followed, but it would be a fitful sleep. She had heavy heart and a sudden need for comfort, but there was none.

CHAPTER EIGHT
Misadventures in a Foreign Land

'Rumors abound in San Francisco of an incredible new find. Diamonds, the rumors go, reported to come from sources very high up in financial circles. It is believed that persons still unknown to this party have in their possession a single gem larger than a pigeon's egg, of matchless purity and color worth at a low estimate $500,000. It is strongly fancied that the diamond field is located in south eastern Arizona. The implements used by the discoverers in extracting the diamonds were ordinary jack-knives. If so much wealth can be turned up by such primitive means, what might be accomplished by shovels and pickaxes? Little else is discussed on California street but diamonds and rubies.'
The New York Sun , March 29, 1872

A carriage sped out of a jam at Aldwych and negotiated the even more dense traffic pressing on the Strand. The carriage was distinguished by a bright baronial crest on its crimson doors, but in the rain and mist currently filling the gray skies of London, few carriages were shown off to any distinction. Even the magnificently-groomed horses up front seemed dismal in this cold, unforgiving day. Progress was slow. It seemed as if the entire city had decided to travel toward Charing Cross all at the same time and stood abreast and in line, immobile, yet with deadly purpose.

Asbury Harpending, a tall, well-kept, almost dandified man with a shock of untamed brown hair, was quite a contrast to his carriage companion, Baron Rothschild, The Baron was perhaps carrying more weight than his moderate height called for; nevertheless with his elegantly trimmed whiskers he looked thoroughly   distinguished.

The two men had traveled in from the City for the purposes of a meeting and luncheon. Though hardly equals in the world of finance, Harpending had, in the short time he'd been associated with the City, carved out quite a niche for himself in London. His specialty was floating American mining shares and publishing a financial newspaper, the *Stock Exchange Review*, priced one shilling.

In association with another baron, Baron Grant (with whom he was now currently in dispute), he had floated the successful Mineral Hill mine. In just one day he'd made a profit of £300,000 and that was impressive enough to catch people's attention. Harpending stayed on to float more mines and start up his financial paper. He was in London indefinitely, and if men like Baron Rothschild sought him out, then he was well in indeed.

So why, then, was Asbury Harpending so agitated this mid day? Certainly he was far from calm. The baron was doing his best to placate him, but it was not easy.

"Yes, I too heard of the rumors published in the New York papers, but I put them down to fancy. "

"You see, Baron, that was my reaction too. Then Bill Ralston's cable came, and they still come. Seven cables now in all. Ralston is insistent."

"Yes, I heard about that too. I hear the first cable was quite something."

Harpending opened his portmanteau to reveal its contents to the baron. "Yards, sir, enough bunting for Regent Street. It was alarming. I'm used to Bill's ways Baron, but this they tell me it is the longest cable ever received in London and must have cost him eleven hundred dollars at the very least. Bill never stints when it comes to business."

"And then six more. He must be very convinced these diamonds are real. How can you be so sure, then, that he is wrong?"

Harpending offered the cables to the baron to read for himself. "You read them, Baron, you tell me, sir, am I crazy or is he?"

The baron received the cables in his lap and registered much surprise.

He was not used to such frankness, yet pleased with Harpending's approach. The English never shared their information, and even if they took you into their confidence it was only because they wanted more from you than they could give.

Harpending was doing his level best to dissuade the baron from having anything to do with these diamonds. As the carriage inched forward along the Strand, Rothschild read the cables whilst Harpending stared out at the passers-by scurrying along the muddy, soaking-wet pavements. The shops looked dull, the homes murky, and the theaters cramped. London was much busier than San Francisco, but the stench from the streets was sometimes quite overpowering. He still missed home, no matter how successful he'd become in the city.

Most of his time was filled by his newspaper and his war against Baron Grant and his paid stooge, Sampson, financial editor of *The Times*. The campaign was hard to wage against such stalwart pillars of city society, but

Harpending had paid a Bank of England official £500 to gain sight of Sampson's financial statements. These proved, without doubt, that Sampson was an insider in the infamous Emma mine and had boosted it for his own personal gain, knowing it to be fraudulent. It was hard to stop those who wished to throw away their money on a useless hole in the ground if they wanted to, but no one who read the *Stock Exchange Review* could mistake that newspaper's opinion about it, and only the reckless took no heed.

Now Ralston's cable was about to alter everything. Ralston was more than just a good friend. The two of them had been friends and financial partners for years in numerous ventures. Harpending had even bought Ralston's old house from him. They'd been in the thick of things in San Francisco for the past twenty years more. So it was a real tug o'war for his heart when Ralston summoned him to take part in this great diamond venture.

The baron put the cables to one side without immediate comment. He yawned, then quickly apologized, explaining he always yawned when he was hungry and he'd unaccountably missed breakfast that morning.

"Your wife is well?" he asked Harpending.

"Certainly."

"She likes living in London, does she?"

" To be frank, although we are welcomed in the finest homes here, she misses San Francisco, and her friends. The fine weather, too. But London is the center of the world, I say, and it's from the center that the world is fashioned. Of course you'd say the same for Paris, I should think."

The baron said nothing about Paris. "Yet, you do know American mines, Mr. Harpending. You have worked often with this banker, William Ralston. He is a lion among bankers, no? Tell me, is he likely to make such a fuss over something like this if it weren't at least a possibility? How much does he assess the field to be worth?"

"Fifty million dollars is his conservative estimate, but I have to tell you, Baron, this time I think Ralston's wrong. His ambitions have outgrown even mine. When he decided to build the grandest hotel in the world, right in San Francisco, on my land on Montgomery Street, I had to withdraw and sell out to him and Bill Sharon. Ralston is the most wonderful man in the world, but when I invest it's my money that's on the table, when he invests he's got the richest bank in the West on his side."

"You say he uses the bank's money for his own gain?"

"I would say no such thing, sir. Everything Bill Ralston does is for San Francisco's gain, California second. It is merely that he has endless backing. But I find the cost of the war sometimes outweighs the fruits of victory. That's all. Besides, what have we here? Two miners who claim to have diamonds when not a one has ever been found before? I even seem to recall the name of one of them. Arnold was a gold miner, I believe. He had some crazy notion the

Indians were sitting on a hoard of diamonds somewhere."

"And this is not possible?"

Harpending shrugged. "I can't say, Baron. What isn't credible is that they haven't ever tried to trade them for liquor or guns."

The baron smiled. "I know of this American dislike of the Noble Savage.

"Well, I'm no friend of the Indian, Baron, but them aside, could there really be a place where diamonds could be picked up on the ground and found in anthills?"

The baron pondered this a moment. "Well, America is a very large country Mr.. Harpending, not all of it has yet been discovered. It has furnished the world with many surprises already, why not diamonds as well?"

Harpending had no reply to that. It was true, America was full of surprises, and this had been a complete one to him. He couldn't help having this feeling about the luck of this man Arnold. In Harpending's experience it was a rare man who set out to find something that had never been found and yet come back with it. Almost as if he'd found the Holy Grail itself.

The baron smiled. "You were thinking, Mr.. Harpending?"

Harpending laughed it off and waved a hand to show that his doubts were mere trifles. "I was just thinking of the quest for the Holy Grail, sir."

"They do not have that also, do they?" The baron asked, then laughed, seeing Harpending's confused face. "Diamonds I can trust a man with, Mr. Harpending. A diamond can be proven. It is either glass or diamond, no? Show me a man with the Holy Grail and I will show you a liar. Of that I am certain."

Harpending brightened up now. "Sir, let me attest to the sure fact that Bill Ralston does not make any such claim, though to be honest, I wish he had. At least that I could reject out of hand with no more lost sleep. These diamonds, on the other hand..."

They were pitched forward suddenly and actually began to make some progress toward the vicinity of Simpson's Tavern and Divan.

"My main concern, Baron, is that we Americans have little experience of diamonds. Ralston insists he has a sackful already, but..."

"Then go and see Tiffany. Never waste time, Mr. Harpending. Go and see the best man in New York. Go and see Tiffany."

"It had been my intention to cable San Francisco and tell them the very same thing."

The baron was interested by now. He wanted to know more about these American mines. He liked Harpending; he always took to a man who didn't try to get him to invest, indeed,did his level best to dissuade him from getting involved. "The Emma mine. I hear so much about it from this Baron Gotheimer, the one who calls himself Baron Grant now. Sampson of *The Times* says one thing, the baron another. They tell me you are against it because you weren't offered the mine. Tell me honestly, what is your side of the affair?"

DIAMONDS

Harpending was suddenly thrown back against his seat. A horse reared up, protesting under the whip as it rode alongside them in the road.

The baron uttered an oath. "Really, the traffic is poorly managed in this city. They tell me the average speed now is just eight miles per hour. Even that I think is an exaggeration. If we get to Simpson's at all we shall be fortunate." Then he appeared to calm and re-addressed Harpending. "You were about to say, Mr. Harpending?"

"Oh yes, the Emma mine. Well, Baron, I've got to tell you that far from failing to be offered the mine, I inspected the claim back in I1870. It's up by Salt Lake City as you might know, about forty miles east of the city. Sam Brannan was the gold miner who owned it and he was famous all over those parts for his running battles with Brigham Young's destroying angels, you know, the Mormons, mighty protective and won't flinch from inspiring a bit of terror in the land. The Mormons sent flock after flock after Sam, but he outsmarted them and took a good deal of them down on his own account. But I reckon all this got a bit on his nerves so he wanted to sell...to anyone but a Mormon, y'understand.

"Well, I got word and together with Bill Ralston we took a thirty day option on the mine. They wanted $350,000. I arrived there unannounced, presented my credentials to the mine superintendent and he does the decent thing and shows me around.

"Got to tell you Baron, it sure looked good, but once you stepped away from it and really considered it, you could see why Sam Brannan stopped digging when he did. The damn thing was a kidney, it was going to pinch out at anytime. It was just a shell, Baron, but with just enough high-grade ore to fool a tenderfoot. But not me, sir, not me. I turned it down flat.

"So when it's unloaded on the London stock market, sir, for nothing less than two million pounds, it's my duty to warn men of their folly. It's mines like the Emma that ruin the market for everyone."

The baron regarded Harpending for what seemed a long time, then smiled. "I like you, Mr. Harpending. You're direct, no charades like the others. I believe you. It is unfortunate that Sampson is a fool and Baron Grant an even bigger one. You can rest assured they won't have my money and I will advise my associates likewise. Those bounders will not have the opportunity twice."

The carriage put in a spurt for the last twenty yards and at last pulled up outside Simpson's Tavern.

By chance another of the dining companions was about to enter the building and so ensued the usual set of introductions, hand-shaking, and trivial words before they were out of the drizzle and up the stairs to the restaurant.

"I have quite an appetite," the baron declared at the top of the stairs.

"Me too," admitted Alfred Rubery, their new dining companion

Alfred Rubery was a long time friend of Harpendings. They'd had high

141

times together in San Francisco and the mining camps . They had met when the influential Englishman had been 'experiencing' American life back in '62. Rubery, the nephew of the statesman John Bright, had somehow gotten himself involved with a duel up on Comstock with a man called Tomkins that July. Rubery asked Harpending to be his second, but had Harpending advised a retraction, and an early death had been averted.

Somehow Harpending had ended up in jail over his southern sympathies. It was only when fleeing justice with Rubery that they'd come across gold in the hills up by Havilah and Clear Creek. It had been the start of Harpending's first fortune. Though he'd lost touch with Rubery until this visit to London, they'd met up again as old friends, and the alliance was as thick as ever. Now there was talk of Rubery getting involved with this diamond game. It turned out he was sick and bored of London society and needed fresh fields. He, like the baron, would be urging the man to speed back and find out first-hand what was really happening with these gemstones. And Rubery fully intended to go along.

And so it was the three of them swept into Simpson's , discharged their coats, and were quickly escorted to a bright window table in the very busy room. The baron instinctively preferred the window table on account of the draft. London dining rooms were always so smoky and stuffy, and to his way of thinking a good lunch needed air to be fully appreciated. For that reason Harpending rather missed the coat he'd given up, but no matter, dining with the baron was an event in itself.

Heads turned when Baron Rothschild entered the room. It was important to see who was with the great man, and there was always the slim hope he would recognize your face and bestow a grim smile your way, thus propelling one up the social ladder (though some mean-spirited types would hold that only the London branch of the Rothschild family were of real consequence). It could be safely stated, however, that no Rothschild was without prestige.

If the room was suddenly full of sycophants, there were at least two major exceptions; two well-dressed gentlemen escorting a young, lavishly-dressed lady seated between them. The men had unaccountably placed their menus right up to their faces when the baron had entered the room and slunk deep into their chairs as he'd swept past with his companions.

If eyes had not been on the baron, questions would surely been asked about the strange behaviour of the two men.

"What has got into you both now?" Alyce demanded to know. "You tell me to behave like a lady and there's you lollygagging under the table like you had been drinking all day. Slack, Arnie, what's going on?"

Arnold gave her such a look she knew she had to keep her mouth shut, but she didn't understand. She'd been thoroughly enjoying her meal up until that moment. God knows it had been hard enough to find a dining room that would admit women.

"It is him, I tell you," Arnold whispered to Slack, his face completely hidden by the menus. "What the hell is Asbury Harpending doing in London today, this year of all years? We are undone, Slack, I tell you, we are undone. One look at us and he'll twig. He has to."

Alyce suddenly understood and naturally she grew quite agitated. She now had fears that the police would be called for, followed by public humiliation.

Slack looked across the room and made a positive identification of Harpending and one of the other two. He groaned. All was lost now, surely.

"Can we run out?"

"No, call too much attention."

"Can't we bluff it? After all he's never seen us in suits."

"You prepared to take the chance? Soon as we open our mouths we are done for, Slack. You cain't hide being from Kentucky. Oh, misery."

Alyce was distinctly pale now. She spoke through clenched teeth. "You said there was no possibility of anyone ever knowing us. You said it was impossible."

Arnold was trying hard to think. To stand up and walk out was the obvious thing, but if Harpending even glanced their way the whole thing was bust. Arnold was no Greek god, but his face was memorable enough. He stayed hidden as he desperately tried to think. He whispered to Slack. "You can git up, he don't know you from Adam."

"What y' mean he don't know me? That there's Alf Rubery. We got into a scrape back in '62, remember? I still bear the scars from his tomfoolery with the 50 caliber Hawkins and that grizzly - remember?"

Arnold groaned. Now he remembered. They knew both Harpending and Rubery, and sure as eggs was eggs, they'd know them. There was no getting out of it.

"You two can't stay down there. Sit up, people are staring."

Arnold and Slack did inch up a little, but their faces remained fixed behind the menus. Slack's heart was pounding. He expected the worst.

"Do something," Arnold implored Alyce.

"Yeah , distract them," Slack urged her. "You always said you were a good actress."

"There's a diamond on your finger if you get us out of this one," Arnold told her, "but do it quick."

Alyce had already made a plan. "Go, soon as they're distracted."

Alyce stood up from the table and began to walk away from it toward the windows. She held a hand to her head and clutched at her dress collar.

"I must have air," she cried in her best English accent. "Please open a window, I must have air."

Harpending, ever the gentleman, was up in a trice. Baron Rothschild sat with his mouth agape as this woman bore down on them, clutching her throat.

"I must have air," Alyce cried out again, before neatly turning and falling into a dead faint, stopped only from hitting the floor by Asbury Harpending's deceptively strong arms.

At first Arnold and Slack were transfixed by Alyce's performance, but sanity was restored by the second time she called out, and they were out of the room at the very moment she fell into Harpending's arms.

They found Mr.. Cuthie at the entrance greeting new customers, but it didn't prevent Slack from dragging him to one side and pressing five guineas into his hands and instructing him to pay for the lady's cab. The man had no chance to protest. They were out of there, down the stairs and vanishing into the crowds before anyone could blink.

"I'm going to buy what we need. You head west, Slack, in case we're followed. Meet you at Thavies Inn at five. Find out what time the next steamer leaves."

Slack walked away without a word, melting into the crowd. He for one couldn't believe their ill luck. They'd been in London just three days and for them to meet up with the only two men who could possibly identify them; well, it was fate, a sign. They should have quit when Ralston had paid them the $125,000. He wasn't even sure if they had got out of the situation successfully or not. What had happened to Alyce? Would they force her to tell who her dining companions were? Surely not, they were civilized men, but even if they suspected the tiniest bit they would surely warn Ralston. He walked on, not daring to look back in case he really was being followed.

Alyce was making a good job of it. Anyone could pretend to faint. Just about anyone could fake an English accent. But could just anyone cry on call and beg Baron Rothschild for forgiveness for spoiling a lunch he had not yet even had a chance to order?

She sat in a chair at their table and dabbed a delicate handkerchief to her cheeks. She had to agree with the men around the table that it was truly embarrassing and humiliating to be so rudely abandoned by her dining companions. The manager Mr.. Cuthie duly arrived. He could affirm that the two men had paid handsomely for their luncheon and a cab for the lady. He assured the lady that he would make sure she was delivered safely to her home.

"I say, this is quite a mystery, " Rubery declared, "just like a Wilkie Collins, don't you think?" He turned to Alyce. "How well did you know the men, my dear? I didn't catch their faces, but if you know their names I'll make sure the bounders are black-balled from every club and eating establishment in town. To abandon such a handsome woman as yourself is plain criminal. I for one would like to see them horse-whipped. What say you, Baron?"

"Horsewhipped is fair," he answered. "My dear, you must stay to dine with us. Tell us your name, let us know what we can do to help "

Alyce did her best to brighten up a little. "You're too kind, sirs. I hardly knew the gentlemen at all, you see. I was to be considered for the post of governess to one of the gentleman's children. He lives abroad you see and he required me to live in his home in the Cape. You know the Cape, sirs?"

"I hear it is as fair as paradise itself, but I've sailed to a few paradises in my time, " Rubery told her. "Not met one that lived up to it yet. You are well out of it, my good lady. Good governesses are hard to find why, families are crying out for such women as yourself to tend their offspring. You stay in England, my dear."

Alyce suddenly paled again. "Gentlemen, I've caused such a fuss, I must leave you. I still need air...." and to emphasize it, she rolled her eyes. The baron had quite enough by now and signaled to Harpending to do something.

"I will get a cab for you, my dear," Harpending told her, quickly leaving the table. This event had quite spoiled his lunch with the baron, and the sooner she was gone, the sooner they could get back to the business of diamonds.

Alyce soon found herself escorted from the tavern by the strong arms of Rubery and Harpending, despite her protests that she could walk it.

"I can walk, sirs, truly I can."

"No, no, we will see you down. Simpson's is a fine place, but you're quite right, there really isn't enough air, wouldn't you agree Alfie?"

"Absolutely, Asbury, absolutely. There is never enough air in London eating establishments." It was difficult to tell whether he was making a joke at Alyce's expense or not, she didn't care one way or another.

She got more advice from them as they bundled her into a cab.

"Get some rest, " Harpending told her , "and lots of hot tea. Believe me, it's best."

"And choose your future employers more carefully," Rubery advised her in parting.

"I will, sir, I most truly will."

As Alyce's cab drew away from the curb she looked back to see the two men staring after her, a look of great concern on their faces. They were really quite sweet. She felt a pang of guilt that Arnold and Slack were setting out to cheat them. But for all that, there was the business of the diamond ring to consider. She'd truly earned that diamond, but could she accept it without it being offered in marriage?

To have happiness, travel, a man to call her own (even if he was a villain) was one thing, but without marriage she'd have to remain childless forever, and it was already getting so late.

"Where to, miss?" The cabbie called down from his perch.

Alyce suddenly had a brilliant idea: she would visit a place she'd read about in the London Magazine. Her own little adventure.

"Chelsea. Ponds Yard if you will. But set me down by the river before it."

"Lor missy, you not about to throw yourself in the river, are yer?"

"Do I look that miserable?" Alyce laughed, more with relief at being out of trouble than good humor.

"You looks fine, my missy. I'll 'ave you at Ponds in a jiffy; road'll clear once we pass the 'ouse of Commons."

Alyce wished she could repair her tear-stained face. She longed to walk and see the sights, but she knew it was not proper. Women could walk in San Francisco and no one would think twice about it. Here it was considered scandalous if a woman admitted to possessing legs. And if she had no escort, then the trouble was even worse. Which set her thinking about marriage again. Would being rich make Arnold a settled man who'd want to take a wife and start a family? Perhaps. Either way, it was unsettling. What if this hare-brained diamond swindle failed? What then?

The cab passed great constructions being undertaken at the end of the Strand. She marvelled at how tall and solid these buildings of stone were. A city built to last a thousand years. San Francisco, by contrast, was made of matchsticks. Suddenly she regretted they'd be going back so soon.

Slack decided the best thing to do was walk. It had been his way for many years and he wasn't about to change now. His nerves were all jangled, to be sure, but he felt they'd escaped Simpson's unrecognized. He didn't recall Harpending so well. but Rubery he'd have known from a hundred feet on a moonless night, the neat cut of his greased hair, the long weasel nose and the bright narrow eyes.

"I'm sorry sir, I'm so sorry sir. You weren't looking at all..."

Slack suddenly realized that oblivious to where he was going, he'd walked smack into a pretty young girl selling violets. The violets were ruined, and Slack could see it was entirely his fault. The girl was a beauty and she was on the verge of angry tears. Violets was all she had between her and starvation, by the look of things. She was a mere snip of a girl wearing only a thin cotton smock.

"I'm the one who's sorry, miss. I wasn't looking, you was right about that. I'm right sorry for crushing your flowers. How much do they sell for?"

The girl was puzzled. She had never heard an American accent, nor indeed had she ever heard an apology before. "They be tuppence a bunch, sir, but you can't buy 'em now, they be ruined. I..."

Slack smiled. "How much the lot, miss. Tell me, how much the lot? How many bunches you got?"

The girl stared at him, his strange, dark brown weathered tan, like a fisherman's, only deeper. She stooped to retrieve the fallen flowers, but Slack kicked them into the gutter.

"Never mind them. There's twenty bunches that's forty pennies and at least four shillings. Here's a crown and I'll hear no protests. You're going to show me the finest tea shop in the area, and I'm going to watch you eat until your bones disappear. Right? I'll not take no for an answer. I can see you're half-starved, girl, and I could do with some company. If you don't like the offer you can say so, but you're going to have to accept it all the same. I spoiled your days work, least I can do is make amends."

The girl, whose name turned out to be Kathleen, couldn't believe Slack's generosity. At first she'd thought that because he was a foreigner he'd mistaken her for a scarlet woman, but then, to march her to a tea-shop and watch her eat, well, it was the most strange, most needed, most gentlemanly thing anyone had ever done for her. She was overwhelmed by his generosity, and patience as he listened to her pitiful life story. No one had ever asked her such things before. Slack appeared genuinely concerned for her welfare. He did not know it, but by his act of generosity, he'd won the young girl's heart.

They sat in Larkin's Eel and Pie Shop, and Kathleen ate as Slack drank sour lukewarm coffee and sampled some cake. They made a strange pair, he dressed like a gentleman, she a mere flower girl.

"Does it hurt?" she asked suddenly.

"What? What hurts? Slack asked, puzzled.

"The scar on your neck. It's very deep. Was it an Indian spear that did it?"

"Indians use the bow and arrow. That way they don't need to get close. I'd not be here if it had been an arrow. Nope, it was a bear, Kathleen, and let me tell you, a bear has the most vicious claws you ever did see, dirty too. This here was two years in the healing. I've got others too. T'aint a pretty sight, my body, I can attest to that."

Kathleen blushed. But she was looking at Slack with distinct interest now.

"Eat, young 'un. I'm not quitting you until I'm sure you can't eat no more, and that's a promise."

Kathleen smiled. This was like Christmas and her birthday all rolled into one. She wondered if all Americans were like this man.

"Tell me more about bears and mountains," she urged Slack. "You've seen so much, I don't even know what a mountain looks like."

"Well, I don't know."

"Oh please. I would love to hear about the bear. Was it big?."

He'd been thinking about how he'd met Alfred Rubery anyways and that was a tale worth telling. He smiled and found he was beginning the story.

"There's this fool of a man, an Englishman I have to say, come west to make his fortune digging for gold.

"The man, I'll call him Alfie, had a grizzly cornered, and angry from a shot that had grazed him when his Hawkins had unaccountably misfired. The one

147

thing you don't do to a grizzly is turn your back on them, especially when they're angry.

"Alfie managed to dodge to one side when the bear came through, but who was coming out of a mining shaft at just that time, why me, that's who. The bear didn't care who it killed as long as it killed someone, and it settled for me because I didn't have a gun or knife on me.

The bear caught me full on and that would have been the end of it, but I fell back down the shaft and the bear had no choice but to follow, roaring and hollering in protest.

Just when I was trying to decide whether the bear intended to dig for silver or tear me to shreds, Alfie put his face down the shaft and says. " Here's a knife, you finish him for me."

The knife landed smack across my right arm, landed hard, and it jarred the bone. There was no harm done, but what with the sudden pain, I let out such a yell, that the bear, who'd been trying to locate me suddenly decided to move in for the kill.

"Now, it was dark. Could I find that knife again? I could not. Could I find anything to strike that bear with, other than my bare hands? I could not. We wrestled, we rolled around, and the bear got in two good bites either of which would have killed an ordinary man, but I bit back and tore the bear's left ear off, not that a grizzly has much of an ear, but it certainly changed the balance of things. There was a pause to catch our breath now and growl a little at each other as we crawled to our respective corners."

The girl was looking at him with excitement and horror, living it all. She could see from the way Slack was speaking that he was remembering, not telling it.

"Well the end of the game came pretty unexpectedly. Just at the moment I discovered I was actually sitting on the knife, there was a terrible roaring and shaking and rumbling. Me and the bear heard the word 'Quake' and then, wouldn't you know it, the shaft fell in. The bear and me were practically buried alive in rock and mud, so much so it was hard to tell us apart.

Upstairs Alfie finally picks himself up and lowers a rope and that would have been that, but the bear got to the rope first with his teeth, and with one sharp tug had Alfie down the shaft as well. I had the satisfaction of hearing him holler out a painful yell. "You'd think one of us would have remembered to bring a pack of cards." I remarked, and the bear growled a little in agreement. Rubery got the jitters, he was really afraid of that bear.

"So it went, all three of us had a wasted day clawing ourselves out of that mess, and even then they weren't out until Arnold got back with fresh supplies.

I was out first, sore as any man could be, but I wouldn't let Alfie up until the bear was hauled out. It protested some, and there wasn't a soul who didn't

148

DIAMONDS

want to kill it there and then, but I wouldn't hear of it As soon as the bear could scramble on its own, it was off without a word of thanks, or an attempt to collect its much-missed ear."

Kathleen laughed and clapped her hands. "The bear was saved. I am so glad the bear was saved."

Slack grinned. He'd told a story and made someone happy.

"More, tell me more," Kathleen insisted.

Slack blushed. "First I need fresh hot coffee, not this slop they served me earlier."

Kathleen was up in a trice to organise it. Slack watched her go. His thoughts went back to the bear again. He never did discover how Rubery got out of the shaft, but one thing was for sure, Alfie Rubery would remember him; no one would forget a day like that.

Arnold had more serious business to conduct than entertain flower sellers. Diamonds had to be purchased and the business completed quickly. Harpending's appearance in London had him worried. If word got out that an American had been out and about purchasing diamonds,... well, it wouldn't take a genius to connect this with the recent discoveries in San Francisco. It was bad enough that Harpending was involved and that news had leaked to the newspapers about a diamond find. Soon there would be no chance to move at all without everyone getting suspicious.

Holland had provided them with quite a haul of small stones, rubies, and sapphires, but these were of poor quality. They'd spent ten thousand dollars on what was really just icing on the cake. It didn't matter if they were practically worthless, what mattered was there being enough quality stones sprinkled over the claim to convince any further investigations. That there would be further investigations Arnold had no doubt. For the scheme to work, there had to be enough stones out there to keep them guessing for some time yet. The problem in Amsterdam had been obtaining quality stones. They had them aplenty, but either wouldn't sell 'em, or, else set a price so high it was plain dishonest. He hadn't wanted to buy in London at all this trip, not with news being in the New York papers, but as yet the London *Times* hadn't picked up on the story. There was word out about a new discovery of diamonds, that much he knew, for he'd heard it himself from a banker when they'd changed American gold for British banknotes. So it was important to complete business quickly. Trouble was, no matter how hard he disguised himself, there was no hiding his American accent. Certainly he couldn't go to the place he'd bought from before. His only worry was in Harpending asking questions of the diamond sellers. If just one said an American had been in to buy he'd cable Ralston immediately,

Still, it was no use placing obstacles across the tracks before it was time.

DIAMONDS

Best to get on with the business and hope luck was still on their side. Alyce had done a good job in the tavern. She was a woman in a million. He'd make sure he picked out a particularly fine stone for her. Something she could treasure all her life.

Hatton Garden was the traditional area for traders of precious stones and fine objects. Since Kimberley had come on stream with their diamonds, business had really picked up in this area. New shops had opened up and trade was brisk. Few customers would be wanting what Arnold needed, however.

He chose D'Arcy and Neewand, for no reason other than the fact that they looked dingy and the most in need of business. He might have been wrong. It might have been better to do business with establishments that looked prosperous, but he figured that they'd probably have better memories than D'Arcy. It was hard to judge on a building.

For his buying he'd made a special stop before hand and bought an overcoat as his disguise. He wanted to look as much like an Englishman as possible, and it was all damn uncomfortable. To look at him on the street, no one would have been able to pick him out from another and that was just the way he wanted it to be. To this he added spectacles, thin wire framed with large thick lenses. He couldn't see a blessed thing with them but no matter, he only intended to wear them for effect when he entered and left the shop.

He entered the premises of D'Arcy and Neewand with sweating palms, his fingers crossed and his wallet tight. They'd not get much of a price out of him, of that he was sure, at least.

It was Neewand who dealt with him. Arnold thought he might be dutch or German. But he looked keen to do business.

"Goed daag, manherren, good afternoon."

"I represent Franklin and Shuster sir. We're about to go into business making rings and charms for the catalogue trade. You might have heard of *Sears* company? Buying all done by catalogue in America. It was Mr. Franklin's idea that we get into the jewelry business. Bracelets, rings, all kinds of fancy stuff. Keeping costs low and prices moderate, we can open a whole new line of customers to fine jewels, sir. Now what do you think of that?" Arnold thought his intentions sounded plausible enough.

Neewand thought it was a mighty fine idea. Such a deal would be just what he needed. Business wasn't good. Since diamonds had been found in Africa the market was flooded with gems of indifferent quality. Fine stones sold easily enough, but few wanted the Indian stones anymore, they all insisted it should be the Kimberley stones, of the very best quality. Now he'd heard rumors of a big American find of diamonds and the whole market could collapse at anytime.

"I'm looking for several thousand stones, more if you have 'em. No quartz mind, I know my diamonds. I want enough to make the bracelets sparkle, but

150

not enough to make 'em too precious, if you get my drift."

Mr. Neewand understood. "Small, good and clear, ja? I understand."

"Exactly so. But that's not all. I want sapphires and rubies, too, all as nature delivered 'em. Now, Mr. Neewand, I want your best prices, 'cause you won't get another customer like me again, and if you do us proud at a keen price today you'll get an order like this twice a year, spring and autumn. Now what do you think about that?"

Mr. Neewand fairly shook with delight "It'll be difficult to get it all together..."

Arnold cut him off. "If it's too big an order, I can try across the road."

"No, no, sir, we can do it. But I must have time. I could possibly do this for you by Friday."

Arnold shook his head. "It's today or not at all. I'm catching the steamer tomorrow. My order isn't finished yet either. I want ten really fine uncut diamonds, ten karats or more, impressive stuff. About this size. " Arnold indicated something like a pigeon egg. "Not only that, I need about twenty rubies of similar quality and the very best fifteen sapphires you can find. Keenest prices mind. The entire order uncut and unpolished. We've got our own boys to do all that. And before you get imaginative, remember, if I don't like 'em or your price, I'm taking the steamer to Amsterdam before I return to New York. I'm sure they're just as keen to sell to me as yourself. This is cash business, o'course."

Mr. Neewand couln't believe his luck. He wasn't about to let Arnold escape. It would be difficult, but he could put this deal together . "I will have your order together by the close of business today, sir. May I enquire your name?"

"Greeley, sir. Ask anyone in New York, most folks have heard the name.

Indeed, Mr. Neewand did seem to have heard of a Greeley, but he couldn't recall what or, why.

"One final thing, Mr. Neewand. There's a young lady...I've promised her a diamond ring. Nothing too special, mind. I can get it set, but I need just one stone, fine cut, a good sparkle, a modest size, I don't want her to get too excited."

Mr. Neewand began to smile. "I have the very thing, Mr. Greeley. A gentleman who shall remain nameless, but highly respected and much admired in the political world, has just broken off an engagement. I have the stone he was due to collect. Arrived from Kimberley just a month ago and it's quite a specimen. Small, a particularly fine ice-blue diamond, it's like no other cut I've seen. It's on sale for three hundred guineas, but seeing as you're trade sir, I'd consider it an honor to sell it to you for two hundred guineas."

"Two hundred guineas?" It seemed a bit steep to Arnold. "Make it pounds, not guineas and it's a deal if I like it. Is it here now?"

DIAMONDS

Mr. Neewand put up his hands. "Pounds it is, you are the customer, sir.." Arnold was looking into a box containing what seemed to be diamonds as small as pinheads. "And these?"

"Nothing, pinheads. Of no value. No use as a gemstone, sir, but they're just as hard as your usual diamond."

"You got a price on these?"

Mr. Neewand looked surprised. "These sir? If you want them, they are yours. I have plenty more."

"You give me all you've got, Mr. Neewand, and mind you don't mix 'em. I've an idea for 'em, but I'd hate to chuck out the wrong ones by mistake. You got an idea at what we're looking at here? I mean a price. The diamond for my lady and all the rest of the business. We're talking wholesale sale here, you understand."

Mr. Neewand had no idea. No one had ever asked for such quantities before. He'd have to buy in from all over the street, but he knew his business and he calculated he could make a profit at five thousand guineas. If this was to be repeated twice yearly, why he'd be a rich man inside two years.

"Five thousand guineas, sir."

Arnold frowned. "I don't like this guineas business, where I come from a dollar is a dollar, not a dollar twenty-five. Talk pounds to me, Mr. Neewand. If I don't like what I see, you can expect me to balk at the price. You'll find I'm a tough man to deal with and I hate a cheat. The best you can do for me in pounds and we will do business for years. So don't cheat me now, eh?"

Mr. Neewand expressed a deep, anguished cry. " I would rather cheat my dear mother, may God rest her soul. You will have the best I can produce at your price, Mr. Greeley, I will personally guarantee the quality of the particular diamonds and rubies and sapphires you want. In fact, I will throw in the Jasset ruby as well. It came from India three years ago and I never found a buyer for it on account of its unusual shape and size. The lapidary refused to cut such a stone. It's flawed, but I assure you sir, if you could find a lapidary of iron nerve and good enterprise, he could fashion the stone into something beautiful.

"It's a pigeon-blood red, sir, and that's a sign of rare quality, believe me."

For some reason Arnold believed him. He congratulated himself on choosing the right diamond trader. "I'll be back by six to collect."

"At six it would be perfect for me, Mr. Greeley. You will have some assistance, sir? I hope so. You will be carrying a valuable load."

"I intend to bring my associates. Never fear sir. They rob Greeley, they take on the might of the United States itself."

Mr. Neewand smiled. "Then it will be a battle worth seeing."

"Aye, that's true." Arnold admitted, and then he turned on his heel, and left the establishment. It was raining, but let it rain, soon they'd be on their way

DIAMONDS

again. Mr. Neewand had just what he wanted, assuming his word was good. Five thousand was a lot of money and he fully intended to beat him down some from that, but if he got what he asked for, then together with what they had from Amsterdam, it would be quite a haul. Ralston would be overwhelmed, of that he was sure. Five thousand guineas was almost twenty-five thousand U.S. dollars, he'd beat him down to four and a half thousand at six, but together with Amsterdam and their first trip well, that was almost sixty thousand dollars they'd spent on this business alone. Not counting the journeys, hotels, the time and planning gone into it all. Well, you didn't catch fish without bait , and you didn't make money without money, so they say.

He walked along the road toward a mess of buildings where there was much activity. He recognized its purpose immediately. Here the next day's paper was being got ready for printing. All it waited for was the latest dispatches from all around the country.

He smiled as he walked by the Standard building . How they'd love to know that the world's greatest hoaxer was killing time outside their very own doors. Slack would be joining him at Thavies Inn at five. Time enough to fill him in on the story, get him a hat and scarf so no one would see his scars. What a fine tale he'd be able to tell his grandchildren. Dodging barons in London and grizzlies in the Rockies. He was smiling as he strolled now.

He noticed a shipping office next to a coffee house and considered London was always so practical. In this small area he could purchase diamonds, a meal or coffee, arrange shipping, and read the very latest news. London was such a hive of activity, it was hard to believe that anyone could be poor or without work in such a place. Yet it was the one thing he'd noticed above all others: the many thousands of menfolk and women who were living dirt poor and reduced to begging. He came to the conclusion that there were too many without any spirit of enterprise. They should get out in the world like he had. Anyone could make a fortune if they set their mind to it.

He entered the coffee house in a self-righteous mood, not an uncommon feeling for a man expecting to garner a fortune.

CHAPTER NINE
Where are They?

Asbury Harpending made a decision and sent a cable to San Francisco care of W. C. RALSTON. Bank of California.

Am persuaded you do need me after all. Stop. Will catch the Cunard steamer Wednesday April 7. Stop. Are you aware of rumours already circulating? Stop. Are your rights secured? Stop. Suggest Tiffany in New York should see the items before any major investment is agreed. Stop. Arrive San Francisco May 2. Stop.
Asbury Harpending.

Alfie Rubery had argued him into it that same afternoon.

"It's like this, Asbury. You can't make a proper decision either way without seeing the diamonds and the diamond field for yourself. Your business here can survive without you for two months, even three, and there's everything to gain if it all bears fruit.

"Listen, you can leave the moment you decide you don't like what you see. We could go, make a judgment, and return as fast as we came, if you like. But I tell you, I'm game to get out of London. It's too soon for me to abandon a life of adventure, and this smacks of treasure trails. What do you say, or will you stick to soft living now?"

Harpending had had no choice but to say yes. He placed his business affairs in the hands of a trusted lawyer, ordered his wife to pack, and booked the Cunard steamer. Harpending was nothing if not a man of decision. Once a decision was taken, he saw no reason to delay. Delay bred doubts, and doubts were the enemy of enterprise.

"Drink on it," Rubery had suggested, producing a bottle of champagne.

"Yes, champagne. I need something to steady my nerves." He smiled, thinking of San Francisco and the diamonds. "If there really are diamonds, Alfie, you may never have to work again."

Rubery laughed at that as he struggled with the champagne cork.

"You forget, I never did get in a full day's work, Asbury."

Harpending didn't feel inclined to smile at that remark. "Well, then, you shall work passage on the steamer. You shall learn all you can about gem stones, Alfie. We both shall. I intend we shall be experts from the day we arrive, and old Bill Ralston will be amazed."

"Capital idea, Asbury. Capital. I never did find a successful way to pass the time on board a ship. If we know all there is to know, then no one will water our whiskey, eh?"

"Right. It's knowledge that makes a man wealthy, Alfie, not imagination and fantasy."

"I'll drink to that, old bean."

Alyce wasn't happy. You could tell by the way she sat and angrily brushed her hair. She didn't know why she let herself get this way. Happy one moment, all awash with self-pity the next. It was so hard to know what was right or wrong.

She regretted having to turn down Arnold's beautiful diamond. She hadn't really thought he'd buy it, and it must have hurt him she'd said no because he'd been promising her diamonds since the first day they'd met. But she'd told him flat: if he was to offer her a ring, it had better be when he was thinking about marriage and all the normal things a man and woman did to make themselves happy and contented. Fact was, she couldn't take the diamond, although she wanted to very badly. It was a terrible dilemma.

On top of all this she'd been crushed to discover they were having to leave England the very next day. She understood why. After the fracas with Harpending, they certainly couldn't risk being in London any longer. But having only just got here, it was so disappointing to have to go home again. She'd barely seen a thing. She felt cheated by it all. To come so far and not even spend a week.

Arnold didn't seem to mind, but she knew Slack didn't feel like going either. He'd come in a very happy man that evening and she'd seen him happy that way only once before, when he'd been smitten by some showgirl. He said nothing.

Arnold didn't seem to resent Alyce's attitude to the diamond ring so much. In fact, he tossed it to Slack and told him it was time he found himself a woman of his own. He wasn't about to marry Alyce, and that was it. He'd done right by her; the ring was worth a good price and he'd bothered to get it. He felt he'd done enough. If she wanted what he couldn't and wouldn't give, then all right; he wasn't about to dash his head against a wall. They were still together. She'd be a fool to leave him and she knew it.

155

That was when Alyce pulled her surprise. She'd got up and from behind the chair produced a small oil painting and unfurled it. It was for Slack. It was worth it to Alyce just to see the expression on his astonished face.

Slack stared at it for a while. He just didn't know what to say. No one had ever given him anything before, still less an oil painting. Heck, he didn't even own a wall to hang it on.

"But why? Why give me this, Alyce? And why this woman lying in a ditch?"

"That's no woman in a ditch, John Slack. You are so ignorant. That there is Ophelia. She's drowned herself because Hamlet treated her so bad. Not only that, he killed her father Polonius. It's a very tragic tale. This is a copy of a work by John Everett Millais."

Arnold laughed. "Slack, you don't know anything that isn't in the newspapers. That's Shakespeare, Slack. The Theater. This is London, where they used to put on all his shows."

Slack stared at his "woman in a ditch" a while and seemed to take a little more pleasure in it now. "Well, it were a waste, she was a bonny creature wasn't she now?"

Arnold smiled. "Now he gets it."

"Maybe I does, but exactly why do I get this picture, Alyce? You never bought me nothing before."

"What day is it, John Slack? Tell me, doesn't this day mean anything to you? Can it be you've forgotten your birthday? Your own birthday "

Slack fell silent. His birthday. He'd not only clean forgotten it, the very last time he'd celebrated it was why, almost twenty years past. He hadn't realized that anyone aside from his long departed mother had known he had a birthday. He just didn't know what to say. Luckily, Arnold did.

"Well now, we have to dine out with the best wine and do some dancing. We have to celebrate. Slack, you old dog, you keep your secrets too tight. What about that girl you was talking about? Don't you think you could find her and we make it a foursome? Hell, it's our last night in London and I'm not planning on ever returning. We have to dance and we've got to eat. Slack what about it, where's that girl?"

Alyce was intrigued. "Slack has met a girl?"

Slack looked embarassed now. "That's all she is," he said. "it uh .. she's just a girl, she sells flowers. I bought her lunch, that's all."

"Find her, get her to join us," Alyce told him. "Slack, we have to celebrate."

Slack shrugged. "I don't know where she lives. I'll never see her again." He looked at his painting again. "Alyce, I got to thank you for this, but it's going to hang on your wall. You'll have to keep it for me."

"You forget you're going to be rich, John Slack," she reminded him. "I

DIAMONDS

expect you'll be living up on Nob Hill."

"We won't be living in California, Alyce. Get lynched if I do after this."

Alyce suddenly realized that that was so. "Why, of course. You'll both leave."

"You too, Alyce." Arnold said to her. "Harpending knows you now. You can't live out there. Not once we have made our sale. I've got to be savvy. Got to be scarce. You'll be with me, Alyce. I promised, and it's tough you don't want my ring, but you're with me good or bad now."

Alyce suddenly felt unwell. She'd never thought it through like this. She was trapped with Arnold now. What a fool she had been for not accepting his ring. Lord, she'd never thought it through. She was in with them whether she liked it or not. She'd have to sell her home.

Slack set his painting down with great care and announced he would take a bath. There were no end to shocks this evening. It turned out he always took a bath on his birthday, or every twenty years, whenever he actually remembered.

"You take a bath, Slack, and I'll fix you up with a lady for the night. Alyce, put a smile on your pretty face, tonight we celebrate."

"No, no.." Slack protested. "I don't need any woman. I ..."

Arnold shook his head and stood up, placing a hand on Slack's arm.

"Slack, you're my best pal. If a man can't have a good time on his birthday, when can he? You leave it to me and Alyce. You'll see. We'll have a grand old time, you'll not forget your birthday again."

"That's what I'm worried about." He picked up his painting again and rolled it up tight, secretly pleased to have gotten the picture, even if he didn't know quite what to do with it.

Alyce smiled again. "Don't worry, John, I'll keep Arnie on reins. And it would be a fine thing if there was another woman at the table."

Slack turned and walked towards the door. He stood there a moment, realising that it was so long since he'd actually ordered a bath, he wasn't even sure how to order up hot water. He turned back and walked up to Alyce, placing a kiss on her left cheek. "Al, I truly like what you gone and done. I always wanted a picture. I truly did. Never admitted it, but it's a fact I always wanted one."

Alyce was touched. Slack had never kissed her before, nor shovn so much emotion. "It was the best I could do, John. It's from a studio in Chelsea. I read about it in a journal. The artist is as poor as a rat, his wife begged me to buy and I just knew that that girl in the painting was for you. "

Slack just nodded. He'd said enough; anything more would be embarrassing. He quitted the room on his quest for a bath, carrying the birthday picture under his arm. He'd have to have his own place now. Alyce was right. Time he got a home together. Somewhere in the mountains, perhaps, with a clear view of the trees. Sonora came to mind...no, no...Monterey, good fishing in the bay.

157

Now there was a place to live in peace. No one would bother you there. Sort of place to have a good woman live with you and help raise strong children. It was all a fantasy of course; he knew he wouldn't be able to live within five hundred miles of California once Ralston paid them out.

Arnold sighed, then offered a quick smile to Alyce. "Buying him pictures,Alyce? What you trying to do, civilize him? Heck, soon you'll have him living in a little white house with a picket fence and as tame as a tabby cat."

"I kind of think you overestimate the power of art, Philip Arnold. I just wanted to give him something he couldn't eat or drink, that's all. And..." Alyce put down her brush and stepped over to Arnold, slipping an arm around his waist, pulling him close to her. "Arnie, I want you to know I appreciated that diamond you bought. I never thought you'd do it. I really appreciate it, I truly do. It was pretty, but don't be angry with me for turning it down."

"It's gone now, Alyce. I knows your reasons and I'm not angry. But I won't talk about the other. Now get yourself dressed; we've got some celebrating to do. It's going to be a long trip back, and there will be precious little to do aboard ship."

"You said you'd arranged shipping? It won't be rough seas I hope."

"Slack found a Cunard steamer leaving Liverpool tomorrow, bound for Boston, but we can't take the chance on that. It's going to be full and we just can't run the same risks as today. I've found us a fast sailing clipper leaving Tilbury at high-tide tomorrow. She's bound for Baltimore carrying new machinery for some cotton mills. Captain was in a coffee house earlier and he says he's running out of Tilbury a day early 'cause word's got out about these machines, and the cotton companies here don't want Baltimore to have them."

Alyce didn't like the sound of this. "A clipper? A sailing ship?"

"Now, don't gripe, Alyce. I've got the cabin right next to the Captain and he's a good fellow. A Cornishman named Pollard. He's bent on making the journey as fast as he can on account of a bonus for fast delivery. The machinery is steam driven he says and can double the capacity of the cotton mills they're destined for. You can be sure England doesn't want them to go. That's why the shipment was switched to Tilbury to fox any spies."

"Cotton machines are secret?" Alyce doubted this story and figured it for one of Arnold's embellishments.

"Birmingham makes a living selling cotton cloth. They'd burn the ship if they knew an American mill was getting faster looms than British mills, Alyce. We got best fare, and what is more his wife is traveling too, so you'll have good company."

"Hmm, I suppose sail is healthier than steam." Alyce stated unenthusiastically.

"No slower. Captain swears he can do the journey in fifteen days, better if there's a favorable wind."

"But didn't you want to go in by Halifax?"

Baltimore is just as good. We can make the train to St. Louis and go from there to Omaha. You will have to travel back alone from Rawlins Springs, since Slack and me will be heading back up to Vermillion Creek."

Alyce frowned. "You never said anything about the diamonds."

"No I didn't. Don't even like to discuss 'em really These walls are mighty thin."

"You've got 'em in the safe, haven't you?"

Arnold showed some surprise. "Lord no, woman. What if some curious fellow in this hotel takes a look? You can't trust anyone. Got 'em safely hid in here. A thief would have to tarry a good long while in here before he found 'em. Slack's got the others in his room. Got to keep the bundles apart. I tell you, Alyce, that Dutchman did us proud. Personally I think he robbed himself to get our business. Straight-arrow deal I can tell you. The stones are better than Ralston deserves. I didn't have the heart to bargain the price down. He's been so keen to get my business it's almost a shame I'm not running a catalogue business. You should see the ruby he sold me. Like something out of the crown jewels. Or would be, if it was cut and polished some. The sapphires were quite brilliant; didn't know they could be so fine. I tell you it grieves me that I have to turn them over to Ralston, but they'll boost the price he'll give me for certain." He smiled. "He'll think he's got the rights to King Solomon's Mines. I'd like to be watching their faces when they see what they're getting."

Alyce was confused now. "Aren't you going to deliver them yourself?"

"I tell you, Alyce, when I cable 'em that we are on our way, which I'll do from Reno, then if they don't come at least halfway to meet us, I'll assume the game's gone cold. We've got to keep 'em keen, Alyce. That's how we'll land 'em."

"Assuming they don't find you out."

"And why should they do that, Al? Nothing blinds a man better than greed. Believe-me."

"I'm sure you're right, Arnie." Alyce wondered if the same now applied to him?

"I am, I know I am." He affectionately patted her rump. "Now let's get Slack a real nice birthday surprise. You any idea what kind of woman he'd go for?"

Alyce pretended to be shocked. "You ask me? You're the one who's lived with him longest.

Arnold pulled a face. "There weren't many women up at the mines and we were usually too broke to pay for the crab apples there were. I think that's what drove Slack to newspapers."

Alyce smiled. 'We'll find him someone. My guess is he likes 'em kind of quiet."

"Well, not too quiet. We're supposed to be going out on a celebration, Alyce. Heck, we don't want no damp squib school marm."

"Well, I wasn't going looking for any school marm, was I? Honest, Arnie, you just don't have enough confidence in me. You taking a bath?"

"Another?"

"You ever hear of anyone taking a hot bath on a clipper?"

Arnold shrugged. He had forgotten to ask about the bathing facilities.

"I'll just take a quick one."

"You'll take as long as you need, Mr. Philip Arnold, and you'll wash your hair. They provide the soap, so there's no excuse."

It doesn't take much of an effort to have a good time in a big city when there's no shortage of money. The music hall is great fun for a sing-song and a good laugh, the Oyster bar is good if you like oysters and brown ale, and dancing is delightful if you have survived the oysters.

The partner Alyce had chosen for Slack couldn't have been a bigger surprise. She'd found her at the music hall where they'd all but given up trying to find someone to suit Slack. He'd made it very clear he was resistant to any painted woman. There seemed no possibility of pleasing him until Alyce met up with Jenny Stiles, a dancer, just like herself. In fact, Arnold wasn't sure Alyce had any intention of letting Slack get a word in at all, but she put them together at last and the woman was so charming and friendly that Slack soon acted as if he'd known her all his days.

She was no beauty. Arnold thought her plain, but she had dark, enticing eyes. There wasn't a scrap of paint or powder on her face, and her jet black hair fell straight back like a waterfall and reminded both men of an Indian squaw. Slack liked her enough to allow himself to be talked onto the dance floor of one establishment they'd wandered into for some fresh steamed haddock and Belgian potatoes. It was quite a sight to see how Slack danced, never putting a foot wrong. Neither Arnold nor Alyce could ever remember him learning the waltz.

They sang, they shouted, they got terribly drunk, and they had an excellent time of it, sampling ten or twelve different places. It's probable everyone they met thought them all a roaring nuisance, but Alyce for one was determined to have a good time, even if she lived to regret it. London was so different from San Francisco, there was simply so much to see and do. The dance halls were a thrill, and the London fashions were so different, so lavish, it shrank the pretensions of San Francisco to nothing.

All in all, Alyce regretted deeply that they had to leave for America the next day. There was another disappointment. Alyce and Jenny had spotted a place offering Ambrotypes (ferrotypes) and suddenly they were desperate to have a record of their outing on Slack's birthday. Slack was keen because he had always wanted to know more about photography and the mystery of how light and silver produced these pictures directly onto glass. Of course in Paris they were already printing photographs onto paper, but how long could paper last? Slack sorely wanted a camera. Something to capture the beauty of the Colorado mountains. The owner of this little enterprise could have probably sold one of these cumbersome wooden boxes to Slack too, if Arnold hadn't came to his senses and gotten them away from there and back into a passing cab. He wasn't as drunk as he appeared.

Alyce sulked. "I wanted a picture to remember London by, Arnie. A picture with us all in it."

"You can git pictures taken in America. I'm not providing Ralston with any evidence that we were ever in London. Imagine if it fell into the wrong hands."

Slack knew Arnold was right, but he was as frustrated as the women.

When they were a mile away Arnold took Alyce's hand and pressed it to let her know he felt her disappointment. "Anyway, we couldn't have pictures taken, Al, not with us improperly dressed." He pointed out three top-hatted gentlemen dressed in black silks, staggering across the road, but not yet ready to call it a night. That was the thing about London at night; the men dressed as if they were about to go to their own weddings. Both Arnold and Slack knew that no matter how much money they made from their diamond scheme, they'd never have the nerve or desire to truss themselves up like Englishmen. It fair made one short of breath just to think about those starched white collars.

"I think John Slack would look a real gentleman in a top hat," Alyce remarked; giggling. They all stared at Slack then and burst out laughing. Slack frowned; he was always the butt of their foolish jokes. What was so funny about him wearing a top hat, he should like to know.

The cab came to a halt and the driver banged on the roof. They found themselves outside the Gaiety. It was time to eat and drink again.

Much later than they'd planned they finally returned from their carousing and they probably woke every soul sleeping in the hotel doing it. Slack's woman stuck close. She was no modest lass; besides Arnold had slipped her ten pounds to stay with Slack for the night. In fact, she rather liked Slack. He was shy, despite the drink. She found his conversation interesting, never tiring of his stories about what went on in the mountains and mining camps. She urged him to set it all down on paper, but Slack laughed at the notion. He didn't think people would believe him, and he himself was no longer sure half the things he'd seen had really happened. Jenny stayed with Slack from preference, the ten pounds notwithstanding.

They tumbled to bed and made great efforts to remove Slacks boots and his shirt and just about rolled his trousers down. Slack was clearly the worse for the liquor, but happy with it. He was never one to feel sorry for himself and besides it had been so long that he'd been with a woman he was concentrating his thoughts on the business at hand.

For her part, Jenny Stiles was out of her dress and corsets so fast it showed some professional aptitude in these matters. Slack liked what he saw, not that he saw much, as Jenny quickly extinguished the gas lamps.

Slack would remember little about his lovemaking that night. He was unconscious from the moment of final passion. Jenny was not far behind him and the snoring was so terrible they must have woken many on the same floor.

Arnold and Alyce were no better. How they'd even gotten up the steps to their room was a mystery, and fitting the key into the door was such a palaver that it needed two pairs of hands just to hold it steady, never mind find the hole in the lock.

And so it was all four slept like old logs on the slopes of the Rockies, never to be disturbed.

It was Jenny Stiles who woke first. This was a long standing habit with her, and she much disliked it, waking suddenly a few minutes before daybreak. Her head was thumping, the walls hardly seemed vertical and her thirst was terrible. She had finished the entire contents of the water jug within moments of rising.

It was only then she noticed Slack lying sprawled across the bed, snoring like an old dog with his enormous feet dangling off the bed. The blankets lay strewn on the floor. She smiled as first light revealed his brown torso and his deep angry scars. Had she not been in danger of losing her head from her neck with any sudden movement she would have kissed him. Slack had certainly been an interesting arrangement . If he'd not been leaving so soon she would have happily seen him again at half the price. But not for free, he'd think her cheap.

It was only after she'd dressed and was looking for her reticule that she came across the strange sack under the bed. Slack's coat had fallen to the floor along with everything else, so although she found her reticule under this pile, the sack had her interest. It sat there next to the commode, and she couldn't but be curious about it. Finally she had to crawl under there and feel it. It was so strange to the touch she didn't know what to make of it. Could have been a bag of beans, but the beans felt too hard, too heavy surely. She swished it with her fingers and poked the sack, but she just couldn't guess. Pulling the sack out from under there was not any easier. It weighed a ton. She pulled it, tugged at it and wrenched it out of there, all the while trying to watch Slack's body in case he awoke and noticed what she was doing.

She finally had it in front of her on the floor. It was too heavy to hump up onto a chair and besides, she wanted to stay out of Slack's sight line. The string was tied so tight it was nigh impossible to work loose. Fortunately she

DIAMONDS

located Slack's knife lying beside his canvas bag. A few deft moves and she had the string cut, the bag open and as the light grew stronger in the room she plunged in her hand, and, like Tom Thumb, drew out a ...piece of glass. Curious, she looked at the tiny tear drops in her hand and puzzled over them a moment. If this were a dream it would be a sack of diamonds, but surely if they were diamonds they'd sparkle and ...she looked again, thrusting her hand deeper into the sack and closing her fingers upon larger cold stones near the middle (the bottom was too dense to get through). She drew out what looked to be a ruby, but again it was as if these had been found at the bottom of a muddy well. If it was a ruby, surely it would shine like it did in the fairy tales? With her last dip into Slack's tarnished treasure trove, Jenny came up with about half a dozen stones; diamonds, sapphires, a ruby or two. It was just at this moment the sun breached the window sill, and few rays caught the handful of gems. Just one stone, a white, pure-white diamond (she assumed), seemed to catch the light, and even if it wasn't polished, it sent the sunlight dashing off in all directions, like a diamond should. Jenny wasted no time. She wore a diamond ring. It was an inferior thing, a hand-me-down from a great aunt who'd once married well but died of consumption some years past. How much nicer would Slack's new, bigger diamond look in that ring than the small stone she owned now. And if a man owned so many diamonds, would he miss but one? Would he even know? Jenny didn't think of stealing it, she was not a common thief. Exchange is no robbery. He'd never know.

She sat up off the floor momentarily and inspected Slack. He snored on, nothing was about to wake him. She returned to her treasure. She worked that knife on the ring with feverish excitement. Why, the diamond she was taking from Slack had to be worth ten, a hundred times more than the one she was giving him. Perhaps she could sell it, once they'd left England. A diamond could get her on a boat and take her to, oh, anywhere, she could see Africa or India, all the places people talked about all the time.

The knife slipped and sliced her finger. She cried out and bit her lip, but still Slack didn't stir. Now she worked even faster, and at last the diamond came free of the ring. She had to keep sucking her finger to stop the blood, but she'd accomplished what she'd set out to do.

Slack's diamond was hers. He had her great aunt's stone in his sack, and she quickly tied it up again, pushing the sack back under the bed with her feet.

She was up on her feet now. She had to leave before he awoke, or she'd not be able to meet his eye without looking guilty.

She'd gotten herself a valuable diamond, earned herself ten pounds, and had a good time in the bargain. If only all nights were such good business. She'd be sure to look out for more Americans should they come to London.

She wiped the knife on the bedspread, located her cloak and without a backward glance abandoned Slack's life forever.

163

DIAMONDS

Jenny was already on the street that was just waking up to a normal day when she began to regret she'd not taken more. It's always that way. You get away with a small crime, and you immediately wish you'd grabbed more. If she'd taken it all, why Slack could never have found her. She could have gone to Rome or someplace. He'd never find her, never.

As she caught an early omnibus to Camden Town, she thought that Slack would never miss just one diamond. Why, he'd be grateful for Aunt Mabel's little stone - if he knew.

Arnold raised Slack from his deep slumbers. It would be a lie to say Arnold felt his usual buoyant self. It was a lesser man who walked the earth this day, a man who looked at least ten years older. The wine, beer, and oysters had all taken their toll. Oddly enough, Slack awoke untroubled by it all. He put it down to drinking four pints of milk directly after the oysters, a trick taught him in San Francisco by a priest who lived in fear of being poisoned. All considered, he felt pretty good.

"Are the diamonds safe?" Arnold inquired as he flopped down in a chair and clutched his head. He could hardly move two footsteps without wanting to fall down. "The woman's gone. You didn't let her leave with our life savings I hope?"

Arnold was attempting a joke, but all of a sudden Slack paled. Right up until Arnold had mentioned her, he'd forgotten she'd ever existed. In one bound he was off and under the bed, sliding out the all important sack. He was relieved to see it was intact and was about to say so when he noticed a trace of fresh blood on the drawstring.

He examined his own fingers for blood and found none. He knew immediately that his night visitor had taken a look for herself. Now he was afraid to open the sack up in case she'd filled it with sand or gravel and robbed them blind. If she'd just taken one diamond he intended to seek her out and personally drown her in the river. He wasn't about to lose everything because of her, no sir.

"You're awful quiet," Arnold stated quietly behind him, his words laden with doom.

"She's cut the knot. Cut herself in the process. She knows what's in here."

Arnold was beside him in a trice. "You showed her the sack?"

Slack looked at him with some annoyance. "No I damn well didn't. You got me so drunk, I don't recall a thing after the carriage ride. I told you that this was a dumb place to hide them."

"Open it," Arnold insisted, fearing the worst.

"I'm trying, bitch tied it too..." The knot suddenly came free again and

Slack opened up the sack. Both men peered in and frowned.

"Don't look any different," Arnold muttered.

"Well, we didn't exactly count 'em. She could have helped herself to a handful."

Arnold spotted a small sapphire on the wooden floor and examined it. "I'm sure of it. She's been in there, got herself a few. That means half of London will know that there's two Americans in London with a sack of diamonds under their bed." He swore. "Curse her. Now we have to go. We have to be at the ship an hour before high-tide. We'd best be gone from here, in case the wench comes back with some sticky-fingered friends. Damn it, Slack, we was supposed to keeping this secret. Damn the wench. Damn you having a birthday."

Slack suddenly felt an enormous pressure in his bladder. "Got to go, where's the pot?"

"What ,she took that too? Just how many stones did she take?" Arnold exploded. But Slack found the pot and relieved himself with some urgency.

"Listen, You got me drunk. I don't even remember coming back to the hotel. We still got a sack of precious stones, sack's still heavy. I bet she didn't take but one."

Arnold wasn't in any mood to be mollified. "Well I'm going to weigh this sack. Just as well this is sack we intended for the mountains. If she'd gotten the other open I think she might have killed you for the stones in there."

Slack finished up and set the piss-pot down. "Let's weigh the sacks anyways. Best we know what we've got, in case we meet anyone else who might be tempted."

Arnold put a hand to his head and groaned. "My head is spinning and I'm sweating up. God knows what they put in their ale here, but it's powerful stuff. Come one. Let's weigh them, then have breakfast."

Slack looked at Arnold and shook his head. "You need the hair of the dog. A good stiff drink will fix you up, at least get you standing up straight. How's Alyce?"

"She's green."

"If you'd listened to me about the power of milk, you'd be a better man now."

Arnold just closed his eyes and leaned against the wall. What a day to be ill. The curious thing was, when they got the sack down to the weighing machine it was the exact same weight as the night before and there appeared to be no substitutions. Perhaps they'd wrongly maligned the wench. Perhaps she'd just looked out of curiosity and then retied the knot. Was it possible there was such a thing as an honest whore?

165

DIAMONDS

Two hours had passed before Arnold was prepared to stand up and walk a straight line. They urgently had to leave for the river, but one of their party had already decided she'd never be ready to depart.

Alyce wasn't speaking. The very idea of a boat made her heave and her head spin. Had anyone mentioned the word ' Oyster' she would have lost everything she'd ever eaten since the day she'd been born. She only left with the men for Tilbury by steamferry because they forced her. She would have gladly have been left on the pavement or lying in a ready-prepared grave. She knew for sure that she'd not last the simple trip down the river, let alone the clipper journey.

Suffice it to say, despite Alyce parting with much over the side, they reached the clipper on time. The Captain was glad to see them, the monies were paid over and the vessel got away on the high-tide as predicted. By evening they had already rounded Kent and were most assuredly on their way back home. It would be a good day and a half before Arnold and Alyce would surface on deck, ready and able to take the air. Celebrating costs, and not just money.

CHAPTER TEN
Of sharks and men

"They say this is the finest way to travel."

"Who says?"

"Well, Prince Albert, for one. God rest his soul."

"Did he ever cross the Atlantic? Did he ever sit breathing in this infernal sulfurous smoke that pours from the funnel? Did he ever taste the water on a steamer? I very much doubt it. Here a man is forced to drink champagne merely to keep from dying of thirst. Furthermore, they said the Atlantic was as smooth as the old bard's head, and we've spent the entire time being tossed from one wave to another. Whoever sold you these tickets, Asbury Harpending, was a damned liar. This business of the steamer won't catch on y'know, people won't put up with it."

Harpending smiled, pulling his coat closer around him to keep out the biting cold northerly air. There was no wind to speak off, but the sea swell was extreme and if there wasn't an iceberg somewhere close, well, it was remarkable. A man would have to be dressed like a polar bear to survive this cold for long. The sea seemed to thrash the Cunard steamer from all sides, impeding its progress as the paddles thrust against thin air on every other turn.

Harpending was thoroughly sick of the entertainments on board. There was only so much deck quoits, shuffle board, and chess a man could stomach. Even his wife was rapidly running out of gossip to repeat and had begun to look decidedly listless. And as for getting Rubery to read anything at all about diamonds, it was a great struggle. The library was for him some great penance. He would keep on saying that he was a man of action, which for him tended to mean endless promenades around the deck, attempting conversations with the pretty young daughters of fellow passengers or, *risque* flirting with other men's wives. There were far too many meals with people he couldn't stand. The entire journey was a necessary ordeal and more than once when he was trying to get Rubery to read or, his wife to be agreeable, he regretted that there was, as yet no method of flying across the Atlantic. There had been talk of a tunnel,

167

but that was just wild speculation. An airship would be more practical if some method could be found to control it. Otherwise passengers might be purchasing tickets for New York and finding themselves in Rio or even Moscow. However much one disliked ocean travel, at least the ship could be confidently predicted to go where it was bidden.

Harpending was impatient to be in San Francisco now that he had made the decision to return. If there really were diamonds to be had, then there would be much to be done. It could be the greatest float of the century. It would be essential to avoid the chaos that was Kimherley at present. A free-for-all, that was ludicrous in its inefficiency, with every prospector in competition with each other and the lack of control of supply and selling meant that profits were heavily diluted. Ralston, he knew from the cables, had some control, but without total control the scheme would be too big a risk. As it was, each miner employed on the claim would have to surrender every diamond found, or else be searched. If just ten percent of the gems were leaked by individual pirates, that would drive the price of the diamonds down. He'd seen this happen to so many silver and gold mines, it would be best to learn from all the mistakes made before. Planning, execution and management, coupled with a controlled selling policy and all would be successful. It was because of his skills at achieving this objective that Ralston had summoned him. He was keen to get started; provided all was well.

A gong sounded from within.

"Elevenses," Rubery declared, standing up and rubbing his hands with anticipation. "Hot bouillon, Asbury, something to combat this infernal artic air with. Then another game of chess before lunch, eh?"

Harpending repressed any sardonic comment rapidly forming in his mind and rather listlessly followed his companion back inside. Another five days of this. It was just too much to bear. He'd definitely have to look into this airship idea.

The same day, but almost a thousand miles farther south, the clipper Oriella Star lay in the Atlantic waters just five hundred miles short of its destination, becalmed under a cloudless, brilliant, starry sky.

Arnold couldn't have been more agitated by this turn of events. He liked to be a man in control, and to be at the mercy of God's own wind, well, he didn't like it and saw the entire venture slipping away from them. They had been drifting like this for two days, all the while drifting farther south, although the weather by day was pleasant for the time of year. Alyce preferred it after the terrible first two days when she'd not been able to leave the cabin for more than ten minutes at a time without needing to rush back to vomit, yet again. The oysters from London had not settled well on the swelling seas, nor on the

DIAMONDS

choppy channel. Arnold had survived , just, but neither of them had eaten a hlessed thing for the first three days Even hot tea was a torture.

Slack, needless to say was untroubled and what was worse, unconcerned at the lack of progress. In actual fact he was sat at the stern fishing, at this late hour on a chilly evening.He had the stars for company and a home made rod and line hung over the side. He'd told the captain flat that the chow wasn't up to scratch and that he intended to do something about it. He couldn't believe that among the sailors on board, not a one was a fisherman and they'd all rather settle for hardtack than exert themselves to get something fresh and tasty from the sea. The only fresh food available on board were eggs supplied from six chickens kept up on the poop deck. Sailing along at a good lick of almost fifteen knots at full sail, fishing was at best risky.

But now, at midnight, the new moon having already settled in the sky, the fish were unsuspecting. Slack had already landed ten mackerel, and he, for one, wasn't about to turn up his nose at them for being too oily. He liked their flavor, and now he was patiently waiting for larger prey. He'd set his heart on tuna or shark, but it would have to be small he knew he didn't have a hope at landing a larger fish. In fact, if it came to fighting for it, the fish could catch him,because his seat was insecure, one good tug could have him off his perch.

Arnold was out on deck taking a stroll with the captain before they turned in. Arnold was hoping there would be better news about the weather. The captain was not very encouraging, however.

"Had a spell like this in '67. Becalmed for fourteen days. We were fresh out of water and damn near out of food before the doldrums were finished. This could be a repeat. Not a drop of air, the sea's flat as a Dutch pancake, and the bird doesn't look happy."

He pointed to the sleeping gull that had roosted in the rigging for the past three days. It had arrived exhausted, probably blown off course by the gales farther north. It must have sighted the clipper and thanked its stars it made it. Slack had fed it scraps of fish, and it showed no sign of wanting to leave. It was common opinion on board the ship that the bird wouldn't leave them until it smelled land again (or until Slack stopped feeding it.)

"You don't think they could fit a steam engine to these old clippers so they wouldn't be stranded like this?" Arnold asked.

The captain frowned, as if Arnold had insulted him. "Steam will finish off all the clippers in time, Mr. Arnold. Heaven preserve them as they are for now. I'll not have a damned steam engine installed in my ship, *The Star* will be no ocean bastard."

"I've got something, " Slack suddenly called out. "Lend me a hand there. "Slack was on his feet now, trying to keep the line as he wound it around a metal hook embedded in the teak deck "It's bigger than a mackerel and fighting fit."

169

DIAMONDS

"Maybe it's a whale," Arnold declared, laughing a little at Slack's obvious excitement.

The captain looked over the edge and tried to see what was down there thrashing the water. "You'll not get it, it'll beat you. It's too big, Mr. Slack. You'll not land it."

"Well, you might be right," Slack answered, leaning against the force. "I've fed it a mackerel with the hook in it and it's swallowed them both."

"Leave it be, or there'll be trouble," the captain told Slack.

"It's coming. It's giving way, it's..."

And then Slack was gone, snatched overboard, landing with a huge splash.

Arnold quickly looked over, the captain likewise, but it was just too dark to see. In a second Slack came up, spluttering, thrashing the water with a damn good imitation of a doggy paddle. Arnold suddenly realized that his partner couldn't swim. " He can't swim, Captain, we'd better get a rope to him."

The captain was quick to respond, but Slack wasn't too happy down there. " It's a shark, god damn it, it is shark! Fetch me a rope."

"Just lay still, float on your back like you do in the creek, Slack, don't thrash the water. Float. We need a lamp. Someone fetch a lamp, I can't see anything."

It's all very well to instruct someone what to do when you're on a dry ship and the other is in shark-infested waters, but it didn't calm Slack so much. They could hear him cussing loudly.

"I can't swim," Slack reminded them, quite unnecessarily. Suddenly he felt the body of the shark brush by him , the tail thumping his legs and thrusting him below the water again so that he came up coughing and gasping.

"Help me, the shark is..."

There was a loud crack from a pistol discharging into the water, and at the same time the captain had a rope over the side. The entire ship was in uproar.

Arnold stared at the ship's bosun as he stowed his pistol. It was quite a sight to see the man in his longjohns wildly firing his pistol, as if he were used to shooting at sharks every night. He saw Arnold staring at him as he anchored the captain's rope line.

"You can tell your Mr. Slack that we're grateful for the fish we get for breakfast, Mr. Arnold, but we'd appreciate it if he'd let us sleep nights undisturbed. " And that was that.

Slack was brought up a desperate man. He'd had a close brush with death and got himself a good soaking for his efforts. He sat in a sodden heap on the deck, much chastened .

"I told you it might be a shark. They get greedy, Mr. Slack," the captain told him as he began to reel the rope onto the deck. "You throw 'em fish, they'll think they've arrived in heaven. You start throwing him men, well, we won't ever shake it. It'll become a blood-crazed killer, and you'll do no one any favors."

"Stick to the mackerel" Arnold advised Slack.

The captain shook his head. "If it wasn't for the bosun's efforts with his pistol, you might be a good meal for that shark. I have to tell you, sir, as long as you are on my ship, there'll be no more fishing. I'd like to think I have your word on that."

Slack looked up, shook some of the saltwater out of his eyes and nodded his head. He'd had a fright, he knew when he was out of his depths (so to speak), and how could he disobey? Captain's word was law at sea.

"Well, I guess we've got ourselves breakfast at least," Slack remarked, hoping to make the best of it.

"Aye, we have, and I'll miss your fish, Mr. Slack, but you have to promise me you'll do nothing foolish again."

"You have my word, Captain. You have my word."

It was only at this time they discovered the gull had gone. It was Arnold who discovered it. "Must have been frightened by the pistol shot. Hell, I know I was."

"Bird had gone afore supper," the bosun told them as he made his way back to his quarters. "Weather's going to change. My leg says so, and it never fails."

The captain seemed to be impressed with this. After the man had gone and they'd gotten Slack up on his feet again, he was looking up at the sky for clues. "Well, I can say this for you, Mr. Slack, I have known the bosun for twenty years now, and never once have I seen him get up after he's gone to bed, and for him to register an opinion on anything, other than a man's value to a ship, well, I guess you've found his mark. If he says the wind is coming, it'll be here by dawn, you can swear by it. He never says a thing unless it is so."

Arnold was happy to hear it. He scooped up Slack's fish and put them into the bucket he'd had ready for them. "Captain, I hope your confidence is well placed. I for one will be glad to get going again. Come on, Slack, let's get you out of your wet clothes before you catch something worse than shark."

That night Slack slept naked in his bunk and dreamt of big fish eating his toes. He was not amused to wake later than usual and discover his clothes drying in the rigging, blowing out with the newly unfurled sails. He faced more than a few sniggers as he finally regained possession of his shirt and pants, but it was all good-natured joshing. They'd even left him a mackerel for his breakfast. The crew wanted to hear of his adventures with the shark and never seemed to grow tired of talking about it. Now that they were sailing before a good blow there was a friendly atmosphere on board, and if Slack was the butt of the joke, well, it was well meant. He was man enough to stomach it.

171

DIAMONDS

Alyce was the disappointed one. She'd slept through the entire adventure, and worse, she'd had this longing to see a shark ever since she'd first heard about those monsters of the deep. She felt desperately cheated, but she did try to comfort Slack some, for he was not the best of men to be the butt of a joke, and above all he much regretted his punishment. Men of Newfoundland would know what it was to be denied the waters of the Atlantic. Once you've tasted fishing there, the cold salmon rivers in the mountains were tame ducks indeed.

"We're making good time," Arnold informed them that afternoon. "We'll make up for the lost days, you'll see. We'll be in Baltimore before we know it. I'll be a happy man to reach dry land, I can tell you."

Only Slack would be the one to miss the ocean. Despite his humiliation at the hands of the shark, he'd enjoyed life on the clipper and he'd never yet seen such skies. He liked to lie on deck at night and just watch them. There had to be more stars up there than diamonds in his gem sack. Millions more. He could watch the stars forever, always wondering if there was someone up there lying on his back looking back at him. He never mentioned this thought to anyone. He'd had enough of their petty riducule. Man should keep his ideas to himself. It's safer that way.

On April 18th, the clipper entered the waters of Chesapeake Bay. A day later they were landed and on their way by railroad. Soon Ralston would have his precious diamonds, presently Arnold and Slack would be very rich men indeed.

"I smell the money now, " Arnold remarked on the second day. "We're home and dry friends, home and dry."

CHAPTER ELEVEN
Apprehensions

San Francisco had never looked livelier. It was a typical warm May morning, and the streets were still in chaos on account of the cable-car diggings, but it was astonishing what almost two years could do to a city. Asbury Harpending quite regretted having left his favorite city at all. His wife had been right when she had remarked that what the great city of London lacked most was an affection for itself and its citizens. Anyone visiting San Francisco could plainly see that the townsfolk loved their city.

It was growing apace in every direction. The harbors were full of steamers unloading their wares from all the ports of the world, and here it was remarkable just how clean the air was. Harpending began to feel sorry for the pain and torture he'd put his lungs and eyes through in sulfurous fogs in London. Returning to California was akin to discovering you loved your old sweetheart after all, and that she felt the same about yourself.

"You look uncommonly pleased to be back, Asbury." Ralston remarked, examining a financial document just this moment handed to him. He passed it over to Harpending for his inspection. " Here, this should keep that smile fixed there for some time to come."

Harpending scanned the figures and seemed impressed. "Mine?"

Ralston beamed. He was proud of them. " I said I would look after your affairs as if they were my own. Well, here you are and here they are. You are worth almost four times more than when you left, and not a penny of it at risk. Any one of these investments can be liquidated now, without prejudice. Nor have I included the statements on your profits from the Montgomery Street sale. Bill Sharon knows you are back, and he has pledged to pay up by June 1st. I trust this is acceptable to you?"

Harpending was astonished. "It's more than I hoped for. It's a honour to be your friend, Bill. If I'm to come in with you on this diamond venture, it's best I'm good for it. You say you're wanting ten investors at $200,000 apiece?"

"That's just for openers. Two million dollar capitalization should see us through. Once we have the company shares floated here, New York and London, it's my estimation that each one of us will treble or quadruple our investment on the first day. Whether you stay in for the ride or sell out at that time is up to you, but if this deal is as good as I believe it to be, well San Francisco will soon have streets paved with gold and trees studded with diamonds."

Harpending shook his head and laughed. "I'd rather hoped to sell the stones than invest in some darned civic decorations, Bill."

Ralston chuckled and slapped his old friend on the back. "Now tell me, how was your journey? Tell me all the gossip of London. I hear old Rubery is back with you. Is he fully informed? Will he invest?"

"I think he's not prepared to go as far as $200,000. But he's here and I trust him, Bill. He's a true gentleman. He's got a jaundiced eye and if anyone of us is in danger of being misled, he's here to bring us up sharp."

Ralston stood up and walked across to his desk, placing a key in the top most drawer's brass lock. "I thought you might take some persuading, so I had some of the better gems laid aside for you to inspect when you arrived. You're not too tired to look at them, are you?"

Harpending laughed and hauled himself out of his leather chair. He looked around the large, comfortable room and seemed to approve. "Got yourself a comfortable place, Bill. Any closer to the bank you might as well be living over the shop."

"I'd like to get home to Belmont every evening, but some nights there is so much to do and there's always cables from New York in the morning that need urgent answers. Lizzie, bless her, says I should move San Francisco closer to Belmont." Ralston smiled, "It's either that or I get myself my own fast train. Now what do you think of that? A banker with his own personal train?"

"Well, Crocker considers the Central Pacific as his own and the passengers a necessary evil, so why not?"

Ralston took a small velvet pouch out of the drawer and bade Harpending hold out his hands , into which he emptied the gems. Harpending looked at them in amazement. He'd never held or even seen precious stones in the raw before, but he was not disappointed. He held two handfuls of diamonds, sapphires, and rubies.

"Not yet cut or polished, mind, but these are the best they found. This diamond weighs half an ounce and it's perfect. I've had it valued by old Kavak. Fifty thousand dollars alone. I didn't tell Arnold and Slack this for fear they'd demand more, but as it is, I have in my possession, both here and at the bank gemstones valued to near three hundred thousand dollars." He let that sink in, then added. "Arnold and Slack sold out for one hundred and twenty-five."

Harpening looked astonished and quickly handed such valuable merchandise back to Ralston. "Sold out their share for so little?"

"No, just for the diamonds found so far. It's my belief they've incurred more than a few debts these past years and matters were pressing. I have secured one third of the entire claim for no cost whatsoever, just for the right to market the diamonds. I intend to secure the other two thirds; at a price, as soon as I am satisfied that the find is everything they claim it to be."

Harpending sat down again, frowning. "And they would sell? Isn't that a little curious? "

"Not so very curious, " Ralston replied, walking over to fetch some red wine from the octagonal cellaret. He returned with the decanter and replenished their glasses before sitting down by the fireside with his old friend. "It's common for a man to sell out, especially at the right price. Arnold and Slack do not know at what I have valued the claim. Even if they did, either they must stick with it for a number of years before they see a profit they can't very well afford to work the mine profitably themselves, not on a commercial scale or sell out. They need the money now, Asbury. They've been hungry prospectors long enough. Arnold wants to settle down, raise a family. They aren't fresh young boys anymore."

"So you anticipate no problems with them at all?"

Ralston smiled. "An investment without problems is like surgery without pain; you know that as well as any man."

"I'm glad to hear you have retained some sanity, at least. Tell me, you have no worries about the claim being genuine?"

Ralston nodded. "I am taking precautions. General Colton has been out there under protest and blindfolded, I may tell you. But he's seen the claim . He's dug for diamonds on the plateau they showed him, plucked them off the very ground and found them in old anthills. He's as convinced as any man and he says Arnold and Slack made no attempt to help him find them. Now what do you say to that?"

Harpending frowned. "Well, all I know about Arnold is that he was trying to raise funds to help him with an expedition to find diamonds about two years back. I was telling Baron Rothschild that it's more a wonder he actually found them than not. You are sure the claim is sound?"

"The General declared it genuine. You say you knew Arnold and Slack from the old days?"

"Rubery remembers Slack. Something about a bear, as I remember. Slack came off the worst of it, and as I recall we all parted ways. It was about the time I founded Havilah, so I don't recall much about them except to say they were hard-working and got by, which is more than you could say for a lot of prospectors at that time."

"So you wouldn't be against them."

"No reason. They sold a gold claim to George Roberts, didn't they? He suffer any on account of that?"

"On the contary, he more than doubled his investment."

DIAMONDS

"Then they are plain fools. Here they are about to do it all again." Harpending smiled and raised his glass. "To prosperity, Bill, to eternal prosperity."

Ralston raised his glass and they both toasted each other.

"One thing bothers me," Harpending declared, after some thought. "Not one of us is an expert on diamonds. It seems these stones are found in Kimberlite pipes, geological freaks that can go down as far as a mile. The ground around them can be devoid of anything of value at all, but find that pipe and you've got your buried treasure. Everything you've told me is consistent with the way diamonds are found in South Africa. Scattered on the ground and then below it in clusters. They didn't say anything about rubies being with them, however. I've been reading up this subject and there are some things to consider. Firstly, diamonds are basically carbon, as is coal. Only diamonds are crystaline carbon, and coal is not. Then there are sapphires, which are part of the corundum family of minerals. Rubies and sapphires appear to be the same thing, excepting that only rubies can be red. But I ask myself whether all these precious stones can be found in one site?

"It would explain why they've never been found before on this continent, but do we know enough, Bill? Shouldn't we get someone out from South Africa who knows the business at Kimberley? Do we know for sure that diamonds and rubies can be found together?"

Bill Ralston sipped his wine as he gave some thought to his answer. He was glad he'd persuaded Harpending to leave London, this professional approach was just what the diamond scheme needed. Yes, questions ought to be asked, experts approached. "Well, take the silica minerals, Asbury. I'm told that if you can find agate stone, then you can be sure you'll find onyx. Then there's quartzite too and the likelihood of opals, all one in the silica family of minerals. It might be like that with diamonds, yes? Lion with the lamb, so to speak. No opals have been found, mind, and only a sprinkle of garnets, but why not the whole shebang? A glory-hole of minerals, untouched by time."

Ralston could see Harpending was still skeptical. He smiled reassuringly. "If it seems a bit too good to be true, well, consider the fact that so far diamonds outweigh two hundred to one, and sapphires are forty to one. I cannot vouch for the laws of nature, Asbury, but it seems that it is primarily a diamond discovery. Do not be discouraged. I fully intend to have the diamonds exposed to Tiffany in New York. If he is discouraging, just a little skeptical, then Arnold and Slack must find themselves other investors. Don't worry, I haven't abandoned my wits, Asbury, but neither will I let this opportunity pass us by if it really proves genuine."

"Then we must also add that I would like the claim to be inspected by a mining expert. I would do it myself, but I claim skills in gold and silver only. I'd like for us to hire the very best there is and let him put the claim to test, even if it means digging it to a hundred feet. Will you take my advice on that?"

Harpending was quite firm about this.

Ralston shook his head smiling. "You really are the most suspicious of fellows, Asbury. If there is the hint of trickery, do you think Arnold and Slack will allow us to see Tiffany and call in a qualified surveyor? I think not. I will have both the claim examined and the diamonds."

"Well put it to the test soon, Bill. I still have many doubts, I truly do."

"I will, I most certainly will, once they return."

"Return?" Harpending was confused now. "You have lost them?"

Ralston allowed himself another sip of his wine before he answered. Harpending gave the fire a kick, watching with pleasure as the sparks showered upwards to the chimney.

"They left almost two months ago now. I sent them back to their claim, told them I wanted the best diamonds they could find. If we are to attract investors, Asbury, we have to have something spectacular to show them, wouldn't you say?"

"Sound thinking. Tiffany will be able to make a better judgment too. When do you expect them back? And where is this diamond claim exactly?"

Ralston stood up and walked over to a map he had on the wall. It showed the western states and was the very latest available. "General Colton said they disembarked at Rawlins Springs, which is here in Wyoming."

"Wyoming? That's some way off. How will you protect yourself so far away from home?"

"The claim isn't in Wyoming. The General was blindfolded, to be sure, but he says the mountain above the mesa is covered in snow all year long. Well, that has to be here, the Unita Mountains, which border between Colorado and Utah. He established that the claim is not in Utah, so we've got it narrowed down to Colorado. Now that's our secret. I'm encouraging the idea that they could be in Arizona for the present, so if anyone decides to go and look for them, they'll be off track by a good five hundred miles or so, at least."

"Finally I hear something that makes me believe you haven't entirely lost your reason, Bill. So when do you expect our prospectors back?"

"Any day now. When I told them I wanted more diamonds, they didn't flinch a bit. They set off on the eastern train and promised me they'd find me two million dollars worth of gems." Ralston smiled, adding, "Arnold is prone to exaggeration."

Harpending sharply inhaled. "Hell, I'd like to see two million dollars worth of diamonds. I shall await their arrival with impatience, Bill."

"No more impatient than I, I can assure you. Now, about dinner. Yourself, Rubery, and I must confer. I have emissaries from Japan arriving, sent by Baron Ikakuri himself. We must dine and make plans tonight. Tomorrow I shall be keen to learn what Japan has to offer."

"Japan?"

"Yes, believe it or believe it not, Japan is making an approach to us with a view to trade. It's never happened before. Baron Ikakuri is a very progressive sort, apparently. He intends to bring an entire Japanese delegation with him to America and they intend to stay at my palace! Well, I can hardly disappoint 'em, can I." He laughed. "If we can open a window to Japan, Asbury, who knows what trade might come of it? If you know any soul who has been there, get them to come and see me. I'd like to know more about that strange country."

"I'm impressed. They sought you out?"

"The Bank of California is famous all over the world, it appears. We must be doing something right, eh? Now dinner. It is past seven, and I, for one am hungry."

The two friends finished their wine, and discussed life and finance in London and whether Gladstone could last much longer. It was Harpending's opinion that he could not and that Disraeli would be prime minister before long. England needed the cobwebs cleared away and the likes of the notorious Baron Grant swept away with it. Now that he was back he saw San Francisco with new eyes, saw its potential was so great surely it would eclipse London one day, and the sooner the better. Diamonds would only hasten the day.

"It's important we secure the diamonds for San Francisco," Ralston pointed out as they strolled toward the Grand Hotel for their dinner engagement. "If New York knew where the diamond field was, we wouldn't stand a chance. They'd grab it for themselves. We must be on our guard and secure Arnold and Slack to ourselves before we go to see Tiffany. If he says yea then they might want to deal with Jay Cooke or others."

Harpending pulled a face. He'd lost out heavily when he'd wanted to develop the railroad north and Bill Ralston had warned him off going up against Cooke who'd wanted the same. "I see Cooke's placing advertisments in Scandanavia now and the Baltics to get people to settle the Pacific coast."

"There was an advertisment in *Harpers* I saw it myself. It compares the coast to the Mediterranean but it doesn't mention the rain or the winters, or its complete lack of civilising features. It's Cooke's Banana Belt if you ask me. It's bound to fail. You are well out of it, Asbury. The lumber alone is worth getting out, but as to living up there, it's a swamp."

"I hear from William Roberts, Jay Cooke's chief engineer, that the railroad is going to cost $50,000 a mile to build in the Cascades. I suppose I'm lucky I didn't get started, but despite your comments, Bill, I think there's a fortune to be made going North. You'll see, one day they'll settle up there." He was wistful a moment, and sighed before recovering his thoughts.

"Now to the matter in hand, Bill. Arnold and Slack, I have a proposal. Take a thirty-day option. Pay them another hundred thousand if you are so sure. They cannot go behind your back once they have accepted your money, and unquestionably you can secure the investment in that time."

Ralston nodded in agreement. "You are right. We must take an option, but not before they reveal where the mine is. I can't pay for some vague mystery that is only perhaps in the mountains of Colorado."

"I am most keen to meet Arnold and Slack again. They have exercised proper caution in this business. It smacks of them having been disappointed a few times before."

"They are not disappointed now. The General seems to think they are honest men. He was telling me that Slack is the real brain and we will make a mistake to underestimate him. He has some useful ideas. It's my impression that he'd like to go into real estate once he's sold out. He's got plans to open up Southern California ahead of the railroad."

"That's your plan."

"He is not to know that. But his idea is sound enough. If this scheme works out, I might work a scheme with him to do just that. Southern California must grow. All it requires is water and the railroad. Everything else will follow."

"And we shall be very old men. Let's stick to what we know, Bill, mining and San Francisco. All the money that needs to be made can be made right here."

"Never a truer word, Asbury. You're right as usual."

Alyce had stayed on the westbound train. She had felt very sad leaving the men after these weeks together, but she had her tasks and they had theirs. Her role now was to sell up, pack up her possessions and move back east. The boys would come to stay with her when they got finished with Ralston. She was not to be seen in San Francisco in case Asbury Harpending got sight of her. Arnold wasn't sure Harpending would return, but he was Ralston's man and diamonds would bring him back for sure. This wasn't fair to Alyce, but she would do as they bid her. Arnold had promised her a good home in Kentucky once all this was over. She would be sad to leave the West, but not stricken. Kentucky was just as good if you were with the man you loved.

There were some uncertainties, of course. If they should be caught out by Ralston or whoever, then she stood out as their accomplice. Whatever happened now, she had to leave. She'd stick by Arnold, through thick or thin; she'd told him as much and he'd said he'd always known it. Still and all, he wouldn't marry her. Sometimes she told herself that it was a blessing. As if God was telling her, stop, think, wait, time will tell. Other times she just craved respectability.

The westbound train sped through the sage brush and with every minute she was that much farther away from them and closer to her fate. It was no comfort either way, and if she'd the courage she would have disembarked at

Salt Lake, and taken refuge with the Mormons as a way out of it. But she didn't. She was just ever so slightly more afraid of them than either Arnold or Ralston.

She was afraid of what she might do to herself. Alyce had a sudden insight in understanding how easy it was for a person to want to jump off the highest ledge to their death. The decision was easier than many might imagine, when all you have is the choice between that of Lot's wife and a plunge to one's death and oblivion.

She sat motionless on the railroad car as it sped toward the familiar Nevada mountains. She knew tears would be wasted. One must just go on.

DIAMONDS

CHAPTER TWELVE
The seeding

There had been quite a change to the plateau since their last visit two months before. The snow was still in evidence on the ridges, but the hot weather of the previous three days had produced a good run off from the mountains and the streams were swollen to over-flowing. Above them waterfalls cascaded off jutting rocks and it was altogether something akin to paradise. The vegetation was lush around the fringes of the mesa itself, and if it hadn't been for the mass of insect life, a better place to camp two men could not have found.

Slack nursed a sore arm. He'd had a brush with a tree. Or if the truth is required, he fell asleep on his mule and fell off some forty miles back. Arnold would have laughed, but he was too busy cursing a bad tooth. His left cheek was swollen and he feared for a septic abscess. Slack had taken a look, but seen nothing amiss. If he'd had whiskey and rope to tie down Arnold with, he'd have attempted to fetch it out, but since they had not, the man would have to suffer.

They made the best of the good weather. Slack was stripped to his pants and working hard on his anthills. It took some skill to make anthills so they looked as though ants had actually made 'em. It wasn't a question of building them up by piling mud up high. The things had to taper just right, and although it was impossible to get a true honey-comb effect, it'd pass if you left sticks and straws in the wet mud until it was half-dry; -then you drew out the sticks and straws, leaving the holes. If anyone got suspicious, well, they'd only have to kick the thing and see it was riddled with ant tunnels. Attention to detail was everything. Arnold had insisted. If they were to be successful, then they had to be more thorough than the government tax collector.

The actual salting required equal skill. Slack had to select a ruby, diamond, or sapphire (but never mixed, an anthill they thought favored rubies in one corner and diamonds in another). He would place a ruby in one of his holes, then push it toward the center with his stick, withdrawing the stick, and then when the entire salting was finished (no more than three or four gems per

181

anthill), he would sprinkle water over the entire construction, slapping fresh mud over all the openings.

He had a similar process for planting gems in the ground. Of course much of the plateau was rock and it was impossible to embed diamonds in rock. The whole area had to be carefully mapped however, so that there was a logic to their planting. Diamonds, Arnold figured, would favor the stream that cut through the plateau finding their way to the swollen creek below. It was logical, therefore, that he had to climb down to the creek and make sure diamonds were deposited under large boulders and in the newly deposited mud from the run offs. When Ralston sent a second man to verify the claim, it was likely to be a jaundiced fellow and he'd certainly take the trouble to climb down here and poke around. He would not be disappointed. The waters were ice cold and swollen, to be sure. Nevertheless, Arnold waded in and took the trouble to bury the most common of his diamond haul deep in the bottom sand. It had to be deep because the scouring motion of the mountain water was taking the top sand farther down stream with every melt. By mid-summer the creek would be down to a trickle, and these pinheads would be near the surface, just waiting for a simple scrape.

By this methodology, Arnold depleted his stock of sub-grade diamonds from the very top of the mesa to the creek bottom. There wouldn't be a patch that didn't have at least one diamond to find. And not all at one level, either. He was too smart for that. If it required him to dig down four feet or even ten feet in some spots, then he did. The skeptical investigator would do as much. He made sure diamonds could be found at every level on the way down. In particular he moved every boulder and heavy rock and sprinkled the better stones under these. He'd noticed how the General liked to poke about under what he called "trapped sand". Now it was more like an over generous treasure trail with booty at every turn.

"Some folks would think us mad, throwing thousands of dollars away like this, Slack. Kind of makes me a sight dizzy to contemplate it myself."

Slack was busy burying rubies and sapphires into the ground at the edge of the plateau. He was following a triangular pattern. It was agreed that the gems had to have a pattern, but it mustn't be perfect. They'd both worked on gold prospecting long enough to know that nothing worked on a straight line. A seam could double back on itself, go anywhere but straight. And they figured it would be the same for diamonds. For that reason, Slack would pace six feet on a straight line and then four feet to the right or left before going straight again. Each time he stopped he'd jab the ground with a metal rod brought expressly for this purpose to get it as deep as it would go, then drop the gem to the bottom once the rod was out. He'd close the hole with his heel before moving on. Seeding was a slow process and you couldn't cut corners, but it was better than planting potatoes, and the harvest would be something to brag about.

"Damn, these gnats are vicious brutes " Slack complained as he slapped another. "Why don't they stay with the mules?"

"You got any more of that oil of cloves?" Arnold called out from the stream. "My damn gums ache so."

"You told me to hold off until you were desperate. It's nearly all gone. I told you Arnie, best to whip it out. One good tug and I could get it free."

Arnold chipped some ice from the still frozen banks of the stream. It hurt like hell but it did provide some relief. There was no question of leaving the plateau before they were completely done; that would be foolhardy. Yet, it was getting so he could hardly think straight.

After a while Arnold walked up the creek some ways to the frozen waterfall and lay down under it, burying his face into what was left of the snow. Slack found him there after he'd finished with the rubies.

"Bad?"

"Bad."

"I've got an idea."

"I don't want your knife in my mouth; John Slack. Life's too short to bleed to death up here."

Slack nodded, Arnold really was bad. His face was quite distended. A man really could die with bad gums; he'd seen it happen before. By the time you found a doctor or dentist, should such a person he within the nearest hundred miles, then the poor fellow was usually dead.

"I'm going to have to truss you up some, but it'll be worth it."

"You are not going to..."

But Slack grabbed Arnold's wrists, got his ankles together and in the time it takes to pucker your lips, he had Arnold bound up like a young calf, his faced buried in the snow.

"You can protest all you like, Philip Arnold, but I'm not about to listen to you moaning yourself to death for the rest of this trip."

With that said, he hefted Arnold up, and staggered with him over to the stream, depositing his carcass in a deep hollow that totally swallowed him up in freezing water. Arnold yelled as the water swirled about him, but Slack ignored his protests. "Open up, open. I'm going to put the oil of cloves on now."

That got Arnold's attention. Oil of cloves would ease the pain a short while. He trusted Slack not to drown him, but Slack was no dentist, that was for sure, and he wasn't gentle. It's a funny thing to see a grown man reduced to terror by a simple thing like a tooth, but Arnold was sorely afraid of pain.

The water was cold for Slack, too, but he didn't seem to mind it.

"Creek will wash the blood away, rest your head back against the rock, there; see, you can't drown. The cold will concentrate your mind."

183

DIAMONDS

Slack rubbed the oil of cloves on his finger then pushed it into Arnold's unwilling mouth, not at all distracted by Arnold's gargled protestations. With the oil of cloves on his gums Arnold felt immediate relief, but it wouldn't last long. Slack waited just two minutes for the pain to ease then wedged Arnold's mouth open with a large pebble before getting his fingers around the rotted tooth. He peered in, and it didn't look so good. The gums were badly swollen, a deep purple and bleeding.

"Infection's underneath. Too much good living, Arnie. You'll end up like George Washington with his wooden snappers."

Arnold couldn't exactly reply. He gurgled and coughed, but Slack wouldn't let him up now he had him down.

"You think it's going to be a hot summer this year? I says it will be." As Slack talked he got himself a good grip on the tooth, and without any warning at all gave it an almighty tug, adding a little twist. He could actually hear the tooth coming away, tearing root and all, and the blood was something terrible. He pulled back, snatched the pebble away and flipped Arnold over so he could cough up the blood quick.

As the cold water flooded his mouth Slack cut him free. Arnold roared with pain into the water, then collapsed with a whimper.

For a moment Slack thought he wasn't coming up for air, but he began to stir at last, blood mixing in the water, sending a copious amount down to the creek below.

Arnold didn't surface in a hurry The water temperature may have been only one degree above ice, but he was actually sweating from from the pain of it all. He lay on the rocks, sloshing the icy water through his bloody mouth. He couldn't remember when last he'd felt something so bad.

"I reckon you're right, there's an abcess under there," Slack told him as he walked back to his gem sack. He picked it up and walked over to the camp fire, still smouldering on a granite rock. He knew the sun wouldn't be enough to get the frost out of Arnold, nor indeed himself, for he was just as soaked. He piled on some branches and twigs until he had the fire ablaze, radiating enough heat to melt the snow off the far peak.

Arnold finally summoned the will to get out of the stream and walk to the fire. He didn't look at Slack, or say a word. Blood still flowed from his mouth and probably would for some hours yet, but it was just a case of spitting and putting up with it. He tore off his clothes and threw them to the ground. They were bloodstained and wouldn't be much use to him the way they were.

"Knew a man who was shot to put him out of misery," Slack stated at length. He wasn't at all put out Arnold sat by the fire naked, or that he didn't thank him. He wouldn't have thanked a man for half-killing him either.

"He begged them to shoot him, his teeth were so bad. Funny thing was, when they laid him to rest they discovered it wasn't his teeth at all. He'd gotten

184

a brass nail embedded in the roof of his mouth. Of course everyone wanted to know how it got there, but there was no chance of that considering how they so readily shot the poor bastard before taking a look inside his mouth. I don't know how a nail got in there, and I suppose he didn't either."

"I hate it when you get talky, Slack," Arnold confessed.

That shut Slack up. He sat by the fire getting red one side whilst the sun burned the other. Anyone who saw the men like this would have sworn they had spent ten years straight out in the mountains and gone crazy with it.

"You remember to sprinkle some pinheads around the roots of the plants?"

Slack grunted that he had. "I've got some emeralds. Did you want emeralds to be here too? We don't want to gild the lily too much."

Arnold winced as the throbbing pain returned momentarily.

"Any more oil of cloves?"

Slack smiled. "Saved a drop." He threw the little brown bottle over. "Don't get it in the hole, go around it. You'll be all right. Tooth came out clean."

"You keep it?"

"No, I did not keep it. It was a blackened, foul thing. Best left in the creek." He grinned. "Another little gem for Ralston to find."

Arnold sighed the sigh of one who feels deeply wronged. "Well, it might have gotten better."

"And Christmas will come twice a year."

Arnold frowned and moved back a little way from the fire, for it was awful hot now. "Put the emeralds in the roots of the yucca plant. Toss a couple into the water. Got many?"

"Just a few. We never had any before."

"Well, we've got 'em now." Arnold snapped. "You're an aggravating man sometimes, John Slack."

"Maybe, maybe I am."

Arnold spat out some more blood, hitting a trail of ants running from the heat of the fire. "You think it will rain soon?"

Slack looked up at the sky. "Not for two or three days, but soon."

"Soon's enough. There's a lot of tracks that need covering."

Slack looked about him and considered the remark. "Got to be some traces of our diggings. Might as well have the place looking worked."

"It will, we're going to dig a trench diagonal to the stream. Tell 'em it was rich pickings, but we think it's even better over by the stream. "

"Better yet, let's dig a trench that cuts into the stream. We can get it filled with water from the run off and cast some pinheads into it. They'll settle nicely into the mud, ready to be good and dry by the summer."

Arnold thought about it. "All right, have it your way. But we have to be away from here by tomorrow afternoon if we're to keep to schedule."

"I'll get digging."

DIAMONDS

Arnold watched Slack walk over and seize a pick ax. The soil was rock hard. It would be back breaking work getting the diggings to look realistic. He was in no shape to help. His head ached and his jaw, cheek and just about everything else in his head throbbed something dreadful.

"Get some sleep," Slack advised him. "Sleep's usually the best thing."

They were on their way to San Francisco two hours after sun-up the next day. Arnold was still full of pain, but the swelling had subsided and he was on the mend. Slack nursed blisters from his diggings, but both men agreed they'd done a fine job. Whoever came next couldn't fail to find something, and even if they were there a week or even a month, every day they'd find more. They were confident the plateau would pass any test.

"Fact is,"" Arnold told Slack as they rode the mules down through the forest, "fact is, there's no one who's ever seen a diamond mine in the entire continental United States. I don't care if Ralston finds himself ten experts , they'll all have to come to the same conclusion. This is a very rare diamond field of perspicacious beauty . Unless they fetch over a Dutchman fresh from Kimberley, we're home and dry, Slack. What do you say to that?"

"I'll tell you when we're home and dry, Philip Arnold."

"You're a hard man to please, Slack."

Slack smiled to himself. It was true, but that didn't alter anything. A man was better being true to his doubts, and he had a few...

CHAPTER THIRTEEN
The Waiting.

Waiting is sometimes the most terrible thing in the whole world. Waiting and not knowing is an open invitation to all kinds of doubts and worries, it can kill a man with the stress of it and there were a few men in San Francisco who were fretting their days most anxiously. It was on of those terrible hot days one experiences in early May. It catches people unawares. No one was dressed for it and them that still stuck to wing collars and the like felt them wilt and the starch grow clammy. The bay was full, a healthy sign of good trade. Three of the sailing ships were immigrant ships, filled mostly with Chinese labor destined for new railroad work or the mines. Summer was early this year and it was a humid day. It was good to see trees giving shade again. There was an altogether expectant atmosphere in the city; a definite reluctance on the part of folks to go back inside their places of work after lunch-break. Trade had recently improved, stocks were at a ten-month high, and even the Central Pacific was running on time.

Asbury Harpending was busy at his home on Rincon Hill. The house had stood empty these past two years and needed not only a good airing, but some detailed attention to decoration and repair. His wife had seized upon the need for a little work to mean she had full licence to re-build the entire home to 'European' standards. She'd gotten her way with a flushing toilet and hot and cold water in the new bathroom. She was all for doubling the size of the house, but Harpending had held firm and confined her to expanding the drawing room so it could be included with the proposed conservatory, where she intended to grow exotic plants. Like any wife in their circle, what she really wanted to do was compete with Ralston's Belmont, but Harpending wouldn't hear of it. He liked the house as it was and was not about to go into debt for some foolish fancy to impress friends and strangers .

All this was yet in the planning stage, but Harpending didn't mind allowing his dear one some leeway on this as he knew he'd not get her back to London. The difference in her since they'd returned just eight days earlier was remarkable. She had positively blossomed. Back among old friends and family she was a changed woman, thrilled to be living in fresh clean air and seeing people who did not always judge you by your breeding,

Harpending himself had noticed his own manner changing back to its former good humor. He too was unexpectedly happy to be in the city and had wasted little time in getting back into business. He'd balanced his books, found himself in excellent financial condition and together with Alfie Rubery had speculated on a gold venture in Nevada . This had proved to be a lucky plunge for them, the shares had risen by sixty percent in four days of trading and they'd sold on the turn, making themselves fifty thousand dollars clear profit. It was always good to know one hadn't lost one's instinct for a good investment. It augured well for the diamond venture.

However, it was his very concern for that business that worried him. He'd seen the diamonds, heard first hand from the General on the physical attributes of the diamond claim, and they even thought they had an idea of where it was in the mountains. Yet, nothing could begin without Arnold and Slack and from them there had been no news at all.

Ralston had confessed privately that he had dispatched two men to look for them: one who followed them on the train, but they'd easily outsmarted him and another, one of the best scouts in the city, had ridden out to Colorado, made inquiries everywhere about them , had ridden up into the mountains but he'd seen nothing and no one.

Everyone was anxious to get on with the business of setting up the diamond company, should it be positively proved beyond doubt. But nothing could be done without Arnold and Slack.

As if by divine intervention, that very moment as Harpending was thinking about the two prospectors, a bank messenger arrived at his front door. He was to expect Mr. William Chapman Ralston at six that evening. Would he be at home?

He would be in and he would be impatient in extremis until that hour came. He sent the messenger back with the positive message.

News at last. He was sure of it, so much so he sought out his wife and gave her the good news. She said she was pleased for him and would he mind not standing in her light while she was choosing material for the new drapes. She neither liked to encourage or discourage him. He abandoned her for his small rear garden, where an apple-tree was in full glorious white blossom. At least the tree was enthusiastic. He paced the ground like a caged animal, too excited to rest or do much of anything until he had news that Arnold and Slack were back.

His wife sighed; he was just as impatient as a child, and no easier to control.

"I'll make you some mint tea. You know how it calms you," she called to him from her boudoir window.

DIAMONDS

"Tea? I was thinking of champagne."

"And I'm thinking of your health, dear. You can celebrate all you want when there's a profit to show, but for now, you must sit, drink tea and consider your plans."

She was right of course. What he really should be doing was reading his diamond book, familiarizing himself with all the different types of stones, so as not to be fooled by quartz or anything else that an unskilled eye might mistake for the real thing.

He was still pacing up and down by the tree when she walked back out into the garden, accompanied by the Chinese servant carrying a silver tray with the hot mint tea in two china cups. The very first thing his wife had done was to hire a reliable Chinese servant when they'd arrived. Wing-Lo was no picture to look at; he had scars on his cheek from a fight or two, but he was reliable and his English passable. Harpending meant to ask him exactly how he'd got his scars, but manners seemed to prevent him. The Chinese led difficult lives and often seemed to be quarrelling among themselves.

In his opinion they were excellent workers and had done a good job of replacing the Irish as household servants in the city. The Irish and the Chinese now regarded each other with some hostility. It did not bode well for the future of the city if one group got the upper hand.

Later as the Harpendings sipped mint tea and enjoyed the gentle scent of the apple tree, Mrs Harpending considered how best to relax her husband.

"Read," she beseeched him. "You know how it calms you."

"Read? My dear one, I am so distraught with impatience I could not tolerate a single page."

"Well, you could cut pages then, for me."

Harpending frowned. He detested cutting pages and could not see why publishers could not accomplish this detail themselves. "Cut pages, my dear? What is it now? Some overwrought tragedy, some female in love with a sea captain who's vowed never to return 'cause he loves another?"

His wife offered him a withering smile. "Not at all, it is the very latest work from Mark Twain. Mr. Clemens, if you recall. We made his acquaintance at Belmont."

"The newspaper man from Virginia City? Him who was with the *Alta*."

"Well maybe he was dear, but he also wrote that book you insisted upon reading aloud to Lord Jenner in London. *Innocents Abroad*, remember?"

Harpending remembered. He'd enjoyed the book; what American wouldn't who was living abroad at the time? The book made him laugh a great deal, which was more than can be said of much of the English fiction he'd been press-ganged into trying.

"What has he written?"

"Something that will find him out, I fancy. Leastways among you and your

189

friends. It's about his days in the mines out West. They say it names names and is really quite amusing."

"Heck, I could write a book about the mines and the miners, myself."

"Yes,dear, but Mr. Clemens actually did. It's called *Roughing It* and it should keep you quiet for a few days, I fancy. It's all of five hundred and ninety pages long and bound in half-morocco. It was Tilly Colton who recommended it to me. Everyone behaves extremely badly, she tells me, but naturally you never did, my dear."

Harpending smiled, enjoying her sarcasm. "I was known as the Saint of Havilah," he told her, straight-faced.

"Tilly said there is a lot of business about the Yellow Jacket mine and Gold Hill and the mismangement by Bill Ralston's bank. She said that Bill's law-yer-should read it too."

Harpending was intrigued. She had his complete attention now.

"It does not mention me, I hope. I never liked old Sutro, but I never said a bad word about him. Adolpho Sutro has been wronged, I grant you that, but I took no sides. I was not part of that squeeze. I never saw why Bill was so against it, but if they get their access tunnel, who knows what might happen? They may get it yet of course. It would be a boon to everyone, save lives too, but don't tell Bill I said so. What else has he to say?"

His wife shook her head and stood up to leave him be. "You must first cut the pages and read it from the beginning, mind."

With that she was gone, and for the first time Harpending noticed the Mark Twain book on her vacated chair. He eagerly reached for it and at the same moment noticed that the pages had indeed already been cut.

He smiled to himself. She'd just got him distracted to calm him down. The happy result was, that when Bill Ralston did arrive, some half-hour late, Harpending was deeply engrossed in the overland journeys men had made in the days before the railroad. So much change in so short a time. What a different sort of life they'd lived then, and how sad it was it had all gone forever, even if life was more comfortable now.

Ralston arrived with much enthusiasm and seized upon the wine and cana-pes, claiming he'd been too busy to eat anything all day.

"Our boys have cabled from Reno," he told Harpending.

They were in Harpending's study,with all his old maps and books lying untidily around them. Ralston had seen Twain's book lying on the desk, but he made no comment. He was too excited.

"I was beginning to lose heart they'd ever return. After all I did advance them a great deal of money."

Harpending shrugged. "They'd be hard pressed to spend even a dollar up in the mountains, Bill. Anyway, a man tends to lose track of time up there. I remember when ten of us had been so long living up in the wilds that we couldn't say whether it was 1865 or '66, never mind select a day or month or hour. In the end it turned out to be Christmas Day and I can tell you we all felt mightily robbed we'd not gotten some celebrating in on that account."

Ralston smiled. "Glory days, Asbury. New hopefuls are up there now. Arnold and Slack will be here on the very next train it says. Here, read the cable yourself."

Harpending took the cable from Ralston's hands and read it eagerly. Both men were intoxicated with the thought of diamonds now.

> SUDDEN FLOODING DELAYED RETURN STOP - VEN-
> TURE SUCCESSFUL STOP - WILL TAKE NEXT TRAIN FROM
> RENO STOP - REQUEST ASSISTANCE FROM SOMEONE YOU
> TRUST AND KNOWN TO US TO SHARE AWESOME BURDEN
> OF RESPONSIBILITY STOP - SUGGEST MEET LATHROP
> STOP -
> ARNOLD STOP -

"I thought of you at once," Ralston informed him. "Arnold is right. We can't possibly let them enter this city unprotected. You'll meet them at Lathrop and escort them in."

"They'll accept me?"

"You know them, and they know you are my partner in many things. I shall furnish you with a document bearing my seal. Remember they are known to certain individuals now. They'll be on the lookout for them. I can't think of why I didn't think of this problem earlier."

Harpending read the cable through again. "Venture successful and 'awesome burden' smacks of rich pickings. You think they've got what they promised?"

"I'm certain of it. Asbury, soon, you and I will be so close to a grand fortune, I can almost touch it now. You'll take the train tomorrow? You will be in Lathrop before them, but I believe they should arrive no more that two or three hours after you."

"I'd go now if it would get them there any faster," Harpending replied.

"Now we must think ahead. There's Arnold and Slack's share to be bought out, a company to be formed."

"Yes, but I think your idea for just ten investors for the original company is too few. Twenty-five each contributing eighty thousand dollars would be a better spread of the risk and still gets you your two million. You can go to common stock from there on."

Ralston considered Harpending's remarks a moment. "Yes, twenty-five is a good number. I have no quarrel with that." He took out a list he had from his pocket. "I've given some thought to the matter. A company needs a name, and I thought the San Francisco and New York Mining and Commercial Company would fit it right."

"New York?"

Ralston poured himself some more wine and drank a little before answering. "We can't shut them out, and besides they'll take against us if we do. We will have to go to New York to see Tiffany anyway, so it would be prudent to bring them in. I've a mind for Thomas Selby as Director; he's solid. Will Lent, of course, as well as yourself. Milton Latham, Louis Sloss would want to come in, and you'll want to bring in Rubery and Maurice Dore. Where is Rubery, by the by?"

Harpending laughed, suddenly recalling his friend. "Oregon. He's gone to Portland. He has an idea to export Oregon timber to England. I say the freight will kill him. After all, it's got to go around the Horn. But he's keen to undercut the Swedes over in England, and Oregon is in need of a steady customer."

"He'll need bigger ships, steamers."

"He says not. Sail is half the price of steam now, and speed is not essential after all. Perhaps it is a way of giving work to the old ships. Rubery has a knack of turning a profit on outlandish ideas, so don't rule him out."

"What about Cooke's rail road? They're going north."

"Rail-freight charges would strangle it. You know how they hate to hear of a man making a profit."

"Well bully for Alfie, I say. The West must be developed or die. Oh yes, I've a mind to bring Babcock and Willis into our camp, is there anyone you think will join?"

"The General?"

"He's already in as general manager. He says he doesn't want to commit himself financially. He's ready to get started. He's keen I can tell you."

"In New York you'll need General Barlow. He's got much influence. Gansl represents the House of Rothschild in New York. I promised the baron that he'd get in on this, so he'd have to be included too."

"Excellent. Naturally, the baron wishes to be involved. I see no reason why we can't offer him the rights to market our gems in England and Europe. It's his territory, after all. I have every respect for the Rothschilds."

"Then all we need are Arnold and Slack," Harpending declared.

"And secure rights to the land around the diamond claim. They must tell me exactly where it is now. It is ridiculous to keep it so secret."

"Not so ridiculous," Harpending replied "There are many rumors about. I'd rather not have the mountains crawling with prospectors, nor the expense of buying into their claims."

"Well I'm still encouraging the idea that there's a big find in Arizona, but we can't keep that story up indefinitely."

"Long enough will do. Now, Bill, you are still a hungry man, I can see. I didn't get to taste one canape. You've an invitation to dine with me tonight."

"Well I'd intended to swim. I like to get my exercise

"You still swim every day?" Harpending was surprised.

Ralston grinned. "A man must always be vigorous, Asbury, or else he loses his zest for life."

"Bill, I'll watch you swim, but I can assure you that the day I lose my zest, it'll be the day I'm carried off in an oak casket."

Ralston laughed. "Asbury, if I thought you'd lost your enthusiasm for making money and taking a risk, well, the very fires in the center of the earth would be dimmed to extinction. Come. I'll swim, then I'll eat. We have much to discuss and I have news from Japan to tell you. Our next days are likely to be busy ones indeed. But first to the Hyde-Street public-baths."

Harpending drove him down in his buggy himself and, true to his word, watched the giant of a man swim out into the ice-cold bay. Ralston seemed to relish the experience, but Harpending almost felt a chill coming on from just watching him. He thought that Ralston was a brave but foolish man. A heart should not be subjected to such extremes. One day it would get the better of him, he was sure of it.

"Come on in, it's warmer than yesterday. Come on in."

Harpending waved back to Ralston, but he made no moves. He had more than enough hard times in his life without volunteering for more. He stood at the water's edge and reflected on the bankers he knew in London. Men who would rather be hung in public than seen swimming in common water. Yes, it was good to be back in California. Jove, San Francisco was going to teach those English something about finance now. Nothing was going to stop Bill Ralston; there was no one of his enterprise anywhere, no one.

Lathrop was a miserable place. In the sun it would be hard to like it, but in the driving, hard mountain rain, it was beyond redemption. The Pacific train was late, as if by intention. Word had come down to them that the line was awash through the Truckee pass and progress was down to five to ten miles per hour.

Harpending spent his time with his diamond book at the Hog's Back Inn. He was trying to memorize the facts. The facts, he knew, were desperately important. A man must know the facts or else wallow forever in ignorance. He looked away from the page and tried to recall what he'd read. He minded not if he received odd looks from the few drinking in the inn. If they wished to stare, well they could. Had they not seen a man trying to learn something before? He recited, "Diamonds are found in er One ounce,,"

It was no good. He looked back at the page. Ah that was it. He quickly looked away again and thought he had it fixed now. In a low whisper he recited,

One hundred and fifty carats in an ounce.
4 carats is equal to about four grains, diamond grains being
a deal smaller than troy grains used in measuring gold.
A carat is valued not only by weight, but by color and purity
of sample, cut and polish being the final arbiter of price."

Harpending looked back at the page and saw that he had it approximately right. It was a little confusing that diamond grains were smaller than gold grains; it would mean a special set of weights would have to he made, many sets of weights. There were always unexpected costs in any investment. Ralston had an idea of recruiting direct from Holland for good lapidaries. Energetic days lay ahead.

The innkeeper came across to Harpending with more coffee. Harpending didn't like to drink when he was on business .

"Nothing to eat?"

"Not hungry, but the coffee's good. Keep it coming. Been in Lathrop long?"

"Since before it got its name. I was a prospector hereabouts."

"How did it get its name? No one famous I know of."

"Blame lies with Mrs Jane Stanford. She insisted there had to be a stop named after an ancestor, the Reverend John Lathrop. Fact he didn't even come west didn't seem to matter to her. Sometimes I think I'll have a station after me when I'm gone, but I don't reckon people will go for it."

"And why is that, sir?"

"Names D'eath sir. A town called D'eath doesn't appeal to most, sir."

Harpending wasn't sure an inn called Death would be entirely appropriate either. Lathrop seemed doomed somehow.

The train was still nowhere in sight some four hours later, and Harpending had read quite as much about diamonds as he could take. Certainly he'd had enough coffee; his eyes had that staring look and his heart beat with some nervousness. Rain or no, he decided a good walk would be the sensible thing, to see the sights of this ill-starred town. What he saw did not impress him. He didn't think it had much of a future, but then he'd never thought Sacramento would catch on, so his opinion was not so very reliable.

When the Pacific train finally appeared Harpending had been soaked, he'd been baked dry again and he'd grown so sick of waiting he was relieved beyond measure to see the familiar locomotive creep along the rails. He even mustered a cheer or two and when it finally pulled in to take on water and discharge a few disgruntled passengers, Harpending leapt aboard and began to roam the cars, looking for Arnold and Slack.

DIAMONDS

Imagine, then, his disappointment when, upon reaching the very end of the cars, he found them not. He felt positively sickened by it. Surely Arnold and Slack could not have let them all down now, not at this stage, not after dispatching a cable saying they'd be on the train.

He walked back through the train a dejected man. He didn't even notice the two men asleep in one corner of the third car. They were dressed in rags and naturally smelled bad, so much so they inspired a man to hurry by them to get it over with quickly.

It was only after he'd gone through one more car that Harpending realized what a fool he was. If two men had been up in the mountains these past two months, digging, getting up to their necks in dirt, subjected to the elements and this infernal rain, why, they'd finish up a lot like those two tramps in the third car. He quickly returned to them and inspected them more closely. One had the bleached blond look a man gets on his hair from being exposed to the sun without a hat. He was as brown as a southern cotton-picker. There was none of the usual prospector's baggage around them and absolutely no sign of any diamonds, but if Harpending was a betting man, it had to be them.

"Gentlemen? Sirs... " He shook Slack. "Er, excuse me sir but are you ..?"

Slacks eyes opened and he caught full sight of Asbury Harpending's face no more than an inch from his own. It was the worst shock of his life. He knew for sure the game was up. Slack started and sat upright, sending Harpending flying.

"Arnold," Slack called, waking him with a jolt of his foot. "Wake up, man."

Harpending picked himself up of the floor and at the same time the train began to signal it was about to leave.

"I'm sorry to startle you gentlemen, but I am right in assuming? ..."

Arnold was blinking, trying to adjust to wakefulness. "Harpending ain't it? Asbury Harpending. Jax mine and the Grand Hotel Harpending."

Harpending smiled, glad to be recognized. "You are Philip Arnold?"

Arnold smiled. "The same, and this here is John Slack. You'll remember him no doubt."

Slack stammered a hello. Surely Harpending wouldn't recognize them from that lunch in Simpson's in London. There was that risk. How foolish of Arnold to cable for someone to meet them. How poetic that it should be the one man who could unmask them. The train pulled out of the station at last. No escape now.

"I am a very relieved man, Mr. Arnold. I had feared you both were not aboard the train. By the look of you you've had a hard time of it."

"It was all in the last few days," Slack told him. "Weather changed. Floods, ice and snow, Arnold's mule bolted. Never seen such weather."

Arnold sighed. "To state the facts, Mr. Harpending, we are very sad men.

We'd hoped to bring back two million dollars worth of," he lowered his voice a moment and tapped his nose "you know what. But that damn mule was determined to cause trouble from the day we hired it. I was crossing a swollen creek when all of a sudden a tree snaps upriver, and if you'd ever heard a tree snap under the weight of water, you'd know it sounds like cannon, only louder. Anyways, the mule takes off like a Chinese rocket, leaving me in the water. I ran after him, but he snagged the saddle and it crashed into the water along with a sack of diamonds.

"Well, I tried scrambling for 'em, and I got a few, but Slack hollers and I look behind me at a wall of water coming down the mountain. I had but seconds to get out of there, and I can tell you, Mr. Harpending, that creek went from being a few feet deep and twenty feet wide to a raging torrent fifty foot deep and sixty across. Trees, rocks, you name it rolled past us, propelled by the rush of water."

"We never did see the mule again," Slack added. "Had to pay twenty dollars for it too. Wasn't worth five."

Harpending experienced a dizziness. "You lost the diamonds." It was a disaster.

"Half, just half, but never fear, Mr.. Harpending, we saved the best half, and I can assure you now, here, that there's still a fortune up there, only don't ask us to dig for it. I'm due for a rest, Slack too."

Harpending couldn't bear this. They had lost half. And they didn't seem so concerned either. He hated the idea he couldn't see the diamonds, but of course, he couldn't very well have them exposed to any prying eye on the train.

"You had no difficulties?" he asked.

Arnold showed surprise . "Difficulties?"

"Finding the, er,.... stones."

"There's more up there than flies on a cow's backside. Practically trip over 'em there's so many. Threw a lot back, of course. Ralston said he only wanted the best."

Harpending swallowed hard. "Threw some back?"

"Give 'em a bit of time to grow a bit more eh?" Arnold joked. Slack enjoyed, seeing Harpending's face go through a range of emotions.

Harpending finally realizing this was a joke, tried his level best to smile. He couldn't get over how battered and weather-beaten the men looked. It really must have been a hard time out there.

"You must get a lot of rest. You have a place to go to? If not I would be happy to entertain you at my home."

Slack started. Was this a trap? It had been Arnold's idea to stop two wretched Irish prospectors and swop clothes. They'd not believed their luck. Arnold and Slack's clothes were dirty and there was a little blood, but they were new and still had a lot of wear in them yet. By contrast the two miners' rags were mere pretenders to clothing, though there was a hint of tweed in one jacket. Everything was held together with hooks and leather patches. These men had obviously been through hard times, and Arnold knew, better than most, that people readily believed what they saw. And what they saw were mountain men in sore need of a change of clothes and a good bath.

"We have a place to go, Mr. Harpending. If it pleases you, we'll be staying over in Oakland. I think that we've done our part in this bargain. If it is all right with you, we'd like to hand over the, er, rocks to you. Naturally, we'll take a proper receipt, but if Bill Ralston sent you, then I'm pretty sure we can trust you."

Harpending quickly produced his letter of authority from Ralston. Neither Slack nor Arnold read it.

"No need to doubt me," Harpending declared.

"Never entered my mind," Arnold told him. "You have someone to escort you over on the ferry? No one is to know what you're carrying, but someone could always take a chance, what with you looking like a real gentleman."

"Your concern is right, Mr..Arnold. I shall cross on the ferry alone, but General David Colton will be waiting for me in his carriage. There is quite a gathering at my house to see your er ... rocks. You'll not reconsider and come with me?"

Slack shook his head. "We're not fit to be seen by man nor beast, Mr. Harpending. We both trust you. Besides, we've got them weighed and counted. Little else to do up in the mountains when you're tired."

"It's a hard life. I know. I was out there long enough."

Slack acknowledged that. It was true. Harpending was one of the few rich men of San Francisco who'd gone out there and earned his fortune with his bare hands. Of course, he'd had the wherewithal to invest wisely, not many could say that, and most were reduced to going back up to the mountains again to start over. Something that Slack was not about to do again in a hurry.

"You a fishing man, Mr.. Harpending?" Slack asked him.

Harpending was surprised. "Fishing? Why, I have dabbled a little."

"Going to get me a boat, I reckon, nothing too fancy, a nice little solid thing that can sleep me and a dog, maybe. Could fish for trout in Lake Tahoe. Then I know there's king salmon in Monterey Bay in June and July. I could chase 'em over to San Francisco Bay during August."

"King salmon is good, but if you want real adventure, Mr. Slack, then you have to go south of Point Conception. You've got barracuda, albacore, black sea bass, leaping tuna. If it's fish you're after, well I can introduce you to a friend who's all for moving south and getting some sport fishing for gentlemen going. There's yellow fin, croaker, cobina and even swordfish. Met a man who's all for settling the Santa Barbara Islands just for that very purpose. Never met a man who was so interested in fish and disinterested in man as

DIAMONDS

Frank Kinney."

"Then you never talked to John Slack," Arnold moaned. " I can't abide it when he gets onto the subject of fish. I reckon he's wasted in the prospecting business. He should have gone out to sea. Leastways he'd never have gone hungry."

Harpending laughed. He was more relaxed now that conversation was flowing. "And you, Mr. Arnold. You staying in the prospecting business, or will you hang up your boots." Harpending studied Arnold's worn hoots and shrugged. "What's left of them."

"All depends. But I can tell you one thing, Mr. Harpending. I could live two life times without missing the mountains. I fancy moving to somewhere flatter than Kansas, where a tree is the highest object for a hundred miles. Beyond that, I couldn't say."

By means of conversation about nothing in particular, the time passed and Harpending was able to make a judgment about Arnold and Slack. They seemed good fellows, and were obviously exhausted: they would need many hours of sleep. He could not doubt their integrity. Had they not just told him they'd hand over their diamonds to him on trust? He could think of few men who'd do such a thing. But then, this was not gold, it was diamonds. They'd soon know if he made off with them, and well, the question just would never arise.

When the train finally pulled into Oakland, almost nine hours late, Arnold and Slack produced a large canvas sack from under their seat and took in receipt a simple piece of paper, on which Asbury Harpending acknowledged the diamonds to be Arnold and Slack's sole property. If he were to lose, mislay, or apprehend the said sack, he would be liable, in full, to the tune of one million dollars in gold coin. It was an onerous and daunting responsibility. Harpending wasn't sure he'd ever held in his hands anything of so much value before. It was a momentous feeling. He understood now what they had meant about sharing the awesome burden.

There were no good-byes. Arnold and Slack vanished into the night and left him to make his way onto the ferry.

The sack was so heavy Harpending had to hail a cab and he was afraid for a moment that he'd never find one and be left standing at the side of the road like a total fool. A station cabby finally pulled in and agreed to take him and his sack to the ferry. Harpending hadn't planned this properly and he was embarrassed. He'd been caught out here. One mistake and he'd be liable for a million. He sweated on this the entire journey. What if he was stopped by a robber? He hefted the heavy sack of diamonds onto his lap and gripped it tightly. He was longing to take a look inside, but only a fool would stop and

198

risk being robbed. It did occur to him that he might be headed to San Francisco with a sackful of rocks in his hands instead of precious gems and this could be Arnold's cunning plan to sting them for a million saying he'd given over diamonds in good faith, but then he dismissed the thought. Arnold and Slack were not rogues; they seemed to be men he could trust.

DIAMONDS

CHAPTER FOURTEEN
Bluff Counter Bluff

No men could have been more impatient than those assembled at Asbury Harpending's house that evening. The debris of consumed wine bottles and half-eaten food was testimony to their siege mentality. They were dug in for the night, or until Harpending returned, whichever came first. Those gathered were an impressive sight , the elite of San Francisco's financial barons. Ralston was present of course, as were William Lent, Will Alvord, the Mayor , Louis Sloss, Alfred Rubery, the very wealthy Maurice Dore , George Roberts, William Sharon and former congressman and governor Milton Latham, whose name would lend an important weight to the enterprise.

The room was well prepared for Harpending's arrival. The billiard table had been covered with a white sheet, and gas lamps were at their brightest over the table so they'd not miss a thing. But there was this awful sense of doom in the room. Rubery was all for sending out a search party in case Harpending and the General had been interfered with. George Roberts wondered if Arnold and Slack had returned at all and if they had weren't looking for better deals, perhaps Flood and Mackay would top Ralston's offer.

Ralston was the only calm man in the room. "They'll be here, nothing has happened, and Flood and Mackay can offer all they want, but I have a legal hold they'll not shake in my lifetime. Arnold and Slack have no choice but to come to us."

Only Lent and Ralston had actually seen any diamonds in the raw, and these associates weren't about to invest their money in this enterprise unless they were properly impressed by incontrovertible evidence.

They were not to be disappointed. At eight o'clock precisely General Colton's carriage drew up outside Harpending's home and Harpending appeared thereafter, unable to suppress a boyish enthusiasm or a broad smile. The General followed him in, firmly closing and locking the door behind him. He took his role as security guard very seriously.

DIAMONDS

"The train was later than usual, gentlemen. All complaints to be directed to Stanford, Hopkins, Huntington, and Crocker, if you please."

"I'll send a cable off this night," Milton Latham announced. "And I'll send Huntington the bill for the cost of you having to feed us twice today, Harpending. It's a disgrace the way the railroad is run."

"And remind them what a time table is while you're at it," George Roberts told them. "What have you, Asbury? That sack looks as though it's been through quite an ordeal."

Harpending hefted the sack onto the billiard table, and all the men crowded around. Ralston smiled as he came up to Harpending's side and shook his hand. "Thank you for accepting the responsibility, Asbury."

Harpending smiled. " There's quite a tale to this." He began to struggle with Slack's knot as the others around him grew impatient to see what was in the sack. "Seems Arnold and Slack found twice this amount and had two sacks of gemstones, but they were struck by a flash flood and lost a mule and half their stones. They send their apologies and ask if you'll settle for a million dollars' worth."

There was much amusement in the room at that remark, for not a man save Ralston, Colton or Harpending could believe a simple sack could be worth so much. "A million!" George Roberts exclaimed. "Arnold's the worst liar I ever heard. I'll wager a hundred dollars right here and now that that sack is full of quartz and they're ..."

Just at that moment Harpending got the sack opened and pushed it over, spilling the contents out onto the sheet.

"I'll take that wager, George," Lent declared with a smile.

An awed hush descended on the room as the extent of the sack's contents were displayed. The colors and the fantastic range of gems were all shown to their best by the bright glow of the gas light. The table was covered with diamonds, rubies, sapphires and a few emeralds. It was unquestionably a monumental haul. Their eyes devoured them with lust, their fingers touched and prodded them with wonder.

"And you say there was another sack just like this one?" Milton Latham inquired of Harpending.

"Yes, all of it lost, though I dare say a man could spend a profitable time in that stream once the floods have subsided. Arnold says they could be washed a mile or more downstream. But it's no easy traveling; ask the General here, he's been up there."

"But what about the claim itself?" Louis Sloss wanted to know. "Are we saying this is the extent of it, impressive though it is?"

Ralston laughed. "My friend, this is but the work of two men with just picks and shovels on the site for a month or a little more. Gentlemen, I am satisfied that Arnold and Slack have proven, beyond doubt, that they are men of good faith, and although I have no way of knowing the true value of these stones, I would be astonished if they were worth less than half a million. With good mining in a controlled atmosphere, I'd say we are on the verge of another Kimberley. What say you all?"

All spoke at once, but the gist of it was that everyone wanted in. Only a fool would turn down such an investment opportunity. Champagne was opened and drunk. Toasts were made by the dozen and every man in the room would have placed their cash down on the table at that very moment if they'd been carrying the necessary amount on them. There were no voices of reason or sanity in that room. The keys to the nations' treasury had been handed to them, and they were not about to relinquish them. Nor were they especially keen to have them put away either. No one seemed to tire of examining the stones and exclaiming their natural beauty and what they thought each one might fetch once cut and polished. There was talk, too, of employing the best lapidary in Holland to come out to San Francisco and train up others in this highly skilled affair. Many plans were made, and if words were deeds, the entire diamond industry would have trembled at the scope of this massive enterprise. Ralston was charged with establishing a company proper, issuing a prospectus, sorting out the legal niceties, and removing the one great obstacle to their control of the mine; the buy-out of Arnold and Slack. Everyone was agreed that Arnold and Slack must be bought out for the cheapest price that could be gotten away with, or at least reduced to a rump holding. No one actually expected Arnold and Slack to give up without a fight, but no one could actually agree what price should be set. Certainly not a million, and even half a million seemed excessive. These men, mere prospectors, stood in the way of them making a fortune. They had to be disposed of, and soon.

There was then the question of authenticity of the gemstones. Everyone was in agreement that though they assumed the diamonds to be genuine, no one in the room was able to state categorically that this was not quartz or colored glass. Expertly produced, but glass nevertheless. A motion was put and carried that Harpending ,as their representative, would take the stones to New York for appraisal by Charles Tiffany; but only a sample of the best ones, as chosen by Ralston and Harpending. The rest would be placed in a secure vault, and perhaps consideration would be given to putting some of the gems on display once the business with Arnold and Slack was out of the way. This would stimulate public interest in the forthcoming share issue.

Milton Latham put forward the proposal that Sam Barlow, a leader of the New York bar, should be retained as counsel in New York an idea that had already ocurred to Harpending, along with General Benjamin F. Butler, on account of his influence in Washington to enable legislation necessary for the exploitation of diamonds in Colorado. It was realized at once by all, that much land would have to be purchased around the diamond area and it was probable that legislation would need to be passed for the company to acquire the "public" land.

Much of the conversation was about money that night. Business, legal matters, commitments, and what rights each had and what role. They all congratulated each other on their wisdom in having the perspicacity in being friends and thus getting this opportunity to make yet more money. It was judged a marvelous evening, well worth the wait, and there was not a man there who didn't think he was well on the way to doubling his fortune within the year. Harpending was thanked by each man in turn for making his home available to them all and Ralston was cheered for being so charitable in letting them all have the opportunity at cracking the whip.

Never did men leave a place so happy and confident.

Never had Harpending and Ralston's star risen so high in their fellows estimations. Maurice Dore was so enthusiastic he was prompted to repay an outstanding loan he'd taken with Harpending two years before, about which both were too gentlemanly to mention. Bill Sharon, Ralston's heir apparent at the Bank of California, was last to leave. Being Ralston's partner in the Palace Hotel project, having supplanted Harpending who had balked at the cost, he wanted to talk to Ralston about the horrendously mounting costs and the possibility of him taking up a healthy stake in the diamonds company on credit. He was a little overstretched at this time, what with the horses and endless demands of the hotel constructors.

Harpending was finally alone in the great fug left by the men. He judged the evening the most successful potential investors meeting he'd ever attended, and as he made sure every last gemstone was back in the bag he reflected that he should have at least one of these diamonds made into a brooch for his dear wife. He'd select one and have it cut and polished by Kavak, if he was up to the job. A dainty thing, a shower of daisies, or an animal perhaps, a leopard. His wife was very fond of animals. It would be a surprise; she was fond of surprises.

He went to bed happy and contented

Not so Arnold and Slack. They had found their way to Oakland and surprises.

They had returned to an unhappy home. Alyce was in tears the moment they stepped through the door. Arnold was angry that she was still there putting their diamond scheme in jeopardy, but by firelight he could see she was clearly distraught, and when a lamp was lit and they saw the ruination of her little home they understood at once. Someone, or many someones, had taken revenge on Arnold and Slack by wrecking Alyce's home. Slack could think of several who could have done it. All those they had ditched on the route to

Rawlins.

The kitchen was gone, completely, the entire section ripped off the main house. Slack was astonished. It looked as though the house had come under attack. Alyce herself was unharmed, but quite clearly the house was a ruin, unless money was spent to fix it.

"I came back and this was it, Arnie. I know you said I was to disappear out of sight, but I couldn't go. No money's been left me and I can't find anyone who knows a thing. The house is all I have."

Arnold was angry. He'd not felt so angry in a long time. He had no proof of course, but he knew that this terrible thing was not directed against Alyce, but against him and Slack. This was stupid. Even up on the mines people would respect another's home. This was knavery of the lowest kind.

"Alyce I promised you I'd see you right. Well, I will. Now I know you were set on selling this place at a profit. It's plain that can't happen unless we fixes it up. Well, they're not going to have the satisfaction of that. I'll not buy a plank of timber in this town, not a darned nail. You were fixing on getting close to a thousand dollars for this place, I know. Well me and Slack will settle that on you, first thing tomorrow. What you say, Slack? "

"I'm agreed. It's the least we could do. Land ought to be worth something."

"Oh,well, we'll keep the land. Oakland's a growing town. A ruin's just the thing to keep on this land. One day I might just come back and find this piece of land is the last of its kind. What you say, Alyce, you accept?"

Alyce walked over to Arnold and hugged him, hard. "Arnie, I knew you'd help. I'm sorry I didn't go away like you wanted."

Arnold held her tight and rocked her a little. Obviously she was shocked, her house being wrecked like this. Funny thing was it didn't look bad from the outside. She'd have to go. Harpending was in San Francisco. Alyce would have to leave and go into hiding. Harpending would recognize her immediately, and he'd know that a game had been played on him.

"Got to send you away, Alyce. Tomorrow. Harpending's here, in town and appears to be running the whole show for Ralston."

Alyce paled, but stayed in his arms. "Oh, Arnie, will you be found out?"

Arnold laughed. "Not us. You should have seen the man when he saw us in these clothes....that reminds me, we got any clothes left?"

Alyce shook her head. "They took everything." She looked over to Slack "Your boots, too. All my dresses, no one ever saw them, or that Mrs Kelly. I could have sworn she was a woman to be trusted."

"Probably got into the wrong hands," Slack ventured. "Alyce, no more tears. You'll live well from now on. I'll make sure Arnie treats you right."

Arnold laughed . "You don't have to worry, John Slack. I'll tend to Alyce without you proddin' my back."

DIAMONDS

They ate what there was that night, then slept on the floor. It wasn't the Grand Hotel, but it was more comfortable than the mountains. Alyce was right to have stayed, but it couldn't have been pleasant to live in a place so ruined.

"Look at it this way, something had to go wrong. I've been waiting for it since we started on this years ago. Everything was going too well. It's no comfort to you, Alyce, but Arnie an' me could be luckier for something going wrong."

Arnold made no comment. "Well, that's yesterday. Tomorrow we tackle Ralston about getting paid for our claim. This is the delicate part, Alyce. That's why you've got to be gone. I've an idea they'll be wanting to get New York people involved, so that's where you're headed. East. When all this is over, Slack and me will be back east and they'll have a trial finding us, I can tell you. You can pick your town to wait in, Alyce, but leave New York out of your calculations."

Alyce lay there in the dark thinking about that. Any place back east. Well, she certainly didn't want to live in any big place, but where? No place too big; she'd be lonely for want of a smile from someone, no place too small, she'd get no peace. Had to be a railroad town. She didn't want to be cut off.

"Philly," She told them. "I never been there, but they say it's a pretty place with a theater and everything."

"Can't go there," Slack pointed out. "Perhaps farther south. Richmond maybe."

"And why can't I go to Philly?" Alyce asked.

"Ralston's got interests in Philly, that's why. We already checked on that. Something to do with relatives and the like, " Arnold told her. "Boston. I like Boston. No one will think of looking for you there and that's where you've got to go. It won't be for long, Alyce. I'll be along to get you soon as this deal is done."

"And when might that be, Arnie?"

"Hard to say. I'd like to ask Ralston for cash right out, but he might not like that. Besides we still have to lead them up to Vermillion so they can stake it out and whoop it up a little."

"Aren't you afraid they'll find you out?"

Arnold laughed. "No woman, I'm not. Ask Slack here. If they dig over that ground for six months they'll never stop finding diamonds. Maybe not as many as the day before and less each day, but there'll never be a day when they don't find something. When they finally figure out there's no more diamonds, well they'll just have to deduce they got them all and that's that."

"It's the truth, Alyce, we spread out the icing real thin, I think they'll never get tired of digging ."

DIAMONDS

"You tell her, John Slack. Something else too, that rock up there holds some of the prettiest granite I've ever seen. There's the irony of this whole enterprise. If you could sell black granite for a price, the whole mesa would be worth a fortune."

"Black granite? Isn't that marble?"

"No, marble is marble, granite is granite. But black granite is prized by some people as a thing of beauty. So Ralston might be disappointed he doesn't own a diamond mine, but one day he might be mighty glad he's got a million tons of granite."

"Of course it might be a very long time," Slack commented, then chuckled some. He didn't rate black granite as highly as Arnold did.

"I think we ought to get some sleep," Alyce told them. "Tomorrow is an important day."

"No bigger ever dawned for us," Arnold added, yawning and stretching. He reached over and kissed Alyce on her nose. "I'm real sorry about this house of yours, Al. I'd come to see this as home myself. I'll miss it."

"But not as much as I will,' Alyce thought to herself. "Not as much as as I.' What was it that nagged at her. The tone in Arnold's voice? The way he'd kissed her? Something wasn't right. A woman could tell these things. But something had changed with Arnold. Had Slack noticed it? Was it all in her imagination? Had she been alone in her ruined home too long with her misery?

It was a long time before Alyce could sleep, and the snoring by the two men lying beside her didn't exactly help.

CHAPTER FIFTEEN
The Snag is Revealed.

Arnold and Slack were beginning to think they ought to quit the rags business and get themselves kitted out with some city suits. If they were to negotiate the best deal with Ralston, they could not do it with the other side sneering at their clothes. There was no time for much tailoring, but suits could be had off-the-peg, so to speak, in the city, and it was to attend to their image they left early the next day, first placing Alyce on a Eastern train. Arnold told her he didn't like to lose her again so soon, but he didn't see how to avoid it with Asbury Harpending around. Slack told her he'd miss her too, and promised her he'd see Arnold kept his word about the money once she'd let them know where to send it. She could leave word in New York at Madame Klein's, an established boarding house that Arnold knew. That done, there were hugs and kisses and reluctant good-byes as the train pulled out of Oakland.

"Well, where are they?" That was the question on every tongue that morning. Perhaps Ralston had expected Arnold and Slack to be on his doorstep when the bank opened that morning. Certainly Harpending did. Yet by noon, neither man had put in an appearance. It was distinctly odd.

Ralston sent out a bank messenger to investigate. More than two hours later (they always linger about their business), he reported that the house in Oakland was abandoned, a ruin.

This certainly made a few hearts beat harder. Ralston was now an anxious man. He had the diamonds in his possession, he could not fault Arnold and Slack in that, but he still had no idea where the diamond discovery was, no idea at all. The venture could hardly go ahead without that knowledge. Arnold and Slack played a canny game, all right.

Harpending was just as agitated. He'd taken it upon himself to sort diamonds from sapphires and those from emeralds, putting the lot into separate velvet sacks made expressly for this purpose. He knew as well as anyone that a meeting was desperately needed with the principals. Alfie Rubery came by to enquire as to their whereabouts. He was as keen to meet them, but he was to be disappointed. He left after an hour to attend to his timber interests. But he'd not stray far, he was so keen to get into this diamond business now, he'd wired to London for funds. He was determined to be part of this adventure. Ralston knew that the business had to be pressed forward quickly. News was beginning to leak out and gossip was rife in Culpeppers. Secrecy had already been compromised. Rumors of 'new exciting finds' had reached the papers, and speculation on diamonds being found in Arizona were surfacing and had not gained prominence only for the lack of any evidence.

But where the devil were the men of the hour? Did they not care for money as much as he'd counted on. Or were they playing hard to get. He could do no work that morning . He could not break for lunch either. All he could do was sit and fret.

And that's just how Arnold wanted him.

"Just when he's beginning to think we've been murdered by bandits or fallen under a carriage on the way to the bank, that's when we pitch up, Slack. Timing is everything in this game. If we'd looked too keen, he'd try to fob us off with pennies. Desperate, he'll give us the keys to the vault."

Slack didn't exactly hold with this philosophy, but he fell in with it. Arnold had been pretty much right up to now.

At three o'clock precisely,(after a splendid lunch at the Grand) two gentlemen strolled into the Bank of California and asked to see William Chapman Ralston. The gentlemen wore suits of the finest cloth and cut and could have passed for bankers if they'd not sported a deep burnished tan, normally associated with miners up in the hills.

Ralston was relieved beyond any measure to see them and at once escorted them into his glass enclosed inner sanctum for consultation.

"My word, you look dapper, gentlemen. Life out in the mountains must agree with you. My friend Asbury Harpending said you were looking worse for wear. I must recommend him to an optician."

Slack smiled as he settled in a high backed leather chair. Arnold remained standing, not wanting to crease up his suit.

"Couldn't come to town the way we was, Bill," Arnold told him, deciding that he was on first name terms again now that the man had his diamonds. Ralston didn't flinch this time, he saw.

They soon got over the pleasantries and settled down to business. It was fortunate, too, that Asbury Harpending arrived, accompanied by Alfie Rubery. They'd come to deposit the diamonds. Ralston took the opportunity to adjourn the meeting to his private office where they could not be observed. Thomas Brown, the assistant cashier,was brought in to properly account for the precious stones (by numbers and weight), appreciating the sorting that Harpending had already done that day.

DIAMONDS

Whether he was surprised by the quantity of stones or the fact that they existed at all, he didn't say. He did issue a proper Bank of California receipt for them, but as is the way with banks, placed a proviso on the value of one million dollars in gold, subject to proper valuation by an authority acceptable to both parties.

Arnold grumbled a little, but only for show. Ralston wasted some time assuring him that he would not be cheated, and it was decided that only the expert authority of Charles Tiffany would be acceptable.

Slack looked at Arnold, but Arnold was smiling. He was confident. He'd predicted this might happen and may have been satisfied to be proven right. Certainly if there was a time to protest, this was it. Ralston waited, but no protest came.

"I'll accept Tiffany's valuation," Arnold told him, "but you're saying you'll only take the best of what we've given you to him. Well that leaves a few buckets unappraised sir. Are you suggesting they are free?"

"No, no. We will assess their value, fairly, once we have Tiffany's estimates. We want to be sure that what we are dealing with here are diamonds and if they are diamonds, which I'm convinced they are, then I want to know their quality. No one in this room is an expert in this field. You cannot expect less."

Arnold mulled that over, and Slack shifted in his seat a little. The meeting wasn't going especially well to his way of thinking and worse, his new suit made him itch something terrible.

"We come now to the actual diamond field. Hereby known as Vermillion Creek," Ralston announced. "Gentlemen, we have an agreement here. I own one third of this diamond field and so far you have kept your word in every detail. I want to thank you for that and also say to you that given the promise of this field, the results shown so far, it would be impractical of you to continue to hold the two-thirds you have, which I admit here and now is preventing the commercial exploitation of this magnificent asset you have. I am saying to you both now that we, through the Bank of California, are prepared to offer-you a generous sum for the entire diamond field if you will relinquish your share. An outright buy."

"And I'm going to stop you right there, Bill," Arnold told him calmly. "I can tell you now, you aren't shaking us out of the tree so damned easy."

Ralston didn't seem annoyed by this at all. Indeed he seemed encouraged. He knew better than anyone, if a man valued something, well, no amount of money would make him part with it. Had Arnold and Slack given it up too easily he'd have to have some doubts.

"Well what have you in mind?"

"I have in mind keeping our two-thirds and getting rich off it."

"But you must know there are millions to be raised just to get this scheme going. You have no experience of raising finance, organizing the massive resources to mine on a commercial scale." Ralston halted a moment and sat back in his chair. "Perhaps we can come to an understanding."

"You should keep a piece of the mine," Harpending intervened , addressing Arnold. "You'll be richer than any man in San Francisco with just ten percent and bear none of the risks or expenses."

"And we will make you a cash offer for the remainder of your share," Ralston added. "A substantial sum."

"I was thinking you already got one third for nothing," Slack reminded him.

"That is water under the bridge and I assure you it is not for nothing, Mr. Slack. You don't know what expenses I am incurring on your behalf, not to mention my time. You don't seem to realize that I'm bringing together the very best financial minds in the West on this deal. In a thousand years you could not secure their goodwill."

"And Flood or Mackay? You think they'd buy my goodwill?" Arnold asked.

Ralston deserved that and took it like a man. Arnold was not to be treated lightly. "You have a price in mind, Mr. Arnold?"

"That depends."

"Depends, sir?" Ralston was being wary now.

"On whether you are making us an offer that includes the diamonds we've brought you or just for the diamond field, leaving us ten percent."

Ralston chewed that over and realized that he had scored a victory of sorts. At least they were talking business now. Harpending's suggestion of ten percent had been an excellent device."

"You have already been paid one hundred and twenty-five thousand."

"With respect, Bill, that's water under the bridge. You paid for some of what you got. We've brought you more and sweated our guts out for 'em too. Now give it to me straight. We retain ten percent free and clear, which we get regular, every quarter right off the top, gross, I'm not even going to discuss net. Right? For the remainder of our share we want a good price cash, in gold coin. For the diamonds brought in yesterday we will take the price settled on them by Tiffany: so long as he and you don't get together to fix a deal to set 'em low. And don't say you didn't think of it, 'cause any man would."

Ralston pursed his lips and glanced over at Harpending and Rubery. This was a delicate phase. Set the price too low, well Arnold could go to Flood and Mackay and they'd grasp this bunch of roses with glee. On the other hand, set it too high and well...

"Well here's how I'll settle this, Mr. Arnold, Mr. Slack. I'll value my stake in your claim at one hundred thousand dollars. Now you own two-thirds, that would be two hundred thousand dollars, less ten percent. But that's calculating prudently for an unsurveyed claim. Should you hold off receiving payment until the claim is verified by an experienced mining surveyor, I'll state here and now, placing it in writing, that the Bank of California will pay you ..." Ralston did some calculating on his blotting pad. " Three hundred and fifty thousand dollars for your remaining shares, excluding the ten percent you retain. "

"Six hundred thousand and you've got a deal, Bill," Arnold answered coolly.

Slack started. He'd guessed two hundred and fifty thousand. Arnold asking for six was crazy. Agreeing to a mining surveyor was sheer madness, surely?

Ralston smiled; this was haggling he was used to. "Four seventy-five, Mr..Arnold. That's a generous offer."

"Five twenty-five', "Arnold countered. "I'm mindful of the diamonds you're holding as security. Remember you ain't paying us for them until Tiffany gives 'em the nod, which *he* will."

Slack was really nervous now. Arnold was playing dangerous poker indeed.

"Five hundred thousand, Mr. Arnold. Is it a deal? Subject to a survey."

Arnold glanced at Slack and smiled, his triumph hard to hide. "Deal." He turned to Harpending. "You are the hotelier here, what say you we take a party of it at the Grand? I think Slack and me can afford the champagne now."

Harpending laughed. "Gentlemen, you are my guests. Mr. Arnold, I must congratulate you on your horse-sense. I couldn't have gotten a better deal out of Bill myself." (This was a lie, since Ralston and he had agreed they'd go to a million, if they had to).

"I hope that I've made the right decision," Arnold declared modestly.

"All monies will be paid no later than the day after the claim has been confirmed by...'"" Ralston was saying, but Slack cut him off.

"You can delay payment depending on a surveyor, Mr. Ralston, " Slack told him, "but we'd want paying immediately for the diamonds currently in your possession once Tiffany is through with them." Slack wanted some kind of insurance. This survey worried him deeply.

A word from Slack was always treated with respect.

"I can see no problem with that. Mr. Slack. John, I'd like you to spend some time with Asbury here and select the best of the stones to your way of thinking. The rest we will have assessed by Mr. Kavak and then made secure. That way you will know Charles Tiffany is seeing the best. All right with you?"

It was. But Slack was still nervous. Arnold had taken a very big risk now.

"There is one matter," Ralston remembered as all were on their feet. "The diamond field. We still don't know where it is, Mr. Arnold."

Arnold smiled, the kind of smile a poker player has before he slaps a winning hand down.

"Well, the way I see it is that you've promised us a lot of money, Bill. And

211

I've promised you a lot of land."

Harpending had to laugh. "You're a damn fine poker player, Mr. Arnold. Get out of this one, Bill."

Ralston was cornered, but he wasn't out of the ring. He took Arnold's point and considered the problem a moment. Finally he had it.

"Mr. Arnold, I believe I can accommodate your request. If I place the entire $500,000, in gold coin, in safekeeping, that is to say in escrow ," he could see they didn't follow-him, "held by a third party, gentlemen, then legally I am obliged to pay you out the moment the claim is verified to my satisfaction. In fact, we can place it with a bank of your choice."

This had Arnold in a fix. He wasn't sure about this escrow business. It sounded like some kind of bird that should've been extinct already.

"And if that money is there, you can't snatch it back?"

"Oh yes I can, " Ralston told him. "If our independent surveyor says no, then you forfeit the money. You'll keep what you've got already mind. The diamonds cover that. The ones we received before. No one loses, but that is the deal."

Arnold looked at Slack and Slack stared back, not quite sure what to make of it. It sounded like they were getting the money. But it was hard to be sure.

"If the diamond field is verified?" Slack asked.

"The money will be released to you with immediate effect."

Arnold stuck out his hand again. "I'll reveal the exact site of the diamond claim the same day Tiffany confirms the diamonds are genuine."

Ralston had been hoping for better than that, but he'd set the conditions, he could hardly ask Arnold to disabuse them.

"Then that is acceptable to me. I'll require your release on the land."

Arnold smiled. "Oh, I think you'll find I've registered the claim, Bill. In Colorado, Utah and Nevada, in case there's a dispute. It's in Arnold and Slack's name, so if you've a mind to forget to put our name on the documents, you'll be fighting in a lot of courts."

"You have my word that you will be protected. I'll swear it legally today." Ralston sounded sincere. It was the best they could hope for, really.

Such was the precision of Ralston's assistant cashier, celebrations began only when documents and receipts and all formalities had been signed for. Mr. Brown was particular about that, and Ralston wanted Arnold and Slack clearly aware of what was happening, just so they couldn't complain later that they were cheated.

Harpending did them proud with a celebration. Champagne flowed, but they declined oysters; their memories of those still too vivid. Ralston looked in, Rubery sang some songs and strangers swelled the crowd. It was an excellent occasion. Slack wished Alyce had been there to join in, but that would have been impossible.

The night was declared over pretty soon, however. Harpending was bent on catching the eastbound train the very next day, and he'd gotten a party together for it. Tiffany had already been alerted. Arnold was keen, but Slack had reservations. It seemed to him that they'd been rushed through in making decisions . He wasn't happy about the conditions at all, but he couldn't say so. There'd been no time alone with Arnold. It was one hell of a risk to show the diamonds to Tiffany, and it was even more of a risk to agree to not receiving the money until the claim was verified by a surveyor. It was one thing to fool General Colton, but who would they pick? What if they really did bring over a Dutchman? They'd be finished. Lucky not to end up in jail. Or broken men in New York's Bowery if Tiffany spotted the diamonds for the trash they really were. Of course some were valuable, but which? How to tell? Who really knew?

"Cheer up, compadre, the world still turns with or without you," Arnold told him as they went up to their rooms in the Grand. They had decided to accept Harpending's offer of a free suite.

"You seem pretty confident," Slack told him.

"And so should you. We are so close to a fortune now, heck, even I believe the claim is worth millions." He laughed, then tottered, bumping into the wall. "Damn champagne, does something to your legs."

"Not as much as it does to your mouth. Feel as though I swallowed a lemon or two."

"As I recall,you did," Arnold told him, then laughed, thinking it was an excellent joke. "I'm a wreck, Slack, get me to bed. I shall be a bear in the morning."

"Well you can be a bear, Arnie, but I'm not sitting near you."

Two would-be wealthy men staggered up the rest of the stairs. Only Slack entertained doubts. Arnold had the money spent already. That would always be the difference between them.

Arnold suddenly sighed, putting an arm around his friend. "I should have asked a million, Slack. I should have asked for a million."

CHAPTER SIXTEEN
Judge Tiffany

The boys had not long left on their journey east when the news got around town about a definite diamond find. The newspapers went wild, of course, and printed all kinds of speculative stories. They could not know the details, but that did not stop the *Bulletin* from drawing a map of the mine, known as "Discovery Claim," citing an informed source close to the Bank of California. Well, it could not be a very close source, for they had the diamond claim sited in southwestern Arizona, repeating the mistake of the *New York Sun* two months previously. When word reached Arizona, the few who lived there, and there were precious few, must have scratched their heads and eyed their neighbors with grave suspicion of concealing this great find. Not a few would have damned their eyes for failing to spot gems "as large as chicken eggs just lying on the ground, ready for picking."

A rush was started by the newspaper, and the articles and rumors caused much merriment in Ralston's circle. Ralston made use of the free publicity, however, and took it upon himself to display some of the diamonds and rubies left behind by the New York party. He placed them in the offices of William Willis, and it took less than an hour for a queue to develop almost a mile long and less than two hours to get them under glass, for Mr.. Willis soon realized there'd be many missing from all the sticky fingers in the crowds. The effect was nothing less than a sensation. Everyone wanted to know where the diamonds were from and how they could buy shares in the mine. The deafening silence was no comfort, and rumors ran wild everywhere. The newspapers received news from every quarter in the United States about persons claiming to have found diamonds. No doubt a few country paper editors were caught out, but not San Francisco editors; they had noted who had placed the diamonds in Willis's offices. From now on, their spies would be watching the Bank of California like hawks.

It is worth noting that at about this time a gem called the Staunton ruby went on display in another store window, but it was a poor thing and not connected with Bill Ralston. It only served to show how just anyone would try to cash in on someone else's luck.

While the fever pitch rose in San Francisco, it also made excellent progress in New York. The *Sun* led with the stories and even offered a prize for sight of the first American diamonds to be brought into their offices. It's possible a few tried to dupe the public, but the genuine articles were being kept under close guard in Harpending's security box.

The party for New York consisted of six men: William Lent, soon to be the president of the mining company; General Dodge; Alfred Harpending; and, of course, Arnold and Slack. The journey had been its usual uncomfortable one, with endless stoppages, inedible food, and indifferent conversation. William Lent had taken a dislike to Arnold and Slack for no reason other than snobbery, and Harpending had nursed a cold for the entire journey. Altogether they would have been more pleased to have arrived at a cooler time. New York was sweltering. It hit them like a fist in the eye. There was not a breeze, just a heavy stench from the mass of humanity and horses that clogged the streets. The men crawled off the train and were instantly bathed in sweat. It was no blessing to be confronted by New York enthusiasm, either. The newspapers were busy fanning the diamond fever and how these men would have been mobbed if they had known Arnold and Slack had arrived in their midst. In actual fact, one newspaper proprietor, Horace Greeley of the *Tribune* was there to greet them, along with his friend General Sam Barlow, the famous legal counsel. Since Greeley was also running for president that year, it demonstrated at once to Philip Arnold the influence of William Ralston.

With Greeley and Barlow was Major-General Benjamin F. Butler, congressmen. Slack had read a great deal about this man. In the heat of the Civil War, it had been Butler who'd been charged by Lincoln to hold New York for him. It had been a difficult time. There were many riots from anti-war, pro-rebel mobs. They used fire to strike terror into the city and it was a ruthless Butler who organised spies to root out these so-called Copperhead elements. Slack also remembered something of tales about Butler holding scandalous orgies on river barges off Fortress Monroe, parties to watch battles in progress, as if the sight of men dying was sport. Hard to imagine this old fat grizzly of a man getting much sport at all now.

Slack was nevertheless impressed. Hot and bothered, but impressed. These men were the most influential in New York and all of them wanted to get a first look at the diamonds.

Greeley was at Slack's elbow as they reached the carriages arranged for the purpose of taking the tired men to their hotels. "Won't you reconsider, Mr. Slack? Surely we can get a glimpse of these stones." Slack said nothing and disappointed Greeley turned to Harpending. "Mr. Harpending you'll let us see them."

DIAMONDS

He was not a man used to disappointment. Greeley was New York, almost nothing happened in the city without his say so. His power was quite awesome; nevertheless, he was not to get his way.

"Gentlemen, we have an appointment to meet with Mr. Charles Tiffany himself at General Butler's residence tomorrow at eleven. We are exhausted and drained. We appreciate you meeting us, but please consider the state in which you find us. Tomorrow, sirs."

Greeley and Butler had to concede the point. It was hard to be patient, but there was no choice.

Will Lent went off with Sam Barlow as his guest. Harpending led the rest of the party to the St James Hotel on Madison Square. It was his choice. The hotels around city hall and the "old" city were too cramped for his taste, and Madison Square was blessed with many shady trees, altogether cooler to the eye, if not the flesh.

Each man repaired to bathe the journey's grime away, once their luggage had arrived.

Asbury Harpending had to accede to Horace Greeleys request that he give an interview to a man from his newspaper. It was the least he could do, but Harpending wasn't giving away much. The less everyone knew, the better chances of keeping the whereabouts of these diamonds secret. It was essential to control the rumors and keep the press with them so that they would be better disposed toward the company once it was launched. This much he'd learned from his business affairs in London. And recalling London, there was work to be done there, dispatches to write and cables to send to his offices.

After washing, a change of clothes, and a small repast, Arnold and Slack ventured downtown on foot, strolling in what passed for air in this city. They had business at 33 Pine Street with bankers *Lees and Waller.* It was here that they had their money on deposit sent by them from San Francisco. Even in this Arnold had been pretty canny. Ralston had paid in gold coin. Gold coin could be changed for paper dollars at almost 210 to the dollar in New York. At one time during the Rebellion it had nearly touched 300. But this year was still a time of financial uncertainty. Gold coin was sure, but paper was, well, paper. Still, the paper dollar was negotiable, and it bought the necessities of life. Arnold thought it worth the risk. Ralston's first payment to them had brought them $125,000 in gold coin. Even taking into account the $59,217 dollars their enterprise had cost them so far, they still possessed $139,000 in paper money, thanks to the exchange. Once Ralston paid on the diamonds following Tiffany's assessment they'd be well into profit, and when the claim was finally verified, why all told there would be over a million to be counted as profit if he and Slack were prepared to go over to all paper.

It was true Arnold had set his heart on a million in gold, but he knew when to fold your cards in this sort of business, and instinct told him he'd gotten the

216

best out of Ralston. It was a real shame it wasn't a genuine mine he was selling, because ten percent of a diamond mine producing ten or twelve million dollars a year in diamonds was quite an income. It made him quite jealous of those folks down in Kimberley making their fortunes, even if his way was more to his taste. As it stood, John Slack and Philip Arnold held sixty-nine thousand dollars each, secure in their separate names. Slack had insisted on that, for although it was unspoken, each knew they'd be going separate ways once the money was divided up. There were small amounts of gold coin safe in London and Baltimore in case they had to take urgent flight.

It was after the bank that Slack realized where they were. "Mrs Klein's boarding house is hereabouts, ain't it, Arnie? Alyce will be anxious for news."

"I'm finished with her," Arnold replied, with a coldness in his voice Slack had not heard before.

Slack could not believe it. He was an old-fashioned sort at heart. He wouldn't believe it. "But... she's your woman."

Arnold shrugged, mopping his brow with a stained handkerchief. "I'll admit she was a good thing while we needed a home in San Francisco, but she's no spring chicken, Slack. I showed her London, didn't I? For nothing. And anyways, she's always on about marriage and babies. I'm finished with all that. She must find herself someone else who'll do as she pleases."

Slack frowned. He would have bet money on Arnold and Alyce getting hitched. "You never intended to set up house with her?"

Arnold smiled, walking on a little way to where an Italian ice cream seller was perched under a shady tree. A block of ice kept his mixtures cold, but you could see the humidity had done him in. Arnold bought himself and Slack some ice cream and laughed as it seemed to sag in the heat.

"Don't look so hard done by, Slack. We're men of the world. Alyce is a good woman, but we've no use of her now. Besides, Harpending saw her. I can't risk it. We don't need her shack in Oakland no more either. We're rich, or soon will be. I'll be damned if I'm going to waste my fortune on raising a family who'll bleed me dry. There's better things to do with money."

Slack ate his ice cream and shook his head. He'd never suspected such heartlessness. If Alyce could have heard this, he knew her heart would break for sure. She'd probably throw herself under a train or jump off a bridge. He immediately thought of writing her a letter, then recalled he did not know where she lived in Boston. He resolved to obtain her address forthwith. He didn't know quite why he felt so strongly about this matter, but he did.

"But you can't just ditch her. She could go to Ralston and tell him everything. You don't know what she might do if she thinks she's been wronged."

Arnold thought about that a moment. He didn't like it, but it made sense.

"Well, it won't matter once we're paid. He'll find out soon enough it was a salt."

"Oh fine," Slack said, stepping back to get a good look at this man he'd thought he'd known so well. Bad business, this. "But you've agreed to a surveyor. It could be months yet and here we are in June. What then? I know she'll feel bitter, I just know it."

Arnold shrugged, waving away some flies. "It's a damn hot city this, John Slack, it makes a man irritable. It puzzles me that folks would want to live in this steamy jungle." He looked at Slack's face then, and knew he'd made an error treating the subject of Alyce lightly. Slack was always wanting things done right. The man had no humor. "All right, all right. Find out where she is and I'll send her the money I promised. Only you'll have to do it for me. I don't want her thinking it was me; I'll not have her hoping. Tell her..." He had no idea of what to tell her.

Slack did. " I'll tell her not to expect anything from you."

Arnold shook his head and wiped the sweat from his brow with his cuffs. "No, listen, she must believe I'm coming for her until all this business is over with Ralston. The money will keep her sweet. Tell her to buy a little place with a garden, like she always wanted. Let her get settled. It might take a while. When I don't come she'll weep a little, but she'll have her home and she'll know I treated her fair."

Slack made no comment.

"I think I must go back now, " Arnold announced. "You coming?"

Slack shook his head. He had to find out about Alyce, they both knew that. "And tomorrow, Arnie, if Tiffany finds against us?"

Arnold laughed, tossing back his head to shake the sweat off his nose. "John .Slack, you are worse than a doubting Thomas. They cannot say anything but what they are, and what they are is diamonds, rubies,and sapphires. Courage, Slack, we are nearly there. The money will be ours."

Slack tried his best to look as though he believed this. "Yes, you're right, Arnie. You go back. I want to walk yet a while. I'm not ready for that charade again. They're too damn enthusiastic for me."

Arnold laughed. "That's what I love about them," he grinned, spinning around and starting to walk away. "Especially Harpending. He's so smitten, I swear I could convince him that they make gold out of butter and coin it."

Slack groaned. "For my sake, Arnie, don't try."

Arnold laughed again and began to walk away, his humor regained. "Don't fret, Slack," he called back over his shoulder. "This will turn out favorably, I promise."

Slack watched Arnold go, but he wasn't convinced. Not at all. He made his way toward Mrs Klein's boarding-house feeling mighty bad about Alyce. There was a note waiting for Philip Arnold, as expected. Been there just two days. Slack claimed he was the man in question and he paid the ten cents fee. Slack took it to a nearby shady spot and parked himself under a plane tree. The city was teeming with people and horses and carriages. The noise was a terrible thing. The horse-drawn trams were crammed tight, folks all talking ten to the dozen and more. Slack thought it was a good place for thieves and pickpockets as well. He knew from just being in New York for half a day that this was as close to hell as any man could get. He was glad they weren't stopping long. He got the letter opened and began to read.

> *Osprey Cottage*
> *Clinton Street*
> *Brooklyn*
>
> *My Dear Arnold,*
>
> *I miss you sorely and wonder if you are safe.*
> *What a terrible journey I had, too. And no amount of trouble with a gentleman who wanted to 'escort' me when we finally arrived. I thought it might be a detective sent by Ralston, but later discovered he was just a lawyer looking for someone to cook and sew for him. Well I managed to shake him by playing one of your tricks at a stop fifty miles from the city. You see, I did learn something.*
> *I couldn't go to Boston. I just couldn't. Instead I'm in Brooklyn, just across the water from Wall Street, your favorite place. I'm living in the quaintest place, on Clinton Street and it's got a garden with apple blossom and I don't mind the heat because I'm on the hill overlooking the river, so it's cooler here than in the city.*
> *I long to see you and John Slack. Are you successful? I do hope so, even if I don't approve of what you're doing. Come and see me soon. I think I can buy this little house for less than a thousand. It needs fixing, but I just know you'll both love it when you see it. I hear talk about diamonds almost every day now. People in this place cannot talk of anything else. I know one woman's son who's already left to try his luck in Arizona, poor soul.*
>
> *Come soon. Tell John I have a new tin bath ready for him,*
>
> *Alyce xx*

Slack felt real bad. He had a lump in his throat and guilt washed over him. Arnie was wrong-headed about this. He'd have to go and see her, level with her. He looked down at his shoes. He'd have to clean up first. He'd take the money to her personally and make it right. He turned towards the street that would take him back to the bank. He smiled to himself. He'd make sure Arnold did right by her, if it was the last thing he did. He made up his mind he wouldn't tell Arnold where she was. He'd panic if he knew she was so close to Manhattan. Slack didn't really believe that Asbury Harpending would recall Alyce at all. Arnold was just using him for an excuse. No, he'd just make sure she had had her home paid for and that she had at least twice as much as when they found her. It was fair, but he knew as he walked towards the bank, she had been led to expect far more.

Another nagging thought seized him. What if Ralston hired a Dutchman to verify the claim? What then? Perhaps it was time to leave? Take what gains he had and leave. He'd not converted his funds to paper, he didn't trust paper. Gold coin was safest. Perhaps it was time to quit before he was exposed for the fraud he was.

Slack stopped at a street corner and looked towards the sun, where at the end of the street he could see tall sailing ships moored at the street's end. Yes, perhaps it was time to slink away, there were ships all around New York. One sailed every day. It would be nothing to disappear to Europe. He'd be rich in Spain with a pocketful of gold.

Arnold had no doubts about anything. He was a happy man, as it happened. No sooner had he left Slack behind him, he had struck up talking with a woman called Flora. At least that is what she said she was called, and she made no pretense at being a lady. She was young, attractive, firm, and for five dollars he could secure her services for a whole night, especially if he threw in dinner as well. Arnold, being a red-blooded man, warmed to the idea and liked what he saw, but he wasn't about to sport the girl on his arm to dinner and told her so. If they ate, well, it would have to be in his room. He was emphatic about that. She argued and Arnold was all for letting her to go to hell when she suddenly caved in and her only remaining condition was iced water and a long bath. Arnold could hardly deny her that, especially for five bucks. Perhaps when the girl saw exactly where Arnold was staying, she regretted not arguing harder, but on a hot muggy day like this, the promise of a fresh cool bath and clean sheets was something she'd have gladly paid him for. To get himself in the mood Arnold ordered iced champagne up to his room.

No more was heard from Arnold and his 'guest' until the next day.

It was Asbury Harpending who thought that there might be a problem. He found Slack after breakfast reading Greely's *Tribune* with his customary zeal. Slack pointed to an article. ' Diamonds in the West confirmed' it confidently stated. "Bigger find than Kimberley?' it asked.

"Where is Mr. Arnold? I've a meeting with him and a gentleman from the press at nine this morning and he's not here. He's generally up for his break-fast before anyone else."

Slack frowned. "I thought he had eaten before me. I'll go up to his room."

Harpending thanked him and went to tell the man from the *Tribune* that there would be a delay.

Slack mounted the stairs wondering what had happened to Arnold. They had barely been apart from each other for more than a few hours since as long as he could remember. He wondered if he was sulking with him because any remark he'd made about Alyce. But when he walked into Arnold's room, one whiff was enough to tell him that it wasn't any sulk that was keeping him abed.

"Damned whore ordered oysters. Everything was all right until we ate and then she was ill, then me. Paid her five dollars, Slack and all I got do was watch her throw up all night." He groaned and clutched his head. "I got my own back. I spewed twelve times, once over her. She'll not fancy doing business in this hotel again. Or eating oysters. Look at me, Slack. All in a sweat and shaking like a dog. I ache and shake. Can't see anyone. My face is swollen."

Slack shook his head. "Five bucks. Women will be your downfall, Arnold. I'll call room service. You need hot milk and rest. Nothing will cure what a bad oyster can do except time and rest. You complain?"

"Complain? I threatened to kill the chef with my own hands. The manager has been up here three times to calm me down and they've cancelled the bill, not that I care since Ralston's paying."

Just to prove he was ill, he vomited again, though little came up. Retching can be painful and he groaned a great deal, possibly more than necessary now that he had an audience. Slack had seen all this before in London and re-minded Arnold of his pledge on the clipper never to eat shell-fish again.

"There's no R in the month. I thought you said..." Arnold spat again and lay back suddenly, a wave of nausea and dizziness over-taking him.

"We have to see Tiffany this morning." Slack reminded him.

"You go." Arnold gasped, then closing his eyes, issued further instructions. "And see that Harpending pays once Tiffany has confirmed their value. I want a bank draft from Ralston today. He knows the agreement. You..."

He struggled with his words and turned over the bed suddenly, gripped by a severe stomach pain. Slack had gotten the message however. He left Arnold to it and on his way down stopped by the front desk to make sure Arnold got a fresh change of sheets and a glass of hot milk and thin slices of plain unbuttered toast later on. It wouldn't cure him, but he'd have something to bring up at least. The Devil's work this, but no surprise. Things had been going too well. Slack sensed doom in the air and he went to meet with Harpending's news reporter with a heavy heart.

DIAMONDS

An hour later, after Slack had posed with the San Francisco party for a photograph, they made progress to General Butler's house to rendezvous with Charles Tiffany. General Bulter's home was built in the French colonial style, complete with exotic plants, high ceilings and much light. Outside the air was as hot and thick as ever, but in this white-washed home all was cool. This was attributed to the cooling effects of the flagstone floors and circulating air. It was all put down to the portly general's French-born wife. It was she who made all welcome and ensured that ice-cold mint julep was always on hand.

All the interested parties forgathered in the walled garden as Harpending set up a table for the gemstones, spreading them out on a virgin white sheet. He wanted to dazzle Tiffany and the others. If he was to secure their financial support, impressing them was everything.

Slack had the difficult task of entertaining the gathering, which now included General George B McClellan, the former politician. He was famous for failing to capture Richmond from the Rebs in '62 and for losing in the presidential election against Lincoln in '64. Even so, the old war horse was still a powerful figure in New York. Present also was a Mr.. Duncan, a banker from Duncan, Sherman and Co. Each and every man new to Slack put questions to him. How had he found the claim? What type of land typified a diamond mine? How did the sapphires differ in appearance to the diamonds, and did one find rubies with emeralds or vice versa? Slack did his best, but he could only answer what he knew, and he had none of the P. T. Barnum style about him. Nevertheless, he did serve to whet the appetites of the "investors."

"Gentlemen, you'll have to excuse me. I'm a man of few words. I went up into the mountains in '59 and I've been a prospector all that time. I could tell you where to look for gold, where's the best place for silver, 1 could save you thousands of dollars in wasted time just knowing which of nature's plants seem to like gold-bearing areas. But as for diamonds, well, it looks no different. There doesn't seem to be any special features, except a quantity of black granite, and that's rare enough. Mr. Harpending tells me there ought to be coal about, but I can't honestly say there's many folks in the west up in the mountains looking for coal, I'm certainly not one of them."

There was laughter in that. It took a rare man to go prospecting for coal, though there was good money in it, especially bunker coal for the growing fleets of steamships.

"I, and my partner Philip Arnold for years thought it was the Indians keeping the diamonds secret. Mr.. Arnold thought it was something to do with the great spirit or a curse or two, but the fact is, although we was in Indian territory how we found the diamonds was completely by accident. That's God's honest truth and I can tell you that I'd already given up on ever finding them when Arnold started panning a mountain creek for gold. The rest is known."

DIAMONDS

General McClellan seemed most impressed with Slack's little speech.

"I'd sooner accept a story from a man who admits to plain luck than any claims to his dedication and skill. I've seen too many battles won by a change in the wind or a sudden downpour to know that it's the man who takes an opportunity when it comes who wins the day. Mr. Slack, congratulations. Now, are we to see these precious stones?"

Everyone took their cue from McClellan. Slack's stock rose accordingly.

"Is it true diamonds were dug up with just ordinary jack-knives?" Someone asked him.

Slack confessed that it was, but added that the emeralds had been found with the effort of a pickax and a good amount of sweat. He didn't want them thinking they were going up there to pick fallen apples.

Harpending came out to fetch them in to wait for Tiffany. He was happy to find to find Slack talking, the men so absorbed and enjoying his modest answers. It was quite a contrast to Arnold's brash behavior. Slack's natural honesty had obviously won them over and well primed to see the great stones .

They entered the large room where the diamonds lay on the table grouped in heaps- diamonds, sapphires , rubies, and emeralds, all to their own spaces. As General Butler closed out the heat, the men gathered to study the treasures and were hugely impressed. They would have been more impressed had Tiffany been on time, but as ever with him, he was more than an hour late. By then they'd drunk quite enough mint julep for their tastes.

They weren't to be satisfied when Tiffany did arrive. He was dressed for the occasion in his coolest French summer suit, but the overpowering odor of his perfume soaked the thick air within minutes of his arrival, and most hung back, content to let him study the precious stones in the full glare of the window's sunlight.

Slack couldn't bear the tension and he'd slipped out to stand in the garden. It was here that General Butler found him thirty minutes later.

"Tiffany is calling for you," he told him.

"You know these roses are infected?" Slack told him. "See, there's black spot on the leaves. They'll wither and die eventually. Got to root 'em out and leave no trace. Dig that soil over too. Get in some good compost before you plant new ones."

The general could hardly believe it. Here was a man whose fate was being decided not twenty feet away and all he could think about was roses.

"I'll have my gardener deal with it. It's my wife's garden, but I'll certainly attend to the matter."

Slack smiled, mopping his brow with his handkerchief. "Tiffany finished?"

"He didn't say." General Butler answered, studying Slack more carefully.

Slack didn't know what to make of that. His heart beating wildly, he did his very best to follow the general back into the house as calmly as possible.

Tiffany was sitting at the table and examining the stone Arnold had named the Jasset ruby. It was definitely the best stone in the bunch; only one diamond came near it for size and clarity. Everyone in the room had their eyes fastened upon him.

"Mr. Slack?" They shook hands. It was all very polite.

"Sir?"

"This is quite a collection you have here. All from one site?"

Slack frowned. He had only one answer really. He could hardly claim they were from somewhere else now. "It's a wide plateau at the top of a long creek, Mr. Tiffany. The diamonds are apart from the sapphires and the rubies are nowhere near them at all. The emeralds are rare and they only occur in clusters of rock. You have to break 'em out with a chisel. Can't say there's many. It's diamonds that's the main feature."

Tiffany thought this over as he pulled on his well-trimmed beard.

"Mr. Slack, gentlemen, these are beyond question precious stones of enormous value, but before I give you the exact appraisement, I must first submit them to my lapidary. I will report to you all further in two days."

Slack's heart sank, but the rest cheered. They had only heard the words ."precious stones of enormous value."

Harpending made the best of it. He praised Tiffany for being cautious and helped him place the stones back into their little velvet sacks. Slack made no attempt at smiling. He thought the game was up.

Harpending tried to dissuade him from leaving, observing Slack's obvious disappointment. "It's best this way, Mr.. Slack. Tiffany will give us an honest opinion. I have every confidence in him. He knows the stones have value, all we need to know now is how much."

Slack shook his hand. "In two days we shall know. There's a bargain to be struck then, Mr. Harpending. We are to he paid for the diamonds you have, and I will give you the exact location of the claim."

Harpending smiled. "That's right, but I'm sure we would not be able to find it, even if we knew. It has been decided by myself and General Butler that for the prestige of the enterprise, once Tiffany has confirmed their value, we will press on toward the claim. You will come, as well as Mr. Arnold. It is only right you show us the way to the claim."

"Yes..." Slack knew they'd request this. He'd been prepared.

"And you will be heartened to know that we cabled Mr.. Henry Janin yesterday, and he has confirmed that he will do the surveying for us. His fee is high. Two thousand five hundred dollars and shares in the enterprise should it be proved, but well worth it I think." Harpending noticed Slack wobble on his feet a little. "I say, are you all right? You've not been eating oysters too, I hope."

"It's the heat, " Slack told him. "I cannot abide this humidity."

Harpending laughed. "Yes, they call this city God's own, but I say the Devil had a hand in it. You're like me, Mr.. Slack, the west is preferable by far. There, a man can at least breathe."

Slack managed to escape, refusing the offer of a carriage. He needed to walk. Matters were getting progressively worse by the hour. He made straight for Arnold.

Arnold was sicker than when he'd left him. Now his eyes and mouth were swollen and he looked feverish. A doctor had visited him, prescribing all kinds mixtures, none of which Arnold would take, sticking to plain boiled milk and Slack's toast. Slack's news shattered him.

"Janin. Henry Janin? Lord, what a blow."

He lay back against his damp pillow and moaned a while as Slack waited by the window (the only place for him to breathe in comfort; a man in sickness is not pleasant).

"Tiffany wants two days and Janin has already accepted. What of your plans now, Arnie? You sure you still want to go through with it?"

Arnold felt black indeed. He'd counted on things going smoothly with Tiffany. All he had to say was that they were diamonds.

Two whole days of doubts and then, on top of it, Henry Janin.

"Henry Janin is the most terrible news we've ever faced," Arnold admitted, groaning further as his fever began to rise again. "He's the scourge of every prospector in the States," he added. "We'll never fool him."

"Janin is said to have examined over six hundred mines without having caused a single client to lose a cent through bad judgment. He'll not risk his reputation on verifying our claim, Arnie. He'd rather say it was a salt than it was true, for fear of being wrong. He's getting two thousand five hundred plus expenses and the right to take up a thousand shares of stock at bottom price."

Arnold digested that. "He don't come cheap. They'll want value from him. Heck..." he spat to clear his constricted and sore throat. " I remember him on Jasper Konrad's silver mine at Hatt's Bluff. There was silver there, I saw it myself remember? He goes down, picks at it, demands Konrad dig in more than seven places and each time silver comes up. Not much, it's true, but enough to convince me or you. Well, Janin says no, the mine's useless. Worse than useless. A mine they'd already taken fifty pounds of silver out of. Fact is, he was right. I don't know how he knew, but Konrad worked that mine another year and he got no more than an ounce of silver for his trouble. It pinched out and Janin knew. And this is the man they want for our mine. My Lord, when things go wrong they go wrong mightily."

"Then what shall we do, Arnie?" Slack had lost confidence in the whole scheme

Arnold had no answer. He had to get sick again. Slack could only wait patiently as the man brought up milk. "Oh, curse the oyster, curse it a thousand times."

Slack wondered about many things as he considered their dilemma. Arnold being ill was a blessing of sorts. It kept him abed, which stopped him doing anything rash.

"Do nothing, Slack. Let's stay out of this a while. Make yourself scarce for the rest of the time until Tiffany reports back. We don't know there's anything bad until he makes his mind up. I'm banking on him seeing things our way. I swear we don't have to worry on account of him."

"And Janin?"

"You tried praying, Slack? I hear it works wonders. One thing is for sure. We don't take them to the diamonds until they've paid for what they've got. I'm insistant upon that. We don't go until they pay. If Janin says it's no good, then all right. We still have a profit. They can't have their dollars back. We traded them good diamonds. Tiffany will say so.

"If things get difficult, well, least we can do is make sure we've got fast horses. You make sure of that, John Slack. If we have to run, we run. We'd be outnumbered for anything else."

Slack understood. "Perhaps Janin won't ... perhaps we did it right."

"We did it right. I always said we only had a Dutchman to fear. I never once thought of Janin. Slack, God will have to be blind on the day we get back to Vermillion Creek, but he's been blind to many things in the past, here's hoping this is one more."

Slack nodded. His sentiments entirely. "Get some rest, Arnie. I'll look in on you later."

"Stay scarce mind. I don't want Harpending seeing your long face."

"Or yours," Slack returned. "You want anything?"

"A hot bath. They say it might help. You can organize that for me?

Slack nodded. "There's one other thing. Alyce. You promised to keep her sweet. If there's Henry Janin coming, we can't afford to have her putting a spoke in our wheels."

Arnold nodded. "There..." he pointed to the dressing table. "It's a letter to the bank. You have my power of attorney. Get money to her, Slack. Send her a letter, say how sick I am. You said you'd pay half."

Slack almost laughed. Arnold at death's door and still he was able to think about how to save half his money. "I said I would and I will. A thousand dollars each. That should keep her sweet enough."

"I was thinking five hundred." Arnold complained, scowling.

"And I'm thinking of Henry Janin. A thousand each, Arnie. She did right by you."

Arnold's face soured and he waved Slack away. Slack paused by the table to pick up the letter. Alyce would appreciate this. Slack fighting on her behalf.

As Slack reached the door, Arnold was coughing again. He sounded wretched. He'd be lucky to be well enough to travel in two days.

Arnold had one last word, though. "Where is she?"

"Boston," Slack muttered as he opened the door and sloped out. He wished it was the last lie he would ever have to tell.

Arnold made no comment. He just lay back in his bed and groaned. It was all he could do. He was a wasted man.

Slack organized Arnold a hot bath, changed his own clothes into something a little more suitable to the climate, and even had himself a haircut and shave. Not for the bank, you understand. For Alyce. She had him proper trained all right.

Only forty minutes later, when at last Slack had the money, he found his way to the Brooklyn ferry from Wall Street to Montague Street the other side. There was quite a delay as a carriage got stuck and Slack was able to study the goings on at Roebling's Brooklyn bridge site in the distance. A one armed man was sat on the ferry watching him for a moment until he caught Slack's eye.

"Used to work on it myself, I did."

Slack looked at him and doubted it. Few one-armed men could be useful on such a construction as this.

"I was there at the beginning, the foundations. That's how I lost this." He indicated his arm. He spat, the contempt plainly evident in his face. "Should've died for all I got out of it."

Slack looked back at the bridge and frowned. "But the foundations are underwater." It was an invitation to a man keen to tell all.

"Aye, they are and I was. You goes down into this air-lock, y'see, and you're working in compressed air. It pains your ears something, awful I can tell you. You're working on the bottom of the river with pick and shovel. It's wet gravel, so you'll know what a sweat you'll work up. You've got six men working down there in this small iron chamber filled with compressed air at eighty, nearly ninety degrees fahrenheit. Now you're sweating on top while your feet stand in icy water, water just itching to rise and engulf you. In ten minutes you've got a blinding headache and they haul you up. They keeps on doing this all day long with different fellas. It's good money, but a month of it you get deaf, six months you'd be dead for sure. I've seen a man drop down dying from the bends, writhing, blood spurting from his nose. They tried to tell me I was lucky only to lose my arm." He spat again and sighed. "Fifty-dollars compensation on account of my other arm remaining healthy. Fifty dollars."

Slack felt sympathetic, but nevertheless he hoped he would live long enough to see them complete the bridge. No braver idea anywhere else he knew of.

When he finally gained Montague Street he made straight for Columbia Heights, following the direction he'd gotten from a gentleman at the ferry wharf. As he climbed above the Brooklyn wharves, he was impressed by the growing view of New York. From this spectacular vantage point you could see Trinity and many spires beyond Hudson Street going north. He stood against the warm breeze and regarded such a panorama he'd not seen anything to match it outside of Nob Hill.

The mass of tall-ships docked at Water Street on the New York side was impressive. As he approached the residential parts proper, Slack thought the folks in these elegant clapboard homes with the flowers and ivy growth on the walls must have fine sensibilities. The streets were covered in fresh straw to dull the grind of the carriages. Grand homes nestled alongside little cottages and quaint shops. It was almost as if time had stood still here. It was altogether much more to his liking than the hustle across the water. Slack remembered too that this had been Henry Ward Beecher country, and he made a note to search out the great Plymouth Congregation on Orange Street.

Finding Alyce's home was much more difficult than he'd imagined. No one seemed to know the cottage, and he'd walked most of Clinton Street searching for it. He didn't like to come and leave without seeing Alyce, but he didn't want to attract too much attention to himself. One never knew what spies there might be and it was best for him to recall that General Butler was running spies all through the Civil War. If he wanted Slack followed it would be a simple matter.

It was just then he spotted her walking along Clinton as if she didn't have a care in the world. She was dressed in clothing he didn't recognize, but there was no mistaking her style, the proud way she held herself, the handsome features.

She must have sensed something, for she suddenly stopped and looked around. She didn't see Slack because he hung back out of sight behind a tree, but when she turned he made up the space between them. He realized with a mixture of shame and pleasure that he was excited to see her.

At the very next corner he caught up with her and confronted her. There was at once a light in her eyes, and Slack couldn't help but burst into smiles. "Alyce, you're looking well, really fine."

She laughed and waited for him to close up to her and although he offered her his hand, she leaned in and gave him a brief and genuine hug. "John Slack, I just knew someone was following me, I just knew it." Her eyes searched his and she looked behind him. "Is it safe? Can you be seen talking with me?"

Slack nodded, took the basket of groceries from her, and walked beside her. "My, you're looking fine. You're a sight for sore eyes, I can tell you that. This place has me all dizzy, there's so many folks. You just never see a friendly face."

But Alyce was looking behind him, slightly confused. "Where's your shadow?"

Slack didn't answer and immediately Alyce grew concerned. "Where is he? Slack? Why don't you answer? Where is he? He is here, isn't he?"

Slack nodded his head once more. "Oh, he's in New York, all right, Alyce. In fact, he's lying in bed sick from eating oysters."

"Oh, not oysters again. If I've told him once, I've told him..."

"But that's not why he isn't coming," Slack cut in , turning his head so she couldn't see his eyes.

Alyce suddenly realized something was wrong. Much more wrong than Arnold being sick in bed. There was nothing new in that. "Something has gone wrong, hasn't it. Tell me...no, wait. Let's go inside first. I have hardly had time to meet my neighbors yet, I just got settled in this week. I was so lucky to find this place. You'll like it. There's no fishing off the back porch, but the air's fresh and the garden is delightful. They tell me the mistress of the last governor lived here, and it's done out so prettily. There's apple trees and plum. There's a noisy old blue jay that squawks at all hours, but I don't mind. It's a place to live, and I just know I could fix it up fine. Tell me, Slack, is he angry with me because I didn't go to Boston? I just couldn't go there. There's been so much rioting with the Irish and all, and then I heard about this place and..."

She led Slack across the street and past an old oak that leaned out over the corner, providing shade for a dog sprawled out in the hot dust. Slack envied the dog his lazy simple life. He saw now why he'd missed the house. It was set back from the street, a thicket of bushes and trees obscured along with the ruins of an old brick kiln left to crumble in the front yard. Alyce led him up mossy cobbled path, and suddenly there were two small homes, side by side, each in neat clapboard, the rear of which would afford a good view of the river below, at least from the upstairs. It was the ideal place to hide a mistress and the walled garden was as private as General Butler's. Cooler, too.

"I have fresh milk here and bread in the oven baking. I hope you're hungry."

Slack smiled . "I have a rare appetite today."

"Good, I can always rely on you to be huungry."

Slack looked about him with approval "Alyce, you have an uncanny knack of finding a real palace to live in. This is a real picture." He handed her the gift of bon-bons he'd brought her.

"I fell in love with this house immediately," she confided. "I was told about it on the train. Can you believe it? An old gentleman was coming to claim his sister's estate and it was his sister who was the mistress in this house. He won't even come to look at it. Says it is a house of sin. I told him I'd buy it if he could see to letting me have it at a fair price and he shook hands on it there and then. Nine hundred and fifty, free and clear. I gave him a month's rent for now and I said I could pay him July. Was I right? Tell me, Arnie isn't going to force me to go elsewhere. Surely Asbury Harpending won't find me here."

Slack waited until she'd exhausted herself with details on the house and her journey and life in Brooklyn. He let her make them a ice cold cordial and cut thick slices of fresh baked bread before he explained the purpose of his visit. And even then he didn't get to say anything much because Alyce suddenly wept and fell into his arms announcing the shame and joy she'd really been keeping close to her heart these past weeks.

"Slack , I'm with child."

Slack was astonished. He reeled back. "A baby? Arnie's baby?"

"Who else's?" She asked, annoyed with his reaction.

Slack just shook his head and groaned. "Oh, this is bitter, luck, Alyce. It's bitter luck. This caps it all, if it just doesn't."

"What are you saying? Slack, aren't you pleased? Arnie is going to have a child, a son most like. Why do you look so sad? You aren't ashamed to know me 'cause I'm not married, are you? I know that's a problem, but surely Arnie will reconsider now that..."

Slack could stand it no longer. He didn't have the knack for lying that Arnold had. "Alyce, I'm happier for you than I look. I know just how much you've always wanted a child. I truly do. I only wish that my visit here today was better timed. I only wish I had better news to give you."

Alyce was quiet now. She knew Slack so well. She sat down, folded her arms, and watched him wrestle with the words. She sensed the worst.

"Alyce, Arnie isn't here because he's never coming here. There, now I've said it. Alyce, he's not coming to you. He doesn't want to get married, he doesn't want children, and he doesn't want you. These are harsh words I know, but..."

Alyce's face fell, her eyes filled with tears.

"Harsh they are, John Slack. I am discarded. Now I am a fallen woman. This child is cursed..."

Slack choked her off. "Hear me out, Alyce. All is not lost. I talked to him. He made certain promises to you. I have made certain that we keep them."

He withdrew the two thousand dollars cash he'd brought with him and placed it on the table. "Two thousand, Alyce. More than enough to buy this property outright and fix it up. One thousand from him and a thousand from me."

"From you?"

"I have lived in your home. I am your friend."

Alyce held her tears. She'd never seen Slack so broken. He could hardly speak right, nor look at her. The money was right, it was good. She was ruined as a woman, a husbandless woman, but she'd never want for a home. All was not lost.

"Alyce, there's other problems. Things didn't go right with the diamonds today. Charles Tiffany wants to delay any decision. He's bringing in other folks to look them over. It might be all right ,or it might be bad for us." He could see she was about to speak. "Wait, yet. They also want to bring in Henry Janin. You'll remember hearing about him ."

Indeed Alyce did. Arnold had once confessed to her that every prospector feared him and his opinion. He had to be the most famous mine surveyor living. It was terrible news. The diamond salt would be discovered for certain.

"Slack, what will happen? I mean, could you go to jail?"

Slack smiled. "They'll have to catch me first. I know those mountains better than any man. I'll not go to jail, and neither will Arnie. We might have to lie low, but I can always grow another beard."

Alyce suddenly realized what was different about Slack. "My goodness, your beard. It's gone. Your hair is cut too. I never even noticed."

"It was the barber's idea. I didn't have no choice, but it's the heat. I can't live with this sticky air. "

"You look years younger. You know that? You look like a young man again. Arnie won't know you. I can't believe I never noticed."

"You were too busy looking for Arnie."

And that was so true she felt embarrassed by the remark. "Oh what am I to do, Slack? What can 1 do? I have a child in me. Will Arnie not change his mind once he hears?"

Slack didn't think so. "No. He is a changed man, Alyce. The thought of riches has him ..." Slack couldn't think of the right word.

Alyce allowed one tear to escape, a fat one rolled down her cheek and splashed on her left hand. "I had always worried about that. I could see how he spent in London. The way he eyed the women. But all men are that way. For shame, my life is in tatters. If only I weren't with child I could face this. I could go on. There's so much shame, Slack, so much shame." The deep anguish she felt was writ plain on her ashen face.

Slack looked at her then turned to his milk and quaffed the whole glass. It was his way of getting up courage. He set the glass down deliberately slowly, then looked at Alyce. "There's another way, Alyce. You could marry John Slack."

Alyce almost laughed and only just checked herself in time. Marry John Slack? And spend the rest of her life hounding him into a bath, or waiting for him to come home from fishing The very idea of it was absurd. It was Arnold she loved, not Slack.

"Oh, you have always been so tolerant of me, John Slack, but how could you do such a thing? I am a spoiled woman. Why don't you find yourself someone new? You'll be rich soon yourself, if they don't find you out. A fresh young girl." Now she was crying.

"Arnie said a cruel thing, Alyce. Said you weren't no spring chicken. But Arnie is a fool. Maybe he wants someone new, but I likes what I see. I know I've never been romantic, but I know something that Philip Arnold doesn't. You are the most lovely and loyal woman a man could ever wish to call his own."

Slack stood up. "I know you won't marry me. But I had to ask." He smiled. "Never say John Slack didn't get a shave and haircut for no special reason." He pointed to the money on the table. "The money's here. Buy your home and be happy. Raise that child well. There's more than one woman in this world who's had to raise a child without a husband."

Slack paused at the door. "I'll always remember you just like this, sat in that chair."

And with that said, Slack was gone. Alyce remained where she was, stunned. Everything had happened so fast. She'd been so happy to see Slack.

She sat in the chair, fixed, quite unable to do anything at all. All she could think of was that the man she loved had said she "wasn't no spring chicken " The room suddenly swayed. Arnie had used her. The entire past three years he'd used her and then just paid her off. And then there was poor Slack left with the pieces, wracked with guilt, that was plain. He was always so loyal to Arnold. Yet he'd come, told her the truth, when it was plain Arnie trusted him not to. And here she was two months gone already, bearing his bastard child. God could be very cruel sometimes. But perhaps it was his way of blaming her for staying with sinners. There was no greater sinner than Philip Arnold. He was taking a risk that she wouldn't seek out Asbury Harpending while they were in the city and tell all.

Alyce was so confused. Why? Why had this happened? How could it have happened? Tears flowed heavily now. Such bloody misery to come.

Slack walked down the hill with a heavy heart. He'd told the truth, to be sure. He tried to make things right. He thought that if he offered to marry Alyce everything would be put right. It was true Arnie didn't deserve Alyce, what he hadn't realized was that neither did John Slack, apparently. Now he had risked the entire enterprise with his foolishness. Alyce could run to Harpending now, if she knew where to look. She could cable Ralston with the truth. Even if Ralston didn't want to believe it, he'd have to investigate and the truth would come out. He'd done a very bad day's work here.

He reached the bottom of the hill and hardly dared go back across the water. He just didn't know what to do. Arnold would probably kill him if he knew what had happened. And Alyce probably wished him dead too for suggesting marriage in the wake of her sudden grief about Arnold.

Maybe *he'd* go to Boston. Maybe it was Slack who should disappear?

Slack watched the ferry come over, laden with horses, frightened and deadly nervous of the water. He just didn't know what to do. He knew he wasn't much of a catch. Alyce was right to refuse him, but it was hard to go back to Arnold now and face him, especially the way he felt. He had every sympathy for those petrified horses crossing the river. They didn't know whether to be scared of what was underneath or what was ahead. Either way, it presented no choice. He thought of what was coming. Tiffany might say yes to the diamonds, he might even give a good price for 'em. But Henry Janin? He was another matter. He'd not he fooled so easy. Arnold had taken on the best. Now he suddenly knew what it was like be a buffalo out on those well hunted plains.

Perhaps it was time to call it quits He was just ahead, his share of the diamond money would see him good, good enough to live a long life without worries. If a man couldn't live on what he had in the bank, well something was wrong. He didn't play the horses, didn't drink more than he had to and the best thing in life was free. Fishing did no harm to anyone except a fish. That's the way it should be. He must pick a spot with good fishing and get himself a log cabin. Why, he'd live ten years without thinking of a reason to spend a dime, let alone a hundred thousand. That was what had always been so crazy about his life with Arnold. The obsession with getting rich. He hadn't really thought about it much, but he'd pretty much done what Arnold wanted these past fifteen years or so, heck longer, ever since they were kids. Arnold had wanted to get rich, so Slack had gone along. It was no use thinking about the farms they'd left behind and sold. No doubt they would have had dull lives, farming wasn't tough like prospecting, but then, at least you'd have time to find yourself a girl, get married and have a family. At least you'd eat once a day, not one out of five, like sometimes.

The more he thought about it, the crazier it seemed that he was Arnold's friend at all. If he'd stayed back on the farm, well he'd be a steady landowning man now, up to his armpits in corn, six kids helping out with weeding and threshing when they had to. A wife busy keeping them all in line. No doubt he'd missed a lot living with Arnold these past years. Of course not all of it was bad. There'd been good times. Times when they'd found gold and spent it like two newly crowned kings. Times when they'd seen sights it had been a privilege, few, if any, others would see. But add up the good times and compare 'em to the bad. Well...maybe that was why Arnold wanted money so bad. He had to have something to show for his scars. Trouble was, Slack just couldn't help thinking that his life had been such a waste. A terrible waste.

He sat there at the water's edge, thinking, watching, depressed, quite unable to come to any decision at all. The horses were got ashore and herded into a corral. Seemed they was to be auctioned. He decided to take a look. Some interesting animals stood there.

He walked over to the corral as the auction began. Quite a crowd had gathered, though the auctioneer wasn't getting much of a price. Slack wondered why there were so many. At least forty, ranging from yearlings to five six year old mares, some in foal and distressed.

Slack nudged a stranger and asked about the horses.

"Mellish's stables burned down. Mellish with 'em. His creditors sneaked the horses over this side to get something for 'em. Against the law to sell them the other side."

"But these are fine horses. Why are they fetching so little?"

"That's the price. That an' the creditors are in a hurry."

Slack couldn't believe that an auctioneer couldn't get five dollars for a beautiful yearling. The same horse would fetch two, three hundred in the West. In fact, the whole bunch would fetch a pretty penny if they were shipped over. It was a crime to sell 'em so cheap.

He felt a desperate urge to buy them himself , though it wouldn't exactly help his situation. He heard himself speak when a particularly fine two year old filly stood watching him with pathetic eyes.

"Did I hear right? Did someone just say you bought all these horses?"

Slack turned and found he was facing Alyce once more. Her face all red from crying. She stood before him , her eyes searching his face,

Slack was quite taken aback. He'd never expected to see her again.

"I've come to say I'm sorry, John Slack. I was vile to you. I can't say how sorry I am for spurning you like you were some common sailor."

Slack frowned. A person saying sorry to him was not something he was accustomed to.

"Alyce, you were right. I was a damn fool for asking."

Alyce shook her head. "No, you were a damn fool for buying a filly that obviously has been sold cheap because someone here is taking advantage of the law. But you aren't a fool otherwise, not to me."

"Well, here I stand." Slack said, smiling for the first time. "I just didn't know what to do. I..."

Alyce smiled seeing his face blushed. "Slack, I'd like you to ask me to marry you again, if you meant it. If you want to marry me 'cause you like me, not because you think you have to."

Slack didn't know what to say. No words came. The horse were restless and he began to call to the nearest ones to calm them. It was easier than saying anything to Alyce. He couldn't believe he'd bought this horse. He had to go over and give his name and pay. Twelve dollars. It was a crime to pay so little for such a fine filly. Alyce followed him over and stroked the animal whilst he settled up. The auctioneer carried on calling, and Slack realized he'd end up buying the lot unless he watched out.

"You like her, Alyce?"

"She's magnificent. Twelve dollars! I'd pay a hundred for such an animal. Look at her coat, look at her face, so sweet."

"Then she's yours," Slack told her. "You've got a stable and I know you can ride as well as any man. I know ladies don't seem to admit to owning legs in this city, but I reckon you'd like to get out on your own."

But Alyce didn't appear to be listening to him. She'd spotted a chesnut colt standing petrified as the auctioneer tried in vain to raise an opening bid for him. She couldn't bear it.

"Five dollars," she called out.

"Alyce what you doing?"

"Five dollars, I have five dollars bid," the auctioneer called.

And he got nothing more. So Alyce got the colt to go with the mare.

She smiled in triumph toSlack. " He's going to be magnificent, John Slack, and he's my gift to you."

Slack looked at her and frowned. Then he understood. "You come looking for me deliberate?"

"You like your horse?" she asked, producing the money to pay for it. "Are you going to ask me to marry you or not? You heard me, John Slack."

"If we marry, Alyce, it has to be our child. Arnie's not to know."

Alyce smiled. "I've had better proposals, John Slack. You don't have to worry about the child. He or she will never know Philip Arnold existed. You'd be the father. Besides, there's always the possibility of another, or were you thinking of producing a foal?"

Slack was smiling now. Things were back to normal with them.

"Alyce,will you marry me?"

"Only if you accept this horse."

Slack laughed. "You're tending 'em. I'm gone for a while, you know that."

"I'll tend them, feed them, ride them, and they'll be the pride of Brooklyn. You'll come back?"

"You know we couldn't see Arnie no more."

Alyce nodded her head. "It would be best if you stopped seeing him now."

"You know I have to go up into the mountains with him."

"After that, if you survive Janin's company. Tell Arnie you're going your own way. Win or lose. He doesn't have to know about us. He always said he'd go back to Kentucky a rich man. Well, let him."

Slack chewed on his bottom lip. She was right, he'd been thinking the same thing. But Arnie wasn't an easy habit to break.

"You think you should take the cottage?"

Alyce nodded enthusiastically. "I'm determined. They'll never think of looking for you here, and besides, who is to say we should stick with Slack as a married name? You can be Frank Smith or something fancy like Richard De la Ware."

Slack laughed. "You'll not turn me into a De la Ware."

"Well, maybe not, but I want you to give up this life. You aren't suited. You never were. Be my husband. I will love you. I will care for you. I already have these past three years. I know you'll treat me fair."

A rough-looking fellow came over to them then and asked them to remove their horses. Most were sold now, mainly to an odd stunted-looking fellow with a glass eye who was busy telling others what to do. Slack rather feared the worst for the rest of the horses.

He gathered the rope tied around their necks and there was a bit of a struggle, but they came when he spoke softly to them, the way he always did to animals. Soon they were all walking back up the hill toward Alyce's home, Alyce examining their gains on the hoof.

"The colt's real distinquished. Someone will be mad to lose him."

"I've an idea we've committed a crime. Never thought we'd end up horse thieves. You hang onto these specimens, Alyce. Feed 'em right and they'll look after you well. I know horses, and these are something special."

Alyce was happy again. All right, she hadn't gained the man she always thought she'd get, but Slack was a good man and the horses were a good omen, she was sure of it. She might never have found him again unless they'd gotten his attention.

"When will you leave for the mountains?" Alyce asked suddenly.

"Day after tomorrow, I think. Soon as the business with Tiffany is settled."

"Then stay over. At least eat supper with me, tell me everything that's happened and what Tiffany said. They don't need you over there."

Alyce found Slack looking at her with one of his half-smiles poised on his face. "What you thinking?"

"Oh, I was just thinking of finding these critters a meadow and how we should get some saddles and ..."

"No, you weren't thinking that. I can tell."

Slack laughed. "Alyce, you've caught me off guard. I didn't reckon on all this happening. We going to get married with a preacher present?"

"Why do you ask?" She sensed he might to change his mind now.

"Well, you being with child an' all."

"Preacher isn't to know that. God does, but the preacher only sees us. You can still say no."

"You think we can find a preacher and a meadow, today?"

Alyce laughed, suddenly growing in confidence. "And I suppose we've got two horses for upstanding witnesses."

"We shall find witnesses. You sure about this, Alyce? I ain't what they call

DIAMONDS

a catch."

Alyce took his arm and squeezed it. "John Slack, you are the world's least romantic man, but I wouldn't swap you for a thousand other men. Now you'll be mine, and soon you'll have a child to take fishing in the bay. I heard there is good fishing in the bay ."

Slack was glad to hear that. He'd been wondering where a man could go to get some quiet in this city. "This bay close?"

"A few miles. You've got a horse."

Slack grinned. "You know how to catch a man, Alyce."

She scoffed at that. "Then how come I ended up with Arnie and you? Still, you were always a rock to cling to, John Slack. I fear it is Philip Arnold who will discover too late who loses most from this."

That was true. Arnie would miss Slack a great deal. They'd been together for so long it was hard to imagine them separated, or that Slack would go off with his woman. But then, strange things can happen.

Later, with the horses installed in the stables and fresh hay given from the house next door, Slack held Alyce's hand as they watched the animals get used to their new homes. He squeezed Alyce's fingers, quite unsure about how to progress with this new relationship. He'd known this woman three years and never once hinted that he even liked her, let alone made a promise to marry, like now. It was a rash thing to have bought the horse, but somehow it had brought him a wife, and for a man who considered he'd be living a life without one, there was a lot to he grateful for. He knew, looking at her as if for the first time, that he'd loved Alyce for much longer than he cared to remember.

Suddenly he recalled he'd brought the one thing that would be of value to Alyce and cement their relationship proper. He fished into his pockets and finally came up with Arnold's diamond, the one he'd tried to give Alyce in London. He squeezed her hand again then flipped it over, placing the diamond in her palm. She looked down in astonishment. It glittered in the light.

"I reckon you can take this now, Alyce. It's unlucky to refuse twice."

CHAPTER SEVENTEEN
"I'll be damned..."

It was June before Clarence King, the great land surveyor, heard about the diamond find in the mountains. He refused to believe it, and his companions out in the field agreed with him. Ordinarily, one man's opinion laid wouldn't matter much, but King thought differently. There was a higher quest here. Knowing America and mapping the continent had long been desirable, but the sheer size and scale of the project had daunted many. Since 1867, when Congress had authorized the famous Fortieth Parallel Survey, Clarence King had led a geological and topographical exploration of the territory between the Rocky Mountains and the Sierra Nevadas, which had included the route or routes of the transcontinental railroad.

It so happened that in the summer of 1872, King and his field men were still at work on the survey. It was the news that someone else had discovered diamonds that had disturbed him the most. Part of his assigned purpose with this survey had been to advise Congress and the nation at large of the natural resources of the area. For them to have missed something as spectacular and valuable as a diamond field reflected on his own prefessionalism and, indeed, showed up the work of the entire Fortieth Parallel Survey. It could even jeopardize future surveys.

Thus, when the news came, it presented an embarrassment that had to be dealt with. King was a high-minded fellow, who demanded and received much loyalty from his assistants and peers. He was an arrogant man, rugged in appearance with long, dark hair. He was particular about his toilet, and was smooth-shaven, leaving only wild grey sideburns. This was a man harder to please than Henry Janin himself.

"I'll be damned if there is one diamond in the whole continental United States," he declared, "not a one."

Naturally, they couldn't wire William Ralston in San Francisco and tell him of their suspicions without proof; still less could they request details about the claim so they could investigate it. They knew from newspaper reports that the location of the diamond find was a strict secret. The 'facts' were that more than ten million dollars had already been invested.' Indeed, diamond fever had spread to all parts of the West. Denver, Salt Lake, and the little station stop of Green River were all suddenly the "sites" of fabulous diamond mines, and perhaps caught out a number of incautious investors keen to buy in at the ground floor. It was this speculation that King wished to dampen down.

"It's just plain ridiculous. We must put a stop to it. If we haven't found any precious stones in all the territory we have mapped, it's unlikely there is any to be had. I declare that we will expose this for the fraud it is."

They gathered at a saloon on the banks of the Yampa below the peak called Rabbit Ears Pass. It was just west of the Continental Divide, and there had been reports of a nickel find, but it had come to nothing. It was here that their own hand-written maps had been spread out and the information pooled. Luckily for them, the newspaper reports held accounts given by General Colton and others who'd been out to the field, but cannily refused to reveal its where-abouts.

They knew, for instance, that the Green and Yampa rivers were involved and the field had to be in northern Colorado, or else Utah, or the bottom corner of Wyoming. They had the area circled and luckily they'd covered much of the ground previously. After all, they were the *only* people on the continent of America with accurate maps. By deduction, they immediately eliminated Wyoming and thought Utah unlikely. King himself favored Colorado, but still and all, it was a massive undertaking. They abandoned all other work and riveted upon the task of proving the diamond claim false. The reputation of Clarence King would stand or fall by their actions.

CHAPTER EIGHTEEN
Westward Ho - Janin Be Damned

Arnold frankly didn't give a damn where Slack was or where he'd been. He just wanted to know when he was going to feel better. He hated being sick and he hated being out of control of the situation even more. He didn't know what Harpending and the others were up to. They'd got word to him, but for the best part of two days he'd been left alone in his sick-bed with no one to talk to and plenty of time to think. That was what he hated the most. Thinking made a man depressed. And he was very depressed. He'd not let on, he was too canny for that, but this sending for Henry Janin to verify the mine terrified him. Once he'd been a hundred percent sure of the enterprise, but not now. It was his private opinion that they would be found out. Whether it ended politely with Janin declaring the mine 'unproven' or a bloody shoot-out, it was hard to predict. He'd seen enough shoot-outs to know that it was usually the perpetrators of the hoax who lost.

He sat in his luxurious bedroom with a throbbing headache, and swollen lips, his mood turning blacker by the hour.

Harpending was much less anxious. True, Tiffany had been awful quiet, but then the silence meant work was being done.. Ralston had sent cable after cable asking what Tiffany was up to, but there was nothing to report.

He therefore took the opportunity to enjoy what New York had to offer. Although the city had the opera, it was too difficult to listen Mozart in this overwhelming heat. The theater was busy, and besides, he'd seen enough melodrama in San Francisco. Music hall didn't appeal at all, so a lucky invitation to visit an estate up the Hudson at Hyde Park couldn't be resisted. It would be cool on the river, and the promise of good horse-riding was more to his tastes. He took his entire party with him and it was quite an occasion.

So it was a Friday, in the middle of the month of June, before Harpending was ready to summon Arnold and Slack to his hotel suite. Slack was newly returned and everyone commented on his beardless face and well-cut hair. It was quite a revelation to discover that underneath it all stood an almost handsome swain. Arnold, still exceptionally weak from his illness, made quite a contrast to Slack, who seemed calm and cheerful, a little red from the sun, but a relaxed man. New York obviously agreed with him.

They were once again gathered to await Tiffany.

Those gathered were William Lent, General Dodge, suffering from hayfever, General McClellan, General Butler. Alfie Rubery, Harpending, Arnold and Slack sat opposite the others. A table lay between them, upon which a jug of water stood surrounded by ten glasses. A bottle of champagne stood to one side, chilling in ice. This was a little premature Slack considered, but was cheered to see Harpending still hopeful.

Outside the building was heard the usual cacophony of city noises, and the palpableness of the unbreathable city air. The rancid stench of the city streets was no joy to the nostrils either. Slack looked out the window and briefly caught a glimpse of a three-masted schooner passing the far end of the street on its way round the Battery. He longed to be out of the room and back at the bay fishing. He'd spent the last day there with Alyce, she exercising the horses and he fishing. He'd caught something he didn't exactly recognize, but he'd put it on a stick and smoked it anyways, and they'd had a kind of wedding supper of fresh smoked fish. It was his idea of good living, though he suspected Alyce had expected something a little more grand. She'd gotten him to a preacher soon enough. He'd thought the preacher would object, but he had done no such thing and married them off quickly, even providing the witnesses for an extra two dollars each. So he had been lassoed and hitched without so much as a struggle.

Funny thing was, being married to Alyce was not so different to living with her before, except now he shared her bed. And that wasn't no picnic either, with her insisting he take another bath before he even looked at her.

For his part, Arnold felt nauseated. He didn't think it was possible, but he still felt feverish. He'd had nothing in three days but milk and dry toast. He was an unhappy soul, half the man he'd been just a week before. The others didn't seem to notice he was being unusually quiet. Each one of them listened only to the sound of the French carriage clock ticking away on on the mantelpiece. Charles Tiffany was already hour late and it was not as if 15th and Broadway was much of a distance to come.

Tiffany finally arrived ten minutes later with florid apologies.

"I am so sorry gentlemen, so sorry, but my son Louis told me only ten minutes ago that I would be late. I was so busy examining a particular diamond that I lost all track of time. Such a magnificent stone."

This apology was readily accepted. His praise for one of the diamonds was an excellent augury for things to come.

"This is good news, " General Butler declared, turning to beam at Slack.

DIAMONDS

"Now before I begin, I have sorted the gemstones into differing piles and I shall make my remarks."

He made quite a fuss over placing the precious stones just so and attaching little labels to each pile, which being in French, few around the table could fathom..

"Now, before I begin, I must say that I will give you only the lowest value. Mr. Ralston requested that he would like to insure the diamonds and other stones and I am obliged to value them only at the insured value as they are now."

Arnold leaned towards Slack and pulled a face. They both knew exactly why Ralston wanted them valued low and it wasn't anything to do with insurance.

"Now, Mr. Harpending, " Tiffany continued, wiping his brow with a delicate handkerchief of the palest lilac. "I must stress that this is not my opinion, but that of my lapidarist Van de Broek. His reckoning is that at the very lowest you could expect one hundred and fifty thousand dollars. Remember please that they are yet to be cut and polished. And..." He paused to survey them all. "I can see in your eyes you are disappointed. But may I remind you all, a finished stone represents exacting precision. You have here gemstones of good quality, the ruby and one diamond in particular of twenty-four carats. This alone will account for almost a quarter of the price. Yet's possible it could be worth two hundred thousand, or twice that. Once it is cut and polished we shall see. Nevertheless, as they are now offered to me, I am not prepared to state that the company of Charles Tiffany will value them at more than the amount aforesaid."

This was caution itself.

"Just one diamond could be worth $200,000," Will Lent declared. "And these were dug out with a pick and shovel? It's remarkable, remarkable."

Arnold was less impressed. There was a scheme afoot here to cheat them and Tiffany was in on it. Either a diamond was worth the money he said it was, or it wasn't.

Harpending stood up to thank Tiffany. He was far from disappointed. It meant that with all the precious stones found so far by Slack and Arnold, the total value could be almost a million dollars, even more once they were cut and polished. It was a good result, all things considered. Especially bearing in mind that Arnold and Slack had agreed to accept Tiffany's valuation, which of course was he lowest one). There was the matter of the stones left back in San Francisco; those were far less interesting than the ones Tiffany had examined, and Arnold would have a tough time getting a good price out of Ralston on those. He was aware that Tiffany had done Arnold and Slack no favors here.

Champagne was suddenly uncorked, a shout went up, and General Butler pressed for Tiffany's signature as to the certified value. Everyone save Slack and Arnold judged the exercise a success.

The toasts were enthusiastic and most optimistic.

"I say we are being robbed," Arnold told Harpending, but Harpending just shrugged.

"You agreed to abide by the terms. Now had you come in with cut and polished stones, then there would be another value."

"If we'd come in with cut and polished stones you would have scorned us."

Harpending mused on that a moment, and could only agree.

"Yes, but think on this Mr. Arnold. You own ten percent of a diamond mine that Charles Tiffany himself will be boosting. Your future fortune is secure. You will be living on Nob Hill in no time at all."

Arnold could not very well argue the point, not did he feel up to it. He was suddenly overcome with tiredness and a wave a nausea. He abruptly left to find a hansom cab to take him back to his hotel, instructing Slack to handle the financial matters on his own.

By two 'o clock Harpending had concluded the deal with Slack. The one hundred and fifty thousand dollars, to be paid in gold coin, would represent the diamonds valued by Tiffany, and for those remaining in San Francisco he would pay an additional twenty thousand. There was of course still a great sum to come to the men once Henry Janin had confirmed the claim. Slack should have argued for more, but he wanted to appear calm and blasé about these precious stones, as if he was already thinking about the ten percent they'd get from every diamond sold from the mine. Only he and Arnold knew that that was nothing more than hogwash. The hundred and seventy thousand would be real money in the bank, at least.

Ralston kept his word. Once he had been wired about Tiffany's verdict, he wired the cash back payable to John Slack. And since Harpending had them booked to leave on the west bound evening train, Slack had no time to do anything other than put the money with his bank, undivided.

They were all assembled in the hotel lobby ready to depart when a cable came from George Roberts in San Francisco. Harpending received it and read it aloud.

Congratulations upon Tiffany result Stop -
Myself and party of friends will meet you at Omaha with intention of joining mountain expedition Stop Do not go without us Stop
- George Roberts Stop -

Arnold rejected the idea at once. "We had an agreement, Harpending. You

243

know that. Me and Slack will take you and Janin to the diamond claim. There is no way I will entertain turning this into a circus. You tell Roberts he can't come. We haven't been paid a dime for our claim yet, and I'll be damned if I'm letting half of California crawl all over it so Ralston can claim it's open season."

Slack supported Arnold on this. He didn't want any more witnesses to their shame than was absolutely necessary. Or so many on site that the diamonds would be depleted too quickly.

Harpending had to agree. Roberts had been no part of this agreement. He would be a major shareholder, for it was he who hadd alerted Ralston from the very beginning, but Arnold was right: this was a professional investigation of a major diamond claim, no jaunt or hunting trip. He rapidly agreed to cable Roberts back and deter him from any action that might jeopardize the handing over of the claim.

With that small battle won, Arnold began to feel a little better. Prior to commencing the train journey, he managed to eat some poached eggs and hold them down. He was determined to get himself well again.

He found Slack in the men's room prior to boarding.

"You could have bettered the price, Slack. Do you have the receipt of the deposit?"

"I do. One hundred and seventy is still a small fortune, Philip Arnold, and there's more to come."

"But you saw how they conspired to cheat us. The lowest value. My God, they'd sell the skin off their own kin."

"Well, we have a profit now. Best to worry about Janin and our own skin now."

Arnold splashed his face with water and rubbed his eyes. "I hope you brought good running boots. We may only get one chance before they form a lynch mob."

"You think it might come to that?"

Arnold was about to reply when Harpending came into the mens room.

"It'll be an excellent journey gentlemen. Got word on the weather, and it is set fair all the way to the Rockies."

"Capital," Arnold replied, buttoning up his flies and heading for the door.

The westbound train left promptly at six. Onboard, the diamond party consisted of Rubery, Arnold, Slack, Harpending and Dodge, William Lent having decided to stay on and do business in the city. The only person still to appear would be Henry Janin and he was to join them Omaha. It would be no pleasure for Arnold or Slack. There would be good odds to be fetched for guessing they were hoping Janin would miss the train. There was little hope of that. Henry Janin was not the sort of man who'd inspire popular legends.

When Janin finally did join the Union Pacific train, he came as quite a surprise to all of them. He looked too soft to have led the life he was famous for, and he'd seen too many good meals, for he was fair to bursting in his clothes. His black leather coat was the only item on him that looked genuine. Considering he'd been associated with the mining industry for near on twenty-two years, it was expected he'd look the part. His hair was long and grey, and he wore a hat that was close to a Stetson, but still had a way to grow yet. The most unusual aspect about him were the four gold rings on his fat, tobacco stained fingers. A man would never guess from looking at those hands that they'd spent years digging and sorting through tons of rocks. His neck was so short, his head seemed to start straight from his shoulders, and he walked like a man who'd spent too long in the saddle. Added to all this, he talked with a New England accent, and this too brought no comfort to Arnold, for he knew New Englanders were a stubborn lot and not easily given over to flights of fancy.

Neither Slack nor Arnold took to him, and he spoke to no one unless he positively had to. He was there to do a job and he didn't like to fraternize much. Arnold got the impression that he'd rather eat a gangrenous sheep than find the diamond claim positive, and no amount of talk was going to sweeten him.

Harpending was glad of the attitude. He was reinforced in his belief that if this man declared the claim sound, then it very much would be.

Slack was of the opinion that he ought to get off the train at the earliest opportunity and run for it whilst he still had a whole body.

After what seemed a week, but had been only three days, the journey settled into a well-established routine. Slack read his newspapers (he'd brought five along for the purpose) and Arnold, read a book about the law. Arnold had had some mighty suspicious reading material to hand of late. Banking and law. It puzzled Slack a little, but he made no comment; a little education would do Arnold no harm. Rubery spent much of his time with a rifle in hand, taking pot shots at wild animals whenever they took the risk of coming too near the railroad. Much carnage was incurred.

Henry Janin slept mostly, but if he wasn't sleeping he would be eating, and if wasn't doing either he'd tell very discouraging tales about the mines he'd rejected and the broken dreams of liars, cheats, and scoundrels. . One could tell from the way he eyed Slack and Arnold that he held them to be scoundrels too. But since Harpending and the others got the eye too, they weren't as kindly disposed toward him as they might have been. Rubery came in for special sarcasm. It turned out Janin couldn't abide the English. Arnold and Slack grew more dispirited as the hours went by.

Finally they came to Rawlins Springs, hired mules and two horses, and loaded their possessions upon them:he picks, shovels, pans, sacks and supplies, and on Slack's advice, netting for mosquitoes. They emptied the little town of everything and soon the great diamond expedition headed toward the mountains, with Arnold in the lead, and Janin taking up the rear.

It was June 25, 1872. They were headed for the mountains, totally un-aware that Clarence King's party was already searching this mountain area with increased determination. They would not give up when so much was at stake.

It was the intention of Arnold to reach the diamond claim a little faster than before, though not too fast, as he didn't want Janin thinking it was too easy. Besides, General Colton had told them of the arduous journey, so why disappoint them?

They'd traveled no more than a day and a half, and had hardly reached the first plateau where the forest began in earnest, when the first problem occured. General Dodge went saddle sore. It annoyed everyone, especially as it was full moon and they'd just taken a vote to ride on as far as they could get that evening before camping.

Dodge was a tad older than the rest of them, and prone to hemorrhoids, but no one liked to stop. The best thing would be for him to call it quits and go back, but he'd not do that.

"Too much easy livin'," he admitted. "Never happened before. Shows how soft a man can get in peacetime."

"Well, heaven help us from another war just to get you fit, General," Arnold remarked, somewhat tactlessly. It was a touchy point, what with Harpending being a southern supporter early on and Slack and Arnold having been vocal supporters of the rebels.

Slack was prompted to recall the time he'd suffered a similar fate and as the others drank water he told them the tale.

"Got chapped so bad once the whole inside of my leg was as a raw as freshly killed pig. Whole thing was afire and it was mighty painful, I can tell you."

"How did you fix it?" General Dodge asked, interested by now.

"Went fishing stark naked in the sea off Santa Cruz."

"In salt water?" the General exclaimed, aware of how drastic this solution was. "It must have been cold."

"Had no choice; General. Arnold here said it would fix it good and it did. I was out there for three days and when I came back in I was cured. scarred up, but cured."

"Why did you stay out so long?" Harpending asked, not sure he believed him.

"Arnold had his rifle pointed at me, " Slack answered with a smile.

"It's true," Arnold confirmed. "I was sick of him moaning and groaning, and since we was panning out a prospect by the ocean, I just knew it had to be kill or cure."

"You stood out there at night as well?" General Dodge inquired.

Slack looked away to spit. "Now, General, even I know a man can't do much with a rifle in the dark."

There was amusement at that. Slack didn't say much, but it was usually worth listening to when he did.

They rode on some more then, glad to be moving. The forest took on a ghostly appearance in the brilliant moonlight. Boulders in the track glowed most eerily up ahead. Nevertheless the mules and horses managed to pick their way without protest. In the distance they heard the howling of coyotes, and all the while the undergrowth was full of animals busy feeding or hunting, wary, but less than interested in the passing strangers.

Henry Janin took the opportunity of a large natural clearing to ride up along side Arnold and talk. "Mr. Arnold? That snow up on the peak, it stay there all year round?"

"Yes, sir. We came up here before but ignored the place the first time. Diamonds are hard to find at the best of times without having to locate 'em under a foot of snow."

Janin made no comment about that. It was pre-supposing there were any diamonds, and as far as he was concerned there were none until he said there were some. "What made you look up here? It's a way off the usual places for prospecting."

Arnold didn't reply immediately, preferring to guide his horse through a difficult path between two large boulders. He was glad to see them and pointed to the broad marks Slack had scratched on the granite to guide future trips. It was just visible in the twilight. A and S. Keep left.

"It's single file for a while, keep left of the path, and don't look down, we're rounding a ravine. Take it real slow and don't let the mules know there's any danger."

There was no arguing with Arnold. Everyone kept well to the left of the path and Harpending dismounted, deciding to lead his mule. He for one was happy he couldn't see how far there was to fall. Fortunately, Arnold did seem to know where he was going after all.

It was almost an hour before they decided to pitch camp and sleep. They were hungry, to be sure, but sleep was needed more. There would be time enough to organize a good breakfast in the morning.

Janin , still awaiting his reply, repeated his question as Arnold sorted out a moss-softened piece of ground to sleep on.

"I tell you, Mr. Janin, Slack and me was following an old immigrant trail. We join it a few miles farther on. It was a damned trail, led to the snow, and if they thought they'd find a way over when summer came, well they were mistaken. The Indians occasionally use this trail, and I thought there was a secret burial ground up here. Heard a rumor the Cheyenne had been hoarding rubies, even heard they wouldn't trade 'em, not even for a Winchester rifle. A man can't ignore that."

"Didn't think this was Cheyenne territory."

"They travel wide, little opposition here. Leastways I never see any other than Cheyenne signs. Didn't find the burial ground. Just some graves of immigrants who starved to death."

"But no diamonds in Indian graves."

"Now, you know they don't bury their dead like we do. No sir, I found no burial ground, no graves festooned with jewels. Actually I was drawing water from a creek when something grabbed my attention. The rest I guess you know. No special talent, but fact is, Slack and me got there first and that is what matters in this game."

Janin had to concede that much at least. "Well, we shall see, Mr. Arnold, but I remind you, I've surveyed six hundred claims and never had a client have cause to complain yet. It's hard to catch me out, Philip Arnold. If there's a snake in the grass. I'll catch it. I'll find you out. Sleep on that, Mr. Arnold, sleep on that."

It was hardly the sort of remark calculated to make a man sleep, but Arnold did. He was exhausted. To hell with Janin anyway. Either he found for 'em or agin 'em. Time would tell. Time would surely tell.

* * * * * * *

Everyone woke early, with good reason. It was snowing. Damn near the end of June and it was snowing, settling too. The temperature had dropped like a stone and Harpending grew worried. He wanted to be rich, but he knew of parties getting cut-off in these treacherous mountains, and there was always the horrible legend of the Donner party to recall.

Slack didn't seem too concerned, however and he occupied himself with the business of organizing a good fire to heat up the oatmeal he'd brought along.

"Sun will melt it off later," he told them ."If it was September, you could get worried, but not in June. You'll see; soon as the sun gets high enough, the snow will melt. Meanwhile, you can fetch some firewood if you wants something to take the worry off your minds."

This they could do, as everyone was keen for something to eat andoatmeal and the coffee smelled pretty good brewing thick over the fire.

"This the only way up and down?" Harpending wanted to know when breakfast was over and they were getting ready to move on. Arnold considered his reply as he saddled up.

"There's two ways, we reckon. In summer a few more. You can follow the creek down, but not in spring or fall. In winter this is the only route and I think it's pretty well impassable for much of December through January and March. I must confess, Slack and me haven't tried the southern route, but you'd have to go a long ways south to round these mountains, maybe as far as Douglas Pass and down to Grand Junction."

Arnold shrugged as he mounted his horse. "Never tried it. Douglas is about eight thousand feet off sea-level, I hear. Slack's estimated and General Colton agreed that our diamond plateau is 'bout seven thousand."

Janin was listening quite intently now. "There's a narrow pass farther south past the Yampa. It's Uintah and Ouray territory. But I know there's a pass between the Yampa and the White River that takes you over the mountain to Green River."

"You mean crossing near Bonanza, that's near the White River," Harpending remarked. "That means we could use the Green River route all the way up to the Yampa. Coming up from the south of Utah."

"Like I say, Asbury, Slack and me never tried it. You still have to figure out how to get through the passes in winter. Slack here figured out there was a way following the Green River south from Wyoming, and taking rafts or something through the gorge to Red Canyon. There's a trail over the mountains there in summer months, but again, it's for men prepared to take the risk. You'd need to get the place surveyed in these summer months so you can find the most economical route."

Janin committed all the details to memory. It was becoming clearer all the while where exactly this diamond claim was. It didn't look promising to him. Not at all.

By the third day it was colder still, and though there had been no more snow, the tracks had been covered and neither Slack nor Arnold could say with any accuracy that they were headed towards their destination.

Harpending was shivering upon his mule as they waited for Arnold. He'd gone to climb a nearby peak to check on their progress. He'd been gone a couple of hours now, and Slack had taken the opportunity to get a nap. Any sensible man would, but the others were restless, anxious to get to the diamonds. They bickered amongst themselves about first one thing than another. Nothing important, but it was part of the general atmosphere. Slack stayed out of it; he wasn't interested in business or politics.

"Where the hell is Arnold? " Rubery demanded to know, taking out his pocket hunter watch and shaking it. "He's been gone long enough. If he's lost, why doesn't he say so? Can't hardly blame him; one rock looks much like another up here."

"Ssh", Harpending called out, listening intently to a far off sound. "You hear that "

Rubery looked puzzled. "What?"

249

DIAMONDS

"That, you hear it?"

Everyone listened, but heard nothing. Harpendinq frowned. "I could have sworn it was the train."

"No trains up here,," Janin told him, smirking a little at Harpending's foolishness,.

"I didn't say it was up here, I said I distinctly heard the Union Pacific whistle. It's an unmistakable sound."

Slack was awake now and he studied Harpending's face. He'd heard the sound too and knew it to be the train. "You know how far sound can travel, Mr. Harpending?"

"No sir, I don't. "

"Well I reckon we are around hundred miles from the railroad. But we've snaked around a lot of hills and it's possible we might be no more than sixty miles away from the railroad as the crow flies. You think you can hear that whistle that far?"

"It's not possible," Rubery stated with some force. "And I might add I heard nothing. It's just not possible for sound to travel that far."

"It would be worth testing such a thing", Harpending remarked, not keen to give in so easily. "What else would make that sound?"

"Any number of birds," Janin told them. "Pintail prohably. This is good breeding ground for them in summer. Might be a curlew "

No one felt like arguing that. None of them were experts on birds.

Fortunately Arnold was sighted descending the slope, and now all attention was fastened on him. It was another twenty minutes before he reached them and he was in quite an exhausted state.

"Slack, get them to put some firewood together. There's precious little of it at the diamond claim."

"Are we leaving soon?" Rubery asked, his impatience barely concealed.

"Two hours riding Mr.. Rubery and you'll finally see what you came for."

There was much surprise and elation at discovering this. The firewood was collected in no time and Harpending had them all on their way in twenty minutes. He didn't like to waste a moment.

Slack took up the rear now, wondering if he should really disappear. How long would it take Janin to discover the claim was a salt. A day? Two hours? He had no confidence at all.

No more than three miles farther on; three long, difficult miles, they found the old immigrants' trail in the narrow canyon and the rotting corpse of the wagon beside the graves. They had arrived. Arnold led them through the natural gap onto the plateau only lightly sprinkled with snow, though the creek was swollen and flowing with a fierce torrent. Slack wondered if it had taken the diamonds along with it. It would be just their luck to discover the creek back to the way nature intended it: worthless.

DIAMONDS

Harpending noted the gap was posted with Arnold and Slack's crude sign-post. He was glad to see they'd taken the trouble to do that. If Janin proved the claim they'd have to post claims all over the surrounding land.

"This is it, gentlemen," Arnold told them, turning about in his saddle. "Slack and me will pitch camp and get a fire going. You folks try your luck."

There were sighs of relief, and Rubery was off his horse with a whoop, telling everyone he'd be first to find a diamond. He ran to the swollen stream armed only with a knife.

Slack watched Janin closely. He was not nearly so enthusiastic. Not for him gadding about with a pick or shovel like Harpending and General Dodge, Janin dismounted, took a long-needed piss, then began to walk over the claim, making no attempt to find diamonds at all. Slack watched him stop at an anthill and observe how the rain had worn it down to expose the honeycomb insides. Satisfied to see the holes, he moved on. Slack was glad of the time he'd put into those to make 'em look right. Arnold was humming to himself as he rigged a tent. This time they'd come with all the right equipment. While they were up on the plateau at least there'd be a measure of comfort. Slack busied himself with making the fire and was amused to discover the smallest of diamonds right beside where he'd dumped the firewood. He said nothing, but picked it up and threw it at the nearest anthill.

It was about four-thirty in the afternoon by now, and the sun had finally broken through the clouds. It was no warmer up this high, but the diamond dust sprinkled on the anthills was a pretty sight. Slack wondered how long it would take for someone to notice.

There was a sudden yell from Alfie Rubery. "I say, I say. Come and see, look here, Asbury, come and see what I've found."

Harpending, Janin, and General Dodge ran to the water and stood waiting as Rubery waded to the sandy bank. "Look here , Asbury, I found two stones under a heavy rock. Must have been there since time began. Imagine it. Look. first honors to me, I think."

Janin was the first to look. He examined them to the light, took out some glass four inches square and proceeded to try and crush the diamond against it. When when that failed, he sketched his initials on the glass with it. He looked at Harpending with some surprise. "These are *diamonds*."

There was much jubilation at that remark, but Janin cautioned them by growling. "Two diamonds the size of peas don't make this a diamond discovery. I want to see what's on the land. Don't expect me to make it easy for them."

By *them* he meant Arnold and Slack, but Harpending and Rubery were already convinced. Especially when, moments later, Harpending stumbled on a boulder lying on the plateau ,and to his utmost delight discovered an emerald only inches from his hand. He scrabbled around the base of the boulder and was soon calling to the others. "Alfie, sapphires, a nest of them. Good God, this place is every bit as rich as Mr.. Arnold said it was."

Arnold only smiled. He was not about to say anything to disturb the building euphoria. Slack watched Janin carefully from behind the cover of his slow building fire. Janin was prodding the ground with a sharp stick. He was taking it very carefully, refusing to get excited.

By the time the light failed a few hours later, and they were gathered around Slack's campfire eating his mess of stew, Rubery had found twenty small diamonds in the stream and had the beginnings of a chill to prove it. Harpending had a little sack of rubies and sapphires, and General Dodge had one large diamond he'd found lodged between the arms of a cactus growing at the fringe of the plateau. He was well satisfied with that. It was hard to tell if Janin was happy. He'd poked around, walked the stream from the top to the edge where it cascaded to the creek below, and found himself a few diamonds. Nothing of particular value, but enough to convince him they were diamonds and that they had the appearance of occurring naturally. He didn't want to say more than that. Privately he was purely astonished that the ground surrendered its riches so easily and, more to the point, seemed to correspond with Arnold's description of the land. He had never once considered that there really could be a diamond find up here. All his instincts told him that it wasn't possible. But one could not ignore one's eyes. The damn things were everywhere. A man couldn't spit for landing on a diamond or ruby or whatever. He hated to admit it, but he was going to have to find for Arnold and Slack. He hated to make another man rich, but there was nothing else for it.

Harpending was so excited he could hardly stop looking at the precious stones, liking them even more in the glow of the fire. He and Rubery were making plans on how to exploit the mine, bring in good roads and even the railroad. If diamonds were so readily available on top, what might the ground bring forth?

General Dodge fell asleep early, complaining bitterly about the throbbing from his nether end. For him diamonds had lost their attraction, unless he could have traded the lot for a cure.

Arnold and Slack took a walk. It had been a while since they'd talked, for privacy had been hard to come by since New York. They walked to the trees to find firewood.

"Things are going well," Arnold declared as he broke a branch to manageable sizes. "Janin is impressed. You can tell. His tone is different now."

Slack had to agree. "He's going to dig tomorrow. Save your optimism for then."

"Can't we get him to dig where we want him to?"

Slack shook his head. "Best he digs a dry hole, that way he'll have more respect for the good spots."

Arnold mused on that a while. Yes Slack was right there. "Now tell me, where did go in New York. I know you stayed a night away."

"You said I was to make myself scarce. I went fishing."

Arnold frowned. "You didn't see Alyce?"

Slack went onto alert immediately. Did Arnold suspect something?

"Now you know I couldn't have got to Boston and back in a day."

"I know nothing of the sort. Train could do it and leave you time to fish."

"If you have something to say, Philip Arnold, say it."

"You sent her the money like we spoke about? You sure you didn't deliver it personally? I know you, John Slack. You didn't get all sparkled up for nothing."

Slack reddened, but Arnold couldn't see that in the dark. He decided half a lie would be sensible in the circumstances.

"All right. I saw her. We met half-way in New Haven. I paid her. She was glad of it. I told her you'd be over to see her once everything is settled. She's renting a cottage in Boston and as soon as she can and will send you the address at Mrs Klein's as before. I didn't tell her you was going to chuck her over. Not while she could do us some harm. You still intend to chuck her, don't you?"

"Why, are you interested? Is that why you shaved?"

Slack was getting angry with Arnold now. Was he deliberately trying to provoke him?

"You're sure quiet, John Slack. You want her, you take her. I'm through. Y'hear?"

."Harpending made me shave. He wanted me respectable to meet General Butler. If you must know Alyce didn't recognize me and the first thing she said was I should grow back the beard."

Arnold chuckled at that. He'd known Slack would do the right thing by Alyce. He didn't think for one moment Slack would go after her. He'd soon find himself embarrassed by her spurning him. He'd not risk that.

Slack sighed and told a lie.. "I don't want her, Arnold. I want a quiet life. A little place up by Lake Tahoe maybe. Once Ralston settles with us, I'll have more than enough to last my lifetime."

"Tahoe? Shit, Slack, that's all you want to do? Live with the critters and fish all day? With your money you could live like a King in Europe. You think they won't find you in Tahoe? You can be sure they'll come looking for us. Believe me. They'll come looking."

"I'll find somewhere farther North. Canada maybe. I really don't care. You still intend to go home to Kentucky?"

Arnold smiled. "I want to live in a place with not a mountain in sight anywhere. Even if they find me, well, Kentucky is a safe as any place else. California law won't be any use to them there."

DIAMONDS

Arnold looked up at the sky and the stars beyond the strees for a moment before turning suddenly and fixing Slack a level stare. "You realize one of us has to stay put up here once Janin finds in our favor."

CHAPTER NINETEEN
Not Quite Eldorado

Progress was being made in San Francisco to float the new diamond company. There had been some technical delays, but these things were natural. The land had to be secured by law, a bill had to be proposed in Congress and passed by both houses before diamonds could be extracted from the ground.

All the time there was persistent clamoring by investors world-wide to buy into the great scheme. Ralston, still mindful of the great bonanza ahead, resisted all boarders. He and the other twenty-four men were not about to sell, and as long the site remained secret, they had no worries. They would not be rushed. The diamonds were just as valuable to them in the ground as out, and until all the legal business was finished, that was where they would stay. Arnold and Slack were still to be paid out, but they were a mere annoyance now and many were already regretting the men had even been allowed a ten percent holding, and gross at that.

As Arnold was making his way towards San Francisco to collect his money in person, Clarence King's men were making their way towards the now unguarded claim in the mountains. King had one hundred dollars on the table that said it was a salt. He had no takers. His men had been around him long enough to know that his instinct about these things was almost always right.

King could have alerted Washington or, at the very least Ralston in San Francisco, as to his doubts. But there was always the possibility that they really had missed a diamond field ,and they wished to be spared the embarrassment if they were to be proved wrong.

So it was that Clarence King and his remaining surveyors came across a snow-covered peak on a pine mountain. They began to scent they were in the right place. When they found notches on the trees they knew they had judged it correctly. No others save the men gone up to view the diamond claims had used this route, and it was a simple job in the end to follow the trail up the mountainside. Harpending having pinned a note to one tree for some scout to read only made it easier. It was in code, but King was no fool. The US Army had taught him and few thousand others the same code in the Civil War. They were to look for a high ridge of trees set against a purple rockface. Two miles further on they found it and the trail used by Arnold and Slack's expeditions. No attempt had been made to disguise where they'd been. Not so very old campfires lay where they'd burned. A child could have tracked these trails all the way to the diamonds.

A day later they found the dead-end pass with the settlers' remains and the broken wagon. The weather was being very kind but unseasonably cold. Nevertheless it was clear, and during the days it was warm, but they knew it could turn at any time and they'd have to get out of the mountains quickly. All of them had experienced the worst these treacherous mountains had to offer.

When Clarence King himself found the first of Arnold and Slack's claim notices, he was jublilant, and when moments later they discovered the entrance to the wide hidden mesa they cheered long and loud. Their confidence in King had made them follow him; now they would set about proving the claim for once and for all. Good or false.

As they made camp and built a fire, King looked the place over. He remarked on how well concealed the site was, how remote. It was no wonder no one had ever been there before Arnold and Slack.

King's party was made up of five men, but all were very experienced in geological matters and hard to please. If they'd hoped to expose the diamond claim their hopes were cruelly dashed almost immediately. One fellow by the name of Gephardt found the first diamond in less than an hour. King himself discovered two rubies in the battered remains of an anthill. He could not have been more discouraged. He had nursed himself with the self-satisfaction he would have in exposing this diamond find, but to find the place littered with precious stones; well, it was galling, an extremely bitter experience.

King surveyed the plateau, thinking it to be an extremely unlilkely place to bear to such exotic fruit, but it was hard to refute what the eyes plainly showed to be true. He ordered trenches to be dug. If it was to be a diamond find, then diamonds must be at six feet below, or more. He himself went down the slopes to the creek below, where he panned the gravel bed of the fast moving waters. Here too, he was disappointed. He worked for only three hours and found more than a handful of small objects that bore a remarkable resemblance to diamonds. He worked more feverishly farther down the creek, and each time he dug or panned or scooped his hands in to clear away silt, there was almost always another diamond for his reward.

It was a crushing blow. They had missed the most significant find of the century. There was no doubt he would have to resign. There was a possibility the entire survey could be in jeopardy.

When he returned to the camp, he was heartened to discover that his men had dug down to six feet in a trench eight feet long and found absolutely nothing. But it didn't prove anything other than the fact that diamonds and rubies were not in that area.

The light had failed by then and they ate around a campfire, planning their strategy for the 'morrow. They'd comb the surrounding area, investigate the remaining anthills, dig in the stream. The diamonds appeared to be natural, the rubies and the one emerald they'd found could be related to the granite in the area. But somehow the presence of all these gems in one place, along with sapphires as well, just seemed a little much.

Yet as King knew very well, at Comstock when the gold had run out and men had all but abandoned the mine, they'd ignored the grey ore that had seemed useless. The fact that Comstock turned out to be the world's largest silver-mine proved that if gold and silver can lie next to each other, why not diamonds and sapphires, rubies and emeralds?

"What puzzles me most," King declared to his men the next day, "is why it is that we have twelve rubies for every diamond found up here. Yet below in the creek there are only diamonds?"

Others had been thinking the same, pondering the remarkable accuracy of the names given to different sections of the claim. Crudely painted stakes pointed the way to Ruby Gulch, Diamond Flat, Sapphire Hollow, each section seeming to hold the one type of stone, never the other. Nature never worked in this manner usually. Of course, just as you were finally ready to confirm your suspicions you'd find a ruby next to a diamond or a sapphire with a ruby, and you'd have to concede that that was the way these things went up here.

Being so late in the year the ground was hard; the floral carpet that had dazzled the men from San Francisco had long ago withered. Winter snow lay thick on the mountain tops. King was acutely aware that their time here was limited. Yet he just could not believe that in all the time spent surveying the Fortieth Parallel they had never come across even a hint of such fabulous precious stones.

Even more awkward for him and his fellow surveyors, was the certainty they had that in what was a predominantly sandstone area, no precious stones could be present. Nowhere else had sandstone yielded anything other than fossils. True, here was black granite outcrop, and geologically it was always possible that when a peak of sandstone was washed away to lay bear the more durable rock below, nature's secrets would be unlocked. The most curious thing of all was the location. Aside from unlucky settlers hopelessly lost, this was a truly desolate area. King considered that if he was looking deliberately for a place to hide something, this would be it.

Gephardt and Arno, another of the surveyors, returned with hands sparkling. Arno sighed, shrugging. "Even the very dust is precious here. See what we got out of the anthill over there? "

"If they are anthills," Gephardt remarked. If anyone was determined to find fault with this diamond discovery it was him, yet he seemed to be confounded each time with bigger and better discoveries.

King was marking off a map he'd drawn of the claim, plotting where each clutch of stones had been found. The most yielding had been the swollen creek, but no man could spend too long panning the freezing water. The trenches they'd dug had yielded either nothing or small amounts just inches down. Just as he was sure again that the diggings were false, another of the party discovered rubies, six feet down. King's hopes were dashed again.

"But it was easy digging, Mr. King," the exhausted man revealed. "I know the ground has been worked over by others before us, but why would they put all the dirt back again?"

'Why indeed?" Clarence King pondered aloud. If this was a salt, it was the most audacious and thorough one he'd ever come across. Someone had literally thrown away thousands of dollars worth of diamonds and rubies. Either that, or diamonds were over valued in America. He had the suspicion that there was some truth in that.

On the very next day, as light snow had begun to fall and King had dejectedly decided that they had to go, it fell to chance to reveal what they had come for.

The German, Gephardt, took a well earned rest from some ferocious digging in the morning, and to the consternation of the others he plunged himself into the icy stream to cool off. He drank long and hard, making a joke of it, trying to get the others to join him, when all of a sudden he lost his lucky coin. Some might mock, but Gephardt treasured that coin like no other possession in the world, and the others knew he'd not leave without it. He'd choose to freeze to death rather than give it up to the fast-flowing waters. It took some time and a considerable amount of panning the gravel, but persistence has its own reward: The lucky coin was found. The three small diamonds he brought out with it were almost ignored, considered a rebuke by him by a land that seemed to say, "So, you refuse to believe" Only, on closer inspection did Gephardt take more interest. He abruptly leapt up and ran over to where Clarence King was strapping a saddle to his mule. Gephardt could hardly contain his excitement.

"Look here, Mr. King, this is the bulliest diamond field there ever was. Not only does it produce diamonds, but it cuts and polishes them too'"

King looked, so did the others, at first astonished, then amused. They fell to laughing. A great weight had been lifted. King looked again. Anyone could see where the lapidary had cut the stone, small though it was. Proof it was a salt at last. King felt a great weight drop from his shoulders. He took out his pipe, surveyed the claim for one last time, and with a look of satisfaction on his face pronounced, "Gentlemen, I believe we are getting out of the diamond business."

CHAPTER TWENTY
Give a man his due

On the very day King was declaring the claim a salt, Arnold was collecting his fortune .

William Ralston had read Slack's power-of attorney and Harpending's letter as to the arrangement on how Slack had been left behind. Now he was so keen to be rid of Arnold, he suspected nothing and released the entire fortune to him.

Ralston had planned a celebration and a public announcement, on the day Arnold had collected the money, but Arnold claimed he was exhausted and although he was careful to thank Bill Ralston and shake his hand many times, he told the banker that he just had to leave San Francisco that very day with the full amount in gold coin, to keep his promise to Slack, who'd be waiting impatiently for him. His only promise was to send Ralston word as soon as he was settled, so that Ralston would know where to send the percentage of the profits once they started mining.

This reassured Ralston and he suspected nothing. He was surprised, mind, that Slack would allow his share to be collected by another, but the men had been partners so long, the trust between them must be strong. Ralston wouldn't just let Arnold go, however, and he had the event recorded by a visiting artist. Much to Arnold's annoyance, since he was desperately keen to get away, they even had a brass band play Arnold out as he boarded the Eastbound train, and held a small farewell champagne party on the platform.

"Will Mr.. Slack be joining you at Rawlins Springs?" Ralston wanted to know as someone refilled their glasses.

"I doubt he'll let me get far with his money before he's there beside me, trying to discourage me from spending it." Arnold declared, doing his best to keep up the bravado, all the time much concerned that someone would turn up to shout 'fraud' and spoil the party.

"You tell John Slack that he scored a big impression in this town, and I for one would welcome him back here. He's man of ideas, Mr Arnold, and San

259

Francisco always needs men of ideas." Ralston continued.

"He respects you a great deal, Bill, and I'll be sure to tell him."

The whistle finally blew then and Arnold felt an enormous sense of relief. In five minutes he'd be gone with Ralston's gold and there was nothing on God's earth that could ever get it back.

Ralston smiling, waved the train goodbye . The man was a fool. Selling out for half a million and ten percent when they could have kept it all. But that was the way of all prospectors, thank the Lord, no vision, no patience, no idea of the long term. That's why San Francisco neded bankers like him, men who could take risks, build a city.

It was towards the end of July, 1872. Diamond fever was just beginning. Now the diamond fields were all Ralston's and his associates. The city was going crazy with the very idea of diamonds, and many were desperate for shares in the newly formed *San Francisco and New York Mining and Commercial Company*. Greedily, the original twenty-five subscribers held fast to their shares, believing that when the company was launched on the Stock Exchanges of the world they would each make millions from the mere eighty-thousand dollars they had each invested.

General Colton took up his position as general manager in lavish new offices built expressly for the purpose. On July 30th, Henry Janin's report was finally released and made public. It was a sensation. The Bank of California was besieged by folks desperate to buy diamonds stocks. Ralston was planning to sell millions of shares at forty dollars each. It would be the biggest stock launch of the century, and net him personally twenty million, by his reckoning. Outside of the bank, people were all prepared to put their life savings into it, if only someone would sell but one paltry share. No one would.

From the *Alta California* Aug 1, 1872:
Report from the American Diamond Fields.
Two thousand diamonds now in this city. Ten pounds of rubies and large sapphires...
Over 3000 acres of land claimed in Utah mountains...
Discoverers of claim, John Slack and Philip Arnold, in hiding.
Mr. Asbury Harpending was the expedition leader to mountains with Mr. Henry Janin to prove the claim.
"It is without question the most fabulous find this century," he is quoted as telling Mr. William C Ralston, of the Bank of California, who has been associated with this find from the very beginning.

That week it is also recorded that the trains leaving San Francisco were full, every one of them, with men laden with all manner of prospecting equipment, each man headed for Wyoming or Arizona, where they believed a fortune was about to be made. Mr. Roberts, the happy general goods merchant, was seen to be placing orders to companies in New York for new supplies to urgently replenish his stocks. Diamond fever had struck and the city was rapidly emptying of able-bodied men.

But from the *Bulletin* the same week:

AMSTERDAM:

Diamond prices in rapid decline.

The recently reported American diamond find has severly depressed precious stones prices in Holland and the market in London. There has been chaos in the diamond fields of South Africa, where over production in the mines has already undermined price support. It is reported that upon news reaching Kimberley of the extent of the American find, many astute mine owners sold out their claims. Investors are warned that unless the Bank of California and its partners in the newly formed S.F. and N.Y. Mining and Commercial Company exercise control over the supply of diamonds, Fingers could be severely burned.

But it would not be the prospectors who got burned.

CHAPTER TWENTY-ONE
"Thank God and Clarence King"

It took almost five days to find the telegraph office, such was the hardship of riding in the unexpected summer snowstorm. It was almost if nature herself had conspired with the hoaxers to protect their sordid scheme. King immediately wired William Ralston at the Bank of California that the mine was a salt.

The shock was so great Ralston could scarcely credit it, and refused to act on the information. Instead, he sent Harpending out by train to meet with King, with the intention of going back up to the claim to investigate further. But Harpending decided to take King's word for it, noting that King had been the first real geologist to see the claim. To Harpending's credit, he admitted almost immediately that enthusiasm had once again got the better of sagacity in the matter of money.

Word had already leaked out by the time Harpending, King, and party had found their way back to a rainy San Francisco. The bad news was given to the awaiting press.

The Great Diamond Hoax, the newspapers called it, and it rocked the world. From all sides praises were heaped upon Clarence King, the "deliverer " of San Francisco.

"We are to thank God and Clarence King for an escape from great financial calamity," the Chronicle exclaimed.

They demanded news of the whereabouts of Arnold and Slack too. Rewards were posted, and some stepped forward, but knew nothing concrete. The Bank of California even requested the assistance of The Mercantile Agency, a division of B. Douglas and Company and R.G. Dun and Company. Between them, it was their self-appointed task to verify the moral standing and creditworthiness of business countrywide. It was William Lent's idea that if either Arnold or Slack invested their ill-gotten gains anywhere in the country, it would come to the attention of The Mercantile Agency.

Clarence King now won a reputation that was to endure for his lifetime and help him secure funds for his massive survey of the Rockies and Sierras. Others were ruined. Henry Janin, for one. His career never recovered, and he died a bitter man. Asbury Harpending also suffered greatly, although it was known that Ralston had had to implore him to become involved in this enterprise against his own better judgment. His reputation suffered, in London, in particular, where his enemies at *The Times* got their revenge on him, fully blaming him for the entire collapse of all American stocks at that time.

William Ralston was magnanimous in defeat. He knew there was little use in going after Arnold and Slack. No one had the slightest idea where they were. Ralston paid back all the investors from his personal fortune, framing their receipts to hang on the wall of his office beside the now redundant maps of Vermillion Creek and Diamond Flat. The net loss, something approaching a million dollars, fell upon himself, Harpending, Roberts, General Dodge and William Lent. All could afford it, but none resented it as much as Lent, who vowed to find the swindlers, if it took a lifetime.

For General Colton, the humiliation was awkward. To have to beg back his old position at the railroad and endure the disadvantage to which he was thus put was almost too much to bear. Harpending, disgusted that he was considered liable for a scheme he'd always doubted, sold up his holdings entirely, everything that could be sold at a profit, and quit the city a chastened man. He went back to his native Kentucky, richer, but wiser.

The Great Diamond Hoax was not kind to anyone, and much was made of it by all those who'd been excluded from the concert party.

But what of Philip Arnold and John Slack, you ask? What became of them?

Philip Arnold returned to his place of birth a rich man. It was entirely logical. He was rich. He'd bested his betters in California, and this being Kentucky they could spit for their money; there was no law to compel him to go back with it. None that Arnold would obey, that is. He returned in triumph, bought himself the Howard building, the most modern in town, and opened a bank. It was astonishing how quickly we all got used to this gentlemen being in our midst, and there was more than one of us who'd pinch himself to recall the young lad who'd run with the horses and dogs on the farms with the rest of us.

Arnold and I took a little time to become friends again; there were more than twenty years missing from our friendship. But in the months he took to settle in and get his mansion built, we all finally accepted that he was here to stay.

Arnold once told me that any fool could make a fortune owning a bank. Yet it was Philip Arnold who was shot down by some fool who'd deposited his money in Arnold's bank and wanted it back before it was due.

Of course, there's many as say that the bank never had any cash anyway and it was inevitable that Arnold would get his come-uppance in hot lead. But

DIAMONDS

I can testify that when they opened the safe there was close to a million dollars in cash and certificates lying there. More than enough to satisfy all claims in Elizabethtown. It was bad luck Arnold died, too. The bullet I fished out of him in less than an hour, but pneumonia is a fickle thing. When the fever set upon him, he knew God was testing him. I nursed him day and night.

"I'm not finished, Dan, I'm just not finished," he kept saying, but he was and more's the pity, for he was good company, and now I come to tell his story there's always questions I wished I'd asked and got answers to.

They say a man is never ready to die. Few could have been as unready as Philip Arnold. I'd heard many of his stories in the time he'd been with us and thrilled to his descriptions of places I'd never see. But now, in the last miserable, terrible two days of his life, he told me the real story, the truth I have now imparted to you all. His confession, if you like.

Arnold began by saying "If you mean to deceive, one must first live like honest men."

In the first few months he'd been back in Elizabethtown he'd suffered nightmares about Slack returning from the dead, walking into the bank to claim his own, but after a time, the dreams receded. A man can get used to being rich, and the more time it is all yours, the more you resent sharing it with others, even your best and only friend for more than thirty years. Nevertheless, I believe he missed him. He gained a fortune but lost his best friend.

The great mystery of John Slack was all the more piquant, for as Arnold began to sink, it was Slack he called out for. I'd like to think Philip Arnold died with regret in his heart, but a conscience was not something he had packed with him when he'd departed Elizabethtown the first time and he'd not brought one back with him.

He lies now in an simple grave beside an apple tree he'd requested I plant for him especially. It is too early to know if they'll be sweet or sour.

DIAMONDS

CHAPTER TWENTY-TWO
The Gentleman Slack

John Slack remained a mystery to me until almost two years after Arnold's death. Just by chance I was in Charleston, South Carolina, to greet the grandparents of my sweet wife, when I came across John Slack at the railroad offices. He was dressed in gentleman's attire and was so transformed from the man I remembered and imagined, at first I blamed my eyes deceiving me. A deep crimson scar across his forehead did throw me at first, but curiosity gripped me, and the first chance I got to speak to him privately, he was quite taken aback. Clearly he had never expected to be recognised. He was there on business for some Real Estate associates, which was another surprise, Slack took me aside and we adjourned to an Inn where he was confident of not being known.

I could sense that he was less than keen to make my acquaintance again, but when I informed him of Arnold's death and deathbed confession, he realized that there was little he could do to prevent the truth being known.

Perhaps he even approved of my plan to publish the story for all to read one day. John Slack had forsaken his name and adopted another, and honorably taken up with the woman Arnold had so carelessly abandoned. It was from John Slack I learned of the favors and affection Alyce had bestowed upon Arnold to no reward, and I heartily approved of his association with this woman. She was the gainer, for I could see Slack talked of her with great affection and was keen that I should note down how she had suffered on account of Arnold.

"If you must write it up, at least tell the truth as it really stands," demanded Slack.

And to be fair, I will admit now that he answered every question I put to him as best he could, and there was much of what Arnold had boasted he'd done that had been Slack's work . Some have said that Slack was Arnold's shadow, but seeing him in Charleston I knew differently. He was an equal partner in the hoax and no plan had been advanced without his participation. He told me too of the fateful night when Arnold had doubled back and attacked him, left him for dead at the bottom of the creek, his head smashed in. It was an extraodinary thing. He had expected trouble. He had expected to be cheated at the last hurdle, when Arnold asked him to stay behind, but had

265

DIAMONDS

never imagined his partner and friend would try to kill him. He was hurt more deeply by the betrayal of Arnold than any wounds, great though they had been.

When Alyce finally saw him, standing before her outside her Clinton Street house, again in rags, with broken limbs and ribs, she nearly fainted on the spot. Slack was already a wanted man, thanks to the prompt action of Clarence King. But one look at the emaciated and scarred wreck that had walked into her home, no description of John Slack would fit as he remained for the best part of a year.

Had he wanted to kill Arnold? Had they entertained revenge? Of course. Who wouldn't. But revenge would have to wait. Slack took ill from the strain and disappointment and suffering he'd been through on account of his near fatal fall and Alyce had had to nurse him through the rest of the summer and winter. It was true they had had entertained plans to travel to Kentucky, confront Arnold, demand their share. But as Slack recovered and time healed old wounds, they found they were not consumed by hate. When Arnold's child was born, any thought of taking risks with duels or fights vanished in a moment. They were a family now and they had to look to the future. Slack would never forgive or forget, but to his way of thinking, he had the love of a good wife and mother, he was a father, and they had a new chance at life. Slack made a decision to stay as dead as everyone thought he was, and that was the end of it.

As we drank the local ale, Slack relaxed a little. He explained to me how he'd not been cheated entirely by Arnold. By chance he'd ended up a wealthy man. They had had more than enough profit from the diamonds. Arnold had not been able to get a dime out of the New York banks because Slack had cannily placed almost all the funds in his wife's name just before he'd left for the rendezvous with Henry Janin. He did not expect his wife to cheat him, for she, unlike Arnold, had a heart. Yet, even so, even after all the pain and suffering Arnold had put him through, he was sorry Arnold was dead and had not lived like a King, as he'd always wanted.

At the end, Slack and I parted cordially. Slack departing taller than when he'd arrived, perhaps glad after all to meet a friend from the past and to be able to set the record straight.

Such is the tale of the Great Diamond Hoax. But let it be a warning to all those who would believe tales of those men who come down off the mountains with diamond dust on their heels and tall stories on their tongues.

Even so, all told, it is my greatest regret that I'd not gone with a young Arnold and Slack that day back in '59 when they'd answered the call of adventure.

Dr. Daniel P. Jackson
Dashaway House
Kentucky, 1886.

EPILOGUE:
THE LAST WORD
The house in Clinton St, Brooklyn.
December, 1886

Once this home had been the modest, yet discreet house of a mistress to a Governor. Had she ever returned to old haunts, she might have been surprised to see the little place so transformed. Not a single feature remained. Now stood in its place a red brick, prosperous merchants home with a holly bush in the front yard and behind stabling for four horses and an elegant sprung coach. Inside the three-storey dwelling changes were apparent also: A rocking horse revealed that a child had grown, and a crib would suggest that another child had been born recently. Indeed, this home now contained five children, one near fully grown. John Slack the man we knew was no more. Here sat an older man, still tall, to be sure, but the years had fleshed him out, turned his hair grey. His name was no longer Slack, but Clay, Henry Clay, in honor of another illustrious Kentuckian. This man, Clay, was reading a book as he sat beside the in his study. The book was titled **The Great Diamond Hoax** and it had been privately printed by Doctor Daniel P. Jackson and taken up by a New York subscription service, so that it was assured of a wide readership in New York at least.

The moment this Henry Clay had heard about the book, he made sure of getting hold of a copy, perhaps fearing memories would be jogged in the city and Slack would be remembered , or worse, recognized. Fortunately so many of the players had passed on by now, and there were new scandals to occupy their minds, more audacious than anything Arnold or Slack had attempted. A woman, older but not yet grey and still very handsome, walked into his study carrying her youngest wrapped in a woolen shawl. She smiled at Clay, and he looked up at her with affection.

"Anything to it?" Alyce asked.

Clay thumbed a page and began to read aloud from the book:

DIAMONDS

"There had been much recrimination in the city when the great hoax was revealed by Clarence King in San Francisco that fateful summer. Mr.. Asbury Harpending, who had brought attention to the diamond claim to Mr..Horace Greeley of the New York Tribune, refused all callers and would answer no questions when visiting New York. When pressed, however, he did remind reporters that this was the city where Mr.. Charles Tiffany himself had pronounced the famous diamonds to be of "outstanding value" in front of several worthy witnesses. Not just he, but Horace Greeley himself and many others had been taken in by these tricksters.

Mr.. Harpending did indeed convey an apology to Mr.. Greeley by telegraph, stating that he regretted involving the great man at all, but would like to say that at the time he saw all the diamonds, sapphires, rubies, and emeralds glittering upon Mr.. Tiffany's table, the thought did occur to him that there ought to have been a few pearls tossed in there as well...'

Alyce couldn't help but laugh and she moved forward to kiss the top of her husband's silver topped head. "It's nice that Mr.. Harpending didn't lose his sense of humor as well as all his money, dear."

At this Clay smiled and set down the book at the opened page, well satisfied that the author had not given Philip Arnold's side of the story completely. "Arnold would have appreciated the remark, to be sure. Now, there is packing to complete and letters to write if I am to make the train on time tomorrow."

Alyce frowned. "You really have to go to California again? Are you sure no one will recognize you? This book will stir the pot, dear. I so much worry about this venture."

He stared back at her, for a moment sharing her doubts, then shook his head, smiling to reassure her that all was well. "I have to go, dearest. I have purchased land in Los Angeles for the company, and it is on my word that they believe we will make a fortune. This is 1886, Alyce, not 1872. California is the boom state I always predicted it would be. Do you know how many thousands are going there daily? The population has doubled in just ten months. I bought many acres there in '83 and I paid just twenty dollars a foot for Main Street frontage. They tell me it's close to eight hundred a foot now. Captain Hessian of our San Francisco office tells me there are more than two thousand real estate agents making a living out there, Alyce, and I know the time to sell. My partners tell me the Los Angeles boom will go on forever and I told 'em, "The moment anyone thinks that, that's the time to bail out. So that is what I intend to do."

Alyce was confused. "But now? At Christmas?"

Clay just smiled. "It's Christmas soon, a time it's turning freezing cold in

DIAMONDS

Chicago and Boston, that makes a man think of moving west. I said to my partners. Either we invest in water or we sell our land to the gullible sheep who just don't know what it is like to live through a Southern Californian summer.

"I'll be gone for two, perhaps three months at the most, dearest. Don't frown. This is your husband here planning to make a legitimate fortune. You wouldn't begrudge me that, surely?"

"No dear, never." Nor did she doubt his intentions. Her man was honest as they came now.

"All cables to the Raymond Hotel in Pasadena. I'll be the guest of the Santa Fe Railroad. And when I return, we'll go to Florida, I promise. I said I'd take the children fishing and exploring, and I will. Besides, with Henry Flagler taking the railroad further south, there'll be real estate opportunities down there by and by."

Alyce sighed and he caught it. He reached out a hand and drew her and the babe closer to him, holding her tight. She didn't resist; she was going to lose him for the winter, and she'd miss every moment he was away. So would the children. She found her eyes drawn to the book he'd left open. She frowned again and he was puzzled by her expression.

"What is troubling you now?"

Alyce shrugged, letting her head fall back so she could look him in the eye.

"Confess you miss those wild days with Arnie. Tell me you think back to those times and wish you were still free to roam in the mountains."

Henry Clay, former prospector and hoaxer, grinned, showing off his fine set of new teeth, one result of the terrible fall he'd survived up the mountains. "Me? You ask me if I miss cold nights by damp fires as the snow packs in around me? You think I would want to listen to even half another of Philip Arnold's wild schemes? You think I liked wearing rags and eating beans, if I was lucky, or roots and berries if I could beat the bears to them first? You think I'd give up even an hour of the life I have now for time in the wilderness? No sir. I have the scars."

He indicated the deep scar on his forehead where Arnold's rock had smashed into his face. " I was so busy staying alive and following Arnold in those days, I never really did get to consider what it was that would make me happy. Arnold could find a lump of gold or silver and he'd shout and holler and sometimes cry he was so happy, but now I comes to think of it, I was always thinking about the land, the trees, the animals and birds that lived off it. I never really took to gold and diamonds."

Alyce smiled, planting a light kiss on her man's warm lips. "Well, I'm glad to hear this, Mr.. Henry Clay, because I want you to promise me you'll not go digging in California this trip."

"Well, a man has to test the dirt now and then. You'd not have me standing on virgin land with my hands in my pockets, would you?'"

DIAMONDS

Alyce laughed and shook her head. "No dear, I wouldn't. But have a care; if you should find diamonds in the dirt there, do toss 'em back, dear, promise me you'll toss 'em back."

DIAMONDS

Welcome to the world of Domhan Books! Domhan, pronounced DOW-ann, is the Irish word for universe. Our vision is to provide readers with high-quality hardcover, paperback and electronic books in a variety of genres from writers all over the world.

ORDERING INFORMATION

All Domhan paper books may be ordered from Barnes and Noble, barnesandnoble.com, Amazon, Borders, and other fine booksellers using the ISBN. They are distributed worldwide by Ingram Book Group, 1 Ingram Blvd., La Vergne, Tennessee 37086 (615) 793-5000. Most titles are also available electronically in a variety of formats through Galaxy Library at www.galaxylibrary.com. Rocket eBook™ editions are available on-line at barnesand noble.com, Powell's, and other booksellers. Please visit our website for previews, reviews, and further details on our titles: www.domhanbooks.com. Domhan Books, 9511 Shore Road, Suite 514, Brooklyn, New York 11209 U.S.A.

NON-FICTION

The Last True Story of Titanic - James G. Clary 1-58345-012-2 156 pp. $14.95
This book reveals startling new information from interviews and diaries never used before to tell what *really* happened that fateful night. This fascinating book comes complete with original illustrations by the author, an award-winning maritime artist who worked on the *Titanic* project. Nominated for the Pulitzer Prize for Non-Fiction, 1999.

Business Advice for Beginners - Victoria Ring 1-58345-044-0 228 pp. $16.95
If you have ever dreamt of being your own boss, this is the book for you. It gives valuable anecdotes about the author's own experiences as head of a successful publishing and graphics company, contact addresses, case studies, and more.

More Business Advice for Beginners - Victoria Ring 1-58345-045-9 248 pp. $16.95
This volume contains further pearls of wisdom from Ms. Ring as to how to set up and maintain your own home-based business.

Action and Adventure
Paladin - Barry Nugent 1-58345-365-2 192 pp. $12.95
Princess Yasmin must go on a quest for a mythical crown, the only thing that can prevent civil war erupting in the exotic land of Primera. Along the way she meets her favorite adventure author Barnaby Jackson, and the sparks really start to fly. This is a taut action novel reminiscent of the Indiana Jones series of films.

Yala - Don Clark 1-58345-561-2 180 pp. $12.95
In the no man's land between the U.S. and Mexico In 1896, a Chinese clan stakes a

claim to a new territory. Two Texas Rangers decide to end their law officer careers and go to New China in order to raise the bankroll needed to start a ranch. Hank and his younger sidekick, Luke, soon meet Yala, a condemned and notorious Chinese criminal: a female assassin.

CHRISTIAN FICTION
The Gospel According to Condo Don - Fred Dungan 1-58345-004-1 216 pp. $12.95
This is an account of the Second Coming as witnessed by a homeless alcoholic. While loosely modeled on the initial books of the New Testament (Matthew, Mark, Luke and John), it interjects humor into the classic story and presents it in a more readily understood contemporary format. Thus, Mary becomes Marva, a poor 16-year-old girl from Central Los Angeles, an evil televangelist takes the place of the money changers at the temple, and our bureaucracy is substituted for that of Rome's.

The Way Found - Nina J. Lechiara 1-58345-017-3 472 pp. $20.00
1532-1558
Matteo and Gianna search for love and truth in university studies, religion and philosophy, from Padua and Venice to Egypt and Arabia. They find it unexpectedly in Yahshua, in the one place they have never looked, the Scriptures. They learn both the truth and the meaning of love and marriage, and become shining examples of Yahvah's way.

FANTASY
The Druid's Woman - Shanna Murchison 1-58345-245-1 120 pp. $10
In this novel of Ireland, Davnat encounters Parthalann, a mysterious druid who trains her up to be his helper and consort. But despite all the powers she is given, their Fates have already been decreed....

The Wizard Woman - Shanna Murchison 1-58345-020-3 204 pp. hardcover $18.95; 1-58345-018-1 paper $12.95
Ireland 1169
The great Celtic myth of the Wheel of Fate is played out against the backdrop of the first Norman invasion of Ireland in 1169. Dairinn is made the wizard's woman, chosen by the gods to be the wife of the handsome but mysterious Senan. Through him she discovers her own innate powers, and the truth behind her family history. She must bargain with the Morrigan, the goddess of death, if she is ever to achieve happiness with the man she loves. But how high a price will she have to pay for Senan's life?

HISTORICAL FICTION
The Wildest Heart - Jacinta Carey 1-58345-041-6 224 pp. $12.95
Rebecca Whitaker is struggling to keep her family ranch from foreclosure by trading with the Indians, working in a saloon, and breeding horses. Enter the mysterious Walker Pritchard, claiming he wishes to stay with Reb to leave the memories of the Civil War behind and learn about the ways of the west. They fall in love, but can Reb

trust Walker? What are his real motives for coming to the Bar T, and how did he know there would be gold in those hills? Reb must fight to save him and her ranch, before everything she loves is destroyed by the men from Walker's mysterious past.

Natchez - Deb Crockett   1-58345-008-4 180 pp. $12.95
Welcome to Natchez, home to whores, gamblers, and anyone out to make a fast buck, no matter what the cost...
The untimely death of lovely young Rebecca Bennett's father forces the feisty girl from Savannah to live by her wits. Alone, penniless, and seemingly betrayed by the only man she has ever truly loved, she struggles to stay alive and fulfill her dream: to buy her beloved Oliver's plantation and have a home of her own, even though he is miles away. But though she tries to live honestly through hard work, she makes powerful enemies. Can she ever find happiness, safety, love, and the people responsible for her father's death and her ruin?

The Summer Stars - Alan Fisk 1-58345-549-3 202 pp. $12.95
Britain's oldest poems were composed in the sixth century by the bard Taliesin. Many legends have been told about he of the "shining brow," but in this novel he tells his own story. Taliesin's travels take him through turbulent times as Britain tries to cope with the disappearance of Roman civilization, and the increasing threat of the Saxon invaders.

Scars Upon Her Heart - Sorcha MacMurrough 1-58345-011-4 232 pp. $12.95
Lady Vevina Joyce and her brother Wilfred are forced to flee Ireland after being falsely accused of treason. On the road with Wellington's army, they meet an unexpected ally in the enigmatic Major Stewart Fitzgerald. Side by side they fight with their comrades in some of the most bitter battles of the Napoleonic Wars. Can Vevina clear her name, protect those she loves, and stop the Grand Army from taking over the whole of Europe in a bold and daring move engineered by the person responsible for her family's disgrace? Is Stewart really all that he seems? Appearances can be deceptive....

Destiny Lies Waiting - Diana Rubino 1-58345-078-5 hardcover 208 pp. $18.50; 1-58345-451-9 paper $12.95
Volume One of *The Yorkist Saga*
Beautiful orphaned Denys has been bought up a member of the Woodville family, now in power thanks to her aunt Elizabeth, wife of the new Yorkist king Edward IV. Unwilling to become a pawn in her aunt's bid for power, she decides to seek the truth about her family and identity.
Valentine Starbury, loyal ally to young Richard, Duke of Gloucester, the King's brother, agrees to woo Denys in order to save his friend from Elizabeth Woodville's plan for Richard and Denys to wed. He unexpectedly falls in love with her, thus earning the enmity of the queen. The secrets both uncover will have dangerous consequences for Denys and Valentine, and the whole of England itself.

Thy Name is Love - Diana Rubino 1-58345-079-3 hardcover 212 pp. $18.30,

DIAMONDS

1-58345-392-X paper $12.95
Volume Two of *The Yorkist Saga*
The story first begun in *Destiny Lies Waiting* continues in this second volume. Denys Starbury and her husband Valentine are thrust into the world of power politics as one by one the royal family is eliminated, until only one man can contend for the throne, Richard, Duke of Gloucester. Denys continues to search for her lost family, but she finds only a trail of murder and destruction. She also seeks the love of Valentine. In a world of shifting allegiances, how can she ever bring herself to trust him?

The Jewels of Warwick - Diana Rubino 1-58345-080-7 hardcover 236 pp. $18.50;
1-58345-413-6 paper $12.95
Volume Three of *The Yorkist Saga*
In this sequel to *Thy Name is Love,* the saga of the Yorkist royal family continues. The "Jewels" are two sisters, Topaz and Amethyst Plantagenet. They are descendants of Richard III, who lost his life and kingdom to Henry Tudor, future father of Henry VIII.
Topaz always felt she was the rightful queen, and would have been, had her father been crowned as Richard's heir. But life holds many strange twists of fate....

Crown of Destiny - Diana Rubino 1-58345-081-5 hardcover 204 pp. $18.50;
1-58345-456-X paper $12.95
Volume Four of *The Yorkist Saga*
In this sequel to *The Jewels of Warwick*, Topaz's rebellion against Henry VIII gets under way, throwing England into civil war and chaos. Amethyst is forced to choose between remaining loyal to her sister, or losing the only two men she has ever loved: the king, and her sister's husband Matthew....

I Love You Because - Diana Rubino 1-58345-082-3 hardcover 264 pp. $18.50;
1-58345-423-3 paper 264 pp. $12.95
Vita Caputo meets handsome Irish cop Tom McGlory at the scene of a crime. This fateful encounter has consequences for both their families as they must struggle together to end the corruption in turn-of-the-century New York City politics before more crimes are committed and more lives are lost.

An Experience in Four Movements - Lidmila Sovakova 1-58345-002-5 124 pp. $10
This is a historical puzzle situated in the seventeenth century. Its pieces reconstruct the infatuation of a Poet with a Princess, culminating in the death of the Poet, and the retreat of the Princess within the walls of a monastery.

IRISH INTEREST
Call Home the Heart - Sorcha MacMurrough 1-58345-072-6 hardcover 244 pp. $18.95; 1-58345-394-6 paper $12.95
Young widow Muireann Graham Caldwell is left destitute by her dissolute husband, Augustine, killed in a shooting accident on their honeymoon. Faced with a choice between returning to her stifling parents in Scotland or taking a chance on running

her own estate, Muireann finds an ally in the broodingly handsome Lochlainn Roche. He has secrets of his own to keep. As the Potato Famine rages across Ireland, can Muireann save her new home Barnakilla? Can she and her estate manager ever have a future together? Does he even love her? Or has he been using her all along?

The Faithful Heart - Sorcha MacMurrough 1-58345-023-8 204 pp. $12.95
Who has murdered Morgana Maguire's brother, poisoned her father, and stolen most of her clan's ships? These are just a few of the pressing questions Morgana must find answers to if she and her one true love Ruairc MacMahon are ever to find happiness in each other's arms. Set against the backdrop of Renaissance power politics during the reign of Henry VIII, Morgana and Ruairc must fight not only to win each other, but also to protect all of Ireland from civil war and foreign invasion.

The Fire's Centre - Sorcha MacMurrough 1-58345-025-4 264 pp. $12.95
Riona Connolly is willing to do anything to save her family from starvation during the Potato Famine. So when she meets the handsome Dr. Lucien Woulfe, who offers her post at his clinic, it seems a dream come true. But their growing attraction is forbidden in the straight-laced society of Victorian Dublin. Riona and Lucien must walk through the fire's centre to secure their happiness before it is destroyed by the evil Dr. O'Carroll and the vagaries of Fate.

The Hart and the Harp - Sorcha MacMurrough 1-58345-030-0 288 pp. $12.95
Ireland, 1149
Shive MacDermot and Tiernan O'Hara agree to wed to end a five-year feud between their clans. Though an unlikely alliance at first, Shive begins to fall in love with her new husband. She soon realises the murderer of her brother is a member of her own clan. How can she win Tiernan's love and prove to him she is not the enemy? Shive undertakes an epic struggle to save her lands and Tiernan's from the ambitious Muireadach O'Rourke, determined to kill anyone who opposes his bid to become high-king of all Ireland. Will she prove worthy of Tiernan, or will he believe all of the vicious lies about her supposed love for another, and become her enemy himself?

Hunger for Love - Sorcha MacMurrough 1-58345-005-X 244 pp. $12.95
Ireland and Canada, 1847
Emer Nugent and her family are evicted from their home at the height of the Potato Famine in Ireland. Forced to emigrate to Canada, they endure a harrowing journey on board a coffin ship bound for Grosse Ile. Emer, working as a cabin boy to help her family's financial situation, meets the enigmatic Dalton Randolph, the ship's only gentleman passenger, who is not all that he seems. They fall in love, but darker forces are at work against them. Emer's duty to her family forces the lovers to separate. Will they ever be able to overcome the obstacles in their path to true love? This incredible saga of love, adventure and intrigue continues in the second volume *The Hungry Heart.*

The Hungry Heart - Sorcha MacMurrough 1-58345-006-8 232 pp. $12.95
Canada and Ireland 1847-1849

DIAMONDS

Emer Nugent leaves her lover Dalton Randall to search for her family in the hell of the Grosse Ile quarantine station. The land of opportunity is nearly the death of them all. Dalton is deceived by his father into thinking Emer is dead, and is about to marry the daughter of a business rival when he meets Emer again. Outraged that his plans for keeping the two apart have failed,
Dalton's father has Emer arrested on false charges and transported back to Ireland. But the Ireland she returns to is on the brink of civil war. Emer finds herself unwittingly embroiled in the 1848 rebellion, and is put on trial for her life. Dalton must travel half way across the world to try to save her before it is too late. This incredible saga of love and adventure begins with the first volume, *Hunger for Love*.

The Sea of Love - Sorcha Mac Murrough 1-58345-032-7 6 hardcover 148 pp. $15.95; 1-58345-033-5 paper $10
Ireland 1546
Wrongfully accused of murder, Aidanna O'Flaherty's only ally against her evil brother-in-law Donal is the dashing English-bred aristocrat Declan Burke. Saving him from certain death, they fall in love, only to be separated when Declan is falsely accused of treason. Languishing in the Tower, Declan is powerless to assist his beloved Aidanna as she undertakes an epic struggle to expose her enemy and save her family and friends. She must race against time to prevent all she loves from being swept aside in a thunderous tide of foreign invasion....

LITERARY/MAINSTREAM FICTION
The Nestucca Retreat - M. Lee Locke 1-58345-009-2 216 pp. $12.95
J. Cunningham Raleigh died in an Oregon rain storm — struck by lightning while playing an electric guitar on a river dock. A mediocre rock musician who never quite left the Sixties, Ham Raleigh was an intimate part of a long-standing triangle. Millie and Jake Prince, a forty-something couple, were Ham's best friends. He was a part of Jake's life from childhood and Millie's since college. He was an intruder in their marriage and also the glue that kept them together. Millie and Jake drift apart after Ham's death, though continue to struggle with staying together, still using Ham as a crutch. Ham's death does not really cause this distancing but reveals the existing rift between them, one that has been ever widening for years. At the ceremony Millie, Jake and Ham's ex-wives hold to say goodbye to Ham, an unexpected visitor turns up who will change their lives forever.....

Eclipse Over Lake Tanganyika - Albert Russo 1-58345-057-2 hardcover 208 pp. $18.95; 1-58345-058-0 paper $12.95
A novel of Rwanda on the eve of its independence.
In this novel of Africa, Russo offers us a wide range of fascinating characters, their hopes, desires, dreams and aspirations, as they struggle against themselves and a rapidly changing society.

Mixed Blood - Albert Russo 1-58345-050-5 hardcover 212 pp. $18.95; 1-58345-051-3 paper $12.95
A moving novel set in the Belgian Congo on the eve of Independence.

DIAMONDS

Leopold, an orphan of 'mixed blood,' is adopted by a lonely American who tries to fit in with his adopted society. Leopold's new mother is the indomitable Mama Malkia, who has a fascinating story of her own to tell.

Falling in Love - Lidmila Sovakova 1-58345-039-4 hardcover 184 pp. $18.95; 1-58345-289-3 paper $12.95
Volume One of *The Jazz Saga*
Set in Prague, this is a poignant tale of love, loss, and the search for happiness of a young girl growing up in turbulent times.

Like a Bubble in a Glass of Champagne - Lidmila Sovakova 1-58345-290-7 hard-cover 164 pp. $16.95; 1-58345-040-8 paper $10
Volume Two of *The Jazz Saga*
Irene's adventures in Prague, begun in the novel *Falling in Love*, continue in this moving novel as she must struggle to find happiness with the very different men in her life.

The Sophisticated Lady - Lidmila Sovakova 1-58345-059-9 hardcover 148 pp. $16.95; 1-58345-291-5 paper $10
Volume Three of *The Jazz Saga*
Irene, growing up in Prague, thought she had it all, and could keep it all. In love with and loved by four very different men, one by one they have been stripped away from her, leaving only Leo, the man she has finally wed. Now her family are stripped from her one by one. Can she maintain the façade of the happily married and blushing young bride? Or is she set on her path of self-destruction?

The Frosted Mirrors - Lidmila Sovakova 1-58345-286-9 160 pp. $10
Volume One of *The Gray Saga*
This is the story of Rinaldo, a young boy who adores his mother and will do anything for her approval. But she is oblivious to all else except the creative muse which drives her poetry, and her cat. The story is also of a painter who is doomed to fall in love with them both.

The Scarlet Maze - Lidmila Sovakova 1-58345-287-7 192 pp. $10
Volume Two of *The Gray Saga*
The story of Rinaldo and his mother, started in *The Frosted Mirrors*, continues in this moving novel. The passionate triangle continues, defying even death, as the three lovers struggle to hold on to each other, even in the face of overwhelming odds.

The Eye of Medusa - Lidmila Sovakova 1-58345-288-5 172 pp. $10
Volume Three of *The Gray Saga*
The sequel to *The Frosted Mirrors* and *The Scarlet Maze*, this novel continues the saga of Rinaldo and his mother, and their search for happiness, which is often at odds with the creative muse that drives them. It also furthers the tale of the painter Christopher Gray and his struggle to win both their loves.

DIAMONDS

LITERARY CRITICISM

The Playmaker: A Study Guide - S. McNally 1-58345-412-8 124 pp. $10.00
A study guide to the book now currently on various examination syllabi. It contains notes on each chapter, sample essays and questions, historical background, and biographical information about the author and his works.

MYSTERY

St. John's Baptism - William Babula 1-58345-496-9 260 pp. $12.95
In this first of the Jeremiah St. John series, the hero is summoned to a meeting by Rick Silverman, one of San Francisco's most prominent drug attorneys. St. John knows Silverman's unsavory clientele and so does not think anything of the invitation—that is until he finds Silverman dead.

According to St. John - William Babula 1-58345-521-9 240 pp. $12.95
In this second St. John adventure, St. John's friend Denise is supposed to be in Frisco appearing in a new production of *Macbeth* with legendary actress Amanda Cole. They arrive at the theater only to discover that Amanda has been murdered and Denise is the prime suspect. St. John soon learns that everyone involved is playing a role. By the time they track down the killer, St. John and his intrepid colleagues uncover some horrifying secrets from the past, and the mind-boggling motive.

St. John and the Seven Veils - William Babula   1-58345-506-X 208 pp. $12.95
In this third mystery in the popular series, St John and his two partners Mickey and Chief Moses are hired to track down a serial killer by a woman claiming to be the killer's mother! Three men have been brutally murdered, but they are without any apparent connection until St. John stumbles across one through a seemingly unrelated case. From the Seven Veils Brothel in Reno to a hideout in Northern California, St John is hot on the trail, crossing paths with a famous televangelist, prominent military man, high-powered doctor, and a complete madman.

St. John's Bestiary - William Babula 1-58345-511-6 264 pp. $12.95
St. John should never have taken this fourth case. But he just couldn't help it—Professor Krift's story of his eight stolen cats strikes a sympathetic chord. After rescuing the victims from a ruthless gang of animal rights activists, the CFAF, he is caught catnapping as the CFAF kidnap the professor's daughter. Suddenly the morgue is filling up, and not just with strangers. St. John's new love Ollie is killed, and he determines to stop at nothing until her murder is avenged. The tangled case drags him through every racket going: money laundering, dope pushing, porno, prostitution, and very nearly drags him six foot under.

St. John's Bread - William Babula 1-58345-516-7 hardcover 180 pp. $18.95; 1-58345-516-7 paper $12.95
In this fifth volume of the series, St. John and his two intrepid partners get caught up in a tangle of missing children's cases after he and Mickey rescue a baby about to be kidnapped in a public park. Mickey tries to tell him that he needs the "bread" to pay for his brand new Victorian stately home which houses him and their detective agency,

DIAMONDS

but this case comes with a higher price tag than any of them are willing to pay.

Venom - Faith Martin 1-58345-374-1 $10
Kate Sparrow is dragged into a world of murder and mayhem when the tranquil neighborhood library is the scene of a brutal murder with an incomprehensible motive.

The Fox and the Puma - Barbara Sohmers 1-58345-486-1 156 pp. $10
This is the first novel in the popular Fred and Maggy Renard series.
When a nude, partly-devoured body is found near a popular beach on an island off the southern coast of France, the small community erupts into panic. Old hatreds and sins begin to surface, and many more ugly secrets will be revealed…

The Fox and the Pussycat - Barbara Sohmers 1-58345-491-8 160 pp. $10
In the second of her Fred and Maggy Renard adventures, the intrepid pair become embroiled in the raunchy underground world of Paris in an effort to track down the killer of her friend Marie-Claude.

POETRY
Cold Moon: The Erotic Haiku of Gabriel Rosenstock 1-58345-042-4 108 pp. $12.95
This is a bilingual book in English and Irish from one of the foremost poets in both languages. Complete with powerful illustrations, this is a must for anyone who loves poetry, elegant books, and all things Irish.

A Portrait of the Artist as an Abominable Snowman - Gabriel Rosenstock 1-58345-124-2 108 pp. $12.95
Another fine collection of poetry in English and Irish from this stunning voice in the world of verse.

SCIENCE FICTION
The Event - Gregory Farnum 1-58345-553-1 176 pp. $12.95
This is a fast-paced technothriller. Prendyk and his girlfriend Jennifer are dragged into a dark world of government conspiracy. "The Event" will have far-reaching consequences for all of mankind.

ROMANCES
Campaign for Love - Michaela Brennan 1-58345-285-0 144 pp. $10
Tired of being hassled over her gorgeous looks, Suzanna Sills dresses down to get a wonderful new job in a top-notch ad agency. She soon regrets her frumpy appearance when she has to work with the gorgeous Quentin Pierce. Quentin hasn't failed to notice that his hottest new star has more to her than meets the eye. But office intrigues get them both into a spin. Can they avoid losing the biggest ad campaign the company has ever seen, and learn to trust one another?

The Right Code - Sharon Holmes 1-58345 118 9 $12.95

279

Jonathan C. Evans is mocked as a computer nerd who lives by logic. Jasmine Banks is the only one who sees Jon differently. She grows determined to make this man realize that logic has nothing to do with a relationship between a man and a woman. But she gets more than she bargains for as the real JC Evans is revealed...

The Picture of Bliss - Jacqui Jerome 1-58345-268-0 168 pp. $10
Just when Candice Edwards thinks she has escaped from her past, she is propelled into a nightmarish encounter with her ex-fiancé. Can she trust the secretive and mercurial designer Lochlainn Alexander, or is he part of the whole plot to ruin her career?

Heart's Desire - Sorcha MacMurrough 1-58345-031-9 160 pp. $10
Nurse Sinead Thomas rescues the hospital's handsome architect Austin Riordan from a life-threatening situation. She accepts his offer to be his private nurse over the Christmas holidays, but gets more than she bargained for as they grow ever closer. A young widow, she never wants to go through the torment of being in love again. But Austin is nothing if not persistent. Can they fight the demons from her past, to secure their hearts' desire?

Star Attraction - Sorcha MacMurrough 1-58345-037-8 168 pp. $10
Zaira Darcy literally bumps into the man of her dreams in an elevator. Dashing Brad Clarke, Hollywood's hottest new director, working alongside her in New York, is everything she could want in a man, and more. But the secrets from her past, and the double life she leads, threaten to destroy any chance of happiness the two might have. Zaira must lock horns with her ex-husband Jonathan one last time to save Brad's life, even if it means sacrificing her own.

Love's Sweet Song - Annabelle Stevens 1-58345-275-3 132 pp. $10
Angelica Castle Murray loses everything in a tragic accident: husband, daughter, and very nearly her life. But in the aftermath of his disaster, she must not only struggle to regain her health, but to come to terms with the fact that ever since her ex-fiancé Winston broke up with her seven years before, she has been living a lie. Winston Murray has never stopped loving Angelica, even when she was married to his brother. Her old life is now in shambles; but how can he tell her that her life with Oliver has been a big lie?

The Art of Love - Evelyn Trimborn 1-58345-001-7 164 pp. $10
Struggling Dublin artist Shannon Butler gives a hugely successful show. Enter her estranged adopted brother Marius Winters, hell-bent on revenge. He accuses her of robbing him of his share of their dead father's estate. Thrown together by circumstances, they try to make up for the mistakes of the past. Despite all their differences, they grow ever closer. But Marius' lying ex-wife threatens any chance of happiness they might have. How can Shannon prevent her new-found love from leaving her forever?

Castles in the Air - Evelyn Trimborn 1-58345-019-X 168 pp. $10

DIAMONDS

Poverty-stricken aristocrat Alanna Lacy is at her wits' end. Enter property developer Bran Ryan, who offers her a way out of her desperate financial situation—marry him! Faced with her father's disapproval, and Bran's spiteful ex-fiancée, can they build a future together, or will all their dreams go up in smoke?

Forbidden Fantasy - Evelyn Trimborn 1-58345-256-7 124 pp. $10

Rose Gray is one of America's top romance writers. So why is it she can't ever seem to meet Mr. Right? Luke Byrnes changes all that when he bursts into her life unexpectedly. Will it be "Happily Ever After" Or "The End"?

Heedless Hearts - Evelyn Trimborn 1-58345-251-6 132 pp. $10

Inexperienced housekeeper Marielle gets more than she bargains for when she takes a post at the house of architect Tristan Fitzmaurice. Sparks fly from the moment they meet, but all too soon, she can feel herself being drawn to him irresistibly. But how can she love him, when he is about to be married to another? But the heart is heedless when it comes to love.

Design for Love - Shirley Wolford 1-58345-594-9 $10

Beautiful interior decorator Ann Seymour gets the chance to prove herself more than capable of running her family's design works when she runs into the enigmatic Adam Frazier, a swashbuckling hunk who has lived abroad for many years and returned home to Orange County. She has a job to do, but can she ever learn to control her feelings whenever they meet?

THRILLERS

Ghost From the Past - Sorcha MacMurrough 1-58345-029-7 180 pp. $12.95

Biochemist Clarissa Vincent's fiancé Julian Simmons was killed in a terrible explosion five years ago. Or was he? Taking a new job in Portland, Oregon, Clarissa sees a man at the airport who could be Julian's double, and is suddenly propelled into a nightmarish world of espionage and intrigue. She must struggle to save her family and the man she has always loved from the ruthless people who will stop at nothing to achieve world domination.

In From the Cold - Carolyn Stone 1-58345-007-6 224 pp. $12.95

Cambridge scientist Sophie Ruskin is dragged into a world of espionage and intrigue when her father, a Russian defector, vanishes. Adrian Vaughan, handsome, enigmatic, but haunted by his past, is assigned to train her as a spy to win her father's freedom, or destroy his work before his kidnappers can create the ultimate weapon. But Adrian's fate soon lies in Sophie's hands, as she travels two continents to save his life, win his love, and fight for the freedom of the oppressed, war-torn Russian Republic of Chechnya.

Spin Me a Web - Shirley K. Wolford 1-58345-598-1 $12.95

Caitlin Cameron, amateur sleuth and feature writer for *Antique Autos Magazine*, challenges her readers to find the thief who stole four priceless antique sports cars. Her life is threatened unless she stops her column. But she's stubborn and has other ideas. She asks Rick Falconer, world-class tennis ace, and new owner of the romantic pre-war, hand-made, antique sports car, *the Princess Eula*, to help trap the thief by using his car as bait.

Rick is appalled at her request and refuses. But then the car is stolen and Rick becomes the main suspect. Both must work together to find the real thief, and uncover a conspiracy which threatens their blossoming love for one another.

WESTERNS

West of Appomattox - Harley Duncan 1-58345-404-7 212 pp. $12.95
After the Civil War, a group of rugged and disgruntled soldiers seek their fame and fortune west of Appomattox in the new Mexican territory, with explosive results. This is a fine new novel sure to please devotees of the western genre.

Blow-Up at Three Springs - Colby Wolford 1-58345-541-8 148 pp. $10
The town took away Frank Gilman's badge, called him a killer, and treated him like dirt when he refused to turn tail and run, and started a stagecoach line with his brother Todd. Frank knew that Deejohn was behind his troubles. The town's biggest rancher, he was arrogant enough to believe he could bend the law any way he liked. Then one day Martha Lexter arrives at the railhead to threaten Deejohn and his empire. Deejohn will stop at nothing to get rid of her. Frank is faced with a choice: ignore Martha, or sell her a seat on his stage, an act which will certainly unleash Deejohn's pack of hired killers, and split Three Springs right down its seams!

The Guns of Witchwater - Colby Wolford 1-58345-525-6 248 pp. $12.95
Winter Santrell is a young peddler who tries to stay out of trouble. But unable to resist a damsel in distress, he comes to the aid of Vivian Kern, desperate for money to save her ranch after her father's death. The whole town of Witchwater is paralyzed with fear as a pack of renegades led by Baird Stark ride rough-shod over them. Santell decides to stand up for the people of the town, even though a few of them are mighty tempted to take up the thousand dollar reward that Stark puts on his corpse!

The Iron Corral - Colby Wolford 1-58345-533-7 160 pp. $10
When drifter Dan Allard takes the Sheriff's badge in La Mancha, he and his deputy Owen Fielding lock horns with Harlan Younger and his tough gang, who are determined to drive the lawmen out of town.
Soon the banker, Jabe Miller, is murdered, and Owen is framed for the crime. Even his own friends and family turn against Dan as he struggles to bring Harlan to justice and clear Owen's name.

Stranger in the Land - Colby Wolford 1-58345-529-9 160 pp. $10
Derek Langton, ex-English cavalry officer, is a stranger in a strange land when he heads out west at the close of the Civil War. He has come to claim his inheritance, the Tower Ranch and fertile Strip with its wild, unbranded cattle. But others covet the Strip, especially Delphine Judson and her gun-toting crew. Derek must fight for his very survival to make a home for himself in his new-found land.

DIAMONDS

Rainbow's End - Shirley Wolford 1-58345-466-7 $12.95

Beautiful widow Prue Jamison saw a rainbow that stretched all the way from Boston to the newly discovered gold fields in California. Prue needed a new place to live, and there was nothing newer than San Francisco.

Ex-Captain Beau Graham wanted no part of a woman who ventured around Cape Horn without an escort. When the Mexican War ended, he had shed all his responsibilities and had no intention of taking on a beautiful, bold-spirited woman who was probably no better than she should be.

Green Grown the Rushes - Shirley and Nelson Wolford 1-58345-522-3 244 pp. $12.95

Lieutenant Boyd Regan is unjustly despised by his fellow soldiers and hated by the Mexicans of Alta Lowa. He is scorned by the woman he loves, half-Mexican beauty Catrina MacLeod, and her blonde sister Jennie. He is unfairly accused, tried and convicted for treating the Mexican peasants cruelly.

Yet if Mexican general Santa Anna obtains artillery, he will destroy Mexico City and all the American troops in it. Only Boyd stands in the way of complete annihilation of the entire city, even Mexico itself....

The Southern Blade - Shirley and Nelson Wolford 1-58345-537-X 168 pp. $10.00

Seven rebel prisoners on a desperate flight for freedom....

The Civil War is in its last days, but these prisoners only know they want their freedom. They are willing to risk hostile Indians and the even more dangerous climate of New Mexico. Lieutenant Sawling leads the motley group on their journey, pursued by the relentless Union captain who has sworn to retake and hang them. The only thing standing between them and the gallows is a beautiful young woman they have taken as hostage....

The Whispering Cannon - Shirley and Nelson Wolford 1-58345-545-0 184 pp. $10.95

Craig Dixon attracted trouble. A war correspondent, he was banned from the battlefield after criticizing Zachary Taylor's 1847 campaign against the Mexicans. But Dixon simply had to be where the news was being made. So he enlists as an officer in the Texas Volunteers, and is chosen as a messenger to get vital information to Taylor. The Mexicans will wipe Taylor's men out unless Dixon can get to him in time and persuade Taylor he is telling the truth.

283

9 781583 456101